Farm Girl

a novel

CORINNE CUNNINGHAM

For Lucas

ACKNOWLEDGMENTS

I would like to thank the many people who have supported my writing in countless ways over the years.

Thank you to my online communities, from the early days of blogging to the invaluable connections I've made on Instagram - your daily encouragement, support, and love is appreciated more than you all know.

To my fellow writers, especially Kristen Ploetz, Faith Raider, Alisha Sommer, and Bethany Stedman, for your emails, texts, skype chats, early morning coffee shop meet ups and pep talks, I thank you with all my heart.

Kylee Foote, Carole Function, and Rebecca Wood – thank you for navigating the waters of being friends with a temperamental writer. Your questions, support, and gentle nudges are perfect and appreciated.

Thank you Crystal Davies, Jen Precourt, and Tatiana Sciancalepore for reading early drafts and telling me I had written something worth reading!

Thank you to Jennifer Hoppins for being my writing partner, for pointing out connections and your thoughtful insights, and for loving Bea, Graham, and Cliff as much as I do.

Thank you Jennifer Booth for the camaraderie, your eagle-eyed editing, and countless texts.

To Mary Lou and Ted Cunningham, thank you for the respite your Maine home offered for multiple writing retreats. Your kindnesses are unending and much appreciated.

To Mom and Dad, thank you for your constant love and support. Mom, thank you for the gorgeous author photos, your endless encouragement, and most especially thank you for giving me the tools to write from the very beginning. I love you both!

Toby Schreier, my brother and the talented artist behind Farm Girl's cover, thank you for the artwork, your feedback, your time, and your enthusiasm and belief in my work.

Fynn and Paige, thank you for your patience and understanding, and for allowing me space to not only grow as your mother, but also a writer.

And to Lucas... thank you for knowing when to bring home gummy bears, for your shoulder to cry on, your feedback, and for always believing in me and more importantly, us.

ONE

B ea Hampton jumped down from the bed of a two-tone,
cream and clay, 1970s Chevy truck. The ground felt
unforgiving beneath her steel toed boots, but the first frost
was yet to come. The softness of summer was fading, green grass
turned to brown more and more each day. Morning dew clung to
her boots and dampened the hem of her frayed jeans. She stared
out at the rows of apple trees lined up like rows of soldiers, a bit
sloppy in the ranks, branches hanging low with an abundance of
fruit. Standing with her hands on her hips she tried to calculate
how many rows the crew would be able to get through by the end
of the day.

Deep in concentration she didn't notice the figure
approaching from the driver's side of the truck. Cliff Finley,
owner of Finley Orchards, stepped next to her and put an arm
around her back. His height swallowed her average five foot six
frame, and as she leaned into him she took in the scent of pipe
tobacco and coffee. Her nerves began to fade.

"What a view, eh farm girl?" said Cliff.

Bea smiled at the term of endearment, the playfulness in his voice.

"It's something. There's a lot of work ahead of us." Still trying to calculate hours and manpower, she sighed. The best she could do was guess. She never remembered Cliff's formula, and didn't have his years of experience. "I don't know how you do it every year, organize everyone and keep them motivated, how you move the orchard through the seasons."

Her shoulders shook as Cliff chuckled.

"No one moves an orchard through the seasons, we follow its lead. And I do it because I love it, as does every single person who works here, you know that. It's too much work unless you care about this place. You've seen me here working the fields year in year out since you were a little one. It shouldn't surprise you." His arm fell to his side and he walked back to the truck. The hinge of the tailgate creaked when he lowered it, then he started moving picking baskets onto the ground. The dozen baskets looked like marching band drums with their straps and handles. White canvas and buckles against a smattering of colors, sun stained reds and blues, yellows and greens.

"The others should be here shortly. Do you remember how to do this?"

She laughed, "I may have been away for a few years, but I haven't forgotten." She picked up one of the baskets and put a strap over each arm, adjusting the length. When she clicked the buckle together it made a loud snap and sent a shiver down her spine in a sweet homecoming sort of way. "It's like riding a bike," she said, grinning at Cliff, "It might not be in my blood, but it's in my heart."

Cliff's smile was full of pride. He looked down at a clipboard he had grabbed from the truck and said, "We're focusing on Macs this morning. Maybe Empires this afternoon. Head on

10

down to the right." Bea followed his gaze and gave a quick nod.

She turned and walked between two trees and disappeared into the rows. As a child she ran through these rows with reckless abandon. In winter months she stomped through piles of snow and rolled snowballs into snowmen to keep the trees company. During springtime she sat beneath flowering trees and made fairy houses out of fallen branches. She sought the shade of the trees during the summer months, and then autumn brought obstacle courses of fallen apples and pickers. Cliff gave her the run of the place, even though she was only his neighbor's granddaughter, a family friend. Her grandmother, Sylvia Eaton, lived across the street from Finley Orchards and Beatrix was sent to her house multiple times during the year, for whole vacations and seasons at a time. Bea didn't mind, though. She enjoyed the comfort and ease of her grandmother's home and the orchard with its whimsy and seasonal changes far more than her parent's stuffy house near the city.

Now, the orchard was just as inviting as ever. The light only hinted at warmth, and she rubbed her hands together wishing she brought gloves and added them to a mental list of things to buy on her first trip into town. She chose a tree and got to work.

It was about time she made her way into the small town of Cumberland to say hello to familiar faces, and maybe a few new ones. Over dinner the previous night Cliff mentioned the additions to the local shop line up: an artisan cheese shop, a craft beer seller, and a coffee and ice cream shop. The old fashioned hardware store, run by husband and wife team Olivia and Steve, still sat on the corner across from the gazebo, where the Christmas tree stood tall every December.

Maybe they'll have work gloves that would do the trick, she thought to herself, picturing something a little softer than the rough gloves she could probably find in Cliff's barn. She wanted something worn in and comfortable, something her grandmother would have, but she couldn't walk in and go through the coat closet like she used to. She couldn't even walk up and knock on the door.

Bea's stomach dropped and her breath hitched. She shoved the feeling down and stepped into the branches, enveloped by the fist sized Macs, ready for picking. She nestled the basket between the branches and the base of the tree, lifted her shin against the tree while the base of the basket rested on her thigh. She reached for a clump of apples and took one by the hand, all of them were the perfect shade of red, no bruises or blemishes. She lifted the apple gently and rolled it off the branch, and though she placed it carefully in the basket, it made a light thump against the canvas.

Four dozen apples later, her thighs ached with weight and immobility. Her standing knee locked into place and she teetered for a moment. She removed her leg from the tree and stood tall, shifting her weight back and forth to release tension. Birds sang and the crisp morning air turned into a balm that caressed her cheek as it whispered through the branches. Bea closed her eyes and felt a sense of peace wash over her. The clenched jaw she hadn't noticed loosened, tensed shoulders pulled down from her ears. Space was made between chest and chin as her head leaned back. A smile played on her lips for no one but herself.

The rumbling of her stomach cut through the peacefulness and she looked down at the watch on her wrist. Not even close to lunchtime.

As she had done a thousand times throughout her life she grabbed an apple off the tree and bit into it. The crisp, tart flesh of the apple left her cheeks puckering as she crunched through skin and flesh. Using the back of her hand she wiped juice from her chin.

"Are you going to pay for that?"

Bea would have jumped at the sound of a voice but the weight of the apples held her down. Her jaw clenched, shoulders pulled up, and the open spaces closed in a second. The songbirds vacated the tree and left a whir of wings against the air behind them. She turned around to see a man walking towards her.

He stopped a few feet away from Bea. He was tall and had a slim but strong build, short wavy auburn hair, and his skin held the leftovers of a summer tan. He wore a red checkered flannel shirt, khaki pants, and his shoes, his shoes were all wrong for the orchard, even on a dry day: loafers, or brogues. They didn't belong in the sleepy orchard Bea grew up in where everyone wore Wellingtons or work boots depending on the weather.

"Excuse me?"

"I asked if you were going to pay for that," he motioned towards the apple in her hand. His voice was stern, but there was a hint of sparkle in his eyes, a playfulness waiting to be unleashed. He pointed towards the basket. "Eating crops and picking don't really go together," he said as he lifted his hand to shield his eyes from the sun.

"Do I know you?" She placed one hand on her hip, the other held tightly to the offending apple. The basket hung low and swayed as she moved her weight to one side.

"I don't think so, I'm a friend of Cliff's. Have you seen him?" He waited only a beat before responding, "No, I guess you haven't, if you're busy staring up at the sky and having lunch while the other pickers are working. Keep picking, I'll find him myself." He huffed off and took with him the peacefulness Bea had found moments earlier.

"Wait just a minute! Who do you think you are?" she shouted and moved to the center of the aisle. Her heart raced as she watched him walk swiftly away. He looked back once, and waved an arm as if to push aside her words. Her irritation grew as she stood staring ahead, watching his flannel back grow smaller and smaller. She took one last bite of the apple and flung it as far as she could. It rolled between trees, lost in the orchard to decompose.

She tried to shake off the condescension and arrogance left in his wake but could only turn back to the tree to top off her basket. After Bea filled it to the brim she walked up the aisle of trees in search of a place to dump the apples and begin again.

The sting from the earlier confrontation left her with a feeling of embarrassment with a side of dread. She had never had that feeling at the orchard, Bea always felt like she belonged here, but today she felt like the new girl. When she was younger working the orchard was easy, but it had been a good ten years - before she started college - since she'd harvested apples alongside Cliff and his hodgepodge team of townies.

The rest of the year Cliff was on his own, save for the days sprinkled here and there when a friend came to help with odds and ends, the jobs that took more than one person. Never once had Cliff hired someone to help off season, he got by with the help of neighbors and friends who in turn benefited by way of bushels of apples, gallons of cider, and the community garden on the edge of Finley Orchards. Cliff bartered for bigger jobs, and even picking hours, trades of skills and time and energy and the occasional pie or a few jars of applesauce.

Voices brought her back to the present, to sunshine streaming across her shoulders, to the dampness growing outward from her armpits, and to the heavy basket in front of her that needed to be emptied.

She looked around for where the voices were coming from, poked through the space between trees to the left and saw nothing. She went through two aisles to the right and saw Cliff's unmistakable height and the breadth of his shoulders.

14

With the basket between her legs, knees knocking the apples with each step, she waddled over to where Cliff was standing with a few other people. She sidled up, unnoticed, to the big bin where the apples were being collected. Carefully she unlatched the hooks on her basket, and reached over the edge of the receptacle to unleash a flow of fruit. Bea stood straight and readjusted her straps, latched the bottom back to the basket. She pulled her shoulders down and back, arching into a slight back bend.

"Bea!" yelled Cliff, "Come on over, I want to introduce you to someone."

Bea sighed, small talk exhausted her. Cliff knew everyone in town, and since she returned it felt like there had been a constant string of introductions, or re-introductions.

She made her way over to the circle of people, a handful of whom she recognized. People from local businesses who made time in their day for a few hours at the orchard here and there, a few jack of all trades men and women, newly retired townspeople for whom this was their first or second year picking as a way to pass the days. But as she approached the group she saw one newly familiar figure. The man in the flannel shirt and inappropriate shoes was standing right next to Cliff.

Bea avoided looking at him as she moved to the other side of Cliff. She nodded at the people she recognized, spoke quiet hello's and how are yous. Though she felt the man's gaze on her, she didn't bring herself to look at him until Cliff put a hand on her arm to get her attention.

"Bea, this is my neighbor, Graham Winters," he said and gestured towards the man who had waved her off in the orchard. "Graham deals in the antique book business, and helps around here in his spare time. He's keeping us all in line." Cliff chuckled softly, the sides of his eyes crinkled as he looked at Graham endearingly. "Graham, this is Beatrix Hampton, long time friend of the orchard and surrogate daughter of mine. My farm girl." He put an arm around Bea and squeezed.

Graham extended his hand to her and Bea reached across Cliff for a handshake.

"Nice to meet you, officially, Graham." Her words were clipped. She went through the street mentally, trying to figure out which house this neighbor could belong to.

"The pleasure is all mine," his words were equally clipped and she couldn't tell if his smile was as forced as her own. To her it looked like he didn't spend much time smiling, between his eyebrows were deep frown lines.

"Officially? Have you met before?" Cliff asked.

"Yes," Graham started, "I was beginning to tell you about a wayward picker when I first joined you all?"

Cliff laughed, "Ah, yes. It's Bea's first day back at picking, she's allowed some leeway. Give her another day or two and she'll be back in full force. When she gets going she's more dedicated than I am, it'd break my back if I picked as much as she's been known to in a day. Ever since the day we met, she's been as in love with this place as I am. Do you remember that day, Bea?"

Bea nodded. She was three years old the first time she met him. She had held her grandmother's hand tightly as she looked nearly to the clouds to find his face. He was as tall and as wide as a lumberjack. Cliff knelt down to her level and his twinkly blue eyes looked right into Bea's. He extended his hand and she let go of her grandmother and watched her hand disappear into his. Her jaw dropped in awe. She looked up and saw his soft smile and it eased any fear she had of the giant man before her.

Now she smiled at Cliff with the memory, "I also remember us talking about how my name was spelled like Beatrix

16

Potter. I couldn't believe you knew about Peter Rabbit."

"And I couldn't believe you weren't allowed to play in your parent's garden, such a travesty," he shook his head and looked at Graham, "so I gave her the run of the place, the apple farm, as she called it back then. That's why I started calling her Farm Girl," Cliff looked fondly at Bea.

"Glad to hear I misjudged," said Graham. His eyes focused on Beatrix, but she escaped them, focusing her gaze elsewhere. On Cliff. On the orchard. On the people who had left their circle right after the introduction was made. A few people were halfway down rows of Macintosh trees in search of more apples to fill newly emptied baskets.

"Bea," said Cliff, hesitating for a moment, "Graham recently bought your Grandmother's house."

Her eyes opened wide and an electric jolt coursed through her body.

"I didn't realize it was for sale again," she turned to Cliff, "why didn't you tell me?"

Cliff crossed his arms in front of him and widened his stance, he looked down to the ground and then past Bea through rows of trees. It didn't happen often, but Cliff Finley was at a loss for words.

Graham spoke before Cliff, "It was a quick sale. I had an offer in before it was on the market a whole 48 hours."

"And do you like it?" asked Bea. She attempted to cross her own arms but the basket in front of her was in the way, she rested her hands on her hips instead.

"I do. Very much. It's a lovely house. Lots of character, very New England."

"Do you have a family?" She couldn't help herself. She knew nothing about this man, except that he was living in her beloved grandmother's home, and that was enough - aside from their earlier interaction - for her to dislike him.

"I don't. It's just me."

"Quite a big house for just one person."

Graham shrugged his shoulders and stuffed his hands in his pants pockets. Bea looked closely at him, at the pock marks on his cheeks, the softness in his gray eyes that flickered with regret.

Cliff laughed softly, "The farmhouse is a big place for just me, but somehow I've managed to fill it to the brim over the years."

Bea took a deep breath and said, "Well, I'd better head back out, it'll be lunch time before we know it."

She kissed Cliff's cheek and gave a slight but pointed nod to Graham before she walked back down and across two aisles of trees to her picking spot. Even though she didn't dare look back, she felt two sets of eyes on her as she walked, and they were at odds. The familiar, concerned eyes of Cliff, and the new, unknown eyes of the man who lived in her childhood home.

She picked basket after basket of apples. Once it reached around twenty pounds she dropped them gently in with the others and then went back for more fruit, again and again. At lunch she ate her sandwich quietly in the shade of a tree, brushing ants off her arms and swatting at mosquitoes. Most of the pickers sat together, chatting amongst themselves about the day, the town, the weather. This first day back, everyone gave Bea room, space to find her bearings. No one asked why she was here after such a long absence. She had braced herself for questions, but they never came, until they did.

While she was chewing a bite of sandwich Ron Taggert walked over and crouched down slowly next to her. All angles and bones, his knees cracked and he plopped as soon as he was within close proximity to the ground. He wore the unofficial orchard uniform: jeans and an unbuttoned flannel shirt open with a tee shirt with Cumberland printed across it in faded letters underneath.

"So, Bea," he said, his eyes narrowing and his voice serious, "are you still seeing the photographer?"

After a pause, she said, "I'm not." But she had to think of what photographer Cliff knew about to pass along the information.

"What was that?" he said with a hand cupped to his ear. Light danced through his thinning gray hair.

"I'm not seeing anyone," she shouted, all heads turned and Bea blushed. She caught Cliff paying extra attention.

"Ahh, that's good. My son Chris is living in town, he's a firefighter, do you remember him?"

She nodded, of course she remembered Chris Taggert. He broke her heart when they were thirteen, and she had been avoiding him ever since. At the time, he was the most handsome boy she had met, blond hair and blue eyes, and Bea fell head over heels in first love with him. He'd dismissed her, though now she wasn't sure if it was because of her, or if it was because he was a thirteen year old boy who wasn't into girls yet.

"When I told him you were back, he wasn't displeased, I'll tell you that." From where Bea sat it looked like Ron winked at her, but she hoped he hadn't.

"Maybe I'll see him around," she said. And with that, she turned back to her sandwich, not wanting to invite any further conversation about her love life. With much effort Ron stood and joined the others.

From her resting spot Bea heard the conversation, and smiled at the familiarity. Nothing had really changed since she'd

19

been gone. Yes, Cliff's hair was now completely gray where it had previously been salt and peppered, the orchard and community gardens had expanded, and most of those that showed up for picking were more stooped than before. But time does that. It changes things in small nearly unnoticeable ways. But the core of life, the heart of a place stays the same. Bea smiled into her turkey and cheese on rye and felt at ease with the familiar and the pull of change. She bristled only when she thought of Graham and her grandmother's home.

Later as the sky turned a faint hue of pink and orange trails swept across the horizon Bea knew it was time to fill her last basket and find Cliff, to call it a day. She was one of the only ones left in the rows as pickers dropped off at different times throughout the afternoon until there were none left. Cliff never asked more of people than what they could give, physically or otherwise, and there was a certain camaraderie and respect that grew between him and anyone who worked on the orchard over the years. In the beginning he could manage the orchard on his own, but as time went on and the lines of apple trees multiplied, he relied on others more and more. Bea was one of many who knew they would always have a place at the orchard, a soft place to land, and though he couldn't afford to pay in the monetary sense Cliff Finley would give you a roof over your head until you found your feet.

Bea was looking for her feet.

After years away she was back at the orchard trying to find her footing. She had always been able to find it in Cumberland, or at least she had in the past and hoped she could now, even without her grandmother.

Bea slowly made her way to the truck. She dumped her apples and found Cliff meandering back as well.

He smiled his slow smile and put an arm around her.

"Ready to head home?"

She leaned into him and said, "I'm ready."

As she opened the passenger side door of the truck, it squeaked and startled a black capped chickadee sitting in a neighboring tree. It's song rang out, chic-a-dee-dee-dee-dee... as it flew away, into another bunch of branches. The familiar hum of the truck engine thrummed through her, she felt rumbles dance from the engine to her thighs that sat flush against the ripped leather bucket seat. They drove back to the farmhouse where they would eat dinner together. There were questions that needed to be asked, unspoken words that needed to be said. But in those few moments between the apple trees and the farmhouse, she let her body sway as the truck followed the contours of the land, her senses overwhelmed by the unmistakable song of the chickadee and the scent of apples wafting from every inch of air around her.

TWO

"Are you sure I can't help?" The sound of Bea's fingers tapping against the worn wooden table rang through the rafters above.

Cliff was bouncing like a small metal ball in a pinball game, ricocheting from oven to refrigerator to cabinet and back to the oven, ending up at the sink. Over running water his voice boomed, "Nope, sit tight. Tomorrow you can help, tonight is a celebratory dinner." He turned his head towards her and flashed a smile.

"Celebratory of what?" Her eyes took in the kitchen. The wallpaper laden with eggplants, tomatoes, peppers, and other garden vegetables. The steel rack hanging from the ceiling heavy with pots and pans. The spider plant sitting on the windowsill, leaves snaking around a glass jam jar holding a cutting suspended in water, tiny hair roots swimming just below the surface.

"Of your first day back on the job!" In two steps Cliff walked across the kitchen and reached up to the shelf above where

Bea sat to grab a pair of tongs from a utensil container filled with spatulas and wooden spoons. Bea leaned into the table and looked over her shoulder as he reached above her, inhaling the scent of hand soap and flour that lingered on his apron.

"I'm not sure that deserves whatever it is you're cooking up, but thank you."

"Chicken Piccata," without missing a beat he was across the kitchen flipping chicken cutlets in the pan. He winced as sizzling oil hit his skin. Rubbing his arm he said, "What'd you think of the day?"

Bea stood and walked over to the white ceramic farm sink, her favorite part of the kitchen. It was the one thing that fit with everything else and tied it all together. Arms crossed in front of her, her eyes followed Cliff as he grabbed for the salt and pepper grinders. She moved out of the way when he needed to drain the capers.

"It all came back to me, picking," she answered. "The sounds and smells, the movements. My shoulders are achy, just like I knew they would be. The people a little older, not unlike yourself," Bea raised an eyebrow as she looked to make sure she hadn't offended him. Cliff chuckled. She laughed and felt the tension she held for the better part of the day recede.

"There's a bottle of white in the fridge, I need it for the sauce. Why don't you open it - the corkscrew is over where the tongs were - and pour us each a glass?"

She searched through a few cabinets for glasses before Cliff pointed to the one on the right of the sink.

"You're slacking," he said, "I haven't reorganized a thing since you were here last."

Bea let out a guffaw, "Only added things."

"Like mugs from a certain world traveler," he chuckled, "which is not my fault. I really haven't gotten anything new since it's mostly just me I'm cooking for, and I don't need anything fancy. I'm happy to have someone to cook for now, Bea."

She handed him a pint sized mason jar filled nearly to the brim with sauvignon blanc and then poured herself a glass.

"Does Graham ever come over for dinner?" She turned to the table, her back to Cliff as she lifted the glass to her lips.

Cliff exhaled, his breath long and low. A silence followed while Bea sat down and crossed her legs while Cliff took his attention to the chicken. She watched him, expectantly. Not for the first time today, he looked old. His shoulders stooped a bit and his gray hair puffed at the sides, matching his unkempt eyebrows and the exposed hair on his arms.

He grabbed his glass from its perch on the counter, turned the burner on low, and joined Beatrix at the table. His legs spread wide, and he wiped his hands on his makeshift apron, a towel he tucked into his pants. Cliff leaned over and placed his elbows on his knees and rested his cheek in a palm.

"I was going to tell you. I really was. But then the sale happened so fast, and you were God knows where on that photo shoot last year, and -"

"He's been in the house for a year," she interrupted, "and you didn't think to mention it over any of our phone calls? Not even in an email?"

Cliff straightened in his seat. "Of course I thought about it, but it was a conversation to have in person."

"And since I've been back? You haven't mentioned him once."

Cliff rubbed his jaw and took a long swig of wine. "Graham was at an estate sale in Maine, so I thought I had a few days to bring it up before he came around," he paused before saying, "but he came back early."

Bea sat up straight like she was going to say something,

but then she slumped into her chair and untied her ponytail. Her hair cascaded down the back of the chair.

"But what if I wanted to buy it back?" She knew she sounded like an angst ridden teenager, but she couldn't help it. Not when it came to her grandmother's house.

"Could you? Think hard on that Beatrix." He stood and moved to the stove and shook the pan back and forth over the burner. "There's nothing you could have done. You couldn't afford the place without your parents help, and you know that would never happen. I tried to think of some way that I could, but other than selling this place, I couldn't come up with anything. So I didn't want you to go through that hurt, that loss, all over again." Bea acknowledged his words with her silence.

Cliff threw some pasta into a pot, the thin wisps of angel hair cowered against the boiling water. He glanced at his watch and moved the chicken onto a plate on the counter. Next he added wine and butter to the pan, scraping up bits of chicken as he went to turn browned bits into a flavorful sauce. Bea watched, mesmerized. She felt the weight of her silence, and the sage undercurrent of his.

"Tell me about Graham. You think highly of him?" Bea took a sip of wine, sat the glass down and ran her index finger along the rim.

Two plates in hand, Cliff came over to the table. Mounds of angel hair pasta topped with fragrant chicken piccata, slices of lemons, and capers in a single line were delicately plated.

"I'll tell you about Graham if you promise you'll tell me why you're back. The real reason."

The color drained from Bea's face. She took a deep breath, and then a gulp of wine. "Is that what the wine is about? To loosen me up so I'll spill the beans?"

He laughed. "The wine is because I'm not sure how to do this, you being an adult and all. You haven't spent much time here since you were a teenager. It feels like new territory."

"Okay, I'll play. You first, tell me about Graham. About why I shouldn't hold it against him that he's living in Grandma's house."

Finishing a bite of pasta and chicken, he held up his fork in protest. "He's the second owner since your grandmother. He didn't buy the house to spite you. That alone should be your reason not to hold where he lays his head against him."

"That's true." She hoped this would buy her some time, that Cliff would go on for hours about Graham Winters and his book-selling adventures.

Cliff set down his fork and leaned back in his chair, his head tilted in thought. "He's a nice guy from New Hampshire, out near Hanover. Commuted to Dartmouth where his father was a professor. He's one of a few children, I think he has a brother who teaches at Stanford. He started dealing in books when his grandparents died. They had an estate full of books Graham's parents didn't want to keep - should sound familiar to you - he didn't want them to go to waste." He paused for a sip of wine, a bite of chicken.

"Why here?"

"Why not? It's beautiful, and there's easy access to Boston but far enough from the city to feel peaceful. There's certainly a population that would spend money on rare books in the surrounding towns. It's the perfect location."

"And he's protective of you."

"As are you, Beatrix Hampton," he smirked, "I'd think that would endear him to you."

She raised her eyebrows and said, "Not necessarily. Depends what his motives are."

"His motives? His only motive is to lead a quiet life, surrounded by good people and books."

"And there isn't a special person in his life?"

"No. He's a grumpy bachelor like me. I think that's why we get along so well," he said with a smile. Cliff rose from the table and gathered both dinner plates, devoid of food except for the lemon slices.

"And why was there never anyone special in your life?" she asked, emboldened by the wine, hoping to stall a bit longer.

Cliff shook his head as he placed the dishes on the counter. He turned to face Bea as he leaned against the sink and wiped his hands on the dishcloth at his waist.

"Of course there's been special people in my life," his eyes twinkled, "but those stories are for another day. And you, young lady, now have the floor." He gestured wide towards the linoleum. "More wine?"

She placed a hand over her cup and shook her head. She sighed with her whole body and slipped her gaze from Cliff to the kitchen walls, the cobwebs in the corners, the stack of cookbooks, worn and tattered. The Joy of Cooking and The Fannie Farmer Cookbook sat on the shelf with post it notes stuck out of the sides, dog eared and food stained pages left the books swollen.

Bea sighed and said, "It's a long story."

"It always is," there was a familiar softness in his voice, and Bea found herself thankful for him. There was no one else alive she'd even think to have this conversation with, no one else she trusted. Cliff removed the dishcloth from his waist and threw it on the counter where it landed in a heap, a mound of wet, woven fabric.

"Does it have to do with Tom?"

"Tom?" she asked, and racked her brain, "Oh! God no!" she'd forgotten that he had been listening intently at lunch when Ron asked about her dating life. His guess was far from the truth. "No, Tom and I were over ages ago. I think we both knew that was going nowhere," she looked at Cliff and found he had relief written across his face.

Tom was a fellow photographer who's path crossed Bea's briefly, but wildly. He was gorgeous, chiseled in every way, and fun to be around. But their romance ended when they had photography gigs on opposite sides of the world, ending before it began, thanks to work schedules. Like all of Bea's romantic relationships.

She didn't have any answers to give Cliff. Just memories that landed on her chest in a mound of sloppy anguish like the dishcloth. That's what she felt like: a used up, balled up, thrown aside cloth. All of her ambitions played out, and now she had to find some new ones. In the past it was always her grandmother who picked up the pieces when she needed someone to talk things over with, but now the duty fell to Cliff and Bea wasn't sure he was up to the task. Truthfully, she had never tried him out in this arena. He was always there for her with a quick supportive embrace but the emotional stuff, that's where Sylvia's expertise came in.

Bea winced at the thought of Sylvia no longer being her confidant. Even though it had been six years, sometimes she forgot and picked up the phone to call her grandmother. The longing to speak to her was a constant ache, one that lessened over time but was always present.

"The dishes can wait," said Cliff. He motioned to the doorway as he walked towards the living room. Bea followed, shuffling her feet across the kitchen floor and into the next room. Cliff started fidgeting with the wood stove. "Do you think we'll need this tonight?"

Bea settled into the couch and the worn plaid fabric covered cushions enveloped her as she shimmied into a comfortable position.

"A fire would be nice."

They were both postponing the inevitable conversation at hand, her in thought, Cliff with fire starters. The sound of crumpling newspaper filled the room. Bea appreciated his tactics. Fire situated, both settled into the couch as it shifted with Cliff's weight. He reached over and put his hand on Bea's arm.

"You know you don't really have to tell me, if you don't want to."

"No, no. You deserve to know why I showed up. I guess I thought I could sneak in with the picking season as an excuse."

"You know you're always welcome, it's not that at all. You've been lost in thought all week. Is it about your grandmother, and now the house?" He didn't wait for an answer, "I really should have said something about Graham earlier."

"Oh Cliff, no. It's not that at all. It's just, I had nowhere else to go. Nowhere else I wanted to go."

The reasons she gave as she sat in Cliff's living room were these: her ambitions crumpled, she was depleted, exhausted, and she feared that she lost her love of photography. It was the truth, though there was far more to it.

For the last few years Beatrix bounced around the world in a whirl of freelance photojournalism. Straight out of college Bea took the work as it came, and it came fast. She said yes to every opportunity, every friend of a friend who needed help, a favor, or a freebie. She did it for exposure, to get her name out, to please friends and potential clients. The travel kept her wanderlust, something that had gnawed at her since childhood, satisfied.

And then one day it became too much. She sat in LAX with a phone full of contacts but all of her contracts and jobs fulfilled. Bea was ready for more than a vacation, she was ready for a taste of home, and she wasn't sure how long she needed to savor the flavors. Not forever, that wouldn't fit with her idea of life. But she knew that for a time she needed to be home. Not the home where her parents still lived, but the place that she went to when she needed a dose of reality, to reset and focus on what was next.

In doing so, in not booking another gig, she found herself homeless. She carried all of her worldly possessions, including her photography equipment, with her from place to place in two suitcases. She knew there were a few boxes of things Cliff had squirreled away at the orchard from her grandmother's house, and sitting in the airport she had a fierce longing to hold whatever was in those boxes. It didn't matter what they were, she wanted to physically hold a piece of her past. Beatrix Hampton needed grounding.

She was starting to feel the burnout that so many photographer friends had talked about. She felt the pressure to be better and faster with everything from pitches to processing, the pressure from clients to be someone she wasn't sure she could be. Tough. In charge. In control. She pretended, in a fake it until you make it sort of way, but that only exhausted her. And now that everyone could easily be a photographer thanks to cell phone cameras, she felt the pressure to excel and that pressure compiled with all the others crumpled her. She knew the risk of dropping out of the business for a season, she knew that she wouldn't be able to jump right back in, but she had to catch her breath. She had to get out while she still could, before the industry swallowed her whole.

Now Cliff looked straight at her, his eyes not leaving hers. Softly he asked, "You brought your equipment back with you?"

"I did." Her shoulders slumped, heavy with the weight of her story, her homecoming.

"And you want to work through the harvest?"

"I do."

"You can stay as long as you like. You know that?"

"I do."

"Have you talked with your parents?"

"No."

"You're not a failure, Beatrix Hampton."

"I know." She looked down at her hands. She folded and refolded them over and over in her lap.

"Do you?" he paused, "Needing a break is okay. Changing your mind about what you want is never a failure." Cliff's voice was strong, steady.

"I know."

"You are not a failure."

Something within her broke, and she looked up at his kind face that had filled with deep creases and wrinkles over the years, but above all it held adoration. The corners of Bea's eyes were damp, and before she knew it tears streamed down her face. She crumpled into the couch, and into him. Cliff wrapped his arms around her, and they sat, staring at the fireplace.

"Thank you," she murmured into his chest.

He kissed the top of her head. "You know, it wouldn't be so bad if you just stayed here, I could use the company. I'm not getting any younger."

She shook her head and sat up. "There's no way. I'd go stir crazy if I stayed for too long."

"That's what you think, but when was the last time you stayed in one place for a while?"

She groaned and said, "Now you sound like my parents. You didn't a minute ago, but now you totally do."

"It's purely selfish." He rubbed the back of his neck. "I'm a lonely man, who doesn't have anyone to share my quiet moments with." He batted his eyelashes and turned his mouth into a pout.

"I'm pretty sure that's of your own accord," she nudged him with her shoulder, "plus, you do have Graham. And the countless people who care about you throughout Cumberland." She stood and checked the fire, for what she wasn't sure, but she didn't like where the conversation was heading.

"Yes, but no one knows the kind of things about me that you do."

"Like how one of your toenails grows into your toe and you have to trim it more often than the others?"

"Exactly like that," he chuckled. "You remember those kinds of things, but they're not the sort I'd share with a neighbor or an acquaintance so I've never had anyone to share those details with. Think about it, it's an option. You never know, you might like being in one place longer than a season." She started to protest but he shook his head and raised his hand, "I know, I know, it's not in your nature. I'll let it go, but I wanted to at least plant the seed. All I'm saying is it's a possibility."

"I appreciate it, I do." A yawn escaped her mouth, her face felt puffy from dried tears. "I think I need to go upstairs. I'm spent."

Cliff stood up. "Go on up. I'll finish the dishes." He began to walk towards the kitchen but stopped in the doorway. "Bea? Thanks for telling me. It means the world that you still want to come here, even though your grandmother isn't across the street. Forget my guilt trip, you can stay as long or as briefly as you'd like and come back whenever. The offer will stand, the orchard will always be here for you."

"Thank you, Cliff," she walked over and gave him a quick hug and a peck on the cheek, "see you in the morning."

She took the stairs slowly, noticing the empty wall leading upstairs. It was not filled with photos of relatives or wedding and birth announcements like at her grandmother's, or the annual family photos that hung in her parents stairway. Instead there was wallpaper covering the stairwell so ancient it peeled at the edges and if she were to run her hand across it, she'd take a chunk of dusty, weathered paper off without trying. The wood floors were ancient as well, but within the cracks of the wide floor boards was a charm and character that no carpet could ever contain.

Upstairs there was a guest bedroom, a bathroom, and Cliff's bedroom. Bea turned right into the guest bedroom, a place that was unfamiliar to her until her grandmother's passing. Before, she had no reason to stay at Cliff's house, no reason to lay in bed and hear his snoring across the hall, which in the past week had been a signal of comfort or annoyance, depending on the hour. The guest room was wallpapered with a calico of tiny pink buds and green leaves against a beige background. On one wall there was a framed print of Winslow Homer's *Girl in the Orchard*: a haunting painting of a thoughtful woman walking through an orchard, bonnet in hand.

Now, as Bea sat on the edge of the bed, she looked up at the painting with sleepy eyes. Before she laid her head on the pillow she made a silent vow to herself that she would not end up alone in the orchard, not like the woman in the painting, and not like Cliff. Her heart ached for him, but she couldn't do it. A familiar feeling of restlessness washed over her, and as she drifted off to sleep her last waking thought was of planning her next move, her escape.

THREE

The alarm on her cell phone buzzed on the nightstand and she groggily reached over to turn it off. Footsteps echoed from the kitchen below, metal on metal rang out as Cliff rustled through the utensil drawer. Bea smelled coffee brewing and swung her legs to one side of the bed, wincing as her bare feet met the chill of the hardwood floor. Outside the sky sat in wait of the sun to peer out from under the horizon.

The world seemed silent aside from Cliff's stirring. Last week when she had yet to begin picking she heard his movements downstairs but stayed in the warmth of the tiny twin bed burrowing under the covers. Each morning she woke lazily as the sun shone its pale morning light first on the floor next to her and then across the blankets in greeting. The house went quiet again after Cliff left for the orchard, the rumble of his truck slowly fading into the apple trees. But this week her alarm rang before the sun could extend a lazy hello, before half the world was awake.

She dug through a small pile of clothing at the foot of the bed and found her jeans from the previous day. She pulled them

34

on along with her favorite threadbare Boston Red Sox tee shirt and a thick hooded sweatshirt to fend off the damp chill of morning. Bea opened the bedroom door and before she could walk through the doorway she stubbed her toe. Rubbing her eyes she muttered a favorite string of words reserved for pain or befuddlement, both situations applied. At her feet were two dusty and yellowed cardboard boxes. She stepped around them, deciding to deal with them later, after a cup of coffee.

"Good morning, sunshine," Cliff greeted her from the kitchen stove where he was flipping eggs in a cast iron skillet. He pointed at the coffee maker, "Grab a mug. Eggs will be ready in a minute."

Bea grunted in acknowledgment and poured herself a cup of steaming hot coffee.

"It'll get easier," he said, his voice light.

Her eyebrows raised in question as she turned towards him.

"The mornings," he clarified, "they'll get easier. It's hell at first, but within a few weeks you'll be awake before your alarm."

In a few weeks, she thought, she'll be on her way. But she nodded and even mustered a faint smile.

"When was the last time you slept in?" she asked.

He thought for a moment, paused midway between the stove and table, spatula in hand. "Three weeks ago on a Sunday I slept until seven," he laughed, "I thought that was something else, my old body getting soft. Started setting the alarm again the next day."

Bea sat down at the kitchen table, pulled her feet onto the

35

chair and rested her chin on her knees.

"The eggs smell good, but I'm not hungry yet."

"Can't go out without breakfast. Like I said yesterday, you'll be hungry before we even get started."

She remembered the day before, how he met her first thing with a bowl of oatmeal.

"Did you see the boxes?"

"How could I miss them?" she scowled, her toe still throbbing. "What are they?"

"You didn't look in them?"

"No, I was pretty focused on coffee." She smiled up at him. The coffee was having the desired effect, the aroma alone was enough to wake her up and lift her tired spirits.

Cliff placed two plates of eggs and toast on the table and sat down across from Bea.

"Have a look when you get back this afternoon," the endearing twinkle in his eyes unnerved her slightly.

"I will," she said through a mouthful of buttery fried egg, "these are the best eggs I've ever tasted, Cliff."

"Would you expect anything less?"

"No, of course not." She finished her coffee in one large gulp, the bitterness left behind in her mouth caught her off guard.

In all of the years Bea knew Cliff and all of the hours she spent in his orchard, she never saw him at his best. She realized this as she witnessed him cook for her, care for her in a more fatherly way than even when she was little and went to him with skinned knees. The way he so easily welcomed her into his life and home and routine felt tender, touching. Maybe it was age and perspective and he was always this way, but these early morning moments were different.

She knew she should feel thankful and honored but suspicion crept in and tainted the kindness of his gestures. She remembered the conversation from the night before, his suggestion that she stay, and how staying wasn't in her plan. But then again, there was no plan. Not really.

She put the mug down on the table and said with a forced smile, "Let's go."

Her resolve to leave after picking season grew by the minute, along with her restlessness. But where would she go next? That question lingered long after breakfast.

That afternoon instead of eating lunch at the orchard Bea walked back to the farmhouse. She said she needed to check her emails, but both she and Cliff knew that the boxes sitting by her bedroom door were calling.

As she walked up to the picturesque white farmhouse with its wraparound porch and weather beaten shingles, she regarded it as one would an ancient relative, with kindness and distinction. A typical New England farmhouse, lilac and forsythia stood in front of the porch, needing to be trimmed back now that the fragrant flowers were no longer and the buds were dormant. The view from the porch was of neat and tidy rows of apple trees for miles until they gave way to the marsh and sand dunes leading to the ocean. On clear nights when the windows were left wide open you could hear the sounds of the ocean meeting the shore, waves crashing, tides ebbing and flowing. It was the same at her grandmother's house, and when she was at her parents' house in the suburbs Bea longed to hear the rhythm of the ocean in the distance rather than cars on the highway.

She noticed the sign for Finley Orchards tucked back from the road that led to Cumberland's only beach, the sign's edges worn and battered, the stain of the wood non-existent. Finley

Orchards was the town of Cumberland's best kept secret. Cliff had seen the toll the business took on the previous owners who tried to grow big and couldn't keep up with the crowds and commercialization long before the days of the internet and social media; from the moment he signed the papers, he vowed to keep the orchard manageable, small, contained and local. Pick your own was a thing of the past at his newly rebranded orchard. The townspeople, normally wary of outsiders, were happy to help the young man with big dreams of keeping the orchard private. And by private, they meant for their community. Cliff quickly became an integral part of Cumberland, donating his time during winter and stretches of spring to other businesses and town projects, and during the peak picking season he struck bargains with the schools and senior housing for his apples, always delivering more than they paid for. Cliff dealt not only in apples, but in humanity.

Bea took the front porch steps two at a time and swung the screen door open wide. She paused momentarily, through a dense amount of trees she could still make out her grandmother's house. Graham's house, she corrected herself.

Upstairs the boxes sat square in front of the bedroom door, exactly where she left them earlier. Dust motes danced in the midday light, undisturbed until Bea's presence shifted the air. She carried them to her bed and sat them down, side by side.

As soon as she opened the first box Bea was greeted by the familiar and comforting scent of her grandmother. A smile spread across her face, and tears pricked her eyes. Instantly she was brought back to her grandmother's guest bedroom to a safe place where her dreams of wanderlust first began and where she was told that anything was possible. It was at Sylvia's house where Bea's height was measured in pencil marks in the doorway between the porch and the kitchen. It was at Sylvia's house where Bea got her first period and had to be convinced that she was not in fact dying, but becoming a woman. And it was at Sylvia's house where Bea sobbed over summer romances that ended in broken hearts, friendships that couldn't stand the test of twenty miles, and parents who simply couldn't understand. Sylvia consoled her granddaughter through it all, and never once made Beatrix feel guilty for her feelings, for being human, for being herself. Bea felt no attachment to the address where school records were sent and her parents lived, but was overcome with emotion when it came to her grandmother's home.

She sifted through the contents of the box, crocheted doilies tucked in and around knickknacks Bea recognized instantly: a handful of porcelain chickadees in all shapes and sizes. Some sat on delicate branches sticking out of painted trees while others were on their own with solid, flat bottoms. Her grandmother's china cabinet was full to the brim with chickadees and china, but a few special figurines resided on a shelf in Bea's room. Sylvia knew how much Bea adored them, studied them, and how careful she was with them, and so she trusted her granddaughter to care for a few of her prized possessions while Bea visited.

Bea carefully inspected each item as she took them out of the box, tracing the outline of each bird with an index finger. The porcelain was cool to the touch, the figurines in perfect condition except for a little dust in the crevices. After inspection Bea methodically wrapped each figurine back in a doily and returned them to the box. She folded the flaps back into themselves and moved the box to the floor and hefted the second closer to her side.

As she opened it, the air outside changed and the wind began to whip against and around the house. The light was no longer bright and yellow, sunbeams and dust motes disappeared while shadows grew dark. Without looking out the window Bea knew the scene that would unfold in the orchard during the next few moments. Heavy limbs of the trees would sway, the clouds would break open and drench the fields, pickers would clutch their baskets with one hand, their hats with another, and walk with heavy steps to the truck, dump their apples with the rest and slowly drive through the fields back to the barn where they would either wait out the storm or disperse for the remainder of the day.

With that knowledge in the back of her head, she made haste and dove into the second box. She found it was stuffed with books full of dust mites and mildew. Dust tickled her nose as she inspected one after the other, stacking them neatly by her side after she read each title: *Birds of North America*, *Wild Bird Guides: Black Capped Chickadees*, and few that look like ancient novels and academic texts that she had never heard of. And a notebook, nearly falling apart, with handwritten recipes. She clutched it to her chest, and a few index cards spilled down onto her lap. When she shifted her weight atop of the overly soft bed the stack of books fell into her. She felt surrounded by her grandmother.

Bea heard the truck driving towards the house and the sound of rain pelting the house, the wind relentless and building strength. Throwing the books back into the box, all except the recipe notebook, she stood and gazed at her suitcases. How could she fit the contents of the two boxes into them? She'd have to store them here longer. Cliff, she thought, had plenty of space and could keep the boxes just as he had.

The front door slammed against the wall as it flung open and Bea heard footsteps in the kitchen. The wetness of the day carried upstairs on a gust and landed at her feet.

Downstairs she found Cliff standing in the kitchen, coffee pot in one hand, the other holding onto the counter.

"Are you alright?" she asked.

He turned and gave her a weak smile that didn't reach his

eyes, "Just filling up the coffee pot. Could use some warmth after getting stuck out there." His hair was drenched and matted down like a wet mop.

Bea walked over next to him and took the pot out of his hand, touched his wet shoulder and said, "You go get changed, I'll make the coffee." His eyes were tired as he nodded and walked out of the kitchen. Bea scooped coffee grounds into the coffee maker, the fragrance hung in the air against the backdrop of damp.

Outside a low and howling whistle called from the distance, and outside the trees swayed and air danced through and around branches. Bea thought she could hear apples falling to the ground, she imagined thumps rising from the ground beneath her and up through her chest.

"It'll let up soon enough," Cliff's voice startled Bea out of her thoughts. His voice held notes of strength and an undercurrent of worry. She poured two mugs to the brim with coffee and brought them to the kitchen table. Bea and Cliff sat and stared out the windows though there was nothing to see but gray sky, raindrops falling on the windowpane, and a blur of trees swaying. A frightening sight for any orchard owner in the peak of harvest season.

He blew steam across the top of his mug and said, "This is going to be one of the best years, crop wise." Not was, is. Bea took note.

"Then I came back at the right time."

Cliff smiled slowly into his coffee, "That you did."

"I went through the boxes," she stated quietly, "thank you for saving her chickadees. Tell me about the rest."

He sighed and rubbed a hand over his coarse midday scruff. Cliff took a swig of coffee and set the cup on the table and leaned forward.

"I didn't know at the time that Graham would come along,

41

but it may be worth having him take a look at some of those books. Not the cookbook, but the others. Even the ancient bird guides. You saw the one on chickadees? She loved those birds almost as much as she loved you."

Bea remembered the vast knowledge her grandmother had about black capped chickadees. Every time one would come to her porch, Sylvia would share some tidbits of wisdom with whoever was sitting with her. The fact that chickadees were actually terrible fliers amused her. She'd share that except for the very young, they didn't actually go very far. It was always the very young chickadees who would take on a foolhardy adventure.

"I didn't look too closely, but I figured they were important to your grandma as they were stacked on her desk." He paused before continuing, "Your parents didn't take a close look at anything when they came to empty out the house. One day I went over and offered to help, but your mother wouldn't look at me. They were just throwing things in a dumpster. Broke my heart."

When Sylvia Eaton died, unexpectedly but from natural causes during Bea's Senior year of college, it was no surprise to anyone that Bea felt the loss the deepest. Not only the loss of her grandmother, but the loss of her home as well. Bea was heartbroken that the house didn't stay in the family, and before Bea could even come up for a breath of air in the depths of her grief, the house was sold and all of Sylvia's possessions dealt with in one way or another. They didn't ask for Bea's help. They didn't consult her. They treated her as a delicate relic that needed to be packaged in bubble wrap, untouched until her grief settled. Eric and Donna Hampton swept in and settled the estate quickly and dealt with it as purely a business transaction. But it was beyond painful for Beatrix. With her lack of closure with the estate came a deeper gorge between herself and her parents.

"Dad never liked Grandma," said Bea.

Cliff laughed, a loud guffaw. "The feeling was mutual, and that's putting it lightly. I thought they would have buried the hatchet, but in order to do that they would have had to talk. Did they ever?"

"Never."

"All those trips up here, your mother did all that driving, dropped you off and turned around and drove home again. All those years she lived with him and barely saw her mother. Barely saw you at times. I'll never understand it."

Bea didn't understand it either, her parents marriage, her mother's choices. Beatrix spent hours plotting her own permanent escape, not just a trip to her grandmother's house, and when she did leave, for good, she never looked back. Her mother reached out, tried to call, but Bea could hear disappointment in her voice, and so the times that she answered the phone grew farther and farther between, and the times the phone rang with the familiar number appearing on the caller ID grew fewer and fewer.

"You know, I nearly punched him at the funeral."

Bea laughed and raised an eyebrow. "I would have liked to see that."

"He made some comment about my taking care of you all those years. Thanking me in his smug way," his body involuntarily shook, like a shiver went through him, "I've never dealt well with condescension, and your father can dish it out with the best of them. Anyway," Cliff got out of his chair and dumped the remainder of his coffee down the drain of the kitchen sink, "Sylvia would have come back from the grave to tell me off if I had socked him." He chuckled, a smile briefly. "Do you ever talk with her?"

"Rarely. When I do it's short, we both share the bare minimum of information at this point."

"Do you miss her?"

43

"I've never really known her enough to miss her."

Cliff looked at his feet and shook his head.

Bea continued, "I still wonder why she stays with him, they don't seem terribly happy. Maybe the alternative is too scary for her."

"What, living at her mother's house? In this awful town?" His tone was sarcastic, but it grew with anger. "We-" he looked away as he corrected himself, "it was never good enough for her."

"I didn't know you gave her that much thought."

He faced the sink and turned the water on, squirted a bit of dish soap onto a cloth and ran it under the water. Suds spilled over his hands as he washed his coffee cup and a few stray dishes. When he finished, they sat, dripping onto a dish towel on the counter.

"I came here the same year your mother got married and I saw the change in her. Your grandmother would have been supportive of her marriage to just about anyone else, but Donna chose a guy who cared more about money than people, even then. What Donna didn't understand was that she would have all gotten over it and accepted him, even welcome him. But he didn't give Sylia the chance."

Bea understood. Her father had never been an easy man to love, let alone tolerate outside of a boardroom.

"And so when you were born, we thought maybe this will be it. Maybe she'll come around and give us a chance. Instead she kept you to herself for a few years when you were a baby, and then used Sylvia as a babysitter. Donna missed so many beautiful moments with you," he sighed. "I can still see you as a tiny thing, walking through the apple blossoms. You used to love picking them up after the big drop. It was like kids do with the leaves in the fall, you'd make a big pile of them, all those white and pink petals, but instead of jumping in them you'd throw them up in the

44

air and let them fall on you. You came alive in the fields, from the very beginning, and she missed all of that."

"He's polarizing. But strong in his own ways, and I think Mom likes that. He gives her a sense of security. I never felt it, I wanted to," Bea paused and then said, "I wouldn't give up my childhood, all the time spent here, for anything."

She put a hand on his across the table. His face, worn like the weathered shingle siding, was cracking and layers were peeling off.

"That's good to hear, farm girl. But even you won't call this place home, for good. You've got your mother in you somewhere."

Bea pulled back, "That's unfair."

He reached for her hand again, "I'm sorry Bea. I shouldn't have said that." He looked at her with kindness and adoration. "You look like her, you know. Especially around the eyes. It's startling. I don't think I ever really saw it before but now that you're grown, it's there."

Bea knew it was the truth. Her features, except for her height, were all from her mother. Her father gave her his height and a touch of stubbornness, but otherwise when she looked in the mirror she saw herself with a hint of Donna, a tad of Sylvia.

"The weather's changing, you can see it in the sky. I need to go check on a few things."

"Do you need help?"

Bea watched as he found and put on a rain slicker, turning into a sea captain with his weathered face peeking out from the bright yellow hood. All he needed was a pipe, and she knew there was one of those in a pocket of every coat he owned.

"No. You stay here, keep warm." He paused with his hand on the door handle, "Bea, I'm sorry. It's the weather. This time of year is stressful as it is, without the worry of storms and other unexpected happenings."

When he left, the door swung wide as a bluster of air filled the kitchen. She sat at the table, still as stone as the weather swirled around her, and then when the door shut and the air dropped there was stillness and the salty, earthy air of the orchard mixed with the ocean. Cliff, for the first time she could remember, seemed ruffled. It might have been the weather, but Bea felt it was much more than that.

Bea hunted around the closet for another raincoat. There were countless waxed canvas coats and a few fleece jackets all in Cliff's size: extra large. The closets both smelled of pipe tobacco. The sweet, smoky scent followed Cliff everywhere he went, living permanently in his clothes and his pores.

Finally her hands ran over the plastic coating of a rain jacket. It was the bright green of a child's rain boots, Kermit the frog green. She put it on and the jersey fabric inside smoothed over her layers and she tucked stray strands of hair into the hood. The wildness of the world outside wouldn't dissuade her. She needed to get outside, to feel the air on her face, and if not to go after Cliff, she would go for a blustery walk in order to check on a few things of her own.

FOUR

L ate Saturday morning Bea walked the streets of downtown
Cumberland, noting many restored brick structures and
widened sidewalks. As with most towns north of Boston,
within recent years the population saw a swing towards
commuters with property taxes and rents increasing as the location
became more desirable.

The town lines of Cumberland extended from the Boxford
river running diagonally from mid state New Hampshire through
the eastern part of Massachusetts to the Atlantic ocean. While
Cumberland's coastline was expansive, the access to it was
limited, which meant that the river was the creator of jobs rather
than seaside tourism until the demand for mill production slowed
after the first World War, and gradually over the course of decades
they all closed, making way for trendy apartments and businesses.
The Boxford Hat Company, the pride of Cumberland for nearly
one hundred years, stayed in business longer than most, well into
the 1970s.

Bea's footsteps fell on the rusty brick walkway at a

leisurely pace, Bea was taking the day off and trying to enjoy it. When Cliff demanded she take some time to herself, away from the orchard, she pleaded with him to do the same. Since the storm the other day he had seemed irritated, tired, fatigued. But he hadn't taken a Saturday off in years, he said, and didn't plan on starting now. When she tried to stay, he sent her into town with a list of items to pick up and the promise of a stroll on the beach later on.

She came to the corner of Main and Taggert Street, and found herself at Sullivan Hardware. An institution, the store had been passed down from one generation to the next. The latest handover was to Olivia Sullivan, a thirty-something-year-old a few years older than Bea. Whenever she and Sylvia visited the store Olivia came to their aid, showing pride from an early age in the family business. Now, as Bea walked into the store she saw Olivia waddling up the aisle in a pair of denim overalls and a can of paint in each hand.

"Bea!" She said with a smile spread wide across her face, "It's so good to see you. I heard you were in town, but I haven't had a chance to get over to the orchard to say hello or bring a pie!" Her words were spoken with a genuine warmth. The paint cans thudded against the counter as she released them, and when Olivia came over to embrace Bea it became apparent that the reason she was waddling was hardly the paint cans.

"I should have made my way in sooner," said Bea apologetically. She took in the scent of the hardware store, of wooden paint stirrers with notes of paint and insulation. "It looks like congratulations are in order! Cliff didn't mention that you were pregnant, when are you due?"

"You know, I'm not sure Cliff knows," she laughed and placed a hand on the side of her stomach, "I haven't seen him in here for a while."

Bea shook her head, "I'm sure he knows. Word travels

fast in this town, and on the orchard. But you know how he gets during harvest time."

"I do," said Olivia as she sat down on the stool behind the counter, the same stool that had been there for as long as Bea had been visiting, "the baby is due in about three months." Bea did the math, a January baby.

Olivia was glowing, from exertion or pregnancy, Bea couldn't tell. Her face still looked the same as Bea remembered, soft and delicate features highlighted by glimmering blue eyes, her uniform was the same as it had been since she took over the shop out of college: blond pony tail swishing behind her, a hooded sweatshirt with the store's logo on the left breast, and leather clog clad fee. Unchanged by pregnancy or time.

"Steve must be thrilled," said Bea, who was thinking about how she herself had never really considered motherhood. It just wasn't in her sights, and while she knew she had plenty of time, seeing Olivia's swollen middle had made her think about all the steps it would take for her to get there. Properly, with an address, a partner, and stability.

Olivia sighed, "He is. He'd like me to slow down. I keep telling him I'll slow down when the baby gets here. He's out back mixing the rest of the paint for this order," she gestured at the cans in front of her, "special order for Cliff's neighbor actually."

Bea stiffened, "Graham?"

"Yes, have you met him yet?"

"I have," she couldn't stop herself from adding, "didn't get all that great of an impression." She thought of his hard features, the thick lines of his furrowed brow, his supposed allegiance to Cliff and the orchard.

When they were younger, Bea looked up to Olivia as she was just that much older than Bea that she hung on Olivia's every word. She wanted to dress like her, be like her, worship her. And

49

so in this instance, Bea looked to Olivia for reassurance, an opinion, when she felt she couldn't trust her own.

"He doesn't give the best first impressions," Olivia laughed and stood up from the stool, her belly bumped into the counter as she tried to neaten up around the register. She picked up a handful of flat, yellow carpenter pencils that sat in a tin can, tapped them on her palm to even them out. When she dropped them back into the can they hit the container with tiny thuds echoing. She rubbed the lower side of her stomach and continued, "It's funny for someone who works with people, but you'll warm up to each other. He's kind. Not always nice, but kind. Kind is more important than nice, though, don't you think?"

"I've never really thought of the difference between kind and nice." said Bea after a pause.

"Spend enough time in the public arena and you'll see it. Maybe the thing about his business is that people seek him out. Most of his clients find him through a friend of a friend, he's very… discreet."

"A discreet bookseller? What need would there be for discretion?"

"You'd be surprised. Give him a couple glasses of wine and he'll loosen up, he's great dinner company."

"Who are we talking about?" Steve came up the aisle towards the register, as he passed Beatrix he gave her a one-armed hug as a greeting before he stood next to his wife and placed two more cans of paint on the counter. Steve had a mop of brown hair he brushed out of his eyes with his forearm to expose hazel eyes and bushy brows.

"Graham," Olivia leaned easily into him, their matching sweatshirts edges blurring.

He nodded, "His order is all set. Four gallons. You'll like him, Bea. Once you get to know him."

50

"I'm not sure I'll be here long enough to get to that point with him." In that moment she couldn't look at Steve or Olivia. Their happiness was contagious. Bea knew their story: high school sweethearts who went off to separate colleges only to reunite back at home after graduation. A quick engagement, then a wedding that nearly the entire town was a part of - planning and attending. Local everything: flowers, food, beer, even the band. At the time Bea was in high school and came up for the weekend of the wedding. She sat between Cliff and Sylvia in a wooden pew on a stiff red-velvet-covered cushion at the Unitarian Church up on the hill across from the center of town, and watched with bated breath as the young couple said their I do's. The hardware store was then passed down to them after a transition period where her parents imparted their knowledge of the business to them in bits and pieces over the next two years. Olivia kept her last name, a source of pride for her parents, as the family name continued and the hardware store would still be run by a Sullivan.

Bea pushed aside the feelings of jealousy and longing for history. The want to have something passed down from generation to generation. The want to belong somewhere and yet at the same time the fear of just such a thing. It could be a gift or a curse depending on who the legacy belonged to. She stared at Olivia's stomach, how Olivia's hands gravitated towards the unborn baby.

"You'll have to stay long enough to see the baby, that's for sure," said Olivia.

"Of course," Bea forced a smile and thought of winter. How the branches of the apple trees look despondent and the sky almost always bleak, even on sunny days. The birth of a baby would certainly brighten even the darkest winter blues.

"So, tell me, what is he painting with this?" Bea pointed at the four cans of paint.

From behind her a voice said, "The office." She turned

around and saw Graham standing behind her, arms crossed, brow furrowed.

"How long have you been standing there?" she turned to Olivia and Steve and said, "Don't you guys have a bell on the door?"

"You know," said Steve, a smile playing on his lips, "I've been meaning to replace that. The last string of bells we had was older than the two of us combined," he gestured at Olivia and himself, "but I just haven't gotten to it yet."

"Add that to your before the baby arrives to-do list," Olivia muttered, nudging Steve with her elbow. "Graham, you've met Bea?"

"I have," said Graham. He walked up and stood next to Bea at the counter. Another customer came in, and the air swirled around them. Bea caught a whiff of shaving cream and used book store, she stifled a pleased sigh. She blushed as Graham looked at her in an unguarded way, and for a brief moment she was glad she swiped some mascara across her lashes, and then she quickly brushed the thought away. He leaned on the counter, like he was a regular in the shop and the familiarity of his movement sent a shiver down Bea's spine as he said, "I just left Cliff in the orchard, I wasn't surprised to see you taking a day off," this time there was a twinkle in his eye, and he flashed his teeth with a wide grin. They were whiter than the coffee stained teeth Bea expected. Her body stiffened and she felt her defenses stand, despite the playfulness in his eyes.

"I practically begged him to let me out there with him today, or for him to take a day off."

Graham stood from his resting place on the counter and straightened, reached a hand to her upper arm, she bristled. "I'm only kidding, really. I think we got off on the wrong foot the other day, I'm sorry."

"I agree."

The four of them stood in silence for a moment as the world continued moving. The door opened again and a man with a Red Sox baseball cap and steel toed boots walked in, accompanied by leaves crunching between his boots and the shop floor. In the distance an ambulance rang out as it raced down the street, the noise was muffled by windows and barriers. There were exclamations from customers down the aisles: "That's exactly what I needed" and "Let's make our way to the register."

"I came in here for something," said Bea, taking her gaze to the aisle heads, willing something to pop out and jog her memory.

"Gloves?" said Graham.

"How did you know?"

"Cliff told me," he shrugged.

She gave him a warning look, measured but fierce, before turning to Olivia, "I'm actually looking for some fingerless gloves, the mornings are getting chilly and I wanted something to keep my hands from getting stiff with cold."

"I've got just the thing, follow me."

Olivia took Bea across the store into the gardening section. "There's not much here this time of year, but there's a few things left. Here are some gardening gloves, you could snip the fingers off of them, or," they walked a few steps and stopped in front of a display full of lively colored mittens and gloves, less utilitarian looking, more cozy hand-knit type of things, "there's these. Not as sturdy, but warmer and softer. The person who makes them calls them 'texting gloves' but they're just fingerless mitts."

"They're handmade?"

Olivia nodded. "Miriam Elliot knits all day. She lives just past the Orchard on the way down to the beach, in an old tiny cottage, you'd recognize it if you saw it. Anyway, she came in week after week asking to put her things in here, and I told her we just didn't have a need, that her stuff belonged more in the boutique across the street, but then one day I was at a doctors appointment and Steve was here by himself. Well, she wore him down with her charm or something, and the display has been here ever since," Olivia sighed and shrugged her shoulders. Bea ran a hand across the various wool goods. Her fingers landed on a brown pair of mitts. Simple, no frills, just a wide opening for four fingers and a simple thumb gusset.

"Don't be too hard on Graham," said Olivia who was straightening a row of paint brushes in the aisle around the corner from the endcap. Bea didn't look up from the mitts in her hand. "He's had a tough go of it," Olivia continued in a hushed voice, "I heard a rumor about him being left at the altar, but he won't talk about it. He's a tough nut to crack, but he's got a heart of gold. You'll see."

"Thanks, Olivia. I'll keep that in mind."

"For the record," Olivia smiled, "he's finally starting to settle in, and he's taking great care of the house."

"You mean my grandmother's house?"

Olivia winced and went back to the paint brushes, sorting by putting the correct sizes together on hangers that fitted into the peg board shelf.

"I should probably make my way out. I want to pick up something at Bert's to take back to Cliff for lunch. He's been spoiling me since I got here."

"I'm not surprised. He's a sweetheart. Take care of him while you're here."

"It seems," Bea lowered her voice, "that Graham does a pretty good job of that."

Olivia leaned against the end cap, arms crossed and her

54

face suddenly serious, "He and Cliff have gotten close over the last year. I think Cliff sees somewhat of a kindred spirit in Graham, with the whole bachelor seeking refuge in Cumberland thing."

Bea wondered what Graham was seeking refuge from, and if Cliff had actually opened up about that time in his life to his new friend, something Bea wished he would do with her.

Olivia stepped closer to Bea and said quietly, "But he's not your replacement, if that's what you're worried about. No one could replace you at that orchard."

"That's just silly, I didn't think that at all," Bea looked down at the mitts and moved her weight from one foot to the other, "Graham just seems hard to read. Shifty."

"He's the least shifty person I know, though I can see having a hard time reading him. But really, Bea, he's one of the good guys."

Bea was skeptical. In her life, she hadn't met many of them, the good guys. Cliff was one, Steve another, but the majority of the men she had come across in both her personal and professional life had been hard on agendas, soft on sincerity.

They walked back to the counter, Bea clutching the gloves in one hand and her wallet in the other. When they reached the register they saw Graham with his cell phone at his ear, his face pale, his eyebrows drawn together. Steve stood silently in front of him, staring intently at the phone, at Graham.

Olivia started to say something, but Steve raised his hand and motioned for her to stop.

"It's Cliff," said Graham, his eyes wild with fear, he looked at Bea and said, "We've got to go. I'll drive."

FIVE

They drove in silence, aside from the rumble of the road beneath the wheels of Graham's Subaru wagon. Bea longed for something to cut through the unknown that hung in the air.

"Where are they taking him?" she asked, even though logically she knew the answer. There were only so many hospitals in the area, and only one in the direction they were headed.

"Perkins Hospital."

He didn't look at her, his gaze was steady on the road. One hand on the steering wheel, the other on the stick shift, she could see his left leg working the clutch as the car slowed down and sped up depending on traffic. Saturday traffic on Route 1A was heavy on a good day, exhausting at its worst. It was the only main road that stretched between six neighboring towns clustered on one side of a major highway. The day was shaping up to be beautiful, clear blue skies, wispy clouds; the roads were full of leaf peepers trying to find their way to pumpkin patches and pick your own orchards, families searching for photo ops. The worst kind of traffic.

She asked, "Was Cliff alone when you saw him earlier?"

"No, Bert was with him." Graham's answer was terse, mirroring the atmosphere in the car.

Bea sat with her hands neatly folded in her lap, her fingers playing with the mitts she unintentionally pilfered from the hardware store. She attempted a sigh, but her breath was too shallow.

Stopped at a red light, she said, "I just don't understand, he seemed okay when I left this morning. Did he seem unwell when you were at the orchard?"

Graham turned to look at her, his cheeks damp with tears, "He was fine. Nothing seemed out of the ordinary."

She searched his eyes and found the same fear she was trying to stuff deep down within herself. His edge was stripped away, the rough exterior gone, and what she saw was tenderness and sorrow. She put a hand over his on the gear shift. Tears began to prick behind her own eyes and she looked away. The light turned green without Graham noticing, and someone in the line of cars behind them honked. He shook his head slightly and turned back to the road, his hand guiding the gear shift - and her - through first to second and then third. She gave his hand a squeeze before placing her own back in her lap.

"There has to be a better way to get there." Graham hit the top of the steering wheel. Bea stared out the window. She knew there wasn't, but bit her tongue. In normal circumstances she loved this drive. The winding roads that wove through the coast, occasionally offering stunning ocean views, were the quickest, most direct routes to many towns - the road to the highway was long and took drivers north before going south, and vice versa.

And so there was no other way to the hospital than the slow, tourist filled road.

As they drove she viewed the scenery she knew so well: old colonial homes with white plaques including the year and the original owner and the family vocation - cobbler, ship builder, postmaster - etched in black writing; unexpected expanses of farm land between towns; strings of small shops mixed with town offices. As they drove, a scene from her memory played in her head of her grandmother's funeral, of Cliff walking towards her, and her parents slinking away as she embraced him. She saw Cliff's face in the trees and houses they passed, his hair less gray and his eyes blue as ever. He smiled at her from just past the car window.

As they got closer to the hospital the buildings became more industrial and Bea watched the image of Cliff disappear, her head became dizzy as the buildings whipped by. She pressed her face against the window and closed her eyes, the glass was cool against her cheek and she found her breath. It had been stuck in the shallows of her upper chest and the first deep breath she allowed herself came with tears. They streamed down her cheeks and onto the glass.

"We're here," said Graham, his voice full of forced calm. He parked the car and put a hand on Bea's shoulder. She sat up and with her shirtsleeve wiped salty streaks from the window and her cheeks. Stealing a glimpse of Graham, at his disheveled hair and red rimmed eyes, she decided they both needed to pull themselves together. Opening the car door she took one last deep breath to compose herself, to set her resolve.

Firmly she said, "Let's go find Cliff."

They walked together, side by side, strangers tied together by the orchardist just beyond the hospital doors.

As soon as they walked into the Emergency Room entrance she knew. Her heart fell, and she knew the state of affairs before anyone could tell her. The resolve she found in the parking lot stuck with her, and she chose to keep her back straight, her eyes dry, and her head clear. Over the years she learned how to do just that, mainly on photo shoots where she was in control of little but needed to give off the air of complete and utter command and measure. To Bea it felt unnatural, but necessary, and she learned from the best how to put her emotions to the side to get the shot she needed, to get the work done. It was one of the reasons she was now on the coast of Massachusetts instead of on location. Bea had never used this skill outside of work, and she didn't like it.

"Can you point us to Cliff Finley? He was just brought in?" she asked a handful of people at the reception desk.

A red headed woman in rainbow covered scrubs looked briefly at the computer before whispering to a blond haired nurse in blue scrubs.

The nurse said, "Follow me, I'll take you to the head physician on duty."

Bea reached out to hold Graham's hand before the doctor told them what she already knew in her heart.

They were too late.

Cliff Finley, at the age of fifty four, collapsed in his beloved orchard. He was pronounced dead upon arrival at the hospital. The paramedics did all that they could, the doctor told them, but when they wheeled him into the hospital he was too far gone, no amount of chest compressions or use of the defibrillator would bring him back.

Graham muttered quietly, "I think he had signed a DNR at some point anyway."

Bea asked, "A DNR? Why would he sign a DNR?"

The doctor, who looked to be about Cliff's age, shrugged. "People have all sorts of reasons to sign a DNR. Your father never mentioned it before?" he asked, looking at Beatrix.

"Oh, he's not my father. Like a father, but not my father."

"In that case I shouldn't even be speaking with you, I was under the impression that you were family."

Graham, who had been silent since they entered the hospital, spoke up, "She is his family."

Taken aback by his words Bea's resolve was starting to crumble and she muttered, "I couldn't even tell you where his extended family is. I think he has a sister."

"Victoria Jennings," Graham said, he rubbed his forehead and looked at the ground. Then he raised his head and said to the doctor, "His sister. I'll be happy to pass along her information to whoever needs it. I have it in my phone."

Bea stared at Graham as he reached into the back pocket of his jeans.

The doctor made a note and said, "Thank you. I'm so sorry for your loss, both of you." Almost as an afterthought he then said, "If you'd like, I can have a nurse take you to say your goodbyes."

Graham put a hand on her shoulder before a blue scrub clad nurse led her into the cold, sterile room where Cliff's body lay flat on a table.

"I'll just give you a minute, I'll be outside the door if you need anything," said the nurse.

"Thank you," said Bea. The instant she walked into the room her eyes didn't leave Cliff, and she didn't notice when the nurse left.

Bea walked up to the table and placed a hand on his chest, still expecting it to rise and fall. The sheet covering him was white, she held the fabric between her fingers and marveled at how thin it was. Her eyes lingered over his pale, cold looking skin and the way his lips hinted at blue, and was compelled to look around for a thicker blanket to cover him with.

There was none.

Cliff's eyelids were closed, the corners of his mouth drawn up slightly. He looked as though he was taking a nap, as though he was simply resting. He looked as though he could wake up any second.

She wished he would.

The sob that left Bea's chest echoed throughout the room and she put a hand up to her mouth to catch the noise, the emotion.

"What are we going to do without you," she said, tears spilling down her cheeks. "What am I going to do without you?"

She leaned over and rested her head on his chest. Her fingers traced the side of his face. Cliff's body was still warm. It hadn't been long, and so when Bea stood up straight, leaned over, and kissed his cheek, he felt no different to her than he had that morning as she left the farmhouse. Except this time she knew he couldn't respond, this time she knew he wasn't going to be waiting for her in the kitchen with a mug of tea, this time she knew she would have the last word.

"Goodbye, Cliff Finley."

She pressed her lips to his forehead. Bea wiped the tears from her cheeks with the back of her hand, leaving the ones that spilled onto his stoic face.

He would never call her farm girl again, and as she walked into the hallway, that was what she already missed. His voice. Being his farm girl.

Who was she without Cliff? Without the orchard?

She brushed by Graham who stood expectantly and when she stopped and leaned against the wall to catch her breath, his eyes searched hers. She couldn't muster a smile. She couldn't find a single bit of comfort to share with him. She shook her head when he walked towards her with open arms, and then she walked away from him, away from Cliff. Away from the only person who felt like home to her.

Outside the hospital Bea waited for Graham. She found a wooden bench to sit down on, it had a small metal plaque with the name of a family, in memory of... she thought about Cliff's lifeless body in the building behind her. She stood and looked to the sky, then sat down again. She thought about how much she didn't know about him. She tapped her foot on the pavement impatiently. She thought about how much time she assumed there was to hear his stories. She stood once more and began pacing. She thought about how much Graham knew. The sky was clear and the air was crisp, perfect picking weather. That was the thought she always had on days like this, no matter where she was: how it would feel to be in the orchard, picking apples and standing on holy ground.

Graham walked outside. He shivered in the sunlight, his eyes were red, his face puffy.

"You're in no condition to drive," Bea said, "give me your keys."

He paused for a moment, concern and strain and loss all flashed across his face, and then he handed her his key chain.

SIX

Bea and Graham were halfway through a solemn drive back to the orchard when the air in the car shifted.

Fueling the tension, Bea asked, "How do you know his sister?"

Graham shifted in his seat and sighed, he leaned into the passenger side door. "She's a client of mine. I had just moved to Cumberland when I started working with her, and she mentioned that she had an estranged brother who lived in the area. It barely registered until one day Cliff mentioned his family situation, or lack of. I put two and two together. I asked him one day about her, said I had her contact info if he wanted to reach out. He just shook his head." Graham looked out the window before adding, "He said he tried to connect with her not that long ago, and she wasn't the sister he remembered. I didn't pry after that."

A car pulled onto the road in front of them, Bea downshifted and the car jerked under her less than smooth control.

"He never mentioned her to me."

"You weren't here," his voice was distant. She gave him a sharp look and he said, "No, no, I don't mean it badly. I just mean, you weren't here for that conversation. It didn't seem like he thought of her, or them, often. Or if he did, he didn't say as much. That was the only time we talked about his family."

They were silent for a moment.

"He hoped you were here to stay," he said, his voice barely above a whisper.

She stared straight ahead and gripped the steering wheel so hard that her knuckles turned white.

"Did you tell him?" He asked as he looked straight at her, she felt his eyes boring into the side of her face.

"Tell him what?"

"Did you tell him you weren't planning on staying long?"

Her face flushed and the only thing she wanted to do was get out of the car. To pull over, throw the keys at him, and walk home. She could do it. She guessed it was another five miles to the orchard. It would be a quiet walk, even with cars whizzing by. She could collect her thoughts. She could process. She could let the reality of Cliff's death sink in slowly.

"I don't know what you mean," replied Bea.

"I heard you, in the hardware store. You said you wouldn't be around long." The tone from when she first met him at the orchard was back. Superior. Condescending.

"That was taken out of context."

"I don't see how," he crossed his arms.

"You don't know anything," was all she could muster.

"So tell me."

She shook her head, "I barely know you."

"Well I know you."

"Excuse me?"

He grew tall in his seat, "I've heard about you ever since I met Cliff. He is," he paused to correct himself, "was, full of stories about you. To him, you were everything. His future. His past. He was so sure you would come back one day, for good."

"Maybe one day."

"But not today. What do you think will happen to the orchard?"

"He's barely gone, Graham. I haven't thought about the orchard, I'm thinking about Cliff."

"They're one and the same. We'll lose both."

Hands on the wheel, she turned towards him, "You've got some nerve, you know that?"

"Bea,"

"You think you know him, us, but you don't."

"Bea,"

"You have no idea how I feel about Cliff, how dare you -"

"BEA!"

Graham was gesturing wildly in front of him. She looked ahead and saw the car stopped ahead of them and hit the breaks, but it was too late.

There was a sound of metal crunching and tires screeching. The airbags went off and suddenly they were cushioned by giant white marshmallows and the smell of burning plastic and talcum powder filled the car.

"Are you okay?" Graham's voice was muffled and distant.

She took stock, moved her neck and her legs, wiggled her spine, "Yes, you?"

"I am. You stay here, I'll go check on the car in front of us."

Left alone she rested her head on the airbag, closed her eyes and waited. For sirens. For Graham. For Cliff to come and bring her home.

Finally, the tears came. She heaved with sorrow. The

smells of the released airbag, and sounds of the cars settling and someone walking through broken glass, it was all too much and she unbuckled her safety belt and opened the door. She wobbled as she stood, gripping the frame of the car for balance. Her legs shook, her eyes couldn't focus as she walked around the back of the car and off to the side of the road. And then bile rose in her throat, hot and acidic. She grabbed her stomach with one hand, steadied herself against a tree with the other, and heaved the pitiful contents of her stomach onto the ground at her feet.

Bea found herself sitting on the curb, head between her knees, the urge to run gone. In a tree not that far off a chickadee sang a sweet song.

A police car pulled up with a fire engine and ambulance seconds behind. The paramedics flew out and huddled around Graham and the person in the vehicle in front of his. Bea saw him waving towards his own car, a puzzled look on his face. She stood up to wave but her head spun and she sat back down, catching Graham's attention. He walked over with one of the paramedics.

"I thought you were still in the car," he crouched down next to her, putting a hand on her arm.

She looked straight into his eyes, "I want to go home."

He held her gaze, and for a split second she felt calmed by his presence. There was a concern in his eyes that took her by surprise, and she couldn't look away. She couldn't explain it, but Bea wanted to reach out and touch the rough stubble on his cheeks.

"Ma'am, I'm Lisa, I need to check out your injuries," said the paramedic, a short woman with black hair pulled into a tight ponytail, deep lines decorated her forehead and the sides of her eyes.

"I'm fine."

"You may have a concussion or other injuries, I need to at

66

least check you out." Bea wondered if this same woman tried to save Cliff, if she rode with him in the back of the ambulance just a few hours earlier. She pushed the thought out of her mind, closed her eyes, and was met with shouts from both Lisa and Graham.

"Bea? Beatrix?"

She tried to protest, to explain that she was just gathering herself, but it only made her feel weaker.

After an examination, a check of her vitals, she refused to go to the hospital.

"I'm not supposed to give medical advice, but," she looked around to see if anyone was watching her, "someone should stay with you all night. You'll need to be woken up every two to three hours, will you...?" Lisa turned towards Graham, who appeared to be unscathed by the accident.

"I can," he paused, ran his fingers through his hair and asked Bea, "or is there someone you want us to call?"

She thought for a moment, of the hints of kindness he had offered, but her protective walls went up and she said, "Olivia. She or Steve can give us a ride to the orchard or to my car in town."

"The police officer or the tow truck driver would be happy to drop you off, and you shouldn't be driving for the remainder of the day," said Lisa.

Graham scoffed, "She shouldn't have been driving in the first place."

Lisa looked uncomfortable, her brow furrowed and busied herself with a bag full of medical tools

"I'm sorry I wrecked your car, but that was unnecessary."

Graham laughed a harsh, tired laugh, and sat down next to her. He dropped his head in his hands. "I just think," he sputtered, "that maybe you shouldn't have been driving. I should have known better."

"And who was going to drive? You? Please. You were in

67

no condition. And forgive me for taking control of a situation. You were attacking me in the car!"

Lisa appeared next to her, "He was attacking you?"

Bea huffed, "No, I mean, verbally, and not-"

"Ma'am, is this your partner?"

Bea and Graham said at the same time, "No."

After statements were taken by the police officer and Olivia arrived, Graham and Bea piled into Olivia's Jeep. The Sullivan's Hardware logo was printed on the side of the vehicle, paint samples and stirrers decorated the floor and an assortment of empty candy wrappers littered the back seat.

"Sorry about the mess," Olivia said as they buckled safety belts and made room for their feet.

The ride home was silent besides Olivia expressing condolences and Bea muttering her thanks. Graham sat in the back, at one point he tried to put a hand on Bea's shoulder, reaching between the safety belt and the headrest of the passenger seat. She shook him off with a shrug.

At the farmhouse Olivia puttered in the kitchen. Bea paced the living room, not wanting to sit down for fear of succumbing to the exhaustion she felt in every bone in her body. Outside the wind picked up, the house creaked and moaned with every gust.

Olivia walked into the living room with a mug of tea in each hand, Bea mustered a smile and took one from her. The warmth nearly scorched her hands.

"It's chamomile," said Olivia, "did the shower help at all?"

Bea sat down on the couch and placed the tea on the floor

as she twisted her wet hair into a bun and snapped it into place with a hair elastic from around her wrist. "I think so," she tucked her legs under her, "I can't believe it was just this morning I was at the hardware store."

They were silent, both stared at the wood stove ahead of them.

"I should light the fire," said Bea. She got up and started placing wood in the stove, just as Cliff had done each of the last few nights.

"Or, we could get you to bed."

"I can't sleep," her hands were working furiously, moving the split wood, crumpling newspapers, feeling the raw edges without slowing down.

"You can, and you should. I'll set my alarm, you need to rest. Steve just texted me this article about the brain needing rest after a concussion. As long as I check on you every little while it'll be okay."

"I don't have a concussion," she thought back to one of her more dangerous photo shoots, one that her ex, Tom, had talked her into involving photos for a white water rafting company. All she remembered now was how reckless she was on the wet rocks along the shoreline and the beginning of a tumble she took leading to a concussion for a souvenir. "I've had one, and this isn't what it feels like."

"Even more reason to get some rest."

"I keep thinking he's just in the other room. Right around the corner."

"Bea, I'm so sorry."

Still crouched down, looking only towards the stove, Bea said, "I can't believe he's gone." And I wasn't here for him, she thought to herself. I was here, but I wasn't.

Standing, Bea wrapped her arms around herself, felt the

tears coming, and allowed herself to feel every emotion that washed over her. She didn't feel anything when they dropped off Graham earlier. She didn't feel anything when they walked into the farm house, or when she wordlessly climbed the stairs and stripped down in the bathroom. She didn't feel anything when she stood under scalding hot water. And she didn't feel anything when she walked by Cliff's bedroom, into her own where she dried off and got dressed and then eventually made her way down the stairs. She didn't allow herself to feel.

But now, she stood in front of the fireplace, arms hugging herself, feet firmly planted in the same place Cliff had stood every night while making the fire, and she wept.

Olivia came up next to her and put an arm around Bea's waist. They stood there, side by side, staring at the cold logs of wood in the fireplace.

SEVEN

Monday morning Bea woke before her alarm. She stayed in the tiny bed and stared at the ceiling, aware of everything and nothing. In the predawn hours everything blended into one large shape of room and house. Endless thoughts swirled within her mind and edged out into spoken words with only the walls to bear witness. When the alarm rang out in the darkness she turned it off and got out of bed.

Downstairs she put on the coffee, made some oatmeal, and reached for the familiar routine established the week before, but none of this felt familiar.

After she finished eating, she methodically did the dishes by hand. Why run the dishwasher for a few dishes, she thought. Peering into the cabinets, she searched for a travel mug to house the remainder of the pot of coffee. Instead she found Cliff's hodge podge collection of coffee cups: an over-sized mug from her alma mata; a few handmade stoneware cups, the ones he always offered her because the texture of the glazed surfaces felt so good in her hands; a coffee-stained diner style mug from Bert's Place; half a dozen I'm-thinking-of-you souvenirs from all over the globe decorated with pictures of landmarks and landscapes, she had a memory for each one. Photo shoots and travel plans gone awry, phone calls home and the rare occasion when she played tourist and went sightseeing.

She touched each mug, and marveled that he kept them all. Behind the collection she found a travel mug at the very back of the cabinet. Standing on her tiptoes to reach it, her side body stretched long and as she returned to the bottoms of her feet a yawn overtook her and the corners of her eyes dampened. She wiped them with the back of her hand before the dampness turned into a threat of full blown tears. Keep moving, she told herself, just keep moving.

She knew that if she stayed put, it would take hours for her to muster up the gumption to get into the orchard, to do the work the day, and the apples, demanded. And so she moved. She put one foot in front of the other and brushed off memories and the familiar scents attempting to pull her into grief. Bea walked purposefully outside and over to the truck, where she knew the keys were sitting on top of the dashboard, waiting where Steve had left them the previous day after returning it from where she left it in town on Saturday.

The driver's side door squeaked and Bea noticed the tell tale designs of salt rust, deep reds and oranges, dancing on fenders and along the edges of both doors and the tailgate. One hand on the door handle, she gazed around the property. The question of what would happen to the orchard crept into her mind often, no thanks to Graham's comments on Saturday. She tried to escape it, to dodge it, but it never really went away. It was a constant companion that only raised its voice when the weight of her grief momentarily lifted.

The sky lightened, and in the distance she could see fog

hugging the apple trees, filling the spaces between them and the rows with a thick layer of gray illuminated by the brilliance of morning.

Though it lay down the driveway, through a hedge of trees, and across the street, she could vaguely see the outline of her grandmother's house. She walked down the driveway, the sand and dirt and rock met her feet as she gently put one work-boot-clad foot in front of the other, dust contained by the dampness of the morning. When she reached the trees she found the path she used to walk through to get to Cliff's house, overgrown with years of vegetation. The leaves would have been fuller in the summer but with autumn came transparency.

She wove between a few branches and found her way to a giant oak that felt like home. It was the one she used to hide behind when her mother came to pick her up and Bea wasn't ready to go. She never was. To Donna Hampton's credit, she sat with Sylvia, had a glass of lemonade, and simply waited. She knew her daughter would come out eventually, there was no need to scream or yell for Beatrix, not here. Donna's presence felt so out of place that eventually it would drive Bea to distraction and she would shuffle her way across the street, head hung low, hands filthy with dirt and tree sap, cheeks tear-stained.

Now she peered through the trees. She wondered if he was waking up, if he was a morning person or if he hit the alarm five times and then needed three cups of coffee to function. She pegged him as a French press type, one that had a system for how long his coffee needed to brew, and at what speed he submerged the plunger. She imagined a miniature hourglass sitting on the kitchen counter, and Graham watching it intently.

She laughed quietly to herself, but stopped as she heard an approaching car miles off in the distance. Birdsong rang out around her, and she heard not only the sweet coos of the morning doves and sparrows, but the distinct call of chickadees. Her legs out in front of her, she drew her knees up and leaned her back against the oak and closed her eyes. The stainless steel mug felt heavy in her hands and when she finally opened her eyes they fluttered with fatigue, at least until a car pulled into Graham's driveway.

Her eyes opened wide and she leaned forward to watch a sleek black car, its engine hummed through the air, intruding brake lights blinked red echoes, and when the passenger door opened Bea sucked in a bit of air in surprise as Graham climbed out of the vehicle. Fully dressed in jeans and a dark sweater with a stack of books tucked into the crook of his arm, he spoke to the driver. Bea couldn't hear words, only murmurs, of a distinctly feminine voice. She watched silently, aware of her body and the stillness necessary to remain unseen. She was not hiding behind the oak, she was in front of it with only a few sparse trees in front of her. Graham leaned into the car for a moment and then closed the door and followed the stone walkway to the front steps. He entered the house and Bea watched as the front windows glowed as he moved through the house turning on the lights.

The edge of the travel mug was cold against her lips, and she scowled as she swallowed the last bit of lukewarm coffee. Bea took a long look at the house before she crawled on all fours around the oak tree and finally stood, curious about what kind of book seller Graham Winters was and who the mystery woman was in the car. She was acutely aware not only of the dirt on her hands and knees, but of her want for a distraction.

The fog was lifting, the road was waking up to commuters, and when Bea reached the truck once more, she didn't pause. She flung the door wide open, threw the coffee cup onto the passenger seat, and hopped into the driver's seat, as ready as she'd ever be to face the day.

EIGHT

The doors creaked and groaned as Bea let herself into the barn. Inside was dark except for a few slivers of light shining through the windows placed few and far between high along the walls. There was dirt, bits of gravel, and sawdust on the floor, barn swallows in the rafters, a long workbench with a coffee maker and stained cups on one side and paperwork piled high on the other, a lump of blankets sat on a chair in the corner for chilly nights spent sorting through paperwork. Bea was reminded of a magazine assignment from a few years ago, the pristine home she shot had barn doors and windows throughout and polished and waxed wood floors, dust and dirt free.

Now, in contrast, she could feel the grime attaching to her skin simply by standing there, grease stains a possibility at every turn and cobwebs awaiting unsuspecting victims. Never one to shy away from getting her hands dirty, Bea loved every inch of the space, griminess and all.

She found a dozen picking baskets and loaded them into the bed of the truck, unsure if anyone else would show up, but wanting to be prepared. There was still a collecting bin in the fields from the weekend when the chaos ensued and the few weekend pickers left the field in stunned silence after the ambulance lights disappeared from view. No one had thought to bring the receptacle back to the barn, no one got in the seat of the tractor to pull it on home, and so it sat in the field waiting for apples. Waiting, like Beatrix, for Cliff to come home and get to work.

It was still early, and from the driver's seat of the truck she could see the fog had lifted and dappled light gleamed daintily on the apple trees. The softness of morning was spreading over the orchard like a blanket, blurring edges with dewdrops and the easy flutter of birds wings as they flitted to and fro in a celebration of daily life. As she stepped out of the truck Bea noted that the natural world kept moving, evolving. Fruit still hung low in need of picking, grass between rows of trees needed mowing, the tractor would eventually need to move back to the barn. Apples needed to be sold, used, and eaten, sauced, canned, made into pies. Bea's brow furrowed and a headache built behind her eyes. She made her way to the back of the truck, wondering how it would all get done, if it would get done. As she lifted a picking basket from the bed of the truck and strapped it onto her shoulders, she gazed out at the seemingly endless apple trees lined up and waiting and thought, it's too much. Too much work. Too much to ask of any one person. How Cliff managed for all those years on his own, she may never know.

From the back pocket of her jeans she reached and found the pair of hand warmers from Sullivan's. She searched for cash to pay for them on Sunday before Olivia left, but Olivia waved her off, "Consider them a welcome home gift," she had said. Bea detected a hint of hope in Olivia's voice, as if a pair of hand mitts would entice her to stay.

Bea slid them over her hands, poked her thumb through the hole and admired the warmers. They were simple, sturdy, and yet had a delicate edge.

She began picking and soon got lost in the rhythm, the movement. In no time she filled a basket and made her way back to the bin where she emptied her load atop whatever was picked on Saturday, before... she couldn't even finish the thought, without the truth of it crumpling her.

She stood at attention when she heard soft footsteps behind her, and watched as a handful of people walked to the back of the truck and chose a basket. In turn every one of them looked Bea in the eyes and held her gaze for a moment to pass along everything that could not be said. None of them were strong enough for words. With a sorrowful exchange and a solemn nod, the pickers got to work, disappearing among the branches into the apples and themselves.

Picking was solitary work, quiet work, especially in New England. Bea spent time photographing field hands and pickers in other countries and what struck her the most was the constant presence of song. Not the birdsong that accompanied apple picking at Finley Orchard, but songs of heartache and hard work and life and love and possibility, sung by people who told the stories of their history by song. It didn't matter if she understood the language or not, she felt the stories. In the past, here on the land she had known for nearly as long as she could remember, she understood the language but she couldn't feel the stories.

Today, she felt the stories, they were held in the eyes of those who came to pick: Ron Taggert, Chris's father, the neighbor three houses over who traded picking time as well as his chicken eggs for apple pie filling, at his wife's request; Anna Henderson, a middle aged woman whose children were in high school and college, and so she filled her hours with the job of being everything to everyone, mostly behind the scenes, and yet still found time to work at the local floral nursery down the road from the orchard, and pick with Cliff each season; William McKinnon had been a friend of the orchard for years, a retired school principal who used to pick only on weekends and holidays but now had time to pick the entire season; Henry Eaton, a scruffy man a few years past Cliff's age, no one knew where he slept at night, but somehow he stayed fed and clothed and there was an unspoken understanding of the wealth of his character, no matter how scraggly he appeared or how many teeth were missing from his scowling mouth; and countless others who showed up now and then or every day of the week. They were a hodge podge crew made up of quiet, sturdy, and loyal people, New Englanders to the core.

At lunch Bea drove back to the farmhouse to find something to eat. The cabinets banged as she opened and closed them looking for something to cobble together. Everyone else had brought a bagged lunch, dropped their backpacks or canvas bags on the ground next to a picnic table Cliff set up near the spot the truck was always parked, where they started their day with nods and ended in waves. Her hunger was barely there, but she knew she needed to eat something - Cliff's voice echoed in her ears - and so she was scavenging around when she heard a knock on the door.

For a moment she thought it was Graham, but as he turned she realized the man before her was a good three decades too old and many pounds too heavy to be him.

"Bert, come on in," she said.

"I'll only be a minute." He walked in and gave a gentle

hug with both arms, she felt something hit against her back and she looked behind her. "Sorry," he said as he showed her a brown paper bag, "Figured you might need something to eat around here as Cliff always did the shopping on Sundays."

They both looked down at their feet.

"I meant to come by yesterday, but with the after church crowd..." he trailed off. She knew.

"The diner's doing well?"

"Steady as always, I can't complain." Handing her the bag he said, "A BLT, made just for you. Remembered you used to like them." He paused as she peered in, the scent of bacon and mayonnaise and tomatoes left over from summer made her stomach feel emptier than it had in days, weeks, even months. "Unless you've gone vegan or something," he chuckled to himself, "I can run back and make something else for you."

"No, this is a treat," she looked straight into his eyes and with the deepest sincerity she said, "thank you Bert."

They stared at each other for a moment until Bea's stomach grumbled and she walked across the kitchen to sit at the table. She took the sandwich out of the paper bag and then used the bag as a plate.

"Want to sit for a minute?" she asked, motioning to the chair across from her.

Bert looked out the door and back into the kitchen. He walked slowly towards the table, and as he did he peered into the living room, as if expecting someone to be there. He looked out of place in a kitchen without wearing an apron, even with his pair of overworked black suspenders atop his well worn Bert's Diner t-shirt and his rubber clogs clomping against the floor.

As he finally sat down in the chair it groaned with the effort of holding him upright. He motioned to her to eat.

"Don't let me stop you, you'll be anxious to get back to

the trees."

The bacon melted in her mouth and mayonnaise dribbled down her chin. "I don't know what my hurry is, but it's there."

"The apples won't last forever. They're ready when they're ready, and they've been ready for a while."

"There's a bunch of folks out there now, just like always."

"Well, what else are they to do? Stop coming? At harvest season?"

She shrugged and sighed, "It's just, without Cliff, I didn't know."

Bert looked thoughtful. "When my Dan passed, I wasn't sure if I could keep the diner going without him," he paused, the wound made fresh again by Cliff's death. Bea had forgotten how much loss Bert had been through just in the last year, his husband had died of a brain aneurysm in the spring. "He was my everything, but the only thing I could do to work through my grief was to open the doors of the diner. The community, they helped me more than anything. Just by being there." Bert reached across the table and patted her hand gently.

"But I'm just visiting, waiting for the next person in charge to tell me what to do," she looked out the window and off into the fields. There was so much she was unsure of, and her grief was mounting. "Is there any word in town about what Cliff had set up in his will?" she asked.

Bert shook his head. "Everyone's speculating. Most thought you'd know," he peered at her expectantly, fidgeted with his hands, wrung them together and then placed them in his sweatshirt pockets.

"I haven't a clue. I guess we'll all find out eventually."

"June was his lawyer. June Mason. You could check with her."

"But I'm not family, I don't know that she'd tell me

anything."

"Beatrix Hampton," he said, his voice raising and cracking with emotion, "you're as close to family as that man had, and the whole town knows it. I'm sure there's something about you in that will, so sooner or later June will be looking for you anyway. I've probably got her number in my phone, give me a second."

Bert pulled out his phone from a deep pocket in his jeans and scrolled through his contacts. He was all thumbs and cursed a few times at mis-swipes of the finger. When he found what he was looking for he stood up and went over to the hutch by the door and opened a drawer, pulled out a pad of paper and a pen and jotted down a few notes.

"Here you go. Give her a call, Bea. She'll help however she can."

Bea finished her sandwich and crumpled the paper bag into a ball. She took the paper from him and said, "Thanks. I'll give her a call tonight. Do you have time for a drive out to the orchard?"

He hesitated, taking a long look out the screen door. "Not today. Tomorrow, I'll try to get out there tomorrow." His eyes were damp and far away. She walked over to him and threaded an arm though his. They walked slowly to the door where she gave him a little squeeze.

"It'll be here when you're ready."

He patted her hand that was resting in the crook of his arm, "I hope so, Bea. I hope so."

She watched as he walked slowly with slumped shoulders down the porch steps and to the light blue Prius that sat in the driveway.

"Bert!" she called after him. He turned his tired, grief stricken face towards her. Bea rushed down the steps and met him in the driveway. She flung her arms around him and whispered,

81

"I'm glad you were with him."

She felt Bert's shoulders heave, a sob escaped, and they stood in the driveway with arms around each other, both silently praying for it all to be a dream.

They were finishing up in the orchard when the sky began showing the first hints of evening. Bea brought her last load of apples to the bin, they cascaded into open spaces resting on each other and the edges of the container. Today's work brought them nearer to the top, and she knew that tomorrow she'd have to figure out how to work the tractor and bring the full bin back to the barn, put it into place and hitch a fresh one onto the tractor.

Bea was talking with Anna about her children, the ones Bea babysat for now and then when she was spending time at her grandmother's, when Anna nodded towards the far end of the orchard. Her forehead wrinkled with concern, and she leaned an arm on the edge of the truck. She looked as if she belonged in the orchard with her button up flannel shirt and puffy vest, blond hair pulled back in a ponytail save for the bangs that brought a bit of youth to her tired, divorced mother-of-four face.

"Poor guy, he's taking this loss as hard as any of us."

Bea turned to see who Anna was talking about, but already knew.

"Do you know him well?"

Graham approached slowly and carefully with his hands stuffed in his pants pockets, assessing the trees and the people in the fields.

"As much as anyone in town does, but not as well as Cliff did. I was surprised Graham wasn't out here today with us." Anna's voice hushed as Graham came within earshot, "I heard you two were in an accident the other day."

Bea instinctively rubbed her neck, the ache of impact suddenly fresh. "I'm sure the whole town heard, Anna."

Graham walked up to the pair of women, Bea mustered a faint smile while Anna dripped concern while giving him a hug. He was rigid, and his end of the embrace was mechanical and almost embarrassed. He looked like one of Anna's sons caught in a hug at an inopportune time, wriggling towards escape the moment she put her arms around him. After she released him Graham ran a hand through his hair and sought out Bea's eyes, but she wouldn't meet his.

"How was the picking today?" he asked.

"It was fine, hun, but we missed you. How are you?" Anna asked with attentiveness from her eyes to her hand that still sat on Grahams arm.

Bea rolled her eyes before looking down the orchard to count how many pickers were still left for the day. She thought maybe she should say something and rally the troops, but she didn't want to, not with Graham around. Her agitation grew and she looked at her watch, barely registering what Graham had been saying to Anna, or that he was now talking to her.

"Bea?" He tilted his head to the side and looked at her, puzzled. "Bea? How's your head, from Saturday?"

She looked at him, really looked at him, and found fatigue written all over his face. Then she remembered seeing him early that morning.

"Oh, it's fine."

Anna looked from Bea to Graham and back to Bea. She said, "I'm going to go check in with the rest of the folks, see if they're going to head out soon and who wants to catch a ride with you." She walked away, and as she did Bea caught a whiff of apples and grass and sweat, nostalgia caught hold and for a moment she didn't trust what she might say next, so she stayed silent.

"I called his sister." Graham left the statement hanging in the air while he stood with his hands in his corduroy pants.

Bea bristled. Nostalgia gone, she felt instinctively protective over Cliff.

"What did she say?" Bea tucked a strand of hair behind her ear.

"She said she was terribly sorry to hear about his passing, and even more saddened that they never made amends. She'll be at the funeral later in the week."

"Oh God, the funeral. I haven't even-"

"It's taken care of."

"What do you mean?"

"Just that it's taken care of. I've been talking with Beverly, the funeral director. She was of course a friend of Cliff's, and we've got it all handled."

"Have you seen a will or anything?"

"No, have you?"

Bea stood at attention with her hands on her hips, "No, I've been out here making sure the apples are being tended to."

"Fair enough."

"I'll get there," she said defensively, "You don't need to swoop in and take care of everything."

He looked down at his feet and then his gaze rested somewhere down the orchard. Silence sat between them like a petulant child.

"I'm hardly the one swooping in."

His words hit her like a ton of bricks, and her perspective shifted slightly enough to realize what he was saying. That maybe she was the one swooping, meddling, confusing things.

He began to walk away when she collected her thoughts

enough to yell out, "I'm not swooping. I belong here!"

Graham turned around and looked right at her with pained eyes. She couldn't look away from him.

"Then prove it," he said, hands once again in his pockets, shoulders shrugged up to his ears. He turned and kept walking, disappearing into a row of apple trees. Down and to the right, where they met on her first day of picking. Maybe, she thought, he's got his own paths through this orchard. She brushed the thought away and assessed the days work. The apples picked and the pickers who were starting to walk towards her. Besides Anna, who had already dumped her last load into the collecting bin, they each dropped their haul into the bin.

They stood around for a moment, looking at Bea and the apples and then each other. Bea thought back on the previous week, how the end of the day happened organically, but Cliff would always say a few words of thanks and encouragement before whoever was left went their separate ways.

She straightened her back, squared her shoulders, and cleared her throat. "Thank you all for coming out today. I didn't know if you all would show up, or if I'd be on my own."

There were collective mutters of "of course" and "we wouldn't want to be elsewhere" but Bea shook her head and said, "You all say that, but I really didn't know. I'm so thankful," her heart caught in her throat and her voice hitched. "I'm so thankful for all of the time I've spent here over the years, with my grandmother and Cliff." She looked up to see Anna holding her hand over her heart, Ron shuffled from one foot to another, Henry with his hat in his hands and a solemn look upon his face.

"Anyway, thank you for being here today. I'll keep showing up in the mornings to work until we find out what's going to happen to Cliff's orchard."

"And then?" whispered William, his eyes were glistening

with tears.

"And then," Bea looked over and saw that to her surprise and irritation, Graham had come back. He was standing with his arms crossed in front of him with an expectant look on his face. "And then, I don't know." She looked at her feet, and by the time she righted herself he was gone. A pang of regret hit and her throat constricted for a brief moment.

She wanted to say that she'd figure it out and she'd stay by their side until everything was sorted. But from where she stood with the realities of running an orchard, keeping up a home, and being a part of a community settling in, Bea wasn't sure that she had it in her. But more than that, she was afraid of who might step up if she didn't, and as she gazed around at the people packing up for the day, at the apple trees, the paths that she once knew like the back of her hand, she was also afraid of losing it all.

NINE

When she came home for the day Beatrix made herself a cup of tea, grabbed a crocheted afghan from the living room, and sat on the porch in an Adirondack chair. The blanket smelled of the house, of Cliff. She wondered how long his scent would last, and if her grandmother's house still smelled the way she remembered, if Bea would smell Sylvia in pockets of air as she walked by the nooks and crannies in the bedrooms and the kitchen, in the root cellar, in the linen closet. If her knees would buckle, or if she'd simply smile and feel comforted by the familiar scent of garlic, lemon thyme, and lavender.

Bea felt the edges of chipping white paint as she ran a hand along the arm rest. She looked down past her feet where the wood boards of the porch were splintering. Every wooden surface around her needed to be sanded, rough edges softened and made smooth to the touch. But structurally, it was all sound, the carpentry was masterful. Whenever she was traveling and people asked her about the people in her hometown, she'd say the same about them. Their rough edges could use some softening, but their hearts were sound.

In front of the porch, Chickadees pranced from one branch of a lilac bush to another sending calls out to the ether. Chick-a-dee-dee-dee-dee... Beatrix heard the familiar call and leaned forward to try and get a closer look, then she closed her eyes and listened as the birds called out again and again. She sipped her chamomile tea, and noticed a slight change in the bird call: chick-a-dee-dee-dee-dee-dee-dee, it lengthened, and Bea instinctively looked around for a threat.

Down the driveway a car was making its way towards the house, kicking up dust. Squinting, she thought it looked similar to the car she saw dropping Graham off that morning. She watched with curiosity as a woman stepped out of the sleek black Lexus, dark sunglasses on her face, wild gray hair springing every which way, and walked confidently in mud colored clogs across dirt and gravel towards the porch.

"It's gotten chilly over here! Must be the ocean. It's a good ten degrees warmer in town!" said the woman in an overly cheerful voice as she rubbed her hands up and down opposite arms. Silver bangles and beaded bracelets jingled on her wrist, the sound echoed against the house. She was wearing wide legged black trousers and a purple and turquoise tunic that flowed in the slight breeze. There was clearly some cognitive dissonance between the woman and her car.

She extended her hand, "June Mason, you must be Beatrix Hampton?"

Beatrix gripped the afghan with one hand, stood, and placed her mug on the railing. Then she shook June's hand. "You're Cliff's lawyer, right? Nice to meet you." She motioned to the set of Adirondack chairs and they both sat down. June moved her sunglasses to the top of her head and crossed her legs at her ankles.

"I am. We've met before, years and years ago. I knew your mother before she was married. We went to school together, up through high school." June did not sound unkind, but Bea didn't know what to make of the woman sitting in front of her. Maybe it was the car she drove in, how different it was from her appearance, or perhaps it was how comfortable June made herself. She was already leaning back in the chair as if she'd sat there a hundred times before. That sense of belonging was contagious, Bea felt the slightest bit of ease in her neck and shoulders.

"And I met you?"

"You did!" she faltered for a moment. "That actually has nothing to do with your mother, I haven't seen her in years. But," she tilted her head and pointed at Bea, "I remember one time I came out to have Cliff sign some papers, and you were in the orchard, bopping around. You lit up Cliff's life, Bea. I'm so sorry for your loss." She reached her hand over to cover Bea's. It was warm and soft and as Bea looked down all she could think about was the warmth June exuded. Bea was willing to bet she gave incredible hugs, warm embraces at just the right moment.

"I'm sorry, I don't remember you at all."

June patted Bea's hand before sitting back in her chair, leaning all the way back and crossing her legs into a pretzel shape.

"It was a long time ago. Listen, I wanted to come out and talk with you before it got to be too much longer. I normally don't make house calls these days, but I've spent all day getting things in order for you."

"For me?" The afghan kept slipping down around Bea's shoulders, she reached for her mug and took a sip before tugging at the edges of the blanket. She pulled her knees up towards her chin. She knew it didn't look professional, or adult like, but she felt cold and tired, her spirit tired and worn down, and something about June made her feel at ease.

"Yes, for you. So I take it Cliff didn't mention anything," June sighed and looked out at the orchard. Beatrix shook her head.

"Well, there's no beating around the bush. The orchard is yours," she smiled and looked at Bea expectantly, as if she was waiting for Bea to start jumping up and down in excitement. As if this was the best news Bea could ever receive in her life.

Bea was speechless. Her mind went blank, and all she could focus on was the mug in her hand, the smooth glaze over clay, the weight of it in her hand. The color drained from her face and she stared blankly at June. With four words her life was changed forever.

"Bea? Are you alright? I know it's a shock, can I get you some water?"

Bea shook herself out of the stupor, blinked herself back to life and said, "No, no, that's fine. Thank you for coming to tell me in person."

"It's a lot to take in. I'll leave you to it." June stood and her bracelets fell down towards her wrists. Bea watched, mesmerized by the bangles and how they looked like they should fall off June's arms, but they didn't. Impossibly, they stayed in the right place.

Bea shook her head, speechlessness turning into blatant disbelief. She looked up at June and said, "But what about his family? Is there nothing in the will about them? His sister maybe?"

"No," she paused and took a breath before saying, "though there is one condition…"

"And that is?"

June sat down again, and looked directly at Bea, her brow knitted with concern. "Would you rather wait until you come into the office to discuss this? Or at least have some water?"

"No, if there's a condition, something I need to consider in all of this, I'd like to know now."

"Well," June brought her hands back to her lap, a film came over her face and suddenly any concern had switched over to legal speak and business, "Cliff's condition was that you work the orchard for one year before deciding if you want to sell it."

"That's it?"

June nodded.

"And what if I'm not willing to stay for that year?"

"The opportunity will go to someone else."

"Who?"

"I think we'd better discuss this in the office, Beatrix."

"No, I'd like to know now so I know what I'm dealing with while I think this over."

"If you decline, the deal goes to Graham Winters. He'd be responsible for the orchard for a year, and then it would be up to him to maintain or sell the property."

Bea was silent, trying to grasp not only that the orchard was hers, but that Graham was a part of the will as well. That if she didn't say yes, Graham would not only have her grandmother's house, but also the orchard. Her heart beat faster, she felt it pumping blood to her eyes and temples as she stifled the rage that was currently brooding.

"And this is all in writing?"

"Of course. Swing by the office at any point and we'll dot all the I's and cross all the T's."

"But this doesn't make any sense. When did he put this together?"

"Probably two years ago, though he added in Graham the last time he came in for a visit. Maybe six months ago?"

Two years ago, Bea thought, I was in the Himalayas.

Two years ago, Bea thought, I was twenty six.

Two years ago, Bea thought, I wouldn't even consider this.

But now, she considered the possibility of staying.

What choice did she have?

TEN

When she was a child Beatrix couldn't wait to leave home for her grandmother's house. She'd sit not so patiently by the door atop her suitcase, kicking her ankles against the hard exterior as her mother moved at an unacceptably slow pace preparing for the hour drive north.

Every time, every visit, it was always the same. Bea would pack her special blanket, named Tiny for it's hefty, plush size, and her favorite clothes: two pairs of ripped blue jeans that she hid in the back of her drawer from her mother, some shorts, a few simple nightgowns, plenty of underwear, a handful of tee shirts, and one dress just in case Grandma wanted to go to church or a fancy restaurant. Neither of those were likely to happen, but Bea liked to be prepared. She never packed books, as she had a stash at the house waiting for her in the guest room, and she didn't need toys. She had the world to explore in Cumberland, but more importantly: her grandmother's yard and Finley Orchard.

Her parents house was cold, sterile. Everything was just so, from the way the throw pillows sat on the couch to the place settings on the formal dining room table. Bea thought her mother kept things that way for her father. Through Bea's childhood eyes she saw the way her mother worked to keep things neat, the way she yelled at Bea if things were done in a way that would upset him, the way she deferred to him in so many areas.

To Bea, all independent and wild and free in spirit from a young age, marriage looked like a trap, for both partners. Her mother wasn't the most pleasant person, but neither was her father. The happiest people she knew were untethered: Sylvia and Cliff. Yes, her grandmother had been married, but Bea didn't know much about her grandfather other than the fact that he had died before she was born. Out of sight, out of mind. And yes, Cliff was married in some ways to the orchard. But that was different than being tied to a person. At least that's what she thought when she was younger.

Bea's parents, she assumed, were more content when she was out of town. As a child she pictured them not worrying about her messing up her grades, dirtying the living room with muddy shoes, or being too loud at a family meal. They ate together every single night. Dinner was always carefully prepared, whether by the housekeeper or more rarely by Donna, and on the table at exactly 5:30 in the evening when Eric got home from the office. The only acceptable noises Bea could make during dinner were the sound of chewing - politely - and the fork and knife working against the plate. When spoken to she was expected to speak clearly and quickly. As an only child, Bea wished for a sibling to take the pressure, the scrutiny, off of her. But another baby never showed up, and Bea was alone in the house with her parents, a wall of silence built around each member of the family that grew as the years went on.

When her mother would finally be ready to embark on the drive to Cumberland, she would grab her keys and sigh and look at

Bea with impatience. "Do you have everything you need?" she'd ask, "Do you have enough clothes? You don't want to make too much work for your grandmother." Bea would nod. "Did you pack Tiny?"

And every time, it annoyed Bea to her core that her mother reminded her about Tiny. As if Bea would forget her only precious belonging.

Tuesday morning Bea sat on the edge of her small bed, looking down at the mess that was her half closed suitcase. A mix of textures and fabrics splayed out, plain cottons and plaid flannels, jeans and wool socks. The only thing neat about it was the simple monogram in white script against the dark blue fabric. The letters stayed crisp through countless airports and airplanes, even though the edges and seams showed fading and fraying. She stared at the empty dresser in front of her, the drawers waiting to be filled, but she couldn't do it. Instead, Bea knelt down beside the suitcase and started folding pieces of clothing and placing them back into the suitcase neatly. Earlier, fresh from the shower, Bea threw on her best clothes from the pile. The floor of the bedroom creaked and moaned as she made her way into a pair of dark wash skinny jeans, performing an elaborate dance of hopping from one leg to the other, squatting and letting out the occasional deep sigh before zipping her slim body into the even slimmer pants. She noted the muffled silence that overcame the house as she pulled a long sleeve tee shirt over her head. She dawned the last layer and a gust of wind blew threw a drafty corner of the window, and she felt a chill wash over her as she smoothed a hand over a soft, camel colored crew neck sweater.

Now she sat on the floor, piecing together her few belongings. A tidy stack of shirts sat next to two pairs of work pants - beat up jeans - while her hooded sweatshirt was crumpled on the opposite side of the room where it landed the night before. She sat back and assessed the room as a whole. The painting caught her eye, the woman walking in the orchard, alone.

Leaning forward, Bea unzipped the very front pocket of the suitcase and slipped out a six inch square of faded pink fabric. Tiny. A faint smile of recognition crossed her face and she closed her eyes and let the tactile pleasure rush through her. Tiny's soft pink satin edges were frayed, it's sheen no longer visible due to years of Bea rubbing the fabric between her fingers. The once plush material was now matted, needing more than a wash and dry to bring it back to life.

Outside the day was unfolding and Bea knew people were arriving at the orchard, but in the bedroom time stood still as she sat on the floor with her legs crossed, rubbing Tiny between her fingers and staring at the dresser. Flooded with memories, she could not move, and with a sigh she watched the memories flash before her like a slideshow, one after the other.

First, she was riding the bus to school, sitting alone and feeling the spring in her seat as the bus drove over bumps in the road. She felt relief when she stuck a finger into her backpack and felt Tiny was hidden, her mother would have freaked out had she known what Bea had packed. She was watching and listening to the other kids on the bus, the kids that her parents wanted her to be friends with. They didn't pay her any attention, Bea liked it that way.

Next she was lying in her childhood bed, the warmth of expensive flannel sheets and deep slumber surrounding her. Her mother was tip toeing across Bea's bedroom floor, the subtle creaks and moans indicating another midnight visit. Donna crawled into Bea's bed, carefully inching towards her daughter's still body. Her mother smelled of sweat and something sweet and bitter. Bea sighed into her mother's body, and was engulfed by protective arms, and she fell asleep gripping Tiny, even at a young age unsure of who was actually doing the protecting.

The next memory was of sleeping alone. Of laying in bed with the beginnings of menstrual cramps, Tiny's edges beginning to fray but still she rubbed the fabric between her fingers, and clung to whatever grounding she could. She remembered being alone. Waiting for the occasional nighttime visits that stopped around the same time her journey into womanhood began.

Next she was on an airplane to Sydney. The flight made ten times longer due the man sitting next to her, Jeffrey, with whom who she just ended a brief, but intense, relationship. He didn't understand monogamy and though she thought she could handle the other women, it turned out to be a deal breaker. On her lap was her camera bag, and when she lifted the flap of a side pocket, the Velcro made an obscene noise that was barely drowned out by the noise of the engines. She reached her index and middle fingers in and found Tiny. A touchstone. A talisman. Used less in the literal sense, but always nearby. She closed her eyes and ignored the urgency of her ex's silence beside her.

Memory after memory of the last twenty-five years of her life flashed by. She grasped to find connections, to find meaning and a trail of breadcrumbs so that she didn't make the same mistakes as before.

Was leaving a mistake?

Was staying?

In the small bedroom of the farmhouse that she may or may not decide was hers, Beatrix sat in an unrestful stillness.

And then she knew. She dropped Tiny onto the still open suitcase and walked downstairs to find her boots. Decisions were often made like this for Beatrix. She ruminated and wondered for a time, and then she made her decision - for better or worse - and went with it. That's how she decided to go to art school in a small

97

town between her parents home and Cumberland, that's how she ended relationships, that's how she decided which jobs to take. She took in all of her options, deliberated over them internally, until her body and mind came to a place of reckoning all at once, clarity came into view, and she knew. It was instinct, and while it took awhile for her to finally listen to it, when she did she knew to trust the clarity. Like clouds parting to show the brilliance of the sun against a sky of blue, the answer was there for the taking..

Bea didn't sleep the night before, and now as she was heading out the door of the farmhouse, she realized that morning had not only come, but was passing by at an alarming rate, and those who were out in the orchard were fending for themselves. She hopped into the truck and drove towards them, not minding the bumps and jostling that kept her body awake and her mind focused.

As she approached them, all Bea noticed was the orchard awash with color. The reds of the apples were especially vibrant, Anna's sweater was a deep shade of purple, William's baseball cap radiated a sunny yellow. After spending the night and morning hours inside the bedroom, she squinted at the colors and the light all around her. With tired eyes, she smiled as she got out of the truck and made her way to the pickers.

Anna walked towards her, "You don't look like you're ready for picking at all, hun. Those jeans and sweater look far too expensive to be out in the muck of an orchard!"

Bea wiped her hands, sweaty from gripping the steering wheel of the truck, on the thighs of her pants in a silent protest. "I've got to run into town, I'm so sorry. I was up all night and I didn't realize what time it's gotten to be. Do you have everything you need?"

William, Ron, and even Henry made their way to Bea. Henry stood a ways back, listening. His face was covered by a wiry snow-white beard, his eyebrows were like tiny birds nests made of stray twigs and thin strips of yarn. Bea made eye contact with him and smiled gently. In the past he had made her nervous, but she knew Cliff had a soft spot in his heart for him.

William said, "We'll need a fresh bin to load the apples into, soon. Otherwise, we're OK."

Bea looked over to the overflowing bin. "Do any of you know how to use the tractor and load it up?"

They all shook their heads.

From the back of the group, Henry spoke up tentatively, "I've done it once or twice, but I don't know, Bea. Cliff always supervised..." his voice trailed off.

As Bea walked over to him she looked him straight in the eye. He smelled of earth and days old sweat, Bea tried desperately not to make a face, not to wrinkle her nose or raise so much as an eyebrow. She noticed the worn areas and patches throughout his khaki trench coat. The coat was not practical for harvesting apples, but it was his signature look, he was never without it, or his fedora.

"If you think you can do it, I'll find the keys in the office and bring them out to you."

"He can do it," said a familiar, though sour, voice from down the row a ways. Bea looked up and saw Graham walking towards her. His shoes were the same loafers he wore the first day she met him. The leather was discolored, the damp morning dew rode up from his socks towards the hem of his pant legs. His hair was messy, his skin sallow, sleep may have been eluding him as well.

Bea sighed and said to everyone and no one, "Is he always sneaking around?"

"Henry, I'll help you. I've got an extra set of keys right here," Graham grabbed a carabiner full of keys clipped to his belt.

He put himself between Henry and Bea. "I didn't want to take the truck if you weren't expecting it to be gone, so we all just walked this morning. I've got a spare for that as well. We'll take care of the bin, we know what to do. You go and do whatever it is you need to do in town. We'll be fine."

Did he know about the will? She asked herself, searching his eyes for an answer but she only found a steely-eyed glare.

Daring him, she said, "Don't you have a job you should be doing?"

"This is where I need to be right now."

He must know, she thought.

She turned her back to Graham and spun to look at the rest of the group. "I won't be long," she said, and then quickly made her way to the truck and into town.

ELEVEN

June sat at her desk and looked at Bea with a mix of skepticism and pride. "You're sure?"

"I'm sure," said Bea with a shaking voice, "I'm in for the year."

June's office didn't look like an office of law, but then, June didn't look like much of a lawyer herself. Today she sported a blazer and a pair of dark washed blue jeans. Various diplomas hung on the wall behind June's minimal whitewashed wooden desk, but there were no fat law journals, no dark leather chairs or mahogany bookshelves as Bea imagined there would be. Instead it looked like a meditation room, complete with a Buddha head on the end table next to an overgrown spider plant, and a corner filled with cushions propped up against the backdrop of a magenta and green tapestry on the wall. There were pictures in over-sized wooden frames carved in tribal patterns, one of June on a sailboat with a man who Bea presumed was her husband, though not who she would have pictured as June's partner. His hair was cut short and styled to match his crisp polo shirt, he looked like he belonged at the yacht club, while June looked like she came straight from a yoga retreat. They were smiling wide, drunken smiles and holding glasses of white wine and June's hair was blowing in the wind.

"Just sign here, here, and here." June leaned over her desk and pointed to a few places marked with bold red X's next to a straight line where Bea's signature was required. "There will be more paperwork in the coming days," she continued as Bea signed with a heavy pen that had the moniker of The Law Offices of Mason & Nealy etched in gold down it's length, "banking info and all that sort of thing, but don't worry too much about that now. Cliff left you in good hands."

"Will you tell Graham?"

"Tell him what, dear?"

"Will you tell him that he isn't getting the orchard?"

June sat back and paused, cocking her head to the side while assessing Bea.

"Unless Cliff told him, Graham doesn't know that he was, or is, the contingency plan. I won't notify him unless you decide you don't want the orchard before the year is up. Now," she leaned forward and rested her ample bosom on the desk, "I have no idea what Cliff told Graham. They were close over the last year. Close enough for Cliff to consider leaving him the orchard if you didn't want it. So I don't know what Graham Winters knows or doesn't know."

Bea finished signing her name with a flourish she tried for years to get rid of. But her hand always betrayed her mind, and her signature looked more flowery than professional.

June took the paper and exclaimed with a toothy smile, "Done! Here's to the first female orchardist of Finley Orchards! Oh!" she paused and grew quiet, "You could rename the orchard. Something with your last name, Hampton Orchards, sounds very polished and chic!"

Bea stifled a groan as she imagined what the residents of the town would think of her if she did that. "No, I think it'll stay Finley Orchards."

June stood and unbuttoned her blazer, she took it off to reveal a white tee shirt with the retro Polaroid logo on display. Bea gave her a surprised look, June looked down at her shirt and shrugged, "Who said I had to dress like a lawyer to be one?" Bea shook her head and laughed. This town and its people never failed to surprise her.

"Well, Bea, if this year works out you'll have a long time to make those decisions and changes as you see fit. By the end of the year you might need to part a bit with Cliff's ghost."

Bea stood and looked around the office once more. "How long were you Cliff's lawyer?"

"Just the last few years." She rubbed her arms with opposite hands and then reached for the blazer. "I can never decide if I'm cold or hot in here," as she shrugged it back on she pointed to the photo of herself and the man on the boat. "Cliff was my husband's client first. But when Rich died, Cliff opted to switch to me instead of changing offices like so many of Rich's other clients. Rich and I had shared this office for years, ever since we were married, but most of my clients were divorcees and more cases of, shall we say, delicate natures. Rich mostly helped the businessmen in town."

"I'm so sorry for your loss," said Bea bowed her head with reverence.

June waved her hand as if she could brush off the emotional exchange and her husband's death, the toll it no doubt took on her, personally as well as professionally. "Thank you. From the outside we looked like an odd couple, he was as traditional of a lawyer as they come. As for me, well, I'm more granola and hippie-dippie than even the health food store owner down the road," she laughed, her warmth resonated through the office. Bea liked her more with every passing moment. "But we complemented each other well, even in our practice. It was kind of Cliff to stay on with the office. It made a world of difference." She paused briefly before adding in a quiet, but professional voice, "And of course, it would be an honor to serve your legal needs as well, even after your year is up, regardless of your decision. Whatever transition you'll be in, I'll be here to advise you in any and all legal services."

Bea thanked her and stepped out of the office. She said goodbye to the receptionist who sat at the desk in the lobby, and walked through the entryway.

Outside, a wall of humidity hit her, and Bea nearly stepped back into the closed door of the office behind her. The deep, endless October sky was full of depth with patches of blue sky and then a sudden blanket of bruise colored clouds unrolled.

She felt an urgency swell in her, a sense of duty and responsibility. With a few signatures, her connection to the orchard had changed dramatically.

Only last week Cliff told Bea about the damage a hail storm had done to dozens of orchards in New York's Hudson Valley, a decade ago. Over two million bushels of apples were lost, and though the storm happened in the early summer, with newly formed apples instead of an orchard ready to harvest, hail was just as much of a possibility in October, and the damage could be even more severe with a bumper crop of perfectly red apples with delicate skin that could easily perish under the throws of a storm.

Bea pushed through the humidity to where the rusty old truck was parked. Her shoulders pulled back, her head held high, she dodged a few raindrops as she headed in for what felt like not only a battle against the elements, but a rightful passage to a new chapter in her life, unwritten and uncharted.

The doors squeaked with rust and time, announcing her entrance to Graham and Henry who looked at her expectantly as Bea stood with the door open, sheets of rain spilling into the barn. Graham was sitting at Cliff's desk with Henry nearby, both huddled over steaming mugs of coffee.

Graham put his mug down on the desk and walked over towards Bea, scowling as he reached around her to close the door. "If you're coming in, come in. Shut the door though, it's damp enough in here." Next, he walked over to a corner where there was a stack of blankets piled atop one another, searched until he found what he was looking for and threw it towards her. Bea's reflexes were slow, and so she stumbled over herself to grab at a towel that landed by her feet. Henry was watching her, but Graham's back was to her as he walked back to the chair at the desk.

"Where's everyone else?" she said as she sniffed the towel before wrapping it around her shoulders, it smelled of sawdust and mold.

"I sent them home. We managed to bring the bin back here, and get it into the storage room before the rain hit."

Henry was quiet, looking down at his coffee, at his feet, anywhere, it seemed, but at her. Bea looked down to make sure her sweater wasn't somehow transparent because of the rain. Thankfully it wasn't.

"Pull up a stool," Graham said, he gestured at a handful of bar stools lined up against the wall by the desk, "we were just speculating about what will happen."

"With what?" she asked as she took hold of a seat, it was covered in a thick layer of dust and her grip slipped as she dragged it near Graham and Henry, the legs scraped against the concrete floor crying out in protest to every corner of the building.

Henry's voice was muffled and solemn, "With Cliff's orchard."

There was a hush that swept through the barn as the rain pelted against the outside walls. Graham looked over the desk, he was at the helm. Papers were strewn about, from where Bea sat it looked like a mess of receipts and notes, the minutiae of a business. Systems in place for one mind, and with that mind gone, others might never be able to crack the code.

Graham was taking stock of the desk, "I'm thinking it'll go to his sister, some blood relative. They won't have a clue how to run this place. I've been running numbers," his hand ran over day old stubble and a scowl, "I'm not sure I can do it on my own, but maybe if a group of us pool our resources we could buy it from whoever ends up with it."

He must not know, she thought to herself. He'll be caught just as off guard as she was.

"Maybe he left it to a charity," suggested Henry.

She wasn't sure if she should tell them. This didn't feel like the time, but the urgency swelling inside of her wouldn't dissipate.

"I was at Bert's yesterday," said Graham, "and no one has a clue. Everyone has a guess. That," he pointed to Henry as if he and his ideas were one and the same, "is one of the more popular ideas. But I think," he turned around to face Bea, his steel-blue eyes looked into hers as he said, "I think Cliff would leave it to family."

The towel around her shoulders wouldn't stay put, and she tugged at it's edges, pulling the sides closer around her.

Henry straightened in his chair and spoke louder than before, "Cliff's family was the town, Graham. Not those folks wherever the hell they are, the ones that never showed up for him in all the years he lived here."

Graham slumped into his chair. It squeaked with the weight held on his shoulders, the tension in his back, and the unease in his face. "You're right," he said. "I don't know what I'll do."

"What you'll do? Graham, I'm sorry, but I don't see how any of this concerns you." She wanted to take back the words as soon as she saw the hurt in his face.

Graham cleared his throat and said, "You wouldn't. Cliff's done more for me than I could ever express, more than I could ever repay. I'm not the only one in this town who feels that way. I don't want his legacy to be forgotten."

Henry looked down at the ground, a tear rolled down his cheek and into his beard. In her head Bea pictured them falling into his coffee cup, plunk plunk plunk. She pictured them falling singly and then a stream cascading from his eyes over his beard and into the chipped white diner mug that held a pool of grief.

"I get that," she moved her hair from under the towel, the back of her sweater was soaked through, a chill ran down her spine. "Cliff did something for every person he met. But I don't see everyone lining up to help make heads or tails of his death and what's been left behind. And I don't know that it's your place to take control of the orchard. You've been here what, a year? Your authority over this place, over Cliff, has rubbed me the wrong way since the day I met you. I don't know where you get off thinking you can take that kind of a role here."

Graham started to say something but Bea stood abruptly, the towel fell to the ground and pooled at her feet.

"I wanted to tell everyone at once," she couldn't look at

either of them directly, her eyes darted from wall to wall of the barn, surveying the property, all that was now hers. Her gaze fell on the two misfits that sat in front of her, Henry with his worn, frayed trench coat, Graham with his soaked brogues, knit brow, and sad eyes that looked too tired to muster anger. At least that's what she hoped.

"Cliff left the orchard to me."

Henry let out a low, long whistle and set his coffee cup on the floor. Graham stood and walked to the other side of the barn, his footsteps fell carefully one after another. A few uncomfortable, full moments passed and then he raised both hands overhead, ran his hands through his already mussed hair and left them atop his head. Elbows framing his face, he knit his hands together behind his head and walked back towards Bea and Henry.

"But you're all of what, twenty? How could he do that? How will you run an orchard?"

She muttered so faintly no one but her could hear, "Twenty-eight," and then she sighed. "But that's not the point, I don't think Cliff thought this would happen so soon. I mean, if he did," at this point she was thinking out loud and didn't realize that she was even speaking the words, "maybe that's why he put in the clause."

"There's a clause?"

She didn't know how much to tell Graham, so she settled for the bare minimum. "I have to stay for a year before I can sell."

He sat back down in his chair just as Henry slipped out of his. Henry put a hand on Graham's shoulder. Bea watched, thinking Graham would flinch or pull away, Henry's fingernails were overgrown and caked with dirt. But Graham didn't flinch, instead he put a hand over Henry's and gave it a pat. Henry turned to her, and through his beard she could see the slight smile that played on his lips. His chin dipped as he nodded, then he pulled the collar of his trench coat up to stand. He turned and noiselessly glided across the floor to the sliding doors, where he opened them only enough for his slender shoulders to pass through to the rain.

"So I have a year to come up with the funds," said Graham. He was hunched forward over the desk, head in his hands.

"You think I won't stay?"

He looked up and laughed a hard laugh that didn't match the sadness in his eyes. "From what I can gather, you haven't stayed in one place for more than a few weeks at a time, because of your job or other reasons. When you live like that, you get used to constant change. And this," he made a grand gesture around the barn, "this is going to be too much of the same for you. Too much monotony. Too little excitement. You can't do this on your own, and I doubt you know how to ask for help."

"I think you should leave."

He stood, and assessed her with a sideways glance. He was looking at her like someone who was looking for the good in something, a reason to stay. He was considering something. Bea, a plan, Cliff's will, she wished she had a clue as without one, his gaze was unsettling.

"Bea, I've been through hell and back and found my sanctuary, finally. I'll say this once. I'm here if you need help through the year, but I'll also be here at the end of the year. Somehow, I'll come up with the money."

"Is that supposed to be a relief to me? That you'll have not only my grandmother's house, but Cliff's as well? Which one is your sanctuary? Or do you need both?"

He sighed, "I keep forgetting. That's what this is about."

"Go, Graham. Go back to your house. I'll be fine," she said it with more conviction than she knew was within her.

"Maybe," he said as almost an afterthought, "maybe it's

time to start over yet again. You and me."

"Now that I have the upper hand, you mean? You want to play nice so I'll sell the orchard to you?"

"No. I just think that we've gotten off to a terrible start, Bea. That first day, and then the car accident. And this," he gestured from himself to her and back again, "isn't going to help. If you only knew-"

"But I don't, and I won't. So please, go."

Graham's shoulders softened and slumped forward, his head lowered, and he walked over to the door. He looked back only once, and found her eyes as he said, "See you around, neighbor," before he slid the barn door shut.

With a rage that had been simmering, she stomped to the desk and reached for Graham's coffee cup. She yelled as loudly as she could, "You can take your goddamn coffee cup with you!" The cup flew through the air and smashed into a thousand pieces as it hit the barn door.

The noise of the crash was lost to the outside world as it dissipated into the rain. She looked out one of the tiny windows, and watched Graham as he walked away from the orchard. He didn't look back.

It took every ounce of energy she had, but she found a broom in the corner, and began to sweep up the sticky porcelain shards. There was no one else to do it, she thought to herself. This was hers. It was time to start taking ownership.

There was a tiny voice that she didn't dare listen to, but she knew what it was saying. Maybe this would be the last time. Maybe this was the beginning she was waiting for.

TWELVE

Bea sat at the kitchen table, staring at her cell phone. The phone, in whatever shape or upgraded form it took, had been her lifeline to work, family, and colleagues. While her address was impermanent, her phone number remained constant.

Now, she knew what she needed to do. Why she hadn't done it earlier, she wasn't sure. Whether it was the unwelcome reception she was sure to receive on the other end, or the potential criticism, or maybe the nonplussed attitude the news of Cliff's death might be met with, any and all of these very real possibilities stared at her from the blank screen on the table.

She scrolled through dozens of numbers in her call history, it might have been easier if she simply searched for Mom and Dad, but somehow she thought they would be closer to the top of the recent call list, dialed or received. They never were.

Bea knew before she called that her father wouldn't answer. She had not spoken to Eric Hampton in a year. She hadn't seen him for even longer. She searched through memories to find him: college graduation, the celebratory dinner after, endless wine and appetizers - the entrees were fuzzy, Grandma's funeral and the days after. All those memories disappeared when her mother answered on the first ring.

"Where are you calling from, Beatrix? The West Coast? Peru? Australia?"

Donna's tone was surprisingly playful, and while her guesses were all plausible, teasing was implied.

"I'm actually calling from Cumberland."

"Oh," her voice turned flat, "how's the orchard?"

"That's why I'm calling," Bea's voice trailed off, unsure of how to continue.

"I'm sure Cliff is busy with the harvest now. The weather's been perfect for fruit this year. The pear trees in the backyard are simply bursting."

Bea took a deep breath and said, "Mom, Cliff had a heart attack. He's gone."

Donna sucked in a breath of air. Bea's arm rested on the table and she slumped over and onto it, ear pressed against upper arm, sweater still damp from earlier.

"When is the funeral?"

"Friday. It'll be at the funeral home in town. Do you think you'll come?"

"I don't know Beatrix. There's so much going on here that I have to take care of. And Dad won't want me driving up all on my own, he has meetings back to back all week long."

"There's more though. He left me the orchard." Donna started to interrupt but Bea didn't let her. Pacing around the kitchen she explained the terms, aside from Graham. She spoke fast and furiously, not giving her mother any room to interject with questions that Bea didn't have answers to. Bea found over the years that it was the only way to convey information to her

112

parents: simply, without any doubt in her voice. Even now, as an adult who held jobs and paid taxes, dealt with many a broken heart, passports and border crossings, international flights, grocery lists, they still knew her buttons, and her mother had been known to push them all.

When Bea finally came up for air she leaned against the kitchen sink and looked out the window to the orchard. The light had faded from gray to nearly black. Rain dripped and dropped. Beams of light from the spotlight on top of the barn door caught in droplets of rain falling down the window. The light reflected and looked like twinkling stars, though the blanket of clouds was so thick it was hard to imagine stars, let alone the heavens, existed.

"Are you finished?" Donna asked.

"Yes," Bea murmured, looking into the sink full of dishes she let accumulate over a day and a half. Dregs of coffee were starting to dry in cups.

"It's a noble thing, what you're attempting to do," said Donna, "but there's so much at stake. Beatrix," she said Bea's name like it was a curse, forced and under her breath, "you can't possibly stay there for a year."

"Thanks for the vote of confidence, Mom."

"I can't even imagine what your father will say." Bea pictured her mother's nose in the air, her eyes rolling so far back they look like they'll get stuck, a tsk tsk inserted after every other word.

"Good thing it has nothing to do with him," said Bea.

"But it will. Don't you see? You won't be able to make it through the year, and somehow he'll have to come in and clean up the mess."

"Dad's never had to clean up on my account, and this won't be the first time."

"But it's business, honey, that's what he does. And your

other jobs weren't in his area. This, this is his forte, saving businesses."

"Cliff's orchard doesn't need saving."

"Well, it will. And Dad will be there when you need him."

"I won't need him, I have never needed him."

Her father was a subject they could never simply agree to disagree on and one reason why their phone calls were so few and far between.

"I'll let you know if we decide to come up on Friday. Do you think you'll be coming home for any of the holidays?"

She hadn't in years, Bea thought to herself, why bother starting now.

Almost as if she read Bea's mind, Donna said, "I just thought, since you're in the same state you may as well stop by."

At this point Bea was the one rolling her eyes.

"I'll think about it, Mom. I'm not sure how everything is going to play out next week, let alone for Thanksgiving."

With barely any parting words - an I love you or see you soon - the call ended in ambiguity.

Bea put the phone down on the kitchen table and started to walk over towards the living room. Just as she walked by the door to the porch, she saw a shadow pass and heard the screen door quietly close. She flipped on the porch light and then opened the heavy kitchen door. The sound of paper sliding against metal surprised her and she felt the skin on her arm prickle, hair stood on edge not only on her arms, but her neck as well.

A manila envelope sat at her wool sock covered feet. As she picked it up she noticed it was not only thick, but heavy and damp around the edges. The light orange color was starting to turn a deep pumpkin. Water had marked it, but age had also softened any hard, stiff paper edges, the whole of it felt like a checkbook that was on it's last check, the register worn and faded. There were no markings on the outside of the folder, but the fastener on the back had lost its purpose along with the metal flaps.

The screen door squeaked as she opened it slightly, the wind took it the rest of the way. Clutching the folder to her chest she peered out and felt the damp air greet her skin, raindrops traveling sideways under the porch rafters to kiss her cheeks and eye lashes. There was no one visible outside, and too much noise from the storm to hear footsteps.

Whoever left the package disappeared into the night, into the orchard or beyond.

After one more look around, she closed the door and locked the deadbolt, twice. Dampness entered the house, and before she even thought about opening the folder she stoked the wood in the fireplace. It lit easily and warmed the living room, comfort reached each corner. With the fire crackling and the soggy envelope at her side she sat on the couch, afghan pulled over her lap, feeling less alone than she had in the days since Cliff's death. Giving the envelope her full attention, she lifted the flap and slid the contents out and onto her lap.

She looked down at the three Moleskine notebooks, the expensive type Bea remembered from early in her career when she attempted to keep a record of her travels. The practice of travel journaling lasted no more than a few months, when she found that not only were the notebooks easy to leave behind accidentally, but also took up space in her suitcase where she could otherwise store photography equipment or souvenirs for a select few people, namely Cliff. He was always in the back of her mind, if not in the front. Not a day had gone by since Sylvia's passing that Bea had not thought about her grandmother, and in thinking about her, Bea thought about home. And home wouldn't be complete without the orchard, and Cliff.

For the first time in what seemed an eternity, a smile

spread across Bea's face as she remember yes, this place had always felt like home. And here she was, with a legal residence, paperwork pending, and a job all in one. She had yet to decide if it was a good thing or not, but for a brief moment she let a sort of joy settle in... until she recognized the feeling and it morphed into the discomfort of happiness through grief. She shook off the butterflies that had erupted quietly and quickly in her stomach.

Bea paused and lifted the notebooks to her nose. There was an aroma that wafted from them, earthy and pungent, familiar. The front of the notebooks themselves were unmarked and unremarkable, but while flipping through the pages she was caught off guard by the contents. Pages upon pages of graph paper filled with Cliff's neat and precise handwriting. Diagrams and charts, foreign looking words and agricultural slang that she was vaguely aware of in the days and months she spent at his side in the orchard. Now, it looked to her like gibberish. There were dates in the upper right hand corner of several pages of what look like diary entries. Different colored pens in all shades from blue to black and the soft charcoal of graphite from dulled pencil tips indicated each entry. The dates of one notebook ranged from the beginning of September to the end, the next notebook held all of October, and the third contained dates only in November. The year was unspecified. The amount of information was staggering, and as the fire popped and crackled she looked up and was easily transfixed by the orange glow in the stove as she processed only a fraction of what she had looked through.

Bea had so much to learn, terms and sales and seasons and equipment. The pressure of what was coming in the days and weeks ahead was enough to make anyone want to flee, and for a flight risk like herself...

The odd thing was that she was not overwhelmed. Instead, she felt pride. Pride for the land, pride in Cliff, pride in the fact

116

that for whatever reason, he chose her to continue his work.

But he had also chosen Graham.

Was Graham the one who left the journals? She couldn't imagine that he would leave without a trace. He'd want her to know that he had the notebooks in his possession. But who would leave the notebooks anonymously? And why?

Buoyed from the delivery, the discussion with her mother was far from her mind. She sat and snuggled into the afghan, it's weight securing her onto the couch, on that spot in the house on the orchard grounds, in a small town in Massachusetts, and she realized that she wouldn't want to be anywhere else.

"Thank you," she said quietly, "thank you for believing in me."

Bea poured over the notebooks, the intricate drawings that reminded her of the detailed, elaborate stories Cliff told her when he was picking and she tagged along when she was no taller than his waist. He'd talk and talk about orchard fairies and sea nymphs, and then back at the farm house they would sit on the porch and she'd beg him to draw her pictures of the characters. He always obliged. No matter what she asked for, he always said yes.

Cliff had never stepped in the way of Bea's plans, never threw caution in her face, or doled out unsolicited advice. He was the only one who held his opinions of Bea's actions to himself, though she knew where he stood.

For all of her warm and caring, determined and spitfire qualities, Bea's grandmother had her ideas about how everyone should live their lives, and Bea wasn't an exception. Sylvia always had a comment about how Bea dressed or her boyfriend, what books she read to her style of photography. "Why not do portraits, dear? Weddings? You'll make more money and be able to stay put!" Staying put was for Sylvia what travel was for Bea. And yet, her opinions never bothered Bea like the ones of her parents. She

117

and her grandmother had an understanding. Sylvia would voice her opinion and Bea would listen and not get upset, unlike her mother. The similarities between Sylvia and Donna were more than her mother would ever recognize, and the differences far greater than even Bea could wrap her head around.

All that on her mind, she was even more grateful for Cliff. For his steadiness, his unwavering presence, even in death.

As the fire died down to embers, she folded the blanket and set it on the back of the couch. Notebooks in hand, she double checked the locks on the doors and made her way upstairs, past the flaking wallpaper, stepping on the creaking stairs, hitting each at it's noisiest point. There was no need to be quiet, no need to tip toe, but still - the sound was jarring and she wished there was a dog underfoot or a cat waiting on the bed for her. Someone to make the dark feel less empty.

The painting greeted her as she walked into the bedroom and turned on the light. Her suitcase was still open on the floor and the contents were piled in the same neat stack she left that morning. She stared at the painting, hoping for a hint of the woman's happiness. Later, lying in bed with all the lights still on, she continued to search the painting. And right before she dozed off to sleep, she found it. Her lips were not cast downward as Bea thought. In the fuzziness of the moments before sleep, she saw the corners of the woman's mouth drawn up in an ever so slight and secretive smile.

Perhaps the orchard, with all of its secrets, was not the prison Bea had imagined.

THIRTEEN

B ea sent everyone home at noon on Friday to get ready for the funeral, but even though her neck ached and her arms were heavy with fatigue she couldn't leave the orchard. The rate at which her emotions were changing was dizzying. When grief swelled she squashed it down. When excitement over the orchard and all of the potential began to grow, she put it into a box and closed the lid. She worked at a furious pace, trying to keep her mind blank as best she could for fear of whatever emotion might escape or crawl out from within her.

The sun beat down, drops of sweat beaded on her forehead and dripped down her back, but she didn't take off her flannel shirt; it was one of those crisp, beautiful days where the sun was warm, but the air was cool. She didn't pay attention to the time, she knew that the funeral was that evening, but she was dreading it and so Bea pushed the thought of preparations to the back of her mind.

The first frost was coming soon, and she had to make sure

the apples were picked so they could move onto the next stage: storage and sales. From Cliff's notebooks she had a good idea of what needed to be done, what steps needed to be taken and who to contact regarding invoices. Cumberland's town schools had already picked up several boxes of apples for their cafeterias, and deliveries scheduled for the coming days to local natural food stores and co-ops. Cliff had it all laid out, month by month, bullet points for how to run his orchard.

"Bea!"

She turned to see Olivia walking towards her. She looked smart in a black knee length skirt and a matching knit top. Her legs were bare and the sight of patterned Wellingtons covered in bright pink and purple flowers against a muted green background brought a smile to Bea's otherwise somber face.

"Nice boots," Bea said as she approached, Olivia's cheeks were flushed and her breathing heavy, but her eyes were bright and her smile infectious.

"Thanks. I've got my dressy boots in the jeep, but I didn't want to risk mucking them up." She paused to catch her breath, leaned up against an old wooden ladder that was placed precariously amid branches and fruit. Bea hadn't used it all day, but she remembered seeing Anna up in the tree earlier. The branches looked bare except for a few at the very top. Someone else would have to reach them the next day. Out of the regular pickers there were few as tall as Cliff. Bea thought of a certain someone who was tall enough to reach them, and she scowled.

"I didn't think it'd upset you that I didn't wear fancy boots out here," Olivia's eyes were concerned.

"No, it's not that, I was just noticing the apples up that tree. The ones on top. I don't have anyone who's tall enough to reach them without hurting themselves. Thank goodness there's only a few really tall trees. Dwarf apple trees are so much easier to maintain." She reached for a few more apples, and twisted them off the branches. They were perfect and she wanted to keep them all that way, to get them inside before it was too late and they were overripe or an extended frost softened them.

"I think I know someone. The same person who told me where I'd be able to find you when you weren't at the house."

Bea dropped the apples in the bucket, they landed with a thud. She winced and looked down to make sure they hadn't bruised.

"I haven't talked with him in days," Bea faced the trees, the apples. She couldn't seem to get rid of her scowl, just the thought of Graham made her uncomfortable.

"I thought as much. He's been in town more often than normal. Guess he's got more free time than usual, without spending a few hours over here each day." Her tone was light, but her words hung heavy like the ripe fruit in front of them.

"That's good for him," she paused before adding, "my whereabouts shouldn't concern him."

"I don't know that they do," Olivia said with a laugh, a warning. Bea blushed. "When you weren't at the house I walked over to ask when he was planning on heading to the funeral home, and who was catering. I shouldn't have been surprised, it's Bert. He's opening the diner up for everyone, it'll be quite the spread." She walked over to the tree on the other side of Bea, then proceeded to pick a few apples, held out her shirt with one hand to make a basket and dropped apple after apple into it. The white of her belly was exposed, the swell of it full and pronounced.

"Anyway," she continued, "I asked if he'd seen you around, since your truck wasn't there, and he said he heard the truck drive into the orchard this morning, but hadn't heard it come back. So we deduced you must be here." While talking, Olivia had walked over closer to Bea. She lifted her shirt to bring the apples up more and Bea lowered herself and the picking basket down, Olivia easily guided her apples in with the others.

"I didn't want to head back with everyone else, there's so much work that needs to get done."

Olivia nodded, smiled and said, "It suits you."

Bea tilted her head, her brow furrowed.

"This," Olivia continued and waved her arms around, "all of this. The orchard, the pressure, it suits you. Cliff knew what he was doing." Then she placed a hand on Bea's exposed forearm, Olivia's fingers and palms were calloused and rough. Not nearly as soft as the rest of her.

"I don't know, Olivia. I'm sure his intentions were good. But, I don't like feeling boxed in, and there's a part of this that feels kind of suffocating. You must understand."

"I'm not sure that I do." She removed her hand and placed it on her hip, swaying to one side, her figure accentuated and dramatized by the forgiving jersey material and cut of her skirt.

"You don't ever feel like you've been trapped with the hardware store?"

Olivia shook her head, "Nope. It was always a choice."

They started heading back to the truck and the bin of apples. Even though the baskets were ergonomically correct, after so many loads and standing for so long, Bea's shoulders ached and her legs were on fire. She had pushed herself this week, and now her body was telling her what her head didn't grasp, it was time to call it quits for the day.

"I always thought it was written in stone, that you would take over the family business."

"It was never a given, there was no pressure. Growing up I knew it was an option, but my parents didn't want me to marry the business if I didn't want to. That's what it is, really, a marriage between the hardware store, Steve, and me. And this town plays a part in there somehow, maybe like a mother-in-law," Olivia's eyes twinkled as she spoke.

A tiny, nervous laugh escaped from Bea's lips, "That's what I'm most worried about, the town. Of not living up to what they all think I should do. I'm sure everyone has an opinion of what Cliff would have wanted. Hell," the flow of apples pitter pattered into the bin as she emptied her basket, each one finding a nook or cranny to fill between the other apples, "June already suggested I change the name. I can't imagine what else people expect me to do. I'll be causing blasphemy in some way no matter what I do. I could keep everything the same, and someone will find fault."

"I had that thought in the beginning. But that's not what happens in reality."

Bea motioned to the truck, they hopped in. The bin remained in the field, it was nearly full again and she would be back later on to hitch it up to the tractor and pull it to the barn. Over the last few days she became a quick study of the daily work, aside from just picking. Yesterday, Henry and William taught her how to drive the tractor, and while she wasn't an expert, she'd be able to get the job done after the funeral.

The truck was a mess, but Bea consoled herself that it was no worse than Olivia's Jeep with candy wrappers and paint cans on the floor. Bea rubbed the back of her neck thinking of the ride home from the accident, there had been a bit of stiffness and maybe some whiplash, but nothing that stopped her from working.

"You don't think people had expectations of what you'd do with the store?" asked Bea.

They passed rows of Macs and Cortlands, Honeycrisps and Golden Delicious, one after another, until they hit a small clearing that gave way to the barn. The house popped into view, and Bea looked over to make sure Olivia heard her. She was staring out the window thoughtfully.

"Of course they had, and still have, expectations. But I made the decision when I took over that I wouldn't care about what they thought. Kind of like what I said before, I think of the town and the people in it as an in-law. Sure, I listen to their requests and thoughts. The store is a part of the community as much as Steve and I, even more so. It's a meeting place, a hub of activity. People count on it to be there not only for advice on all of their home repair needs, but also for the place it holds in the towns history. But we do what's best for the store, and ultimately for us. Most times it ends up being one and the same. "

The truck jolted as Bea turned the ignition off. It rocked back and forth and Bea unhooked her safety belt and slumped down a bit in the driver's seat. Olivia looked over at the house. Bea tried to see it through her eyes. It was an old house that needed work, but was charming even with its fatigue.

Olivia broke the silence with a hushed voice, "The orchard is like that, too, Bea. It holds a piece of the towns history, but you're in charge of it now. Follow your gut. The people here will respect your decisions, they have no other choice. It's not as if you're planning on ruining it. You've got support, and you will have as much help as you need, or are willing to take." Olivia lifted her gaze, Bea didn't want to follow it, but she did. It lead to the familiar yellow siding and front porch across the street. Just then the front door opened and Graham walked through. If she was standing upwind, Bea wondered, could she catch a whiff of Sylvia? Or would it be a new scent of musty books, aftershave and whatever it was Graham surrounded himself with in his home?

He was wearing a dark suit, and there was a sense of recognition in his movements. He lifted a hand, a simple, neighborly gesture. Olivia and Bea both waved back, only one of them smiled.

"All you need to do is ask, and help will be there. All of us in this town? We've got our quirks, and it might take some time for us to warm to new ideas and changes, but we won't let you fail on our watch."

Bea looked over and smiled at her. Silently they watched Graham back his new car, another Subaru, out of the driveway and start into town. Then they both opened the creaky truck doors and stepped outside. Bea walked around to see if Olivia needed help, but of course she didn't. She wasn't infirm, Bea told herself. She was already on the steps of the porch, pointing to one of the Adirondack chairs where a pile of dresses had been flung over the side.

"I wasn't sure if you had anything appropriate for a funeral, or if you had time for shopping. I brought a few things for you to try on. I don't know that we're the same size in shoes, but if you happen to wear a size seven and a half, I've got a few options in the car."

As Bea walked up the steps it occurred to her that she hadn't even thought of what to wear to the funeral. She wore her dressiest clothes to the meeting with June, and she flushed with the thought of showing up to Cliff's funeral in jeans and a sweater. What on earth would her mother say? The good thing was that Donna most likely wouldn't be there, Bea hadn't heard from her since their conversation the other night.

"You, my friend, are a lifesaver," said Bea as she piled a handful of dresses in her arms, their plastic dry cleaning covers crinkling in the wind with her movements. Olivia followed Bea inside the farmhouse to play dress up before attending to the business at hand. The business of commemorating Cliff Finley.

Bea told Olivia to leave without her, to pick up Steve, and she'd meet them at the funeral home. "Save me a seat," she told her, as if they were meeting at Bert's for a quick bite to eat. "I'll be along in a minute," she said.

It took more than a minute.

After Olivia left, Bea took a quick shower. She slapped on some make up, a quick swipe of eye shadow and a bit of mascara, and wrapped her damp hair into a less-than-normally-messy bun. Her mother's voice nagged at her, to not leave the house with wet hair, let alone go to a social event with dripping locks.

And that was what a funeral was, to her mother, a social event. There was a time where her parents seemed to attend a funeral at least once a week. Bea remembered her father making note of who would be in attendance, a business partner in the firm, or a competitor, a mentor of a coworker, a potential investor. He'd implore Donna to look her best. "Wear the pearls," he told her countless times. Wear the pearls meant it was time to impress. Donna Hampton played her part, fixing her smile as she air kissed her daughter's lips before leaving Bea with a sitter. God forbid she'd mess up her lipstick and have to reapply.

Bea slid Olivia's dress over her head, careful of the hair and makeup. She chose a simple long sleeved black wrap dress, hemmed at the knees. Olivia left her with a set of black suede pumps, not Bea's typical fare, or what she thought was Olivia's either, but they did the trick. When Olivia handed them over, Bea looked at the barely worn insole, "Jimmy Choo?" she exclaimed, shocked to see a label she'd only tried on in stores on a whim, never bought because of the price. And where would she keep a set of pumps more expensive than her favorite camera lense? Olivia just smiled her easy smile and said, "You'll feel like a million bucks when you wear them," and then winked at Bea like she'd just shared the biggest secret in the world: the hardware store owner walked around in Jimmy Choo's in her spare time.

Sitting on the edge of her bed, Bea slipped on one shoe and then the other. The tallest heels she wore were her riding boots, and those were only an inch high. These were three inches. Practicing her walk, she stepped one foot gingerly in front of the other, staying close to the wall for support. In the hall she eyed the flight of steps to her left. She walked to the right instead, down the small hallway that led to a window overlooking the orchard. The door to Cliff's bedroom was shut, as it had been since the day he died. She couldn't stand to look at his bed, made perfectly as was his habit. But this evening, dressed in her borrowed funeral outfit, she felt compelled to step inside.

The air was cool, a hue of evening had settled over the white bedspread turning it a dusty blue. The room was made up of simple lines, no clutter, no fuss. A few photos on Cliff's bureau: one of the two of them at the graduation party Sylvia threw for Bea the summer after she finished high school - her parents hadn't invited any of her Cumberland friends to the party they hosted for her, and so when Bea's summer in Cumberland commenced, it started off with the party; a black and white photo of a child with a fishing pole smiling over his shoulder at the camera, she leaned in closer to the photo, wobbling on her heels and steadied herself by the bureau, and saw Cliff's eyes staring back at her; a photo that she published in a local magazine she offered to have printed - signed and matted - for Cliff after he told her how much he loved it, just a simple photo of a beach rose lined path to a private beach down the coast, but instead he clipped and framed the magazine copy; and finally a photo she had seen a thousand times at her own parents house, a photograph of a young Bea, arms wide, walking away from the photographer into a blossom filled orchard.

Without thinking, she grabbed the photograph and headed toward the hallway, but as she turned she caught a glimpse of the windowsill, and on it sat a small figure of a chickadee. She walked over and used her free hand to pick it up, it didn't seem to fit the aesthetic of the various chickadee figurines that still sat in the box from her grandmother. This one was different. Bea remembered it from the kitchen at Sylvia's house. It was the only wooden figure, and she remembered how Cliff would stand in the small kitchen, his figure towering over Sylvia as she made dinner, how he would hold the chickadee in his big hand almost like a worry stone. Now it was smooth and well oiled from Cliff's fingers. Bea smiled, grateful the wooden figure ended up here with him instead of packed away in a box.

Instead of further investigating the bedroom, she walked unsteadily down the stairs, framed photo in one hand, the other clutching the railing. She placed the photograph in the center of the kitchen table, noting the perfect alignment, the framing. She had always assumed her mother took the photograph, and in some way that tied her to Donna in the way one photographer acknowledges another, in creative spirit. Though her mother never mentioned a love of photography, and scoffed at Bea's Masters of Fine Arts degree in photojournalism, Bea always assumed Donna harbored an interest. One of those interests that maybe happened before marriage and a baby, before settling down.

But now, looking at the photograph on the table, it was all too clear to Bea that the photograph couldn't have been taken by her mother. First of all, Donna hovered, she practically invented helicopter parenting. Bea thought the act of following a small child around, expressing opinions about said child's every movement, exhausted her mother so much that she needed the breaks given by Sylvia. Bea always wondered how Donna could so easily drop her off for weeks at a time, but couldn't let her daughter out of her own sight at home. Bea may never know, or understand how her mother could have done the things she did,

128

and continued to do. Daughters aren't meant to know all of the whys behind their mother's actions.

After one last look at the photograph she grabbed her keys, cell phone, and a canvas field jacket. It didn't go with the dress or the shoes, but the pockets doubled as a purse and no one would pay attention to her coat.

Funerals were for saying goodbye. Funerals were for the living. But as she looked around Cliff's home, at the corners filled with dust, the side tables with his unread library books punctuated with bookmarks, his pipe still on the shelf next to the door, she felt a calm settling in. Her goodbye would not happen tonight. She was still coming home to Cliff.

FOURTEEN

The funeral home was on the outskirts of town, and when Bea arrived it was packed. The truck's clutch creaked and moaned with each break and forward motion through the five point turn she made in order to get out of the full lot, and onto the street to find a spot. After ending up two streets over, in a space she could slide into instead of attempting to parallel park, she walked and hobbled up to the steps of the funeral home. Large planters filled with seasonally colored mums in maroons and oranges lined the walkway and steps. Her face fell as soon as she walked through the door, faced with the noise of hundreds of hushed voices that amounted to a wave of sound.

The walls of the funeral home were cream, the molding was cream, the ceilings were cream, but the drapes were the same maroon as the mums out front, and the curtains were trimmed in gold, as were the frames throughout. Artwork hung at eye level, unassuming landscapes and fruit bowl still lifes that were as generic as tomato soup on a rainy day.

It was too late to wander in anonymously. Her days of

blending into the background, camera in hand, looking for a story to tell, were gone. As she walked past attendants she was offered kind smiles, and it seemed that even those she didn't know, knew who she was. She saw Anna turn and whisper to two young men, Bea had to do a double take to recognize the boys she had babysat years ago, and then Anna's sons both gave Bea looks of sympathy. She returned the looks with a permanent tight smile that had appeared on her face. She was afraid of catching herself in the mirror, afraid of who the smile would remind her of. Bea didn't think that someone was there, and she wasn't sure if it was with dread or hope that sought out her mother's face in the crowd.

Instead she found Olivia and Steve, sitting with an empty chair and Olivia's parents.

"Hey you, I thought you'd gotten lost on your way here!" said Olivia. She was sitting on the end of a row, and moved to stand in the aisle to let Bea pass to an empty seat beside Steve. Olivia placed a hand on Bea's shoulder as she walked by. Steve stood as well, gave her a quick hug and whispered, "Nice coat." Bea gave him a fake punch to the arm and said her hellos to Olivia's parents. Bernice, or Bernie, as the whole town called her, and Nathan were retired, though they filled in for Olivia and Steve at the hardware store when needed and were as big a part of the community as ever.

Bernie put an arm around Bea and gave her a squeeze, she smelled of lemon drops and rosemary. She extended her condolences, Bea passed along congratulations on the baby. They were the kind of people who were born to be grandparents, kind and nurturing and with a sense of humor that allowed for fun and just the right amount of doting and indulgence.

Bea saw a woman who she assumed was the funeral director, Beverly, standing in the front, assessing the room, the flow of guests and chatter. Graham appeared by Beverly's side

131

and was introducing her to a woman in the front row, where family was normally seated. It was the first time Bea thought about Cliff's family since the day in the barn. She considered the town his family through all of this, and there was no distinction between where the more important of the bunch, the more affected, sat verses someone who knew Cliff casually.

Bea was peering around the heads in front of her, trying to catch a glimpse of the woman Graham was talking to, when he looked straight at Bea. His brow furrowed. She turned to quickly ask Bernie if she thought Olivia would have a boy or a girl. Bernie started to answer and then looked up to find Graham trying to get Bea's attention with a wave as he moved up the aisle of seats towards her.

"I think you're wanted, Bea."

Her shoulders slumped as she turned to face him.

"Bea, there's a seat for you up front," said Graham.

"I'm fine where I am, thank you."

He paused and looked ahead and then back at her. His deep navy suit was perfectly tailored, he tucked his blue tie against his crisp white shirt and into his suit coat as he said, "Please, you should be up front. Cliff's sister is here. She'd be honored to have you with her. I've told her all about you."

"I'm sure you have. But we're all Cliff's family. So I'm fine here." She felt a jab in her side, coming from Steve who passed it over from Olivia. Bea scowled and looked over to Olivia who mouthed, "Go," to Bea, who then looked up at Graham. His eyes were pleading, and the next thing she knew she was standing in front of Victoria Jennings with her arm extended.

"None of that," the tearful woman said as she stood and embraced Bea so tightly that Bea couldn't move her arms. There was a sob and Victoria eased away from the embrace, Bea patted her gently on the back. Victoria was wearing a dark gray skirt suit, her frosty blond hair was done in a short, stylish pixie cut. Her forehead was covered by side swept bangs, mascara caked eyelashes batted tears away as she waved her perfectly manicured hands in front of her eyes. "Sorry, love, it's just so much. All of this," she waved her hands and circled them around, "I'm getting to know my brother through all of you, and it's just so emotional," she dabbed her nose with a tissue. "I'm glad you're here, with me," said Victoria, "right where you belong."

Bea felt a hand on the small of her back and Graham gestured to two empty seats next to Victoria.

"Where are you sitting?" she asked him, he rolled his eyes and sat next to her. Victoria had wandered up the aisle and was turning her tears towards anyone who gave her a kind, or questioning look, telling them who she was. Bea heard her tell another person how much it all was, and was starting to turn to see who Vicky was talking to when Graham cleared his throat.

"Will you say something?" he gestured to the podium.

"In front of everyone?"

"I meant to come by and ask you earlier, but I, well, I wasn't sure you'd speak to me."

Bea looked at him with wide eyes and said, "And so now you're putting me on the spot."

They spoke in hushed voices, the murmurs from behind them faded to whispers.

"Hey, I didn't call you up from the podium. I'm just asking if you'd like to say a little something about Cliff. I think a handful of people agreed to, but I know you're the one Cliff would want to speak."

She sighed, knowing it was the truth. She should say something, but there was little Bea despised more than having to speak in front of crowds as her face turned red and blotchy, the heat from under her arms growing and the sweat spreading, no matter how warm or cold the air.

Graham crossed his arms in front of him and tipped his head back to look at the ceiling. Fatigue and impatience crossed his face.

"I'll say something," said Bea reluctantly.

"Thank you." He uncrossed his arms, and smiled at her. A genuine smile, even though there was sadness lingering around the eyes.

"So, your new car looks nice."

"Thanks, I just picked it up today."

"Sorry about your old one," said Bea as she looked down at her feet.

He raised an eyebrow and stared at her with trepidation and questions, "Nothing we can do about it now. I'm sorry about the other day, in the barn."

"Nothing we can do about it now," she returned his gaze and added in a small smile, a peace offering.

Victoria came to sit down just as Graham leaned forward a bit and his hands rested on the sides of his chair, an inch away from Bea's. He bowed over his legs, his eyes closed, as if praying. Maybe he was finding some peace in the moment, maybe practicing the words he was planning to speak of his friend, their friend.

She sighed and tried to wiggle out of her coat without touching Victoria on her left, or Graham on her right. Graham reached his left arm behind her to help take her coat off. He didn't mention that it didn't go with her dress, let alone the occasion. He handed it to her and she folded it in half and tucked it under her chair, out of sight, out of mind. He was a gentleman, Graham Winters, she was realizing this now. Maybe, she thought to herself, if they had met under different circumstances, things would be different between them. If he hadn't bought her grandmother's house. If he wasn't the contingency plan for the orchard. If he had absolutely nothing to do with the life she remembered at Cumberland. Maybe, just maybe, if he hadn't gotten in the way of her memories, they'd be friends.

Then again, in certain moments and light there was an arrogance in him that shined through stronger than any gentlemanly manner. She thought back to the first time she met him, standing in the orchard, and the arrogance she heard and felt. Looking at Graham, she reminded herself that the only times she heard that tone was when he was upset, angered or frustrated. No one sounded like their best self when put on the spot. There were a handful of times just in the last week Bea recalled acting so unlike herself under pressure, maybe even a few from today, in the last hour. She smoothed her dress down as the funeral director stood at the podium. Graham inhaled sharply and the silence of the room hung heavy.

FIFTEEN

They all took turns at the podium. Quiet voices, loud voices. More stories were told than Bea could recount later. Stories of Cliff and his quiet heroism. Stories from people no one believed in, except for Cliff. Stories from people everyone believed in, but Cliff's support mattered the most. Bert shared a story about two young men drinking too much hard cider and ending up in front of a bonfire on the beach, the fire dancing higher than the dunes, and how they laughed until they fell over when the fire department showed up. Anna was solemn and teary, until she chuckled and said what they were all thinking, that Cliff wouldn't have wanted sad eyes, tears and moans, or would've, could've, should'ves.

Victoria stood up. Call me Vicky, she said. She told the room she wouldn't know what Cliff would have wanted her to say. She hadn't known him as an adult. He left their family before she had grown, but she was glad to know them all and through them she felt closer to Cliff. There were sighs throughout the room, and

Graham sat up straighter. She felt his arm against hers, and without realizing it she found herself leaning slightly into him.

As Bea Watched Vicky talk about Cliff, she noted zero familiar gestures and little to no resemblance in siblings. Where one would expect to see some similarities, there were none. Bea searched Vicky's face, wishing to see something of Cliff in her, but the layers of makeup and the fancy suit paled in comparison to the memory of Cliff's soft worn cargo pants and sweatshirts, his wrinkled skin, laugh lines and crows feet that enhanced his generosity and spirit.

Bea scowled just as Graham looked over at her, they locked eyes and he gave her a look of reprimand. She thought to herself about how his arrogance was coming out, but maybe it was more his age and how he viewed her. Maybe he thought she needed guidance, that her youth would be a hindrance when it came to surviving in the community as an adult, not as the child she once was.

If she could go back to those days, she would. The ones with no responsibility, where she showed up at the orchard with a sense of adventure and a wild spirit. The summer she turned eight was the one she remembered best, it was the first year she had complete freedom. She walked across the street without holding anyone's hand or attention. She went in and out of her grandmother's house as she pleased, heading indoors only for meals. The single request Sylvia had was that Bea washed up as soon as she came inside. In the first floor bathroom the soft light danced through the window overlooking the backyard. After she finished washing, the bowl of the white, porcelain pedestal sink would be covered in filth. She remembered being mesmerized as the water cleansed her hands, the avalanche of dirt and mud falling away, swirling around and around and finally down the drain.

Only once each visit was she told to wipe out the sink.

Always on the first day, when her body was tired from fresh air and the open fields, the endless running and climbing, she forgot to clean out the sink. Muddy fingerprints were left behind on the water faucet handles, the C and H marks barely visible through the dirt. Grandma's laughter filled the air, "Beatrix Hampton," she'd say, "get back here and mind your dirt and dust!" After that, wiping out the sink became a habit, until the next visit when she'd need another reminder. She wondered if the pedestal sink was still awash in that soft light on summer days.

Her attention was drawn back to the unfamiliar woman speaking, and just in time as it was now Bea's turn to take the stage. She stood, walked carefully in her borrowed shoes as her borrowed dress swished around her bare thighs, and she took a breath as she looked out in awe at the residents of Cumberland. It seemed they were all there, and then some. Her palms slipped as she gripped the podium. There were no notes in front of her, and she had only the image of the dirty sink at her grandmother's house and the photo left on Cliff's kitchen table to fill her mind. She closed her eyes, imagined the crowd in front of her as just one person, a sympathetic audience, and then she took a breath and started.

"Hello. Most of you know me, I'm Bea Hampton. My grandmother lived across the street from Cliff when I was growing up, and Cliff became my best friend in Cumberland," her heart beat in her throat and her palms were sweaty as she looked out at the people seated in stiff chairs, all eyes on her. For a moment she didn't know what she was going to say, Bea ran her hand across the edge the podium, a splinter caught on her finger. Brushing her thumb and index finger together she loosened the shard of wood, but it stuck in her heart as a memory surfaced, "When I was ten or eleven, Cliff gave me my first pocket knife. It was one of those red ones, with multiple blades, and a toothpick," her cheeks burned as she remembered. "He taught me how to use it safely, and I only used it in his sight. I kept it at my grandmother's house, as it wasn't something my parents would have wanted me to have," she looked up briefly and saw Graham looking at her with tenderness, "I was pretty good with it, very careful, but there was this one time when Cliff asked me to help him break down some boxes in the barn. I was telling him about the flowers behind Grandma's house, how I wanted to pick some for his kitchen, and I wasn't paying attention and I pressed down on the wrong side of the knife blade," she winced with the memory, and she heard others in the room do the same.

"I didn't notice at first, but then I caught a glimpse of the blood dripping down my hand, and dropped the knife and the box. Cliff heard, and then saw, and he stayed so calm," she shook her head gently, smiling as she looked down at her index finger, at the faint scar, and how Cliff had put his arm around her and she knew that even if she needed to go to the hospital for stitches, she'd still be okay because Cliff was by her side. "He walked me over to his house, into the kitchen, a trail of blood behind us. He stayed calm, all the while I kept thinking, and finally said, that my parents were going to be so mad when they found out. After he had bandaged up my finger, he laughed his deep laugh, you all know the one," there were nods throughout the room, and in that moment, Bea felt the community supporting her.

"He said to me, 'Now Bea, if you went home missing a finger, then they'd be upset, but this is just a little scratch.' He patted my head and we went straight back out to the barn and finished the job." She laughed and shook her head and then she paused, not sure what else to say, or where she was going. Her cheeks flamed, her hands shook, and she didn't dare look at a single person in front of her.

"But that was Cliff. He'd calm you down, patch you up,

and make you laugh before setting you upright again. He was good at it. He was good at everything he did. He was a man full of generosity and love, kindness and compassion. Cliff Finley will forever live in my memory as the type of person we should all strive to be. All of us in this room are lucky to have spent time with him. He was loved dearly, and will be greatly missed."

And with that, she walked down from the platform with wobbly steps, landing in her chair with tunnel vision and her heart in her throat. She looked straight ahead, past the flower arrangements and the podium where closing remarks were being made by the funeral director. Bea barely took a breath until others stood and began to mingle.

She walked past Graham and Vicky without making eye contact. She made her way from the hall to the bathroom, all the while being stopped by various people who wanted to tell her how brave she was to take over the orchard. People who told her how her words brought them to tears. Bea was asked if she had any photos of Cliff, were any of hers up on the entryway table? She shook her head and said no, she hadn't had a chance to look for any, but aren't the ones up there lovely? They agreed and shrunk away, mumbling about what a shame it was that she didn't have any at the ready. Bea heard murmurs of what a beautiful service it was, how pleased Cliff would be, and how his sister spoke of him in such a moving way.

She excused herself over and over again until she reached the bathroom, dodging into a stall and sitting on the toilet, fully clothed. She just wanted a moment to be alone and a toilet stall was the best option. The bathroom was tiny, though there were three stalls crammed in the space, two square boxes and a long rectangle handicap stall. They were all full and Bea could hear the chatter that came from a line of ladies in waiting, and so she tried to take a deep breath and pull herself together. It wasn't the grief

140

she hid from, but the noise. She sat back with closed eyes, taking in the scent of potpourri and aerosol fresheners, Dial soap and paper towels.

"What did you think of Vicky's eulogy?" she heard a voice ask. Curious to hear the answer, Bea leaned over and put her head between her legs, deep breaths in and out. As she stared at her feet she wondered if anyone would recognize her from the black heels.

"The poor dear, I can't believe they weren't in contact for all those years."

"Did you see how Graham was with her? So kind."

"He and Bea looked quite a pair sitting next to each other."

"What on earth are you saying?"

"Nothing. I just have eyes, you know."

The whir of toilet bowls flushing drowned out the voices for a few seconds.

"Beatrix surely can't do it alone. She's such a young thing."

"That place needs some young blood to keep it going."

"I worry about the changes she'll make, though. You don't think…"

"I do think. She'll make changes because she doesn't know better."

Bea wondered how much longer she could sit there, if she could wait them out. There were two or three different women speaking, one soothing, melodic voice, one shrill one, and there could have been another, or it could have been a combination of the two speaking at the same time.

"Gentrification. That's what will happen."

"You're a fool to think it hasn't already. Just go in to Bert's any day of the week and see all those unfamiliar faces! It

141

wasn't like that ten years ago."

"But it hasn't reached the Orchard. Cliff made sure of that. He kept it running all those years for the town. The old town, not the city people with their expensive cars and their telecommuting and their grand ideas."

"If only Cliff had a child, someone who grew up at the orchard. Knew the ropes. Knew the town."

Bea's heart dropped and a lump grew in her throat so big it nearly choked her.

"Graham was the closest thing."

"You can't say that! Bea really was like a daughter to him."

"But she hasn't lived here, like Graham,"

"Graham's only been here a year. But after all that Cliff did for him," the voice trailed off.

"But he's money. His is a white collar to our blue. How is it different than the city folks?"

"He's good people. One of us."

"And you heard her speak, she's overwhelmed already."

"Already? Wouldn't you be if you inherited a business you had no idea how to run?"

"How could he do this?"

"Cliff was the life of that orchard. Without him…"

They talked between the stalls and then over running water. They talked even as they walked out the door. When the sound of silence reverberated off the walls Bea let herself out of the stall, slinking out like the eavesdropper she was.

Out of the bathroom she paused in the corridor in front of a mirror. She noticed the dark circles under her eyes, the strain in her gaze. She was overwhelmed by an ache for home, for a warm fire and a hot mug of tea, for the musty blankets that sat on the back of the threadbare couch. Her head was tired, her neck ached, and so she unwrapped the bun from atop her head, the weight instantly lighter as her hair fell down the back of the dress. Her eyes were closed and she was giving herself a little neck massage that ended with wrapping her hair back up in the tidy bun when she heard from somewhere behind her, "It looks better down."

She opened her eyes and saw Graham leaning against the wall next to her, arms crossed. Upon closer inspection Bea noted that his suit was not only tailored, but well crafted, and expensive. White collar to their - no, our, she thought - blue. She wondered how this man seemed so very much at home among these people after such a short time. How he could be better suited for running an orchard than she was, how he already had more credentials, more belief rallied behind him, than she did.

She looked back into the mirror and futzed with her hair, trying to decide to leave it up or down. In the end she turned away from the mirror as it cascaded down.

"You're in high demand," he nodded towards the main room, towards the noise and endless people.

Bea shrugged her shoulders, "It looks like you organized the funeral of the year."

He took a long look at the crowded room. "I had a lot of help."

"What's your secret, Graham?" Graham bristled, no longer leaned against the wall. She specified, "How did you get in with everyone so quickly?" As she waited for a reply she smiled politely at a handful of people who walked in and out of the bathrooms. The location was hardly discreet, and Graham and Bea were given curious glances by all who passed.

Graham touched her elbow and led her out of the quiet nook.

"My secret is showing up. Listening," he paused, his hand still on her elbow. She resisted the urge to shake it off, "doing what I can when I can."

She raised her eyebrows, "That's it? That's how you infiltrated Cumberland?"

"Infiltrated? You make it sound like it was all some sort of grand plan."

"Wasn't it though?" She was thinking of the contingency plan. Of his book selling business that couldn't possibly afford him a house in this seaside town, let alone a bespoke suit. But what did she know? Maybe he could afford to putz around town, helping whenever the need arose. She knew nothing about antique book dealing, it could be the sort of thing that made for an easy, early retirement. A life of ease. One that afforded the choice of hard labor in the margins.

"I think maybe you need some air. Let's walk over to Bert's."

She hesitated before acquiescing and saying, "I need to go grab my coat, I left it under my chair."

She zig zagged through the crowd, avoiding eyes and bodies. There were so many people, so much noise. Graham was right, she needed air, not conversations. And, most importantly, she wanted to avoid a conversation with Vicky. She knew she'd need to speak with her eventually, but she wasn't ready. She hadn't prepared for any of this, and the last time she was in this spot she was too young to be expected to handle grief with any decorum. This time, there was expectation after expectation, and no matter what Olivia said about doing whatever Bea felt was best, the weight of judgment felt heavy upon her slight shoulders.

Graham was waiting for her in the lobby where he was gathering the few photos left behind on the entryway table. He tucked them under his arm as she approached, and with his free hand he walked in two steps to the door and held it open for her. Outside they were greeted by a soft Autumn breeze; a few stray

144

dried and crumpled leaves scraped across the sidewalk. Wordlessly, they walked down the street towards Bert's Diner. In this area of Cumberland the houses were densely placed, they sat an inch from the sidewalk with only a driveway between them. Bea tried to step softly so her heels didn't announce their presence to the people sitting behind curtained windows. She looked straight ahead, avoiding peering into dining rooms and lives.

With a deep sigh she looked at Graham and considered him quickly. His strong profile. Cleanly shaved, his jaw was chiseled, and in his auburn hair there were a few flecks of gray glistening in the low evening light. Son of academic parents, friend of Cliff and all of Cumberland, neighbor of Bea's. The realization that this man was destined to be a part of her life, that she couldn't ignore him or push him away altogether, was needling at her. He could be an ally, an asset, and perhaps there was some softening that could be done. A second, or third or fourth by this time, opportunity for an olive branch to be passed.

"Tell me something about yourself," she said boldly. They had another few minutes to walk, and her pace was slowing as her feet ached and her toes pinched in the precariously high heels. There was beauty in quiet, but silence among acquaintances was uncomfortable at best. Give her a room of strangers and she would revel in the unspoken, but with someone that she didn't know where she stood? No thank you.

"Beatrix Hampton, are you trying to get to know me?" He smiled and searched out her eyes, his upper body turning toward her. She shrugged her shoulders and rolled her eyes. They turned down Main Street, where a church was just barely visible up on the left. Ahead it looked as though the street came to an end, but instead it dipped down steeply and ended up in the center of town where the diner waited. Historic plaques decorated the siding of colonial after colonial as well as a handful of old boarding houses turned bed and breakfasts.

"I've never felt as at home as I feel in Cumberland," said Graham. He was looking at the library with its ancient stone wall across the street. There was a dreamy tone to his voice that Bea hadn't heard before.

"Me, too," she said as she looked down at the ground to navigate around pebbles and cracked bricks.

"Why don't you just take them off?"

She scoffed, "Walk down the street barefoot? I can't go into the diner without shoes on."

"It's Cumberland. I'm sure walking barefoot isn't a scandal. You can put the torture devices back on when you get downtown. Here, lean on my arm," he offered his arm and without too much thought she used one hand to steady herself against him and removed the shoes. She felt relief instantly.

"Thank you," she said. He smiled and nodded at her, their eyes met for a moment and they both turned their heads forward and resumed walking. Her feet fell flat on the pavement and though she felt every pebble and every crack in the sidewalk, the ground was like an ice pack on her swollen feet.

"It's funny, when I bought the house," he paused and said gently, "your grandmother's house, I didn't think I'd fall in love with this place. But I fell, hard and fast. I wasn't in a great place emotionally when I moved, and I wasn't looking for anything amazing to happen. Quite the opposite, actually. I wanted a place where I could drown my sorrows. There's been a lot of healing that's taken place here, and I don't know that it would have happened without Cliff."

"This town has always felt like a safe place, a soft landing. I basically threw my career away a few weeks ago, and this is the place I came to recover and sort things out. Because of him."

Silence sat in the narrow space between them as their arms

swung and their bodies nearly bumped into each other with each step.

"So you're staying?" he asked as they paused to cross the road, having arrived at the center of town.

"I am."

"I haven't scared you off, then?" His face was pained and full of regret.

"You'd have to try a lot harder to scare me off, Graham," smiled Bea.

"In that case, may I extend a neighborly invitation to dinner?" Bea didn't reply right away, and he noticed her hesitation, "I'm sure you're dying to see what the place looks like now. It's a mess, to be honest. Books all over the place. I'm still organizing. I want to create a space for clients to visit, and more than one climate controlled room for the business, but I haven't gotten there yet. I have most of the special editions in cases. The marsh and the ocean air aren't great for collectors items, which is what I mostly deal in. And, from what I understand, the people who were in the house before me didn't change much at all, no home improvements or do it yourself projects. I'm not even sure they lived there. When I first saw the place there wasn't any furniture inside, only a few boxes in the attic leftover from your Grandmother with Cliff's name on them."

She wasn't sure that made it any better. Maybe it would be easier to swallow if the house was completely different, with the smell of fresh paint lingering in corners instead of the scent of lavender conjuring memories.

She was curious, and had been since the other owners bought the house, and so ultimately she said yes, and he smiled a genuine smile and with a hand on the small of her back he guided her across the street. As they walked down the sidewalk past the hardware store and down to Bert's she saw Henry linger just past

147

the entryway of the diner, holding his hat in one hand and combing through his hair with the other.

Bea paused and slipped her shoes back on, toes screaming. She straightened and shimmied her toes and ankles into place, only realizing as she removed her hand that it had been holding on to Graham. But he wasn't watching her, he was looking directly into the windows of Bert's diner. His brow furrowed, his eyes were dark, lids appeared tired and his mouth was drawn. From the outside looking in it looked like a celebration. It was a celebration, Bea reminded herself.

"Ready?" she asked.

He sighed, and somehow it seemed like the last moments they shared had been a show. His back straightened as if he was preparing for battle. He looked like he was steadying himself outwardly as she had begun to inwardly.

"Ready," he said.

SIXTEEN

They walked into the diner and were met with laughter and warmth and a sea of bodies and the smell of food. The counters were lined with platters of sandwiches and casseroles, salads of all varieties - potato, pasta and garden greens - and pie. Apple pies for miles.

"On your right, Bea," Bert interrupted Bea's thoughts as she stood starry eyed in the waiting area of the diner. She moved out of his way, he had a tray of drinks balanced overhead and was headed for a group of mourners in the back room. Graham muttered something about catching up with her later, divide and conquer, and left Bea's side.

This was the first time she'd been to Bert's Diner since she came back, and it hadn't changed a bit since the days she and her grandmother would swing by for BLT sandwiches and root beer floats.

And of course, Cliff also brought her here. She looked over at his favorite corner booth where Cliff would sit across from her, his big hands holding the laminated tri-fold menu, already knowing what he was going to order. He knew the daily specials by heart, and how to cook them as well. When the diner got really busy, he would stand up and wave off the waitress who was up to her ears in orders, and walk behind the counter to pour himself a cup of coffee and get Bea a root beer. Cliff had been known to jump behind the counter and flip burgers on the grill, and he could make a turkey club just as good as Bert's. He said he learned from Bert, but truthfully he was simply a natural in the kitchen.

Bea looked around the diner, at the rows of booths on each side wall, and evenly spaced chrome edged tables throughout. They were the real deal, sturdy legs and heavy tops, unlike the replica ones found in bulk stores. On each table sat a napkin dispenser, a container with four compartments full of small boxes of jelly or jam, and a wire holder with a bright red bottle of ketchup, maple syrup, and other condiments. Tucked between the clear salt and pepper shakers with metal screw tops were four menus per table. Bea didn't have to count when she looked from table to table, she knew they were there like she knew the different mugs that sat in the cabinet of Cliff's kitchen. She knew the place by heart.

Bert walked toward her, empty tray tucked under his arm. He wore a nice pair of slacks and dress shirt, rolled at the sleeves. The diner staff were all out of their usual uniforms of Bert's Diner logo shirt and jeans, all wearing their funeral garb, dark colors and dress shoes. He gave Bea a one-armed hug and kissed her cheek.

"Are you going to slow down at all?" she asked him.

Bert slowly shook his head, "I can't slow down, if I do, I'll remember why we're all here."

She understood, so she changed the subject, "It looks the same as I remember."

Bert chuckled, "All except for the napkin dispensers."

"Are they new?" asked Bea.

"New to us, but probably older then you are. Found them at the flea market this summer. They add some color, don't you think?" he said with a wink.

Bea smiled, "As if you needed more color in here."

The diner's walls were painted a light gray, brightly colored vintage signs and neon, retro clocks decorated every available space. Bea's favorite metal sign was the one with a gigantic curved arrow. It brandished the words "Eat here, it's cheap and homemade," and was hung so the arrow pointed to the area behind the counter where the waitstaff yelled back to the cook, and if you sat at the diner counter you could watch your food being made and smell the grease from the fryer.

"Can I help with anything?" she said, nearly shouting to be heard above the chatter around them.

"Absolutely not, try to enjoy yourself, Bea."

Bea looked at him skeptically, and he shrugged his shoulders, gave her another squeeze and walked into the crowd.

From behind her she felt a familiar presence. She turned to find Henry standing behind her. He looked no taller than Bea, but if he were to stand up straight he would tower over her. Life had shrunk Henry Eaton. Experiences that Bea, nor many others, couldn't imagine nor gave much thought to had made him world weary.

"Quite the spread," he said softly.

"I'm sure it's exactly what Cliff would have wanted," Bea said with a slight smile.

"Guess we should make the rounds?" his question caught her off guard, the imperial we most certainly meant her.

"We should, but I'm not ready to jump in."

"It's better to jump before you're ready," said Henry in a matter of fact way. His eyes were set straight ahead. He, like

151

Graham, was readying for a sort of battle.

Without another word he slunk into the crowd and disappeared. Some people could do that, disappear into a crowd. The only way Bea had ever been able to do that was with a camera. For Bea, her camera, up until recently, felt like an extension of herself and she used it to fade away. It was a tool for observation and the focus or attention that came from it was never on Bea, but on the apparatus.

In this moment, she wished she brought the camera that sat untouched in the corner of her bedroom, tucked away in its bag.

She looked around the diner and mentally took the photos she otherwise would have snapped: Olivia and Steve sitting on the stools at the counter, holding hands; Bert hustling around, weaving between people caught in conversations; quick embraces among friends, long embraces among family. Even with edges blurred by grief, they were a wide angle shot of Cumberland's heart.

Bea focused on the early evening light of Autumn streaming into the restaurant from a far corner window, how it played on the edges of the tables and on faces, and when she held her palm up to shade her eyes it illuminated her flesh with a rosy glow. Her hand was a ball of fire as it held the sun and Bea's face lit up in a quiet smile that was to be shared with no one except the remains of light and air and dusk. All at once she felt held and coddled, surrounded and loved.

She felt Cliff. And she wished he would stay.

Bea's eyes closed heavy with tears, a few escaped as she willed them back into tear ducts.

"There you are," said a high pitched, sweet as maple sugar voice, "I've been looking all over for you Bea!"

She opened her eyes to find Vicky standing right in front of her.

152

"Oh, sweetheart, you must be beside yourself," Vicky's eyes grew wide within a blanket of mascara and eye shadow, a pout came across her face as she stared intently at Bea.

Bea wiped under her eyes, "It's just the sun, I've been squinting."

"It would be understandable if it wasn't the sun," said Vicky. Her eyes dripped concern but her voice carried a sing song type of note that was reserved for preschoolers and the elderly.

"I'm fine, really," said Bea, nervously looking around for someone to help divert Vicky's attention. An absurd amount of people were gathered, Cliff on the tip of their tongues and in their tearful eyes. There was hardly any standing room, let alone breathing room, and Bea's brow was starting to sweat.

"Well, I wanted to get a moment with you to myself before you got swept away. From what I can tell, everyone here wants to talk with you."

"I'd say the same about you. Cliff's sister! Everyone has speculated about his family for as long as I can remember." Bea crossed her arms for a moment, and then felt unbalanced by her shoes. Her feet teetered a bit and she uncrossed her arms and rested a hand on the nearest table, giving the people seated around it an apologetic look.

Vicky sighed, "It's not like I didn't try," she had a handkerchief in her palm and she dabbed at an eye. Bea could swear she didn't see a tear anywhere near Vicky's eyes or cheeks - though she did notice the smooth skin on Vicky's forehead stayed in the same place, no matter the expression on her face.

Bea found herself in the position of consoling Vicky, whether it was authentic or not Bea was unsure, though she was leaning towards not. She was standing stiffly next to Vicky, patting her arm uncomfortably as Vicky leaned in for a hug, and then Bea caught Bert's eyes a few feet into the room and she motioned him over.

"Bert, have you met Cliff's sister, Vicky?"

Bert wiped his palms on the apron tucked into his pants, put his order pad in his back pocket and tucked a pen behind his ear. He could yell out orders at the top of his lungs at the diner, but outside of the diner Bea thought he was the most soft spoken man she ever met.

"I haven't had the pleasure," he said as he extended his hand. "Bert MacDonald, owner of Bert's Diner. I was with Cliff..." his voice trailed off and his face fell.

"Vicky Jennings, I'm glad someone so kind was with Cliff during his last moments," she said as she placed a second hand over their handshake. She bowed her head a bit and Beatrix couldn't bear to be in her presence any longer.

Bea gently touched Bert's shoulder and slipped away into the crowded room.

As soon as Bea started to feel lost in the crowd she felt a hand grab onto hers. She looked up and saw Olivia, who had left her seat at the counter.

"Mom and Dad grabbed us a table, will you come sit with us? Let's get you a plate."

"I don't know that I can eat. There's plenty of casseroles in the refrigerator at the house for later," her voice was flat and tired, her feet were sore and while she wanted to sit down, more than anything she wanted to go back to the orchard.

"You need to eat, I know you have food, I think I even supplied a shelf of it, but just have a few bites of something now. You know what? Go sit down with Steve and Mom and Dad," Bea followed Olivia's extended hand to a Formica table filled with platters of food, an order of french fries and a pile of sandwiches cut into quarters, "I'll get you a drink."

At one of the bigger tables in the back room Steve stood

and pulled a metal chair out for Bea. The legs of it squeaked against the floor. She scooted herself in before he had a chance to do it for her. She mumbled her thanks.

There was polite conversation until Olivia returned and took her seat between Bea and Steve.

"Look, but don't stare. Over my shoulder. Do you see her?" Olivia's eyes were full of gossip and suspicion.

Bea saw Vicky where she left her, only with a plate of pie now in her hands. Bert had left her side and Vicky leaned against the wall for a moment, taking in the scene, sizing up the crowd.

"What?" asked Bea.

"There's something about her that just rubs me the wrong way. Maybe it's how she's picking at the pie on her plate."

Steve laughed, "You're starting to get as nosy as the retired crowd that comes in every morning supposedly looking for things to finish the odd project, but really they just want to get a heads up on the town gossip from the weekend."

Olivia playfully shoved her husband and scowled. "It's like she's putting on a show."

"Wouldn't you be?" said Bea, trying to sound magnanimous even though she agreed with Olivia, "Coming into a situation as strange as this, your long lost brother's funeral, there's an orchard at stake that you should have inherited." She took a bite of a quartered turkey club sandwich, the mayonnaise covered lettuce felt slippery in her mouth.

From her other side Bernie rested a hand on the back of Bea's chair, "Now, I wouldn't say that. I for one think he made the right decision. A bit of youth always helps a business," she nodded towards her daughter and Scott.

"Here here," said Nathan, mouth full of something. He sat up and continued, "but that doesn't mean you won't need some guidance, and I'd suggest-"

155

"You will suggest nothing, Nathan," said Bernie, "if you'd turn your hearing aid on you'd know that's not what this conversation is about."

"You know I had to turn it off because all the noise is too much in spots like this."

Bernie rolled her eyes and turned towards her daughter and Bea, "My point is, Cliff made that choice for a reason. And his sister and whoever else has an issue with that, that's their business."

Bea started playing with the corner of her paper napkin, folding it in either direction until a triangle fell off. "I just wish he were here to talk me through it."

Olivia put her arm behind Bea, and Bea felt the support of the women on either side of her.

"You've got a town full of people to lend you a hand, endless advice, and free coffee," Olivia said as she nodded towards Bert, who was flitting from one table to the next, checking on everyone, topping off mugs of coffee along the way.

Bernie was looking at Bert as well and then glanced up, and was now adjusting her glasses, "Is that? No, it can't be," Bernie's mouth was open and she squinted her eyes, "I haven't seen her in forever, but I swear that woman talking to June looks exactly like your mother."

"Where?" asked Olivia, she pulled her arm from Bea's shoulders.

As Bea looked up panic and something akin to love swelled in her chest.

"Just past Bert," said Bernie.

Bea stood, her eyes never leaving her mother. It was like tunnel vision, and she couldn't help herself but focus solely on her mother's eyes, waiting and hoping to catch them, to see a glimmer of grief or a reason as to why she actually made the drive from the city up to Cumberland. But her mother was focused on whatever June was saying, annoyingly so, and Donna didn't see around the attorney to notice Bea approaching.

"Mom, you came," she said, trying to get her mother's attention. She felt like a child, all of her awareness of who she was and how far she had come went out the window and she was focused only on how her mother saw her. Bea smoothed her dress down and her shoulders shrugged towards her ears, hiding her height, hiding herself and reverting to the last time she saw her mother, or even farther back to when her mother was in control of Bea's life. It was easy for her to slip into that place, and she waited for not only her mother's attention, but for her instructions as well.

June turned around and shared a warm, genuine smile with Bea. Her eyes were concerned, "Bea, I'll let you and your mother have a moment," she turned back to Donna, "Donna, it was so good to see you after all these years." She reached her arms around Donna and gave her a hug, bangles jingling and the sleeves of her kimono style top billowing.

"You as well, June. We'll catch up soon."

Donna Hampton had barely aged since Bea last saw her. Her hair was cut straight and styled neatly in an age appropriate bob. She was dressed in a black skirt suit adorned with a string of pearls at her neck that she couldn't stop touching. It was her tell tale sign of nervousness, Bea remembered, the only sign of weakness Donna ever showed. Bea remembered many instances where her mother seemed cool as a cucumber, calm and collected, her voice never rising, but her long slim fingers against her neckline told those closest to her that something was wrong.

"Why didn't you tell me there was a way out? A contingency plan?" Her mother's eyes were like steel boring into Bea. No hello, no hug, no nice to see you, it's been so long.

"I, well, I…" Bea stuttered, trying to find her ground.

"You should have told me, but even still, it makes no sense as to why you didn't take it."

"Why was June telling you about my inheritance?"

"I'm your mother, why wouldn't she?"

Bea laughed, a harsh laugh full of the reality that her mother hadn't played a mothering role for years, "Because it's illegal, Mom. No matter how you sweet talked her. Client confidentiality and all."

"I merely said I was surprised that you committed to the place, and she offered that it was only for a year and then mentioned you were adamantly against the contingency plan."

From behind her a voice popped up, "Contingency?"

Bea closed her eyes and shook her head, "Graham Winters, let me introduce you to my mother, Donna Hampton."

"*The* Graham from the contingency plan?" Her mother's words struck like a hot poker and Bea looked up to see her mother's eyes actually glistening with pleasure and malice.

"Bea, what is she talking about?"

Bea shook her head, "Not now."

"Graham, it's nice to meet you," said Donna as she shook his hand.

"I feel like I must know you a bit already, living in your childhood home," he offered the information freely, and surprisingly Donna flinched as though she was momentarily caught off guard.

"Graham bought Grandma's house from the first buyers. He's an antique book dealer, and has become quite a fixture at the orchard." Bea hoped to soften Graham a bit, but as she looked at him she was now convinced that he never knew about the contingency plan, that he was never aware that he was part of Cliff's will.

"Bea, I hate to interrupt, but can I steal you away for just a minute?" His eyes were questioning and pleading all at once.

"Surely you can speak to my daughter in front of me," said Donna.

Graham cocked his head to the side and assessed the situation. "Okay, well, Vicky is looking to speak with you, Bea. She wants to set up a time to come out to the orchard for a visit. To see where Cliff lived and to try and put some pieces together for herself."

"Vicky, as in his sister?" said Donna, her voice incredulous, her fingers permanently attached to the pearls around her neck.

"Yes, his sister. Bea, will you speak with her?"

"I don't know, I don't know that now is the time."

"When do you think will be?"

"How long is she in town for?"

"I'm not sure. You'll have to ask her, she's right over there," he said, turning his head towards Vicky who stood across the diner, waving at them.

Something within Bea snapped and she felt a fight or flight moment coming over her, and she flew. She turned and walked straight through the diner, only stopping to pick up her coat from Olivia's table. She walked quickly, and knew without a doubt that her mother was on her heels, full of questions and accusations, and she was okay with that. She was even okay with the pain she felt shoot through her feet with each step she took. What she was not okay with was being accosted by Graham and Vicky and having to share her memories of Cliff. She wanted solace. She wanted to grieve. She wanted to sit and cry and lose control of her emotions in a safe environment.

And so she walked out of the diner and onto the street.

"Beatrix Hampton, wait just a second. Don't walk away

159

from me."

Bea stopped in her tracks. Tears started to fall, and her shoulders heaved.

Her mother paused behind her, waited a moment, and then hugged her from behind. She whispered, "Let's go home."

"I'm not going to your house."

"No, I know. Take me to yours. Better yet, I'll drive."

Bea stepped back and faced her mother, "But it's the truck."

"So? What do you think I learned how to drive on? Don't you remember where I grew up? Your grandfather had a truck." She smiled, and Beatrix tried to find the malice she saw earlier, but there wasn't a trace. She reached into her coat pocket and found Cliff's keys and handed them to her mother.

"Let's go," said Donna as she linked arms with her Bea.

Neither one trusted the unfamiliar sensations they were experiencing. But both had cheeks flushed with possibility and a little bit of comfort. Perhaps that was what hope was, finding comfort in the unfamiliar and strange. If that was the case it was exactly what Bea needed.

160

SEVENTEEN

"Not much has changed since the last time I was here," said Donna as she walked around the living room.

Bea scrunched herself into a ball on the couch, trying to get as far into herself as possible, snuggling the blankets around her with one hand as the other cupped a mug of tea her mother made for her while she changed out of Olivia's dress. The heels were sitting, one leaning against the other, near the kitchen door. Bea took them off in the truck on the ride to the orchard, though she welcomed the pain they caused her feet as a distraction to hide the shame she felt from running away from the diner.

"When was the last time you were here?" asked Bea, steam drifted across and away from the mug in her hands, words pushed and pulled, playing with the hot air.

Donna stopped to stand by the table behind the couch, she picked a generic crime novel Cliff had been reading, a bookmark now permanently held his place. Bea's first instinct was to take it from her, but instead she bit her tongue and cupped the mug closer.

"It wasn't that long ago, just after your Grandmother died," Donna paused, and Bea's head raced with thoughts as to why her mother would come over here at that point, "but really it's been the same since before I left Cumberland."

"I didn't realize you spent any time here, a few years ago or even before."

Donna put the book back in place and dragged her long fingers along the wood of the table until she reached the end. She methodically brushed her hands against each other and moved ever so carefully to sit on the other side of the couch with her feet crossed at the ankles, her hands neatly in her lap.

She sighed, "Cliff moved here just before I got married, I spent a good deal of time at Mom's that year. Cliff didn't know anyone," she looked around the room, her eyes a bit misty, but then she shook any sentimentality off like a bad dream, "he was a mystery," she paused to look at her hands before continuing, "no one knew quite what to make of him, a bachelor from out of town. No ties. No history. No wife or family. Nothing to stop him from dropping a seemingly large sum of money into a failing orchard. He wouldn't tell anyone anything except he wanted to make a quiet life for himself."

Bea smiled into her tea cup, "That sounds like Cliff." She took a sip of the tea, winced as the scalding water hit her tongue.

Donna nodded, "Yes, he didn't change much over the years. And from the sounds of it, no one ever quite figured out the mystery of his family. You'd never met his sister before?"

Bea shook her head, "No, he never even mentioned her to me. But Graham met her through his business and in conversation they realized the connection."

"And still she never got in touch?"

Bea shrugged, "It sounds like she tried, but when Graham

brought her up, Cliff asked him to drop the subject."

"He certainly took whatever haunted him to the grave. No mention of her in the will?"

"No. None."

They sat in silence, Bea sipping her tea and Donna looking over every inch of the space she could see without turning her head fully around. Bea watched her mother, and wondered.

"So you were friends? You and Cliff?" The thought of this baffled Bea, and she couldn't help but ask.

Her daydream and gaze broken, Donna looked back at her daughter, a sadness crept into the corners of her eyes, "Yes, we were friends. This couch," she leaned her head back, scooting her bottom to the edge of the seat, she closed her eyes and said, "this couch smells like him. He always smelled the same. From the moment he stepped foot on the orchard, he became the orchard himself." She paused and breathed in deeply. "Apples and pipe tobacco," she said wistfully.

In the following moments they shared a silence full of grief. There was no way for Bea to know the depth of her mother's pain, her regret, her remorse for words left unsaid. But somehow Bea felt a deep sense of loss in her mother. And it not only surprised Bea, it angered her.

Bea rose out of her cocoon and stood, the blanket cascaded from the couch and onto the floor.

"Beatrix?" implored her mother.

In front of her eyes Bea only saw red, and as she looked around the room her mother was completely out of place. She shouldn't have been comfortable in his home. She shouldn't have been reminiscing about how he came to the orchard. She shouldn't have been romanticizing his lingering smell. Bea thought of all the times throughout her childhood that she was shushed upon speaking of the orchard, of Cliff. His name was a dirty word at her

163

parents house. And now Donna was breathing in more than her share of Cliff's memory. Bea wanted her mother to leave, and if she couldn't ask her mother to leave, than she herself would find a way out.

"The apple bins, they're still out in the orchard," her words came out forced, they stumbled from her mouth and fell flat on the decades old carpet under her feet.

"Can't they wait?" asked Donna.

"They can't. I'll be back in a bit. Will you be here?" she spat the last words, aware of the anger and force she said them with. She reached for the coat she draped over a kitchen chair earlier, and caught a glimpse of the photo she left on the kitchen table earlier in the day.

"I, I don't know, I didn't pack a suitcase," said Donna.

"Well then, thank you for coming. If you leave before I get back please lock the door behind you." She hastily put the coat on, grabbed a flashlight, slipped on her steel-toed-boots that sat by the door, and in a last minute effort she moved the frame from the table to behind a container of oats on the shelf. Bea didn't know if her mother saw it while making tea, but she didn't want to think of Donna standing in Cliff's kitchen, staring at a photo that belonged to him.

Only when she was out the door she remembered her mother's car was in the center of Cumberland. Of course she'd be there when Bea returned.

Bea stumbled through the darkness towards the barn. The laces of her boots were loose and the leather tongues spilled forward. She'd tie them when she got to the tractor.

The tractor. She had never operated one on her own, but

164

this was as good a time as ever to prove she could do it.

The vehicle sat outside the barn, and once she got into it she looked down at the wheel, at the dashboard, and it all seemed foreign and yet surprisingly familiar. She thought back on a work trip she was on a year or so ago in the Amazon jungle. She once navigated through the bush and then drove an ATV when her guide became incapacitated by the effects of an insect bite. The tractor looked to Bea like a cross between that vehicle and a Jeep.

She balanced the flashlight on her shoulder and under her chin, the cold metal warmed next to her bare skin. She should have grabbed more layers, a scarf or something instead of just Cliff's old coat. Instead, she was hat-less, glove-less, and scarf-less, with just an over-sized coat on top of her yoga pants and a long sleeved tee shirt. More layers, she thought, no matter the hurry always grab more layers.

The air felt as dark as it looked, deep and treacherous. The engine sputtered, then purred and she took off, the path narrowly lit by the beady eyed headlights of the tractor.

She found the bins easily. They were not far from the barn, and luckily it would be a straight shot to tow them back. She had seen Cliff hitch the bins up to the tractor a thousand times since she was little, but she never had to do it herself. The night surrounded her quickly, and the trees whispered sweet nothings and warnings. She jumped down to the earth and slipped the keys into a coat pocket where she found a knit beanie cap. Without hesitation she pulled it over her head, covering her chilled and windblown ears.

"Do you need a hand with that?"

She jumped up, stumbled backwards and nearly fell into the hitch.

"No, I think I just got it, thanks. What are you doing out here?" she asked Graham as she assessed him. From what she could see in the dim light afforded by the tractor, he was bundled up, wearing a dark pea coat and a hat similar to the one she wore.

"I heard the tractor, and got worried. After you ran off, I didn't know what to make of things." He looked at her intently. He was wearing thick, dark rimmed glasses that magnified his tired eyes. "The battery," he said, turning his body towards the tractor, "you won't want to keep the lights on without the engine going for long. It'll go out and the bins will be the least of your worries."

"How could you hear the tractor from inside?"

"I was on the porch," he busied himself by inspecting the hitch. He leaned over, hands in his pockets. He fished for something, and then pulled out a set of keys with a small flashlight attached.

"In the dark?"

He stood up and looked at her, daring her with his words, "With a cup of tea and the sky and the stars all to myself. Yes, in the dark."

She stood back and sighed. "That's exactly what I'd like to be doing now," the words left her mouth and she blushed, not meaning to suggest she wanted to spend an evening with him.

"You're welcome to come over any time," he said softly. "I like the look, by the way. Cliff would approve," Graham smiled as he walked past her to the other side of the tractor, pointing at her hat. Bea looked down at her feet, heat flooded her cheeks and at the same time she felt swallowed by the coat, the heft of it. It dwarfed her, and she hugged her arms tighter around herself, defining her waist to show that she had one, even in the dark. Graham looked up at her as she shivered in the cold, and then he peered back at the hitch and nodded approvingly, "You're all set," he said.

Bea started towards the front of the tractor.

"What was the contingency plan in Cliff's will?"

He was staring out at the orchard, his back turned away from her. His voice was calm, subdued even. The air was so thin his words flew quickly, darting towards Beatrix. She stopped in her tracks.

"You," she said, "you were, are, the contingency plan. If I don't make it a year here, the orchard goes to you."

"Why wouldn't you tell me?"

"Why does it matter? I'm here, I'm going to last the year and then some. I have no plans of leaving."

"But I could have helped, maybe it would be a better option if," his voice trailed off and landed somewhere far away through the trees like a gentle thud of an apple falling off the branches.

"What is it about me that bothers you?" she interrupted, "Why does it bother you that he chose me? Is it that I'm young or that I'm a woman?"

She watched as her breath hung in the air and he turned and walked towards her. His face at first exasperated, eyes towards the sky, but as he came closer to her they landed on her face. His eyes were full of heat, fire, and a tenacity she wasn't sure she could match.

"The only thing that bothers me about you," he stepped close enough for her to feel his hot breath on her cold cheeks. She didn't dare blink. For a moment she thought he was going to come unhinged. He was going to say everything she not only expected him to say, but that she had been telling herself: she was unqualified, she was too young, she wasn't strong enough mentally or physically to take care of an orchard let alone manage the ins and outs of a business. That Cliff liked him better, that he deserved the orchard more than she did. That Cliff didn't know what he was doing, and should have changed the will. Bea uncrossed her arms and planted them firmly at her sides, her hands

167

balled into fists.

She stared into his eyes until he broke their gaze and looked down to her lips. Bea's face flushed.

He looked down to the ground, stuffed his hands deeper into his pockets and shook his head gently. He stepped back, Bea exhaled.

Graham continued, but his voice softened, "Neither of those things bother me. What bothers me is your undependable nature. The fact that you weren't here for so long, and then you show up, a week before Cliff dies, with no intention of staying longer than the picking season, and then you have a change of heart when there's property involved."

"That's not true," she protested, but she knew she didn't have two feet to stand on, she knew how it looked.

"It's not? From where I'm standing it looks pretty damn accurate."

"And from where I'm standing you look like a jackass who's trying to lecture me. A sore loser."

"A sore loser? Is that what this is to you, Bea? Some sort of game?"

Feeling herself begin to shake with cold and anger, she started walking toward the tractor and hopped up onto the cold, unwelcoming and uncomfortable seat.

Just as she put the key in the ignition, a scream pierced through the darkness, she looked back at Graham who looked as shocked as she felt. His eyes were wide and he ran up and stood on the running board of the tractor, hung on and nodded at her. She turned the engine on and drove slowly through the orchard back to the barn, their eyes searched the darkness for the body that belonged to the scream.

"Use the flashlight," Bea yelled to Graham over the sound of the tractor engine, she was following the path of the headlights, but managed to point with one hand to the flashlight that laid on the dashboard. He turned it on and sent beams of light through the apple trees.

"I don't see anything!" he shouted, his voice looming large and wide as they slowed to approach the barn. He started to say something else, but as they pulled up to the building they were both stricken speechless.

EIGHTEEN

Bea parked the tractor and ran to where her mother stood, silhouetted by the faint light of the farmhouse.

"Mom, are you alright?" Bea looked from her mother to a disheveled pile of rags on the ground and then to Graham and back to her mother again.

As Bea's eyes adjusted to the lack of light she realized that the pile of rags was moving, and had a face.

"Henry?" muttered Bea, in disbelief and confusion.

Graham rushed over to help Henry stand up.

"Beatrix, did you know you have vagrants living on your property?"

"Mom," she rushed over to her mother's side, "are you alright? What are you doing outside?"

"I'm fine," Donna Hampton raised her chin and brushed off invisible dirt from the arms of her coat. Which, Bea noticed, wasn't her coat at all, it was another from Cliff's collection. "I came outside to try and find you, it had been so long since you left, and I was trying to find the door to the barn."

"It's right on the very front of the barn, mother, you walked right past it."

"It's rude to interrupt. The door was locked, so I thought there might be a side door. When I came this way I tripped over," she motioned towards Henry with a look of disgust. "I thought it was just a pile of tarps except it made a noise and so I nearly jumped out of my skin. It took you long enough to get here."

Graham's voice was irritated and gruff when he spoke, "He has a name. Henry, Donna Hampton. Mrs. Hampton, Henry Eaton."

Donna looked with wide eyes at Henry, and then glared at Graham. Henry extended a hand but Donna crossed her arms tighter, as if he was contagious.

"Bea, I'm sorry," Henry's voice was timid and hoarse, it shook, "Ma'am," he nodded towards Donna, "I never meant to frighten you."

"Well, I would hope not," said Donna, indignation flowing freely in her voice.

"Bea," said Graham, "was the barn locked?"

She nodded, remembering how she locked up before she got ready for the funeral. She had made a habit of it, a ritual, so she wouldn't forget.

"Well that's your problem," said Graham. His arm was around Henry, vigorously rubbing Henry's shoulders.

"I don't understand," said Bea, looking from Graham to Henry for an answer.

"And what were you doing in the orchard with my daughter?" asked Donna.

"Helping," said Graham. He guided Henry away from Bea and her mother, "Bea, will you open the barn?"

Inside the barn Bea fumbled to find a light switch,

Graham reached over her shoulder and with a quick flick of his fingers light filled the room from a single bulb hanging off of a long electrical cord resting on a hook above the desk.

"Would someone please explain what is going on?" Donna's voice cut through the silence, leaving space only for apology and explanation, neither were offered.

"Mom, why don't you go up to the house, I'll be there in a minute," said Bea. In her mind a picture slowly began to form. One of blankets piled in the corner of the work area, of doors left unlocked, of Cliff always peering out to the barn in the morning as if to make sure the coast was cleared. She thought he was simply checking the trees, but maybe there was something more. Donna's foot tapped the dirt floor impatiently.

"I most certainly will not. Not until someone explains why there was a strange man lurking in the dark on my daughter's property."

The air grew tense and just when Bea was starting to gather her thoughts, the words started to flow quickly from Graham's mouth, "Mrs. Hampton, if it's not obvious to you, Henry occasionally sleeps in this barn. Mostly when the weather is harsh, otherwise he likes to sleep under the stars. He was a good friend of Cliff's, and Cliff always left the door open for him. Since Cliff is no longer here, and didn't impart that bit of knowledge on to Bea, well, Henry was sleeping outside," he stopped for a breath but just as Donna opened her mouth to interject he put his hand up to stop her, "And furthermore, he's not a strange man. He's a friend of the orchard, and he wasn't lurking, he was settling in for the night."

With a "humph" Donna turned and walked back up to the house, leaving Bea alone with Graham and Henry.

"Henry, can I ask you something?" said Bea.

Henry, from the far corner of the room walked slowly

over towards them.

With a look of warning from Graham she continued, "Henry, do you want to come stay with me? There's an extra bedroom, and it'd be so much more comfortable than out here." She didn't know she was going to ask until the words were out. The logistics of sharing a house with a man she barely knew were far from her mind, she was thinking of the cold night, the dampness of the barn, the way the barn might save someone from wind, but not from a chill.

"It's never been about comfort," without making eye contact Henry stood equidistant from Graham and Bea, the three of them formed a triangle. He stared straight ahead, while the other's eyes were on him. "Cliff offered his house, that second bedroom, more times than I can count. But I couldn't."

"At least come in for a night and get warmed through, take a shower?"

He nodded. "Thank you Bea, but I'd rather stay out here, if it's all the same to you."

She returned his nod.

Graham shifted slightly. "Is there anything you need tonight?" he asked.

Henry shook his head.

"Well then, we should leave you in peace. You've had enough excitement for the night. Tomorrow morning?"

"Bright and early," replied Henry. At first Bea assumed they were talking about picking, but when she saw the look shared between the two she was unsure, and remembered Graham's early morning a few days prior. She found herself bristling at Graham inwardly, feeling out of place in her own home, on her own property. She felt the weight of all she didn't know, and how much she had to learn.

They said goodnight to Henry, and Graham closed the

barn door behind them.

As they walked up to the house the sounds of the night surrounded them, the wind rustled through the trees, a lone car whizzed down the road towards the ocean, tiny feet scampered behind their path. Bea turned and looked at the barn, the light switched off and she shivered.

"He's okay in there?" she asked, searching Graham's face. When she came to his eyes she took a quick breath. His eyes were piercing, and yet filled with kindness, and she wondered, not for the first time, about his actual nature.

"He's more than fine. And honestly, the orchard is probably safer with him here," Graham looked ahead toward the house, shoved his hands in his pockets, "He's a good man. He went through hell and back years ago. If he opens up to you, listen."

"And Cliff took care of him?"

"Cliff took care of everyone."

They walked the rest of the way in their own minds, neither one offering a glimpse into their thoughts.

When they reached the porch Bea turned to Graham and said, "I'd better go in and see about the state of things."

"Listen," Graham inched closer to Bea, "there's so much that you don't, that you can't know yet about this place, how Cliff ran things. Henry knows, and I know some of it, too. I don't want to take the orchard away from you, I want to protect it. I want it to be successful, to thrive."

"And you're afraid I can't do it."

"No, I'm afraid you won't accept help," his eyes pleaded with hers, and he raised his hands almost as if he were to cup her face in them. But instead he caught himself, and shoved them in his pockets again, "Please, let me help. Can we call a truce?"

She sighed, "I thought we did earlier," Bea paused and

174

then said, "obviously, if Henry has been living here and I didn't know it, there's a lot going on I'm unaware of." She thought of the journal she already poured over, and dots began to connect. Henry, she thought, must have left those for her.

"And you're staying?" he asked, eyebrows raised.

She tipped her head back and watched her breath float up to the sky. When she looked back at Graham she gave a quick, small smile.

The lines around Graham's face crinkled, and he exhaled audibly. "Dinner Sunday? My place?"

She nodded.

He opened his arms wide and she accepted, she tried to keep her balance, but she ended up falling into him a bit as fatigue washed over her. She pulled back for a moment to look up at him, and a flicker of emotion crossed his face.

"I'm ready to go," Donna's tone was sharp. Bea jumped back and nearly tripped, but Graham steadied her.

"Mom?"

"I'm ready. You need to take me back to my car."

"I thought you might stay the night?"

"No, I need to get back to your father. He just called and reminded me of an appointment we have first thing in the morning."

"Mrs. Hampton, it was a pleasure meeting you," Graham took the porch steps two at a time and was up next to Donna in a leap, extending his hand. Donna shook it tentatively, her mouth drawn tightly in a straight line.

"I'm sure. And the other man? Where is he? Sleeping on a moss pillow or something?"

"Mom, have a little compassion," Bea scowled as she ducked inside the house for her wallet. The last thing she wanted was to get pulled over and not have her license. The police in

175

Cumberland had little better to do at night than pull over any cars going over the conservative speed limits.

Bea shut the door behind her and watched her mother pick up her purse, and walk away from Graham without a word. Donna then stood at the passenger side of the truck, waiting.

"Sunday night then?" Graham leaned his head towards her, and smiled softly.

"Sunday. Stop by and let me know if I can bring anything."

"I will. I have a few clients to tend to tomorrow, but I'll be in and out."

"Ahem," Donna cleared her throat.

"Goodbye, Mrs. Hampton."

"Goodbye, Mr. Winters."

Graham touched Bea's arm and he gave her a sympathetic smile before following her down the steps, then he walked quickly down the driveway and across the street. From inside the cab of the truck Bea glanced at the rear view mirror and watched his figure grow darker and darker. Engine running, she drove around the U of the driveway and back out to the street. She glanced over and saw Graham just as he sat down in a rocking chair on his front porch. He lifted an arm and waved.

"Don't let that man fool you," said Donna, "you know he's just after the orchard. What could he possibly want to help you for? Always out for themselves, men like that."

Men like what? Bea thought to herself.

She turned up the dial on the old radio and drove the rest of the way with NPR reports playing in the background, drowning out any thoughts Bea had left in her tired mind, and Donna believed she had the last word. Donna Hampton always got the last word, Bea thought, even if it might not be true.

176

"Thanksgiving?" Donna said on her way out of the truck, one foot out the door.

The one word held more of a command than a question. Bea didn't take the bait, but she turned down the radio.

"I'm not sure, I'll have to see where we are, where the orchard is, at that point. I might have to stick around." She said it with an airy tone, as the holiday didn't mean much of anything to her.

But Bea knew the holiday was her mother's favorite. The traditional meal, the gathering of family and statements of gratitude. Forced for some, but it gave Donna a day to feel appreciated by those who may not mention their gratitude enough. A husband. A daughter. On that one day, she made everything from scratch, turkey and all the trimmings. Her special gravy, the pumpkin pie recipe passed down to her from her mother-in-law. Thanksgiving was a holiday that Donna kept, she took ownership of it from the year she left Cumberland and from then on she wrapped it up and served it every year like it was something holier than Christmas or Easter because it was fully about perception.

For Bea, the holiday was a reminder of what her mother left behind. There was never a mention of her grandmother. Sylvia had never been invited to the big house in the suburbs, her recipes were too commonplace, and Sylvia was too rough around the edges for Donna's curated life, and so she was left behind. Sylvia said she didn't care, but Bea knew, deep down, that it bothered her. Now, her grandmother's hurt lived on in Bea.

And so even if it was the truth, even if she did need to wait and see if she could get away from the orchard, Bea knew her words stung.

Donna stepped the rest of the way out of the truck, leaving an imprint in the leather seat and the smell of expensive perfume and obligation in her wake. Almost as an afterthought, she said, "Take care of yourself, Beatrix. Be careful."

They locked eyes and Bea nodded her head in acknowledgment.

Donna continued without an ounce of kindness, "You're entering a whole new world. And there's more riding on this than just yourself or your own bank account. Your father will want to hear all about this, you obviously don't have things under control."

Bea tried her hardest not to roll her eyes, but it was a strain. Her head hurt; dealing with her mother, the funeral, finding Henry, all of it weighed on her shoulders and she was rendered exhausted.

She leaned over the steering wheel, and rested her chest against it, turned towards her mother and said, "I'll let you know about Thanksgiving."

Donna slammed the door and then peered through the window, she gave Bea one last look. A raised eyebrow, a warning.

Bea recoiled into herself, feeling shame and pride, conflicted and sure, all at once.

Donna walked over to her car and slipped into the soft, hardly worn leather seats. Bea knew exactly what it smelled like. New car smell mixed with a Summer Breeze scented air freshener. It had been Donna's signature car scent for as long as Bea could remember. It didn't change with the seasons. It was timeless, that's what Donna would say. So even though her car changed every two years with a new lease, they all smelled the same. There was comfort in predictability, but it came with a price.

Bea waited until she saw the rear lights of her mother's car turn on, her mother pulled away from the curb and she couldn't see Donna's car any longer before she shifted the truck into drive and followed the dark side streets through town and out

178

towards the orchard. Friday nights in Cumberland were like every other night, quiet. The take out joints closed at nine, there was one bar that said it stayed open until eleven, but they rarely keep their doors wide past ten. It was a far cry from the cities she traveled to and called home for even a few short days at a time, holed up in Airbnb or hotel rooms. But now this tiny town on the coast of Massachusetts was the only place she could imagine as her home.

But it was also the only place that asked something of her instead of her simply existing, and it was the only place she ever had to fight for.

Maybe that was the key, the orchard was not an easy place to live and work, and it never would be. Her photography was easy, and she was good at it. This felt different. Maybe, she thought, the path of least resistance wasn't always the best route to follow. Perhaps, she thought, the path of least resistance was littered with easy, with okay, with padding and security blankets, with never really knowing what you were fully capable of. Maybe it wasn't the path she wanted.

So she would fight, she decided, for her place in this space, for her sense of belonging and worth. She would fight with every ounce of herself.

But first, she needed to rest. She pulled up to the orchard and put the truck into park. She didn't bother locking the truck, but double-checked the locks on the house before heading up to bed. Not because of Henry, but because of all the other unknowns.

NINETEEN

B ea slept fitfully that night. The quilts on the bed lay heavy and unwelcome. The coils buried within the mattress felt as though they were flush with her bones.

When she knew sleep wasn't coming to save her and light hinted behind the curtains she blinked the bedroom into focus and stared at the painting. Bea's sigh filled the room, annoyance seeped into the quiet corners and hung heavy in the shadows.

The woman on the wall haunted her, she was there when Bea closed her eyes and she was there when Bea woke up. Every day.

Bea toyed with the idea of moving the painting, of stuffing it in a closet or in the attic, but what would Cliff think?

With much effort, she sat up and rubbed the lack of sleep from her eyes. She didn't want to stretch, and so she stayed hunched over, her shoulders slumped and curled, as if straightening and standing tall would cause some kind of cheer she wasn't ready to invite in yet.

When she eventually made it downstairs, the groans of the house were her only companions. She watched the sky fill with light through the kitchen window and felt the absence of everything. Of Cliff, her mother, her grandmother.

In the background the plink plink of the water dripped through the coffee maker, grounding her as she watched the orchard come alive. The weather threatened to turn for good, the last of the late summer days were behind and winter was imminent. She had never spent a winter in Cumberland, only a week here and there around Christmas and school vacations. There were a few years where friends invited her along to ski chalets, and her parents urged her to make those connections and take advantage of family condos and mountain homes, but Bea always declined. "I'd rather go see Grandma," she told her family time and time again. Her friends never understood. "Are there other kids to play with there?" they'd ask. "No," she replied. "Does she take you places?" "No," she'd say again. After more questions and stark answers her friends would give up and move on. By the time she was in junior high Bea was known as the girl who liked to be alone. It wasn't nearly as bad as the kids who sat by themselves, or even the kids who clung together for safety. Bea knew everyone, and had a home in the cafeteria no matter the lunch period, and always had people to pair up with for science class. But there was something about her that led the other kids to believe she was different. Not a bad different, but a unique, mysterious different. Self contained.

Middle school and high school aged Beatrix Hampton had long legs and long hair and teeth that never required braces. She had a gentle voice, a calm demeanor, and a killer serve in volleyball. She studied hard and did her work and kept out of trouble. She declined cigarettes and booze, not because she disapproved, but because she didn't like the feeling of losing control. Bea Hampton never judged, and it was the lack of judgment of others that won her friends, even though she kept them at a distance. No one could really penetrate the walls she held up, though they weren't brick or pliable, they seemed transparent. But only those who looked close enough really understood that they would never be able to break through, no matter how hard they tried. Maybe there was more judgment there after all. Or maybe it was fear.

Bea stared out at the barn and watched closely for movement. Her mind wandered to Henry. Was he warm enough? Was he hungry? Was he comfortable through the night?

There was a space heater in the hallway she walked by daily, and she made a note to take it to the barn later. She'd leave it by the desk, a quiet offering.

The coffee stopped dripping and she got to work on bagels. She split one and placed the two halves into the toaster. She did this twice and both times she flinched as the springs popped and the bagels jumped and the noise sliced through the kitchen. With ease she slathered cream cheese liberally, added a vine of grapes to the plate, filled a cup of coffee and found a stash of trays at the end of the counter to carry it all on. Cliff had a collection of four different trays, the kind used while sitting on the couch and watching TV while eating supper. Alone.

Her grandmother had trays like them, too.

Bea dragged her hand over the remaining three that were lined up in a row, leaning against the wall. The edges were smoothed with age, the laminate seemed worn of any varnish. Were they hers? She wondered and pictured the folding stands that sat in front of the couch while they watched Jeopardy after dinner, snacking mindlessly on popcorn and M&M's.

She wondered what happened to those folding stands. She'd have a look around in the basement later, she told herself.

But for now she focused on the task at hand instead of the growing list that she was unsure she'd remember later.

She slipped into the tall boots by the door and then walked back to gather the tray in her arms. Even though she walked quietly up the driveway, birds scattered in front of her. No matter how silent she was, they still knew she was there.

Only a lone chickadee watched and sang as she passed, chick-a-dee-dee-dee.

With the morning air swirling around her, she stared and hesitated at the barn door. Partly because of the precariously balanced tray in her arms, and partly because she didn't know what awaited her on the other side of the door. There was no sign of life through the dirty windows, but that didn't mean that Henry wasn't still piled up in lump of blankets sleeping.

"Can I help you with that?" Henry spoke from behind her.

She jumped and steadied the tray, assessing the contents for spilled coffee or a toppled bagel. All intact, she turned and there was Henry. He was wearing his same clothes from the night before, but they were neat and crisp, and his face freshly scrubbed.

"I'm fine, thank you, I just," the lines on her forehead furrowed as she took him in, trying to figure out where Henry had come from. His eyes were hidden behind his full, gray brows, but his smile twitched beneath his mustache. Bea smiled at the very sight of him, and then in embarrassment when she realized she was staring. She said, "I brought you breakfast," and looked past him to the house, to the road, "but it looks as though you've been up and about already."

Henry walked up closer towards her shyly. His

movements were deliberate, the swish of his long trench coat was louder than those of his footsteps. "I was at Graham's," he nodded across the street, "for breakfast and a bit of clean up. The bathroom in there can only do so much," he pointed towards the barn, to the small bathroom in the corner Cliff had installed maybe ten years ago. He ran plumbing to the building with the help of Olivia's father, Nathan.

She raised her eyebrows at him in question as he took the tray from her arms. He smelled of freshly bathed children, soapy lavender and something she couldn't quite put her finger on.

Tray in one arm, he opened the door to the barn swiftly, and stepped back to let her walk past.

It was mint, she noticed as she walked by Henry. Lavender and mint.

Inside the barn was dim. If the windows were properly sealed it would probably smell stale, but there must have been space, gaps in the windowsill, and so it smelled just as the orchard did, only with undertones of sawdust and machine oil.

Henry placed the tray on Cliff's desk. It was still cluttered with papers, stacks and stacks of papers.

Another thing that Bea needed to take control of, the endless paperwork.

He stood back from the desk, pulled a chair over towards her. She took it and sat, the squeak of metal on metal as it adjusted to her weight echoed off the rafters.

Henry walked through the barn with his eyes, she followed his gaze, noting the pile of folded blankets.

"Are you hungry?" she asked, "I know you said you already ate, but do you still have some room left? The coffee might have gone cold, but I can refresh it," she stood and started to move towards the tray.

"Thank you Bea, that's awfully kind of you."

"It's the least I could do after how my mother treated you last night. I hope you don't mind, but I'm so curious," her voice trailed off again as she looked over his appearance.

"Graham," he said, and then took a swig of the coffee.

"Graham?"

"Graham came by again last night, when you took your mother into town, and grabbed a few of my things. He washed them, and I picked them up this morning when I went over."

"Graham," she said again, evenly.

Henry finished both halves of the bagel quickly, and was brushing crumbs from his beard. "Between the two of you, Cliff's shoes are being filled nicely," he said, his eyes smiled at her.

"But I don't understand, why didn't you just let me know Cliff was helping? I would have stepped in." Bea stood and put her hands on her hips. Her head was spinning and couldn't quite catch up.

"Graham had started even before Cliff was gone, Bea," his voice wavered a bit, "the orchard was getting to be too much for him, for Cliff. And then when you came, I didn't want to be in the way. Cliff assured me I wasn't, but he'd never tell anyone they're being a bother even if they were."

Bea reached behind her to find the chair. Her fingers bumped up against the cold metal and she shivered. The chill in the barn caught up to her and she wondered how anyone could sleep out here. She scanned the room again for a source of heat and came up empty.

Finally, she nodded her head in agreement. Cliff would never tell anyone they were a pest, a bother. He welcomed all with open arms, the more of a misfit, the more welcome.

"Does it ever warm up in here?" she asked, rubbing her arms with opposite hands.

Henry laughed, a quiet chuckle, "It feels downright

185

pleasant to me."

He drained the coffee cup and put it down on the tray, walked over towards one of the dirty windows. He took the arm of his clean jacket and wiped a bit of dust and grime from the windowpane.

"Did you find the notebooks useful?"

He was timid, and even with the bravado that came with clean clothes and a fresh face, she instinctively knew not to shout, to push. She didn't want to scare him away. This was the first time since Cliff died that it felt as though she had an ally, someone to stand by her side and prop her up without anything to gain in the process. And someone who was telling her the truth, without an agenda.

"I did. But they left me with more questions."

Balancing on the chair, she brought her feet to the seat and her knees up to her chin. She curled up, trying not to take up space, trying to blend into the scenery so maybe he'd open up more.

From across the barn he looked back to her. "I'm sure. Where to start, right?"

"Yeah, where to start," she said with a sigh. "Henry, can I ask you something else?"

He nodded.

"How long have you been here? And how much did you help Cliff? I mean, do you know the business side of things? I'm so lost and," she only meant to ask one question, but the rest tumbled out, her voice lifted and she watched him recoil within himself. She paused and she rested her chin atop her knees. Through tearful eyes she looked at the floor and muttered quietly, "I'm sorry, but I can't do this alone."

"I don't know what I can do."

She looked up and met his eyes, "Everything. Anything. I

think you know more than you think you know. And I think you have been helping in ways you haven't even realized."

"No, Bea. I'm just a homeless old man who needs a place to rest his head."

"And you've rested your head here for countless years. I think Cliff relied on you. Maybe you didn't expect it, or want that responsibility," she paused, "maybe he was relying on you to bridge the gap. Did anyone else know about his journals? Did anyone else spend the hours with him that I'm guessing you did? At his side and watching his methods?"

"I don't know, Bea. I don't know that I'm the answer to your questions."

"You might not be, but we could help each other. And I bet Cliff was banking on that."

Henry paused, considering Bea's words. Then he said, "I'm not sure I was the one he imagined helping you." He shook his head, "Did you know that he turned 56 this year?"

Bea nodded.

"Every other year, on an even year, he renewed his will." The words fell out of his mouth like a slow trickle. Bea hung on every one, willing him to continue, "I remember a few years back he asked me how old I thought someone had to be to inherit property. If twenty-five was old enough. I said thirty, but what did I know?" he looked up and smiled softly at Bea as he caught her eye.

Bea's cheeks warmed, and she noticed that the cold had seeped into her bones.

"He told me he was near thirty when he bought the orchard, so that made sense to him."

"I guess I hadn't put two and two together, that he was around my age. Did he ever tell you why he came here in the first place?"

Henry shook his head, "Just that he followed his heart, and it reminded him of his childhood. The sea and all."

"I hoped that he told someone a few of his secrets. I didn't realize he had so many, and that he wouldn't be here to let me in on them eventually, in his own way," Bea stood and stamped her feet on the ground to warm them up.

"You're cold," said Henry.

"You must be, too. Want to come in for another cup of coffee?" she cocked her head towards the door of the barn and the warmth of the house.

He shook his head. "No, I'll get started on some work, if it's all the same to you," he walked over to a stack of picking baskets, grabbed one from the top and started to adjust the straps.

"Do you think others will be over today?" she asked.

"Maybe a couple," he said, "Cliff would be out every day of the week this time of year rallying the troops."

Bea walked over to the desk, rustled through some papers. She ran her hand over the top of various stacks. The ink in the pens must have been half frozen. There were yellowed papers, ages old no doubt, mixed with crisp white papers that looked relatively new. There must have been invoices and bills needing to be paid, money to be sorted, phone calls managed. The past week, she thought, went smoothly enough, but she knew that people - organizations who relied on the apples and orders needing to be fulfilled - probably went easy on her. There was a mourning period even though the orchard didn't pause for grieving.

"I can't believe it's been just a week," muttered Bea.

Henry walked over and put a hand on her shoulder. She didn't flinch, and the warmth of his hand seeped through layers of clothing to her skin. She patted his hand and then he retracted it. She looked over and noticed he was taller than she thought. Cleaned up, he was even handsome. His eyes were sad, but bright.

188

And she wondered if there was any way to make everything right again. If there was, she knew Henry would play a pivotal role.

"Thank you for my second breakfast, Bea," he said after a moment's pause, "Cliff knew what he was doing, leaving the place to you. Graham told me this morning about the contingency plan. But you know what I think? I think Cliff knew you'd stay. This place gets in your bones, even if it's not in your blood. But you, it's in your blood."

"You knew my grandmother, didn't you?"

He nodded, "There was no one else like her," he smiled and gave a soft chuckle. "She and Cliff were cut from the same cloth," he said, "sometimes the three of us would have dinner together," his voice turned to a hush and then he ramped up again, but Bea could tell this much conversation was tiring for him. He asked, "Have you been over there yet?"

She shook her head, "No, but Graham invited me for dinner. Tomorrow."

"Good," he said with a firm nod. The picking basket swayed in front of him as he moved, the slightest movement exaggerated by the canvas bucket.

Bea rolled her eyes, "Please don't tell me he's such a wonderful guy. I know you all think he is."

Henry laughed. It was starting to delight Bea when he did so. It was a warm sound, and she felt privileged to hear it. "I don't blame you. It took me a while to trust him," he walked over towards the door, "but I do now. And Cliff certainly did. You'll find out soon enough, Graham is as messy as the rest of us. We've all got our quirks and our faults, but he's got a heart like you wouldn't believe," Henry turned back and looked at Bea, really looked at her. His eyes were clear and his voice firm, "the toughest exteriors give way to the softest hearts."

Her face flushed once more, thinking about Graham and

how she had been a bit unkind, or at least uneasy with him. Maybe she shouldn't have been so quick to judge.

"It looks," said Henry as he peered out the door, "as if you've got some company."

"It can't be past what, eight? Pickers?"

"If she's here for picking, you'd fool me."

Bea walked quickly to the door and saw Vicky walking up the front porch steps to the house.

Bea and Henry looked at each other, both with raised brows. "Did Cliff ever say much about her?" she asked.

"No, to you?"

She slowly shook her head and said, "I've got a bad feeling about that one."

She watched as Henry, right in front of her, started to shrink. His shoulders slouched and he reached for his fedora and placed it on his head. He sunk a few inches, his eyelids drooped, and the corners of his mouth drew downward. "I'd trust that feeling, Bea," he said before his feet carried him off around the barn and down into the orchard where the trees surrounded him like a blanket.

Bea walked back to the desk and picked up the now empty tray. She stacked the coffee mug atop the plate, smiling to herself about the efficiency at which Henry cleared the food and drink. And then she steeled her nerves as she walked out the barn door, and over to the house.

TWENTY

O n the way from the barn to the house a conversation flickered in Bea's memory. She and Cliff were the only two people left in the orchard at the end of her second day of picking, and they were working side by side. Their arms were tired, but conversation kept them moving.

"Why don't you ever talk about where you came from?" asked Bea.

"I don't think about it much," he said without hesitation, the basket of Cortland's hung heavy in front of him. "If anyone asks, this is where I'm from."

"But your family," Bea persisted, "do you ever get in touch with them?"

She wondered if he heard her, the silence gained momentum and carried through the trees and down the orchard rows and back again.

"There were letters, once upon a time. Attempted phone calls. But it was mutual, the estrangement. It wasn't as though I

191

wanted to go back, and they certainly weren't holding a torch and tying yellow ribbons around trees for me."

"But you weren't at war."

Stepping out from the branches he caught her eye long enough for Bea to feel reprimanded. "Everyone is at war with someone, something. For me, in those early days, I was at war with myself. I should have tied ribbons just so I could have untied them when I realized what mattered to me." He sighed a long and hefty sigh. "You find peace, Bea. You do. And then you don't think about it as much. You don't think about the people you left behind, or those who left you. In any given lifetime we live a thousand lives, hell even in one day. The fact that we can start over again, any day, any moment, that's a gift. One that not everyone takes advantage of."

"But the people," asked Bea, "don't you have a sister? Your parents?"

"My parents are long gone. I went to their funerals. My sister, she's not who I thought she was. I gave her more chances than she deserved."

His voice was stern and held just enough bitterness to send an icy chill down Bea's back, the sort that made you wonder exactly what the people you love are capable of.

"Bea, you'll find that at some point you'll be faced with a decision like that. And you'll either let it consume you, or you'll stand tall and strong and leave a burning bridge in your wake. Maybe you'll be lucky, maybe you won't have to make that kind of decision. But, knowing a few of the people in your life," he paused and Bea looked at her feet, "and how much of your life you have left to live, something like that could come up." His voice and eyes softened, "Don't judge an old man, if anything, learn from me. I've gained so much more than I lost all those years ago." He straightened, arched his back and started walking towards the tractor and the bin of apples, ready to haul it in for the night.

"What was it that really mattered?" she asked.

"Family," he said, "is so much more than blood."

As she watched him walk up the row, the light glowed around him. The setting sun brought the orchard to life in a different way than the rest of the day. It danced. The land they stood on was a sanctuary for so many, herself included. She never really thought about how Cliff may have cut ties in order to preserve it.

Her own relationship with her parents had been strained, but there was never a blow out, never a heated exchange. It was a slow progression to where their relationship had ended up, more like it disintegrated rather than was severed. There was still a hint of a thread there, and perhaps it needed a clean cut to break, and once severed the ends would dance in the wind. One end in celebration, the other in a desperate grasping movement, misconstrued as dance.

"Can I help you?" Bea asked at the foot of the porch steps.

Vicky was standing at the door, the screen propped open by her side, poised to knock for the third time. She turned, looked behind and down until she saw Bea standing with the tray of crumbs, dishes piled and balanced.

Vicky stood above her, dressed to the nines. Bea thought of the time it would take to create her look, adding in an extra half an hour if there was a flat iron involved for her hair. She guessed that type of work, the work it took to look like Vicky, would be upwards of two hours. Her eye makeup was heavy and overused, but it was spot on for the look Vicky had going. She wore a black pencil skirt with a plum cardigan twin set, the sort of thing her mother would have and had worn, with kitten heels that wouldn't last longer than a few minutes in the driveway without getting covered with dirt and dust.

"Bea! Good morning," she let the door go, and jumped as it slammed against the house.

"Good morning," replied Bea, her eyes narrowed and her back straightened.

Vicky looked around, stared down at the tray in Bea's hands, and started down the porch steps. Bea walked up, passed Vicky and in one movement she whipped the tray against her hip and under one arm, flung open the screen door and held it open.

Vicky looked at Bea with a strained, tight smile.

"Would you like to come in?" asked Bea, "I can make us a fresh pot of coffee and then we can come back out and enjoy the view," she paused while Vicky considered, "that is, if you were planning on staying a while," Bea shrugged as if it didn't matter to her.

"That sounds perfect," said Vicky, and as she smiled she revealed a bright white grin with teeth so straight they could only be veneers.

The house was quiet, and the kitchen was just as Bea left it earlier that morning, dishes in the sink, dish cloth in a heap on the counter, bag of bagels open and growing stale. She replaced the soggy mess of coffee grounds with new dry ones, and moved around the kitchen without considering Vicky behind her.

At one point Bea glanced over her shoulder and saw Vicky taking in Cliff's home, the knickknacks and cookbooks, the ephemera left behind on the refrigerator door. While her mother seemed to look over everything with sentimentality, Vicky assessed with curiosity. She looked as one might in a strangers home, not one of a loved one, even one lost for a lifetime.

Vicky looked over and she and Bea locked eyes for a moment. Vicky opened her mouth to say something, but Bea was quicker.

"Have you had breakfast? I can make us something."

"I already ate, the food at the bed and breakfast I'm staying at is very impressive."

"Where is that?"

"The Yellow Inn, right -"

"Across from the Unitarian church?"

Vicky nodded, "that's the one." She looked at Bea, but Bea turned back to the coffee, to the dishes in the sink, "Bea, I wanted to talk with you, to get to know you a little bit, especially after last night."

That ship had sailed, thought Bea to herself, but she knew it hadn't. Not really. She knew that she should at least give Vicky a chance. But at the same time, when Cliff had given his sister a chance, it left him hurt. Bea's protective walls formed and stood in front of and all around her, though she hoped for Vicky's sake they weren't visible.

The scent of coffee filled the kitchen as she grabbed two fresh mugs. "I'm sorry about last night," said Bea as she turned around.

Vicky rushed to her side and placed a hand on her back, "No, no, Bea. You've been through so much, I can't even imagine dealing with everything, and then add in Cliff's family, you've got a lot on your plate. Plus, from what I gather the orchard and all of the responsibility that comes with it is all new for you."

Bea shrugged, "It is in some ways, but I've known Cliff and the orchard for nearly my entire life. I know the land, but I've never dealt with the business side, and it's quite different from my own area of expertise."

195

"Photography is it?" asked Vicky, Bea nodded.
"Commercial? Portrait? Magazine? Wedding?"

"A bit of everything," laughed Bea, "but mostly travel photography up until recently. I'd like to think that managing my own business gave me some frame of reference for the orchard, but to be honest at this point I'm pretty far out of my comfort zone even in terms of invoicing." She surprised herself with the admonition, and when she looked up from her coffee service she found warmth in Vicky's eyes and an unexpected pressure from her hand that now sat on Bea's forearm, and realized it brought comfort rather than annoyance.

"All while grieving," said Vicky, sighing. She took her hand back and tucked a stray hair behind her ear. "Can I help you with that?"

Bea replaced the dirty dishes with a container of half and half and a dish of sugar as well as two steaming mugs of coffee, she refused help with a shake of her head and started towards the porch. Wordlessly she waited for Vicky to open the doors for her, and they made their way to the Adirondack chairs.

In front of them, the orchard was a musical. A chorus of birdsong gave way to a solo here and there, and flocks of birds fluttered across the driveway and beyond. It was a show Cliff never tired of, and one Bea was starting to appreciate more with each day.

They settled into the chairs that were close enough to one another for the tray to balance on both of their wooden arms.

Bea grabbed a mug and sat with her back and shoulders against the tall planks of the chair. She pulled her feet up as the chair dwarfed her.

There was a certain honesty hangover that Bea felt when she infrequently gave too much away too soon with people. She barely knew Vicky, and yet there was something about her that was familiar. Bea brushed the thought away, and sat quietly with her coffee cup. The distance between the two women was full of the kind of silence of acquaintances, full of second hand stories and assumptions.

"How late did everyone stay at the diner last night?" asked Bea.

The bottom of Vicky's coffee cup sat on her lap, and she was sitting far enough forward in the chair so that her feet touched the porch floor. She tilted her head in thought.

"I guess a few hours after you left. People were telling stories about Cliff, and asking me lots of questions about our youth. Cliff's childhood seems to be quite an anomaly around here."

It felt like a trap somehow, an invitation for questions, and so Bea sat quietly and waited for Vicky to continue. She looked out past the barn, and wondered where on the grounds Henry was picking, if she should offer a tour of the orchard, if she herself should be picking instead of chatting on the porch. She sat quietly as the questions passed through her head, the silence building.

"I didn't know where he went, when he left all those years ago," at that statement Bea turned to look at Vicky, who was now looking out into the trees as well. "No one knew," Vicky continued, "and we were devastated. This feels like losing him a second time." There were tears in the corners of her eyes, and Vicky dabbed at them with the middle finger of her right hand.

"I'm sorry," said Bea, she looked in the direction of the ocean in the far distance.

"Well, he made his choices. I just felt like I didn't have a say in his leaving, and then when you lose a family member with so much unresolved, it leaves you with a sense of unrest. There's no closure, I guess you could say."

"He died so suddenly, none of us had closure," offered

Bea.

"But you had a lifetime with him. He chose to be here. I hadn't spoken to him in years."

Bea heard a hint of bitterness. Vicky sat up a bit taller, straightened herself even more. The line from her neck to spine was rigid, straight out of a posture textbook. A far cry from the ease of Cliff Finley.

"Cliff never spoke about what happened when he left the Cape, how he came to this place." Bea looked over the property and imagined Cliff out there, what he'd be doing now, what had happened just the week prior. Her eyes misted a bit as she remembered how he urged her away from the farm to have some time in town. Almost as if he knew what would happen and he wanted to protect her.

"Never?" asked Vicky.

Bea shook her head, "I guess I was hoping you could help with that mystery."

Vicky stood up and walked over to the porch railing.

"Cliff was independent, strong-willed, and left home as soon as he could after high school graduation. He lived in an apartment not far from us, he was doing odd jobs around town. We barely saw him. Same thing happened every summer when he came home from college. And then after his graduation, Dad wanted him to be a part of his accounting firm, but Cliff resisted. Eventually Dad won and Cliff helped, he had an accounting degree from college, and worked at the family business. And then one summer Cliff changed. He became more restless than before, and he just left. We weren't sure where he went, but he left a sea of emotionally crushed people in his wake."

"That doesn't sound like Cliff," said Bea, bewildered and quiet. Her words hung in the tension, they sat and marinated as Bea thought about Cliff. What she knew of him when she was younger and the man she looked up to and cherished as a friend and mentor in a sense. His loyalty. His kindness. The way he never made a rash decision, always thinking through logistics and consequences. She raised her eyebrows at her own thought process when she got to the decision regarding the orchard. Leaving it to her seemed to be one of the rasher decisions he made.

"It was the Cliff we knew," said Vicky.

"Did you work for your father as well?"

Vicky turned her head towards Bea over her shoulder and said, without missing a beat, "Until Dad died, and then I closed up the shop and started my own business."

"In accounting as well?"

"No, in marketing. I went to college for a dual degree in finance and communications. I have my own company, which my son is involved in as well."

"Keeping it in the family," muttered Bea, mostly to herself. There seemed to be a theme here. For a fleeting moment she felt a surge of pride in her inheritance, but then she remembered the bonds were only in friendship and not blood.

"Yes, so you can imagine my surprise when I heard Cliff left you the orchard," she looked back out at the orchard, the expanse of acres ahead of her, her mind calculating, "but of course, without a wife or children of his own, I guess it was the only thing to do." She sighed, "It's just a shame he didn't feel like he could count us as family."

After a few minutes Bea broke the silence and said, "Accounting?"

Vicky turned and sat back down next to her. "Excuse me?"

Bea shook her head, "You said the family business was accounting?"

Vicky nodded.

"I just can't picture Cliff sitting behind a desk day in and day out. No wonder he chose to come here." She smiled to herself.

"But it was our father's business, our father's wish that his children carry on his legacy."

Bea laughed, "The one that you sold?" the coffee was kicking in, and her strength was collecting. The self employed, business savvy Beatrix Hampton was coming forth and noticing red flags all over the place.

Vicky, smooth as silk, said, "That was purely business. It made sense to sell his accounting firm and move forward with something that was my strength. And it paid off, my father would have been incredibly proud of what I've done."

"Marketing, was it?"

"With a side of property management. Actually," Vicky looked right at Bea and said cautiously in an overly familiar way, "have you thought of the potential here? You could take a chapter from my book, and either sell or turn this into a more modern facility. Give it a Facebook page and a bigger sign, turn that barn over there into a farm stand or a wedding venue, and you could make a killing."

"Ah, I see," Bea put her coffee cup down on the arm of the chair and stood. "For the record, I can't sell. That was part of Cliff's will," she left out the part about for how long, Vicky didn't need to know the details, "and modernize? The town would have a fit."

"From what I could tell last night, the town," Vicky got up to stand next to Bea, "wants change from you. They want you to give them something Cliff never could. I told that man from the greasy spoon, what was his name?"

"You mean Bert?"

"Yes, Bert. He reeked of bacon grease," Bea bit her

200

tongue, her cheeks started to turn a brilliant shade of red, "Anyway, I told him that I thought I might be able to help. With my expertise, you could take Finley Orchards to the next level. Cumberland is changing, growing. Look at Graham Winters," Bea stifled a groan. "Transplants are choosing to come here for the small town vibe, but want so much more than that. I walked around the downtown area yesterday and was blown away by the potential. Times are changing, and you have the perfect opportunity to carry Finley Orchards into the future, and I can help."

"And you'd do this out of the goodness of your heart?"

Vicky shrugged and put on a confident smile of someone used to getting her way.

"It's family. I'd do anything for family," she said firmly with an unwavering cold stare.

But the spell was broken and Bea had had enough. Her hands were aching for apples, her limbs to stretch into a tree, her heart for space only endless rows of apples could afford.

"I think I'd better get to the field, the apples don't know the difference between weekends and weekdays."

"Please consider what I'm offering, Bea. A fresh start for the farm could breathe some life into it."

Bea seethed, "It has plenty of life in it. Cliff knew what he was doing, and the orchard is reaching its potential."

A condescending laugh filled the air, "Honey, Cliff's ambitions were far from what they could have been. You are sitting on a goldmine. It looks as though Cliff didn't want to cash in. Remember that as you consider what it is you want your life to look like. Do you want to be slaving away in an orchard seven days a week, or would you like to enjoy your life while you have a crew working for you, working regular hours and providing a good income for you and other townspeople. From what I can tell this is mostly a volunteer operation, which can't be sustainable if most of your volunteers are older than I am," she paused briefly and then added softly, "and maybe you could even continue to pursue your photography career. I've seen your work, you have talent."

After having decided that she was going to stay, Bea hadn't given much thought to anything other than surviving - learning how Cliff ran the orchard and continuing on in his footsteps was part of that. The journals that she'd poured over provided a set of guidelines, and she was set on making sure that everything he did, she did. And after overhearing the ladies in the powder room of the funeral parlor the night before, change and updating anything was far, far from her mind.

But. The idea of how she would spend her life… she hadn't really pictured what her days would look like beyond the next week or so. Yes, she could certainly sell the place if it wasn't what she wanted to do, but there was a part of her that already knew that selling at the end of her year would feel like a betrayal. If she was here for the long haul, wouldn't she want to change a few things here and there, and make the orchard her own? And her photography. She hadn't thought of picking up her camera since she packed it up before the trip to the orchard. It still sat in its expensive camera bag, wrapped up with regret and not a shred of hope.

Vicky's answers weren't the right ones, she knew that, especially as she couldn't get rid of the newfound nagging suspicion that entered the conversation.

Across the driveway and down towards the barn a body appeared, Bea saw it out of the corner of her eye and squinted.

"You'll have to excuse me, Anna is here for picking, and I'm not sure the barn is unlocked." Bea stood, leaving the tray and coffee cups on the porch, "You can manage to find your way back to town?"

Vicky said, "Of course. Consider my offer, Bea. I'm staying a few more days," she reached down to the purse she left by the chair and fished around, "here's my card. It has my cell number and email. I'm assuming you have some sort of internet connection here," she said with a wry smile.

Bea took the card and placed it in the back pocket of her soft, worn jeans. Without a smile she said, "We even have indoor plumbing," and ushered Vicky down the front porch steps. She left Vicky at her shiny car, and continued on to where Anna stood waving at her. She didn't wait to see the dust and taillights before she headed into the barn, but the car was gone by the time the pair headed towards the orchard, buckets in front of their bellies, backs ready to bear the load they were about to pick.

Saturday passed in a whirlwind of bushels of apples and getting into the swing of things at the orchard. Anna spent most of the day with Bea catching up on the happenings of the funeral and Anna giving Bea the nitty gritty of who was really helping out at the orchard, which people to count on and who would come by only on a whim. Anna's blond pony tail swished from side to side as she talked, her face animated. Bea knew she was trying to be helpful, but at the same time she also knew you could never trust a gossip farther than you could throw them. That was something her grandmother told her.

Regardless, it was nice to spend the day chatting easily with Anna. After Vicky left, Bea reeled as she played back the conversation. Was Vicky trying to get something from Bea? She couldn't trust her. Bea wanted to, oh how she wanted to. She wanted someone to sweep in and help her navigate the new situation of owning not just property, but an orchard. Bea hadn't realized how much she longed for a guiding hand until Vicky offered one, albeit a slightly overreaching one with a side of guilt.

Anna and Bea picked side by side in neighboring trees, working at a swift and even pace. Bea didn't talk much, but once Anna finished filling her in on how often Bert, Ron, William, and Henry actually showed up (though Anna had no idea how often Henry was there), she shared stories from her day job at the nursery. Bea asked what sort of plants might spruce up the area around the farm house, or if she needed to look out for any flowers coming up in the spring. She hadn't been there at that time in years, and was curious about what to expect, and she had a hunch that this line of questioning would get her talking through picking another few trees.

"Cliff used to love having beds of impatiens," said Anna, she brushed her hands on her long jean skirt and then took her pony tail down and readjusted her hair into a messy bun. Her dusty blue tee shirt was tucked into her skirt, on her bare feet were brown clogs. "He always ordered at least a truck full of flowers every spring. I'd spend a whole Saturday helping him plant them. But the last few years he wasn't able to order them, and instead we used Lobelia and Begonias. Pretty, but a little more fussy than the impatiens you probably remember."

"Why no impatiens? They're such classics, and so sweet. When I was a child I thought the petals looked like fairy skirts," said Bea, smiling at the memory or Cliff knee deep in a flower bed telling her a story about the garden gnomes and fairies that played when they weren't looking. How the petals of the flower got lost in his thick, labor hardened hands, his giant palms.

"Starting a few years ago a type of mildew, a blight, swept through the country, targeting impatiens in particular. It's called downy mildew. It actually doesn't affect the New Guinea impatiens, but they're so highly sought after that we can't keep them in stock at the nursery. People are attached to what they know, and they know impatiens. At least Cliff was always willing to try something different in the garden if he needed to. The mildew leaves fuzzy white spores on the underside of the leaves, and makes the flowers look wilted, like you haven't watered them in days. It can reside in the soil for years, causing quite a big problem unless you get creative and try to grow something else."

"But it doesn't hurt the apples or anything?"

Anna turned to face Bea, hands on her hips, "No, but that's a great question. Have you given much thought to your stance on IPM?"

"I P what?" Bea laughed nervously.

Anna smiled kindly at her and turned back to the tree she was methodically working through, "Integrated Pest Management. It's a system designed to protect the apples and control damage from insects and other creatures. There's different steps you have to go through each season, I'll see if I have anything in my office at home about it, but I bet Cliff has information in the barn somewhere."

Or his journals, Bea thought to herself, though she hadn't seen any mention of it thus far.

There was a learning curve to all of it, and Bea would have liked to feel as if she was getting ahead. Instead, every turn brought more unknowns, more to learn, and more to be unsure of. Even at that moment in Anna's company Bea felt completely alone. And she missed Cliff.

205

TWENTY-ONE

H er feet felt heavy as she crossed the road. Her torso leaned forward to propel herself, but her legs were stiff and unyielding. By the time she reached the yellow lines in the middle, her body was more in line with itself, but her senses were overrun by familiarity as well as the palpable taste of the unknown. She heard a car coming in the distance and hurried across the rest of the way. The road, full of curves and twists, acted like an echo chamber, giving plenty of warning for oncoming cars. When Bea was old enough to cross the road it helped Sylvia feel a little safer with the combination of slow traffic and the long warning period, giving Bea more confidence and freedom to run from her Grandma's house to Cliff's. Between those two properties, it felt like she had the entire world at her fingertips.

In the driveway sat a new dark blue Subaru wagon next to a meticulously cared for lawn. A contrast from the days of Sylvia and Cliff, when it was always the other way around and Cliff would nag Sylvia until she let him come over and blow leaves into big paper bags. They'd be lined up neat and orderly, just like rows of apple trees, on either side of the road come trash day. Bea looked back across the road through the thinning trees to see the farmhouse and the property that looked like no one had touched it in months, the overgrown grass and shaggy hedges. It went to show how meticulous Cliff had been in his gardening as well as orchard management.

When she stood in front of Graham's front door, bottle of wine in one hand, a stack of books tucked under her other arm, she broke out in a cold sweat. Her legs shook slightly from the cold air and nerves. She looked down at her shoes, a pair of Converse she picked up at the box store earlier in the day when she went in search of toilet paper and new bathroom towels, baby steps towards making the house her home. The shoes were stiff and her feet wanted to dance barefoot back across the road. Anticipation fell over her and she was just about to turn and run back to the farmhouse when the door opened.

Graham wore dark blue jeans, a soft looking gray tee shirt with a Kelly green flannel button up, and moccasin style slippers. His hair was tousled, and behind him the glow of the living room was inviting.

"I'm glad you made the long trek over," Graham said with a smirk, "come on in out of the cold." He stepped aside and Bea walked in. Not flooded by a million memories like she thought she would be, she took in the room without a word. In her head, nothing had changed since her Grandma's death and she expected everything to be the same. But in reality, through two changes in owners, everything but the house itself was different. Graham's eyes studied her as she looked around the living room and peered up the stairway, eventually landing on the kitchen in the back of the house.

"I brought wine, I wasn't sure what would go with dinner, but you can stash it away if it doesn't work." She handed him the bottle of Cabernet Sauvignon and he looked approvingly at the label and then toward the books now in the crook of her elbow.

"Can I take those for you?" he asked with an outstretched hand.

Bea handed the stack of a half a dozen books over, "I thought maybe you could take a look at these. They were my grandmother's, and Cliff brought them out a few days before," her voice trailed off and she and Graham were both silent as he looked at the spines of the books.

"I'll put them in my office, I'll be right back." He disappeared after depositing the bottle of red on the kitchen counter.

Bea took the opportunity in his absence to give the place a thorough once over. The wall beneath the stairs was lined with photographs and artwork. Landscapes and architecture, nothing too personal. On the far wall of the living room was an expanse of bookshelves the length of the wall, all full but not bulging. There was a large brown leather armchair and a peacock-blue wingback, as well as a white sofa with overstuffed cushions. The room looked as though it came straight out of a Pottery Barn catalog, perfectly folded afghans and well placed color coordinated throw pillows included. The dark wood paneling that Bea remembered from her youth had been painted white, and even though the sun was setting the room was still warm with the essence of natural light, the glow of late afternoon. It would make for a perfectly moody photo-shoot, she thought to herself.

Graham walked back into the room and smiled at her, following her gaze.

"Come on into the kitchen, I need to finish up dinner," he gestured with his arm and before leading the way, calling over his shoulder, "Should I open the wine, or would you like to try some cider?"

"Did you press the cider yourself?" her voice carried through the room louder than she intended, the hint of laughter was subtle and she hoped he caught it.

"It's actually from a neighbor up the road," he said, "Gabe lives with his wife and kids in an old farmhouse, similar to the one that's on the orchard. They're trying to break into the hard cider market, but it's an uphill battle as the market is saturated."

She watched him, at home in his surroundings. "In that case I'll have cider," she said with a confident grin, "where do they get their apples from?"

As he poured two glasses from a wine shaped bottle, her gaze stuttered over his arms. His sleeves were pushed up to his elbows, exposing lean muscle and strength. Bea blushed when he pushed a glass towards her.

"Actually, from your orchard, he got a bunch early on in the season. Cliff must have a record of it somewhere."

"I'm sure it's in the stack of papers somewhere on his desk." Bea took a sip and enjoyed the cold, crisp taste of apples and light fizz.

"I heard you had a visitor yesterday," he said off handedly.

She took another drink before answering. The cider was tart enough to make her eyes water and her nose tingle but it had a subtle, sweet kick at the end.

She wiped her eyes and said, "Nothing goes unnoticed in this town."

Graham shrugged, "Could be worse. Better to have people watching out for you, I think."

"Rather than not having everyone all up in your business? I don't know. I might go for solitude."

209

He looked at her and a wash of sincerity filled the room, "Maybe so, but then you're in the wrong town, and certainly at the wrong address for that. You'd have to put up physical barriers around the place to keep everyone out."

The room went quiet. Bea looked over at the big dutch oven simmering on the stove, it bubbled and filled the silence. Graham followed her gaze and swore under his breath.

"I forgot about the sauce, sorry."

"What's cooking?" She sat on a bar stool at the counter.

"Spaghetti sauce. Thought I'd keep it simple."

"So you're making your own pasta from scratch?"

He looked at her over his shoulder with a puzzled look, and then at the box of pasta sitting on the counter to his right.

"I'm just giving you a hard time, Graham. It smells delicious," she paused for another drink of cider. It was her nerves that brought out the poor attempts at jokes, "but yes, I had another visitor. Vicky is certainly persistent."

"She seems nice enough."

"She seems opportunistic to me."

"When I spoke with her she seemed to have a genuine interest in getting to know Cliff through the orchard, and you." He stirred the sauce slowly, took the wooden spoon to his lips for a taste, then reached into a cabinet and grabbed a bottle of sea salt. He expertly poured in his palm before sprinkling it into the pot.

"Perhaps. How did you meet her? You said she was a client of yours?"

"She was. She lives in the same area of the Cape where my parents spend the summer, and Dad overheard her talking in a coffee shop about needing to have some books appraised. He gave her my card. It's a small world."

"So book appraisals are a big part of your job?"

"Yes. I buy, sell, and appraise old books. It's all part of it.

Are you interested in books?"

She shrugged, "Aside from the ones I brought over today? I guess I was a big reader back in college, and when I was traveling I appreciated the ease of e-books."

Graham grimaced, "I'm not talking about reading. I'm talking about books. The smell of them, the feel of them. The weight of them in your hand and how the words written inside only tell part of the story," his eyes were dreamy and his voice passionate. He was making Bea swoon in her chair.

"I haven't thought of books like that. I've only really read them for the story."

"We'll have to change that."

She took another sip of her cider, wishing it would go to her head quickly and take the edge off of her and the situation. It was all too much, where she was, who she was with, and more so who wasn't there but should have been.

"Have you seen Henry at all?" asked Bea, "I hope he wasn't scared too badly the other night. I checked on him yesterday, but I haven't seen him today. I thought he might want his space again."

"He's fine. Though your mother had quite the reaction to him."

Having been surprised by her mother's harshness herself, she conceded to Graham, "She's not the warmest, most compassionate woman," she gave a sad smile that didn't reach her eyes. "You can imagine what it was like being her daughter. My father isn't much better. I'm sorry she was so rude to Henry, he didn't deserve that."

Graham stirred the sauce and didn't look up when he said, "He's used to people not being open to his presence. He's a good man, cut from the same cloth as Cliff. You're lucky to have him over at the farm, watching out for the property."

211

"Because I'm not able to?" She said quietly looking sheepishly into her cup, feeling as though the wind had been taken out of her sails.

He put the wooden spoon down on a ceramic rest on the stove and turned to face Bea. She didn't look up, but she could feel his eyes. He came to stand next to her and put an arm around her shoulders, she didn't bristle. "No, not at all, it's just that he's like a stealthy older protector."

That one word made her bristle. It kept coming up, and she felt like her age worked against her more than her gender. "I know I'm young, but I can't help that. I wish I could."

He laughed a warm laugh, and gave her a squeeze before he headed back over to the other side of the counter. "And just how old do you think I am, Bea? Do I seem that much older than you?" She stared at him blankly, not wanting to embarrass herself or him. "I don't think you're young," he continued softly, "and for that matter, I'm not that much older than you are. Cumberland was supposed to turn around the aging process, take away stress and all that," he ran a hand through his hair, "but I guess the effects of life can't be reversed." He smiled, a hint of dimples displayed on his cheeks hinting at a sense of boyishness.

"Some people are just more mature than others," Bea offered, "I've been told I'll look twenty-two forever. So I guess I'm self conscious about that."

"And I aged about five years when my fiance ran off with her co-worker. So you and I are quite a mismatched pair."

His words hung in the air. He turned and filled another stock pot with water and placed it on the stove.

"I didn't realize, I'm sorry, Graham."

"Can't do anything about it now. Doesn't stop it from stinging though, even over a year later."

He swung back to the counter, his face was tired, the

dimples were nowhere to be found. She cupped her cider with both hands. It was cold, and at that moment she would have preferred a cup of something warm, but she needed to hold onto something.

"Thirty-three," he said.

Her eyes gave her away and he laughed deeply. "That bad? How old did you think, honestly?"

She took a sip of her cider to buy herself some time and then said, "Oh, you know, thirty-five?" She lied and smiled up at him. She thought he was at least forty.

"And you? What? Thirty?"

"Now you're just being mean. Twenty-eight."

"Here's to youth," he said, and they clinked their glasses together, "and to not being middle aged quite yet. Let me dump the pasta in the water, and then want to see the rest of the house?" he winced. "You probably already know the house like the back of your hand, but if you want to take a look around, feel free. I know it's been a while. Plus," he smiled widely, "the books. If you're going to be converted, you'll have to see the books. The good ones are in the office down the hall."

He turned, maybe to avoid her eyes, and dropped a handful of spaghetti into boiling water.

She lowered herself down from the bar stool. Past the kitchen to the left was the dining room, but she didn't start there. Instead she turned right, and went past the bathroom and towards what used to be two spare rooms. Now it was one gigantic space, closed off with two sets of French doors.

"I thought you said you didn't change anything?"

"I didn't, aside from a few tweaks to keep my books safe," he followed her down the hall from the kitchen, "It wasn't like this when your grandmother was here?"

She shook her head.

"Maybe they previous owners did more than I thought,"

213

said Graham.

She opened the doors and entered the room, finding it took up the width of the house. There were trunks lining the edges of the room, heavy ones with leather handles on either end, ornate brass corners, and a hefty latch. There were a few prints on the walls, one of a pen and ink drawn map of what looked like Cape Cod, another of the state of Vermont. A desk looked out the window facing the backyard, and archival boxes were stacked everywhere. They were the same type that she would use for her photographs, if she printed her work instead of keeping it on flash drives and internet clouds.

Graham closed the doors behind him and said, "This is my office. Welcome to Rare Books R Us," she looked at him with raised eyebrows, "that's not really my business name, but it certainly feels like it in here. I haven't unpacked the books, only because there's more work to do."

"Shelves?" she asked.

"Absolutely, shelves," he nodded with excitement, "I want it to feel and look a certain way in here, but," he said, pointing to the far corner where paint cans and a drop cloth sat, the paint he must have picked up the day Cliff died, "I want to paint the room first."

"Do you see clients here?"

He shook his head, "Never. I do consultations mostly at clients homes, and I do the majority of buying and selling online. I've never wanted a storefront business, though maybe someday. I'm using one of the other bedrooms upstairs for books as well. When I get myself organized I can probably fit everything into this one space."

He walked around the room, running his hand over boxes to check for dust, "This is actually a climate controlled room now, that was the one modification I had to make. Especially with the room just down from the kitchen, all the moisture and smells and whatnot. But the view," he said turning to look out the window, the tree lined marsh performed on queue with hints of a pink sunset, "the view sold me on the house, regardless of the layout. This is also the one room that stays meticulously clean. Dust is a rare book's worst enemy."

"I'm sure," said Bea, "it's not a photographer's friend either. It wreaks havoc on lenses."

"Do you miss it?" he asked. He crossed his arms and leaned back against the edge of his desk.

She shrugged and continued looking around, "I haven't thought much of it since I got here."

"And then everything changed," he said softly.

She stood in the uncomfortable silence that followed, eyes searching for somewhere to land.

Graham jumped up, "I actually have something for you," he searched around his desk, past the pile of her books and sifted through a stack of hardcovers. "It's a second edition," he said, handing Bea a slim text with a worn brown cover, it's pages stiff with age.

"Robert Frost?" she read the title, "Isn't he the one who wrote the poem about the two roads, and picking one?"

"Yes, and he was local. You can visit his farmhouse over in New Hampshire, just about forty minutes from here," Graham got lost in thought for a moment, like he was visiting the property in his mind, "but I saw this yesterday when I was perusing one of my favorite antique book shops up in Portsmouth, and thought of you."

She held the book against her chest, "Thank you, Graham," she said as she searched his eyes.

The kitchen timer went off and they walked back through the hall. Graham closed the doors tightly behind them, sealing up

215

the room.

She watched as Graham moved swiftly from sink to oven, from counter to fridge and back again.

"Point me to the glasses and a corkscrew and I'll open the bottle I brought," offered Bea.

"Above the sink and to the left," he pointed.

She took two long stemmed glasses and a cork screw to the dining room. She let the wine breathe while she looked the room over. This room was the only one so far that rang familiar in a way that made her stomach drop. The sheer off white curtains were similar to the ones that hung so long ago, the paint hadn't changed, unlike the rest of the house, and pockets of air still smelled slightly of lavender, of her grandmother.

"On your right," he said, and Bea moved slightly to let Graham pass with a steaming bowl of spaghetti in hand.

The long farm table was already set with maroon place mats and matching napkins.

"Do you entertain much?" she asked as she filled the wine glasses. The table looked expansive with only two place settings, the bench on one side and several seats around created a look that begged for guests and dinner parties.

"Not as often as I'd like," he replied and headed to the kitchen.

He came in with a bowl of sauce in one hand, and a salad in the other.

"Sit," he said, his smile was warm. She took a seat opposite him.

They served themselves and each sipped their wine before digging into the pasta. Bea was grateful for the feeling of warmth running through her chest from the wine, she put the back of her hand to her cheek and felt the flush of her cheeks.

"This is delicious," she said after a bite, she meant it.

"Thank you, the sauce is Cliff's recipe."

That bit of knowledge warmed her heart, to think of a piece of Cliff at the dinner table.

"Before this trip, he'd never cooked for me. I was always," she paused and glanced around, "here. And my grandmother cooked. Cliff would eat here now and then, or she'd send leftovers across the street to him."

"Was she a good cook?" he asked, his eyes were on her, his forearm rested on the table, fork hovered over his plate.

Through a mouthful of spaghetti she said, "The best." She felt sauce dribbling from her mouth and dabbed her chin with a napkin.

"Grandmothers always are. I've yet to meet one who is a terrible cook," he said and laughed a bit. "I've found it a bit more rare to find a bachelor of a certain age who cooks well. You really missed out, because Cliff was an excellent chef. I think Bert was always a little jealous and worried that he'd open up a restaurant on the farm and he'd take away all of the diner's customers."

"There will always be a place for the diner."

He nodded, "This is true, there's nothing that matches Bert's BLT's."

"With extra mayo," added Bea. They shared a smile.

She sat back and put down her fork, "He made me Chicken Picatta to celebrate my first day back at picking," she smiled at the memory and could almost taste the lemon on her tongue. "It was the best I'd ever had, outside of Italy that is."

"Cliff was a good man. Possibly the kindest person I've ever known. I feel so grateful to have ended up being his neighbor, and then his friend."

Graham grew quiet and for a few moments the only sounds were spaghetti being slurped and chewed and the grandfather clock ticking in the corner. Once she heard it she looked up and saw the walls, barren of the shelves her grandmother kept in this room. The far wall, towards the back of the house, had been lined with pine colored shelves, simple and bright, it was where Sylvia had kept her favorite of her chickadee figurines, the same ones that were packed up in Bea's bedroom.

She put her fork down suddenly, "Are we really doing this?" she said.

He looked at her with a puzzled expression, one eyebrow raised. He put his fork down and pushed his plate forward a bit, leaned his arms on the table. "Doing what?"

She threw her hands in the air before crossing them across my chest, "This. Being friendly, neighborly. Are we putting everything that's happened behind us?"

"I'm not exactly sure what you're talking about."

"The car accident, your new car. Cliff's will. Henry living in my barn. Me running the orchard. The weirdness of you living in my grandmother's house."

"Bea, I've been through enough to know that I can't control everything, and there's so many questions that I will never know the answers to. But I do know that we're neighbors. That you're dedicated to being here, at least to fulfill Cliff's wishes. That I have a new car because neither of us should have been driving after finding out a man both of us loved and respected died suddenly. I know that," he paused and fidgeted with his wine glass, "we need to get along. For the sake of the orchard, for the sake of neighborly relations. And I'm willing to, no, I want to get to know you as a person and not just the woman who came here for a vacation and was planning on leaving. You're a Cumberland resident, a property owner, and could be an asset to our

218

community."

She sat back, a little stunned, a little in awe of his perspective.

"So you're not upset about the car?"

His eyes lit up with playfulness, "Hardly. I got a new Subaru out of it, what more could my native Vermont heart desire?"

"Thank you," she said quietly.

He shook his head, "Cliff really took me under his wing at my lowest point, and the least I can do is extend the same sort of courtesy to you. You're, admittedly, over your head in all of this, and I'm sure it's not easy for a lot of reasons I probably know nothing about. But I'm here if you need a friend. Or just an emergency contact." At that he smiled, as did Bea, and she offered up her glass for a clink.

"Right back at you. I may know nothing about antique books, but I'll gladly look out for smoke coming off your roof or any suspicious activity."

"That's all one can ask of a neighbor."

"That, and a good home cooked meal. Really, Graham, this was amazing."

He humbly waved off any recognition, and they rose to clear the table, together. It could have been the wine, but there was a lightness in both of their steps, and a glimmer in their eyes possibly signaling a true new beginning.

The quiet of the night unnerved Bea. She tossed and turned in her bed, it squeaked and the springs dug into her hips. Tiny found its way onto her pillow next to her, and like a dance they orchestrated over the years, a ritual of the sleepless, it's worn satin edges felt cool to her cheek each time she turned. Finally, she turned on the bedside lamp, the room glowed with a sepia tinted light. Outside she could hear the wind whipping through the trees, an edge of the tarp that covered a stack of firewood clung to a current of air.

On her nightstand, next to a glass of water and the alarm clock, was the book that Graham gave her earlier. Bea sat up in bed and inspected it, the cover was yellowed and there was a heft to the hard copy even with it's slender size. It was a slight collection of poetry; Bea searched the pages for a few of Robert Frost's poems that she had memorized in school, The Road Not Taken and Stopping by Woods on a Snowy Evening. She was turning the pages quickly, hardly paying attention to the unfamiliar titles, searching only for what she knew. She was about to turn yet another page when she noticed the corner of a page folded down.

Bea read the title of the poem: After Apple-Picking. She scanned the page with delight until the words registered.

My long two-pointed ladder's sticking through a tree
Toward heaven still,
And there's a barrel that I didn't fill
Beside it, and there may be two or three
Apples I didn't pick upon some bough.

Tears pricked behind her eyes and she could picture Cliff standing in the orchard, his sturdy frame taking in the harvest at the end of the day.

But I am done with apple-picking now.
Essence of winter sleep is on the night,
The scent of apples: I am drowsing off.

220

At first she was indignant, and read with a ferocity that only came with anger. Adrenaline did a good job of waking her up completely, sleep would certainly not come for hours at this point.

For I have had too much
Of apple-picking: I am overtired
Of the great harvest I myself desired.

Bea wanted it all to make sense, but each time she came up against death, it hadn't. It was a photograph that couldn't be framed, there were too many working pieces for it to come together in a cohesive manner, too many variables and places one could look.

A second and then third reading brought her heart rate down. She was not angry with Graham for delivering a painful reminder, she was thankful for the gift in her hand. An acknowledgment of her grief, his grief, and a reminder of the great orchard keeper they both knew and loved in their own ways.

It was now the wee hours of the morning, too close to sunrise to bother trying for sleep.

At the foot of the bed was a bathrobe she had found in Cliff's closet. She knew she needed to start finding things of her own, items of clothing that fit and weren't over-sized and hung off her shoulders and pooled at her feet. But nothing new would comfort her the way those old, worn articles of clothing did.

After she put on the bathrobe she stuffed Tiny into one pocket, the book of poems in the other. Downstairs she put the kettle on and after it boiled, made a cup of chamomile tea. Mug in hand she walked around the edges of each room, staring out each window one at a time. The floors creaked and groaned under her weight, and her feet were cold against the wood and tile of the kitchen and living room floors. She peered out the window that opened toward the road, and somewhere past the trees she swore she could see a light. A smile played on her lips, thinking maybe he was awake too. Maybe they were sharing a sleepless night.

Her cheeks flamed. It was from the warmth of the tea, she told herself.

She stood at the window until daylight edged in and the chickadees began to sing.

TWENTY-TWO

It was the beginning of November and the wind howled. The afternoons were gray and there was a bowl of candy, still filled to the brim sitting on the kitchen table, leftovers from Halloween. Graham told Bea not to expect many costumed children but she wanted to be prepared, just in case. So she piled a bowl high with a variety of king sized candy bars, filling in the edges with mini versions of classic treats, and tucked an extra two bags of candy in the pantry. On Halloween she sat on the porch with a flashlight and a mug of tea and jumped whenever she thought she heard feet coming up the driveway, bowl of candy at the ready. Earlier that day she had told everyone who showed up for picking to send their kids or grandkids over. Truthfully, the only kids who made it up the driveway had ties to the orchard. For their troubles Bea gave them extra candy, and some for whoever drove them down the sidewalk-less road.

When Ron brought his grandchildren over he told Bea that Graham was sitting on his porch, just like she was. After they left, taking with them no less than ten candy bars between them, Bea stood on the edge of the porch and looked through the thinning trees and darkness, past the street, to Graham's house. She caught a beam of light, it flashed in a pattern that she assumed was Morse code, and then sent a few back. They passed the next ten minutes or so in such a way, and when the night was perfectly still she could hear his deep laughter coming through the air, and the hair on her arms stood up at attention and she smiled.

After the dinner at Graham's Bea started smiling more. It wasn't that grief had left completely, it was still there lingering in the corners, but she felt less alone. When Sylvia passed, Bea was devastated. Looking back, it was a combination of things: youth, her parents acting as if she had nothing to be upset about, loss of a home, and the solitary nature of her college experience. During her four years at school, Bea was often alone, and at the first chance she opted to have a single room. She studied abroad, whetting her appetite for travel, and when she was on campus Bea spent the majority of her time in the darkroom, huddled over her portfolio, or behind a camera. There wasn't much room or time for friendship.

But this time, her grief felt different. Maybe because of age, but more likely because in losing Cliff, she gained a community. Opening herself up to others had made her less lonely.

Now, she was standing on the porch with an over-sized mug of coffee, waiting for Olivia. It was mid morning on a Saturday and Bea had already made her rounds through the orchard. The season was winding down. When they weren't picking the dwindling crops, Bea and the volunteers spent their time cleaning between the rows of trees, the grassy bits and edges. She carried Cliff's notebooks with her at all times and boldly started adding notes in the margins. Each time she scribbled a note to herself, she paused. Both of their handwriting looked like chicken scratch, except that hers had extra loops here and there. At first Bea didn't want to mar his work but then she realized what the notebooks were, working journals of the orchard. And if she were to move forward with the orchard she would want her own notes. Bea hadn't picked up her own Moleskins yet, that was on her to do list for the next time she was in town, but when she did, she'd begin the process of making her own system to include what she did this year, and what to expect for next year.

Olivia was coming over to sort through paperwork with Bea. The previous day Henry helped move the desk from the barn into the study. It was a small space off the living room and partly under the staircase. In it were two windows on the far wall, and another across from the closet, all with expansive views of the property. Cliff had kept the study as a catch all room, there was a bookshelf, an old sofa bed, and boxes of extra paperwork. His filing system was in disarray, half in the barn and half in the study, and so Bea thought it would be prudent of her to get all of his - her - ducks in a row. So Henry helped Bea lug out the sofa bed to the barn, and the desk into the study. Instead of sorting as they went, they brought each drawer in, one at a time, still filled with endless paperwork and half used pencils, sticky notes with the stick no longer on the back, and countless half empty boxes of business cards.

As she sat on the porch she watched her breath hang in the air, birds fluffing their feathers. The chickadees in particular found the bushes right in front of the porch to their liking, and they kept her company. It seemed like they had gotten used to her, and if Bea stood still and didn't look directly at them, they would call to each other. Chick-a-dee-dee-dee, they sang.

Olivia's Jeep pulled into the driveway and the birds flew up and outward, cutting through the far end of the porch towards the orchard.

225

The dust settled and Olivia climbed out and made her way to Bea. Every time Bea saw her, Olivia's belly grew and her face softened more. Today was no different. Olivia grabbed hold of the railing and walked quickly, as if she had something to prove. Pregnancy, Bea heard her tell Scott at least three times in the past few weeks, was not a handicap. Olivia's cheeks were rosy, her ponytail low, and strands of blond hair framed her face.

"How are you?" Bea asked with a smile.

"Tired," she responded with a huge grin, "tired but wonderful," she rested a hand on her belly and the other one on her lower back.

Inside Bea freshened up the pot of coffee and grabbed a kitchen chair and dragged it into the study. She motioned to the comfy chair, the office chair. It swiveled and swayed as Olivia settled herself.

"Just another few months?" asked Bea.

Olivia sighed, "Two. I already feel as big as a boat, I don't know how the baby is going to get any bigger."

"But it will?"

Laughing, she said, "Yes, it will."

Bea settled into the chair beside her, and started to fidget with the papers at hand, "Well that's good, I think?" Olivia nodded and smiled kindly at Bea, who admitted with an apologetic smile, "I don't know much about all of the baby stuff, aside from pregnancy being nine months."

"Don't you have friends who've started having babies?"

Bea shrugged "No, not really. I never kept in touch with people I knew from high school, or even college. There weren't many I was close to. And in the photography world, especially travel photography, you're never in one place for long. Doesn't leave much time for building families and community."

Olivia looked thoughtful for a moment, and then said,

"Would you do a maternity shoot for me?"

Bea beamed, "Of course! I've never done one, but I'm sure we can figure something out. I'd love to. And maybe a newborn shoot," she started daydreaming, and realized she had never done a newborn session either. More new territory.

Olivia nodded her head, decidedly. "I love your work. Cliff would always bring in the latest magazine you had a spread in," her voice softened, and her eyes were misty, "he was so proud of you."

Bea put a hand on Olivia's arm, tears were pricking at her eyes, too.

Olivia cleared her throat, "You have a way with your subjects, especially landscapes. And I want to show how Cumberland is a part of our lives, mine and Steve's. Maybe we could do some here, and also in town."

"Maybe in the snow? For your winter baby?"

Olivia's eyes lit up, "That would be magical!"

They shot a couple of ideas back and forth, and while portraits had never been Bea's specialty, she was excited - possibly for the first time since coming to Cumberland - about getting out her camera.

"Thank you, Bea," said Olivia, her hand on her belly, "the baby is kicking, give me your hand," she grabbed Bea's hand and yanked her over as she slid her shirt up the shelf of her stomach.

She placed Bea's hand on her abdomen, and Bea could feel her stretched belly button, the warmth of Olivia's skin. Olivia pressed Bea's hand firmly against her with such force that Bea was afraid of hurting the baby.

"If you press right here," Olivia said, "you can feel the baby's bum. And then here, just wait," after they gave the baby's rear end a push she moved Bea's hand over to the other side, where Bea felt the push and pull of something, and then a foot pressed against her hand, through layers of fluid and skin.

Bea gasped and Olivia smiled at her warmly.

"It freaks Steve out," Olivia said with a shake of her head, "but my mother won't keep her hands off me whenever she's in the same room."

"That's incredible. And you don't know..." Bea's voice trailed, asking a question that she was unsure whether or not it was okay to ask.

"No, we didn't find out. We'll be surprised, like the rest of the world. It's really the one true surprise in life, if you think about it. Regardless, we'll be happy."

"Of course," said Bea sitting back in her chair and trying not to stare at Olivia's exposed stomach.

"It's so warm in here, I feel like a furnace," said Olivia.

"Do you want a window open?"

Olivia shook her head, "No, it'll pass. But," she said with a mischievous grin, "if you can keep a secret I'll tell you what I think the baby is."

"Absolutely!" Bea said, with too much excitement. She felt like she was a preteen again and was trying to keep up with Olivia. Any attention from her felt golden.

"I think it's a girl. It goes against most of the old wives tales, but I'm pretty sure. Just a feeling."

"I couldn't even tell you an old wives tale about pregnancy if I tried."

Olivia pulled her shirt back down, rested her hands on the top of her stomach and said in her most matronly, prim and proper voice, "If you crave sweet foods, then it's a girl. If you carry high and all in front low and all around, it's a girl. If your face is breaking out like crazy, then you're having a girl." She gave Bea a side glance and said, "I've craved Reuben sandwiches since I found out I was pregnant, I'm carrying low and all around, and my skin has never been better. All signs point to a boy, but I swear, it's a girl," she laughed before adding, "Cliff said from day one that it would be a girl. While all the old ladies around town have been predicting a boy, he believed me," she smiled and settled into the swivel chair, "It was like our little secret, and now you're in on it, too."

Bea smiled, happy to be in on someone's secret, especially one involving Cliff.

"Are you taking much time off from the shop when the baby comes?" she asked as she started to sort papers into piles: file, shred, recycle.

"The plan is for me to take at least three months off. Between Steve and my parents, it shouldn't be an issue."

"Do you have many people on staff?"

"Not really," said Olivia. She was working on the drawers, the big brown paper bag between her legs was filling up quickly. Bea tried to glance at the things Olivia was throwing out, to make sure it wasn't anything sentimental, but Olivia knew what mattered. She may have known Cliff better than Bea did. Olivia had time and proximity on her side, familiarity simply by seeing him in town and in a business capacity. She continued, "We have a few high school kids who help out with stock and at the register, but for the most part it's just me, Steve, and my parents. They cover for us when they're available, which is most of the time."

"It must be nice to have them around, and so willing to help."

Olivia stopped what she was doing and looked at Bea, both hands still full of desk minutia. Erasers and pencils, paper clips dug out from corners. "I don't know what I'd do without them. Though I've been able to call on other business owners to help in a pinch when Mom and Dad were traveling and something came up. There's a network in town for business owners. We need to get you plugged in, I'll take you to a meeting soon, before the baby comes." She turned back to her sorting and nodded her head with decisiveness.

"The meetings wouldn't happen to be at about five in the morning would they?" Bea asked, remembering Graham coming home in the wee hours of the morning a few weeks ago.

"Actually, they start at about 5:30, and end between 6:30 and 7 in the morning. To make sure all the business owners can attend before everyone's workday gets started. It's basically a support group, almost like Business Owners Anonymous," she laughed to herself.

"Graham's included?" asked Bea, attempting to look busy and not waiting for the answer.

"He is," said Olivia, staring at Bea with a playful grin. Bea's cheeks turned red and then she got up and went across the room where she gathered another stack of papers.

It made sense, piecing together the glimpses Bea had of Graham, that he was connected to the inner circle of the town businesses, the community. A wave of jealousy disappeared, the question about what he was doing with a woman at that early hour of the morning had plagued her for far too long. Attention to detail had benefited her as a photographer, but not so much in her personal life. She was not always able to let the little things go, and tended to nit pick, and in turn not completely trust others.

"5:30," said Bea, "that seems,"

Olivia looked straight at Bea and finished her sentence, "Insane?"

Bea raised her eyebrows, "something like that."

Olivia laughed, "Welcome to small business ownership. We're all a little crazy, but it's worth it. Honestly though, in a perfect world we'd meet at four. As it is, Bert often has to leave early unless he can find someone to open up the diner for him."

Bea noticed just how comfortable Olivia was behind a desk. She was the type of person who exuded a simple confidence wherever she was: in the orchard, behind the wheel of her Jeep, in the hardware shop making spare keys and mixing paint, at a funeral home comforting the bereaved.

"How is Bert?" asked Bea, "I haven't seen him around much since the funeral."

Olivia sighed, "I think it's hitting him hard. He and Cliff were close. After Dan died, he relied on Cliff probably more than anyone else in town. Mostly because Cliff showed up for him, without being asked. If you ever needed anything, I bet Bert would be willing to help out and give you a hand."

"I think he's a little afraid to come back to the orchard."

"You may be right. It must have been awful, seeing Cliff like that." She shuddered, and her voice cracked with emotion. After a few moments she said, "What are you doing for the holidays?"

Bea looked outside, at the gray sky. "I don't know. My parents invited me for Thanksgiving, but I'm not sure I want to go."

"You're always welcome at our place, well, at Mom and Dad's place. They put on a huge spread every year. I think Graham is joining us, among a few other stragglers."

"He's not going to his parents?"

She shook her head, "No, I think they're already in Florida. And this time of year picks up for him. People love buying old collections of books for Christmas gifts."

"My mom would be devastated if I spent the holiday with someone else's parents, especially since we're currently in the same state."

"So why don't you go?"

"I'm not sure I could get away from all of this," Bea

231

looked back outside, at the barn. She thought about Henry, not that she did much to help him, but she wasn't sure she wanted to leave him.

Olivia leaned back and thought for a moment. "You do have a neighbor who knows the ins and outs of the orchard. And it's not like this is the busy season. Things are winding down, right? And by Thanksgiving you'll be getting ready for a quiet stretch anyway. Cliff was always twiddling his thumbs from Thanksgiving until February. He was in town way more than any other time of the year."

"That's true. I've been reading through his notebooks, and there aren't any action items after everything gets stored away for winter. I don't want to impose on anyone though, or look like I'm running away."

"Bea," said Olivia, her voice a concoction of firm tenderness, "by this point no one would begrudge you a little escape, and no one would think you were giving up. You made it through the harvest, you made it through the funeral, you made it through the first few weeks."

Bea gave Olivia, or herself, that.

It was quiet in the office aside form the shuffling of paper, and a steady stream of music coming from the living room where Bea had set up a bunch of CD's in Cliff's old disc changer. There was a mix of classical music, the Beatles, and Dave Matthews Band on random. They all screamed Cliff: eclectic, constant, and classic. The two women thumbed through pages of bills and invoices, following the rule of throwing out anything seven years or older. Seeing one of June's invoices reminded Bea that she had run into Cliff's lawyer at the organic co-op earlier in the week, and she wanted to know how things were going at the orchard. Bea lamented about the state of affairs in terms of paperwork, and June laughed, commenting that at least he kept his appointments and was true to any word he gave, including updating his will every other year on the dot.

"Snacks?" Bea asked when it got too quiet and the CD's needed restarting.

In the kitchen she stopped and took a breath. Olivia's humming filled the house, all the way from the study. Bea could finally picture Olivia as a mother. To Bea, she'd always been just Olivia, even when she got married to Steve, and so it took Bea a bit to warm to the idea of Olivia becoming someone's mother. Olivia was her own person, an individual, which is why it surprised Bea when she took on the store. When she stayed.

Maybe staying said more about a person than leaving.

As she waited for the kettle to boil, she grabbed an ancient teapot from the cabinet and added in some peppermint tea. On a tray she arranged sliced apples and cheese, crackers and a handful of grapes, all from various shops in town. Except the apples, they were as local as they could get.

Outside was still gray. November felt like that: dark, dismal. Even from childhood she remembered November with a bit of a pit in her stomach, an ominous feeling. Thanksgiving always seemed too little, too late to save the month from itself.

The kettle whistled and Bea poured hot water over the peppermint tea - steam wafted and disappeared into the air.

The tray was heavy with the weight of the food and tea pot, but Bea noticed her arms felt stronger than they had in years. She prided herself on agility with the camera, with squatting for long periods of time to get a shot, and being nimble enough to climb into trees, but after a month of being back at the orchard, Bea's body was strong in places and ways she didn't expect.

In the study Olivia was sitting up with attention, staring at a photo in her hand. She looked at Bea who walked towards the desk and put the tray down on an even stack of papers. Olivia's face was puzzled, her brows drawn together.

"Take a look at this photo, Bea. It looks just like you, but it can't be."

"It's my mother," said Bea as she held the photo and marveled. What struck her most was Donna's smile, it looked genuine. It was foreign to Bea.

"Why would Cliff have a photo of your mother?"

"I don't know," Bea said, sitting down. It felt as though the wind had been knocked out of her and her reality began to swirl.

The woman in the picture was her mother, but it wasn't the woman Bea knew. Her hair was full of 1980's flair, big bangs along with her shoulder length bob. Legs a mile long and smile a mile wide. Her eyes were happy, they glittered even in the sepia and fingerprint soaked photo. The edges were curling, it had been touched with too much orchard and salt air for it to age well.

And yet, her mother was staring back at Bea. Full of something Bea had never seen in her. Happiness.

"Maybe I should go to my parents for Thanksgiving,"

"Maybe you should," said Olivia. She watched Bea closely, as if she was going to snap, as if her whole world changed.

But Bea didn't snap. She put the photograph aside and poured two cups of tea. They drank their tea and ate their snacks and finished their work for the day. Olivia went home to her husband, and Bea finished the night in the bathtub. There was an old claw-foot tub in the upstairs bathroom where she soaked for hours, looking at the ceiling, emptying the cold water and then refilling it again and again, thinking of the last time she was at her parents' house.

The last time.

Her father made it known that Bea was foolish. Her

234

mother made it known that Bea couldn't do or say anything to counter his statement. Bea lost her voice, her steam, and left feeling defeated as always, and vowed ever so silently not to return.

But then, she always made the same vow, and she always broke it.

She pulled the plug and as the water drained out of the tub it pulled her skin along with it, and she wanted to sink right down into the pipes with the mini tornado that spun around and around. Instead she sat and felt the weight of the water pulling, tugging, grounding her.

She thought about her mother standing in Cliff's living room, looking wistful. She thought about how Donna never spoke to Cliff, at least around Bea. She thought of how her mother never wanted Bea's time at the orchard mentioned in their home. She thought of the double life Bea felt she lived. Maybe she wasn't the only one.

With Cliff and her grandmother gone, there was only one person who had the answers to her growing list of questions. The problem was, she wasn't so sure Donna would want to answer them. What Bea did know was that she would have better luck finding answers after turkey and endless amounts of wine softened her mother than she would over the phone. Thanksgiving had always been Donna's favorite holiday, and Bea was certain this one in particular would be memorable.

TWENTY-THREE

Bea had a row to herself on the commuter rail to Boston. The red vinyl seats felt stiff and uncomfortable against her back and under her legs. Upon her arrival in Boston she waited for another train out to the suburbs that would take her another twenty minutes farther down the tracks towards her parents.

Graham and Henry had taken her to the station that morning. They sent her off with hugs and promises of the orchard's well-being. Graham's hand lingered on Bea's arm and she blushed when she saw that Henry noticed.

Work had continued at the orchard in the weeks leading up to Thanksgiving. The equipment was cleaned, the apples stored or dispersed, and the grounds were groomed and prepped for the upcoming winter. It was heavy duty work, but the promise of a slow winter made the long, post harvest hours worthwhile to Bea. That, and getting to know both Henry and Graham, her two right hand men, a little better. They worked well together, and she saw why Cliff had relied on them, Graham for his business sense and youthful step, Henry for his steadfast work ethic and loyalty. At times Graham was still hard to read. He was quiet, a little awkward, bookish was too cliche a term to use for someone whose business was books, but Bea would definitely say he was bookish. He never dressed entirely appropriately for labor, the standard uniform didn't apply to him, and at any given moment he looked ready to head off to his real job where clients paid thousands of dollars for decades and centuries old books.

After a quick connection, she was on the final train out to her parents' house, steeling herself against the impending visit. Bea knew she needed to play nice in order to gain the information she came for. Forget giving thanks and grace and being around those you love, she came for the sole purpose of finding out why Cliff had a photograph of her mother hidden in his desk drawer.

She saw him before he saw her. Bea's father stood tall and dashing in a dark suit, looking as though he came straight from a meeting. He was glancing at his watch, and then his cell phone, because he never looked at his phone for the time but he always looked at his phone for updates, business or the weather. His hair was gray and his sunken cheeks were rosy from the cold. While the sun was shining, it only gave the illusion of warmth. Late November outside of Boston was brisk, no matter the temperature.

"Dad!" she said, trying to bring a smile to her lips.

Eric Hampton looked up and recognition flashed across his face.

"Bea. Is that all you've brought?" He said, pointing to the canvas tote bag slung over her shoulder with one hand and putting his phone in the breast pocket of his suit with the other. He reached towards her and there was a sterile, formal embrace followed by a stiff arm around Bea's back as he guided her to the car.

Inside his sleek navy blue Buick sedan the buttery leather bucket seats were a far contrast to the ripped vinyl and lingering smell of body odor and three day old pizza the train boasted.

"Your mother is pleased you decided to grace us with your presence for the long weekend," he said flatly.

"It's been a long time," said Bea, "it'll be good to get away from the orchard for a bit."

He sent her a sideways glance before turning back to the road, "Looking to get away already, are we? It's been what, a month?"

She sighed, "Nearly two. It's been a lot though, all at once. We finished out the harvest season and now everything is packed away for winter,"

"We?" he asked. Bea couldn't tell if he was feigning curiosity or if it was genuine, it was hard to tell with him. Even when she watched her father with business associates Bea could never imagine why people trusted him. He never got excited for much of anything, was relentlessly even keeled, unshakable and unemotional, which didn't always translate to trustworthy in his daughter's eyes.

"I'm not alone on the orchard all the time, Cliff had an army of volunteers," she exaggerated, "and my neighbor, Graham, is a huge help."

She noticed that Eric shifted in his seat when she mention Cliff.

"Your mother told me about your associates, the homeless bum she tripped over."

"Henry. He's actually a huge asset to the orchard." The car went quiet, and for a moment already Bea wished she was back in Cumberland. She had been thinking about how to keep Henry warm all winter, as he still refused a bedroom in the farm house or a couch at Graham's. When the temperature dropped last week Bea took the space heater out to the barn for him, but she didn't know how much of a difference it made.

"And Graham Winters, is it?" asked Eric. He pulled into their neighborhood. The houses were all at least two stories high with expansive lawns, fenced in grounds, the occasional gated property.

"Yes, Graham Winters. He's an antique book dealer."

"The name sounds familiar, but I can't place it," her father's voice was distant, but that was nothing new.

Bea looked out the window, wishing she felt a connection to this place, but instead she felt an ache slowly spread across her chest. She pushed it away as soon as they pulled in the driveway.

Eric carried her bag into the house and dropped it in the foyer. From inside the front door Bea took in the expansive entryway leading to nearly every room on the first floor, and the staircase to the second. There was a sitting room to the right, the living room to the left, down the hall towards the back sat the kitchen, and off to the side under the stairwell was the entrance to Eric's office. Bea couldn't help but compare her childhood home to the modest farmhouse: the ceilings were higher, the light more available, the decor more modern and the paintings larger. It was a home of quiet wealth, modest for Eric's position in business, it spoke to his conservative nature.

Autumnal decorations were spread throughout. The antique table in the entryway held a bowl of cinnamon crusted pine cones and gold dusted acorns. A leaf garland wrapped around the banister on the staircase, reds and oranges danced up to the second floor.

"Welcome home," said Eric his voice full of fact, "your mother must be around here somewhere." He disappeared down the hall.

Bea's feet felt planted into the floor. She looked up the stairs at the wall of memories, photos lined the stairwell. School photos and family shots, posed with tight, rigid smiles. There she was at five, six, seven, and eight, all the way up to high school graduation. They were the type of photographs that were as natural as the sterile painted backdrops.

The sound of her mother's high heels clicking down the hall rescued Bea from going any further down memory lane. Donna walked up the hallway, wiping her hands on a decorative apron that was protecting a crisp white button up shirt and a dark wide legged trousers. Her hair was perfectly blown out, the ends curved in soft rings around her shoulders. The collar of her shirt gave way to Donna's signature pearls.

"I thought I heard the car pull up. Well," she said, "don't just stand there, come here." She walked towards Bea with open arms and a tight smile. They embraced out of formality and Donna ushered her into the house.

Donna brought her into the kitchen and then hurried over to the bubbling pots and pans that covered every burner. A mixing bowl sat on the flour dusted island, a ball of dough and rolling pin at the ready.

"Wow, Mom. Looks like you're getting ready to feed an army."

Donna laughed, "No, just the three of us. But I wanted to get a jump start on things for tomorrow," she said lightly, but Bea knew there was a master list somewhere, a tried and trusted schedule her mother was following.

Bea glanced at the stove, "What's cooking?"

Without looking up from stirring, Donna said "Cranberries and apples for a pie, sausage for the stuffing, and on the back is something new," she picked up the pace and was darting around the kitchen with precise movements. "It's a housewarming thing, the woman at Williams and Sonoma swears by it. It's got citrus and cranberry, cinnamon sticks and rosemary, and it simmers for hours and hours. It's supposed to make your home smell like the holidays. What do you think?" She stopped and looked at Bea with wide eyes, the eagerness in her voice threw Bea, who smiled and nodded encouragingly.

"It's nice, it really makes the place smell like," she struggled for the words and then it was out of her mouth before she could take it back, "home."

Donna put the spoon she was stirring with down and looked straight at Bea and smiled, her eyes looked a little misty. But then again, thought Bea, maybe it was the steam coming off the pan of crumbled sausage.

Donna cleared her throat and turned back to the pans.

"I'm sorry about the way we ended things in Cumberland," she said into the stove top, "I'm glad you're here. It means a great deal."

"I'm glad, too," Bea paused before adding, "I actually have some questions about something I found in Cliff's office,"

Donna waved a wooden spoon in the air, sausage fat dripped and landed on the island counter, "No work talk, at least not until after Thanksgiving," she said.

"It's not work talk," said Bea, but Donna was flitting about in the kitchen and didn't hear her. It was unusual for Bea to see her mother as a domestic goddess. Donna normally didn't enjoy cooking except for Thanksgiving. Most of her dinners were usually catered, or picked up from a specialty shop.

"Why don't you go upstairs and unpack," said Donna, "and I'll make some drinks. Coffee? Tea? Something stronger?"

Something stronger, Bea thought to herself, but she wanted her wits about her. Too many visits had dissolved into pouts and passive aggressive fights and her father closing himself into his study while she and her mother bickered.

But, it was mid afternoon the day before a holiday, a little something couldn't hurt. It might even help.

"I'd love a vodka tonic," said Bea.

Donna turned and gave Bea a smile fit for happy hour at the country club, "Cheers to that. Go unpack and freshen up, and I'll mix up the drinks."

Upstairs Bea didn't have much freshening up to do, and even less to unpack. She slid a few shirts, her pajamas, and undergarments into the empty bureau drawers. The jeans she was wearing would get her through the rest of the visit, though she hadn't decided exactly when that would be. Earlier today she told Graham and Henry to expect her by Sunday at the latest, but she was already missing the comforts of the orchard.

Bea looked with wide eyes around her former bedroom. There were no shelves lined with school trophies. No stacks of her books. No memorabilia on the walls by way of photos or posters. Instead an innocuous nightstand sat next to the bed, an antique wash basin adorned the bureau, and the walls were decorated with Fleur De Lis speckled wallpaper and ornate crown molding around the edges. In the space between two large picture windows was the only frame in the room, and within it, an illustration of Peter Rabbit in Mr. McGregor's garden. Peter's jacket was a water color filled blue and his eyes were tiny and focused on a cabbage that sat in wait. Bea eyed the picture, it was new to her bedroom, but she remembered it hanging in her mother's walk-in-closet. Bea could feel the long dresses she used to hide in while stealing a glimpse of the picture, how she felt held within the layers of fabric.

The print made her think of the first time she met Cliff, a memory that became less and less clear as the years went on. Bea was three or four years old, and when Cliff came into view, she held her grandmother's hand tightly and had to look nearly up into the clouds to find his face. He was as tall and as wide as a lumberjack, with dark hair and a beard that, she would later find out, could hold a dozen pie crumbs. Cliff knelt down and his twinkly blue eyes looked right at Bea, at her level. He extended his hand and she let go of her grandmother to place her own daintily in his and felt the rough hills and plains of calluses. Bea watched as her hand disappeared into his and her jaw dropped in awe. She looked up and saw his smile. Soft, gentle, and kind, it eased any fear she had of the giant man before her.

"Beatrix?" he said, "now, is that with an x or an i-c-e?"

Her hand still in his, she replied, "With an x,"

His smile widened, "Like Beatrix Potter. I once knew a girl who loved Peter Rabbit and Mr. McGregor's garden so much, she went in search of the big wide world for a garden of her own."

"I have all of the Peter Rabbit books," the words tumbled out and then Beatrix scowled at herself. She knew she wasn't supposed to boast.

But Cliff's smile remained, "And is there a garden at your house?"

"Yes, but I'm not allowed to play in it." She let her hand drop from his, and looked to the ground as she kicked the dirt with her shoes. Her grandmother sighed. Her grandmother always sighed when Bea talked about her parents' house.

243

"Beatrix," said Cliff, "do you see that orchard across the street?" he pointed, and Bea craned her neck. She nodded her head even though all she could see were a bunch a trees and a yellow house, "Whenever you're at your grandma's house, you can play at the orchard. Any time. There may even be a few gardens to explore."

They shared a conspiratorial smile, and looking back, Bea could pinpoint that moment as the one that Cliff became Beatrix's friend and protector.

"Dinner will be early tonight," said Donna as she handed Bea a tumbler of fizzy tonic water mixed with vodka, ice cubes clinked against its sides. Bea glanced at the wet bar, it's inventory was plentiful, inviting.

"I have no plans, Mom, so whenever things are ready, that's fine. You'll have to let me know if I can help with anything," she took a sip of the cold, crisp drink. The bitterness of the seltzer, hint of vodka, and a punch of lime all played on her tongue in harmony. The bubbles fizzed up her nose and she searched the table for a coaster to set her glass down on. The coffee table in front of her was filled with perfectly placed tabletop books full of art history and wide angle photos of Europe. Over the years Bea continued to send her published photographs to her parents, whether they were in book or magazine form. None of them were visible. She pushed down the bitterness and disappointment that swelled.

"No plans?" Donna asked.

Bea shook her head.

"Oh," said Donna as Eric walked into the room. Donna straightened her back and fixed her posture, craned her neck a bit.

"I thought maybe you'd want to meet up with some people. Isn't the night before Thanksgiving the biggest night for getting together with old friends?"

Bea laughed into her glass, "What friends?"

Her father went to the bar and poured himself a bourbon. More ice cubes, more tinkling against glass, more tension.

"What about those girls you hung around with in high school?" asked Donna, challenging Bea's blank stare with a wide grin. "Eric, don't you remember? Who was it that used to come over? There was a group of girls,"

"I don't remember, darling."

"Oh, but wasn't one of them a client's daughter?"

Eric shrugged, "I really can't recall, Donna."

"Maybe you're thinking of a few study groups, Mom. But there wasn't anyone I would call a friend."

"Oh, please, you can't tell me you were friendless in school. There has to be someone you'd want to catch up with."

Shaking her head, Bea downed the remainder of her now watery vodka flavored tonic and set the empty glass on the table.

"Another one?" asked Eric.

"No, I'd better pace myself."

He gave her a small smile.

"Really, Mom, there's no one I want to catch up with. I knew people, but I don't think anyone remembers me."

"What about on Facebook? Do you keep in touch with anyone?"

"I don't remember the last time I went on Facebook, Mom."

"Hmph. You should get your head out of the sand now and again, otherwise you'll end up alone at the orchard."

"Donna," said Eric.

"That is, if you stay there long enough,"

"Donna, that's enough."

Bea looked from one to the other, unsure of what was happening. How many drinks did Donna have while in the kitchen? And her father, he was never one to stop an insult from flying Bea's way.

Donna looked at Eric with a pout.

"How is your garden, Mom?" asked Bea, desperate for a change in subject.

Donna's face transformed into softness, she beamed, "Now it's mostly just mums and squash, we're getting it set for winter, but this summer it was heaven. The vegetables did so well, didn't they, Eric?" Eric nodded.

"You planted vegetables?" said Bea, from her memory, her mother only ever planted and maintained flowers. Blossoms thrived under Donna's careful pruning.

Donna nodded, "Yes, and I became quite the Mr. McGregor to the little Peter Rabbits that tried to sneak in to steal my lettuce, sneaky buggers," she chuckled a low, conspiratorial laugh and gazed at Eric.

He said with a hint of pride, "You should tell her about the pumpkins."

"Your father didn't say anything when you came in?" asked Donna. Bea shook her head no, and sucked the last of the alcohol out of an ice cube. "We grew the pumpkins that are on the front steps, as well as the ones across the street on the Smith's porch," continued Donna, her voice proud.

"Wow, that's great, Mom," said Bea, and she surprised herself with her sincerity.

"So things at the orchard," said Eric, "are they going well?"

"They're getting there. Like I said in the car, we finished out the harvest season, and are ready for winter. I'm starting to look through Cliff's journals and notes-"

Donna interrupted, "Journals?" her fingers reached for the pearls at her neck.

Bea explained, "Cliff kept a diary of sorts to keep track of work. What got done during each season, each month, even down to each week."

Donna let out a sound of relief, and slumped into her chair.

Eric gave his wife a look, Bea couldn't tell what it meant, she'd never seen it before. Maybe a blend of pity and disgust, whatever it was she was glad she wasn't on the receiving end. But Donna missed it, she was sitting with her eyes closed and didn't see her husband glaring at her.

"Was it a profitable year?" he refocused his attention on Bea.

"From what I can gather, it was. The orchard has never been about profit, but more about serving the community," Eric raised an eyebrow, Bea ignored it, "so from that standpoint, we were able to make sure all the accounts were taken care of in the community, and we weren't in the hole."

"It's always about profit," he said firmly.

The alcohol had gone to her head, and Bea was starting to feel a bit fuzzy, the edges of the room blurred, "I guess it depends if you're looking for a monetary profit, or a soul satisfying profit."

Eric's laugh was thin. He was still standing, and towered over Bea even from the other side of the room. "Satisfying the soul has never saved a business," he said.

Bea let his remark hang in the air. The bar was looking more and more inviting, and so Bea made her way over and helped herself.

247

TWENTY-FOUR

Thanksgiving morning arrived along with the smells of roast turkey and pumpkin pie. Laying in bed, Bea imagined the ovens full and her mother frantically moving around the kitchen like a worker bee.

The clock on the nightstand read nine, later than Bea had slept since her arrival at the orchard. Her head felt heavy, and her tongue coated with a nasty film, she couldn't remember if she brushed her teeth before falling into bed the night before. Last night there was an early dinner of steak tip salads prepared by the caterer down the road, followed by many glasses of wine and much talk of Bea's lack of friends.

Bea didn't realize she came home for any social engagements besides visiting her parents, she thought that was enough.

She shielded her eyes as she pulled the curtains back and light filled the bedroom, the sky was crisp and blue. In the bathroom she searched the medicine cabinet, it was full of band aides and mini shampoos and lotions, but no pain reliever. Bea twisted her hair up in a messy bun, brushed her teeth quickly, and headed downstairs.

Eric was at the breakfast nook with a cup of coffee and the newspaper - even on a holiday - and Donna was bustling around, her brow furrowed and streaked with flour. It was a sweet, unexpected scene. Bea wondered if this was their norm, if there was a harmony they had reached that was never attainable when Bea was present. Maybe Bea was the odd one out, the creator of stress and tension, the problem.

She shook the thought out of her head and quietly walked over to the coffee maker where there was half a pot waiting for her.

Eric looked over his newspaper and raised an eyebrow, "Morning, sleeping beauty."

"Bea, please, I'm trying to get the second pie in the oven," said Donna without making eye contact while shoving Bea aside with her hip. Bea's arms flew up, hot coffee splashed over the side of her mug and on to the floor.

"Happy Thanksgiving," muttered Bea as she mopped up the coffee with one swoop of a paper towel before escaping the war path and walking over to the table.

"It'll be a happy Thanksgiving when all the cooking is done," huffed Donna.

Eric put down his newspaper, "Tell me again why you go through this every year?"

Donna stood tall with her hands on her hips. She was wearing the same decorative apron as yesterday over a black crew neck sweater with the collar of a white button up peeking out, and a pair of gray slacks. Bea looked down at her own pajamas, if you could call them that. Yoga pants and a tee shirt would never live up to Donna Hampton's standards.

"I do this every year," Donna said slowly, "for tradition's sake. To celebrate all that we have to be thankful for. For you, for Beatrix, for our home, friends, and security."

"It's a lovely thought, dear, but I'm not sure it's worth the aggravation you put yourself through."

"But it's my favorite holiday!" she exclaimed with indignation.

"It sure looks like it," said Eric as he went back to reading his newspaper.

Bea sipped her coffee and looked out the window at the fenced in, contained yard. A longing for the orchard swept over her, Cumberland felt a lifetime away.

"So it's just us today," said Bea, mostly to herself.

Eric lowered the newspaper and looked at her with eyes that she hadn't paid much attention to over her lifetime. More accurately, eyes she had spent a lifetime avoiding. Today she noticed they were lined with fatigue and impatience.

"Who were you expecting?" he asked, his words clipped.

She shrugged, and looked back outside. "No one," she said. Bea half expected, or hoped for, someone from Eric's office or a neighbor. Someone, anyone, to take the focus off her.

But it looked to be a Hampton Family day. Her mother would cook in a storm, and they would give thanks and eat, and then they would all go to their separate corners of the house, only to reconvene at the end of the day in front of the television for the Wizard of Oz. At least, that's what Bea and her mother always did on Thanksgiving. A smile tentatively played on Bea's lips as she remembered the only part of Thanksgivings past she thought of fondly, leftover pie eaten right out of the dish with mounds of whipped cream on top, tartan blankets on the couch, and her mother humming Somewhere Over the Rainbow. But they had to get through the day first.

She escaped the kitchen after finishing her coffee with the promise of coming down to help after a quick shower. It appeared Donna was fixing to feed an army, so the work was plentiful.

While Bea felt bound by duty to rush through a shower and get dressed, her phone beckoned. At the orchard there was hardly any time to waste scrolling. She had finally managed to import Cliff's contacts into her phone and had forwarded his calls to her number. In doing so it initially rang off the hook. But the combination of the change in seasons and the holiday had brought with it quieter times. Still, at the orchard, there was always something to do. But right now, the phone looked like a beautiful distraction, and she scrolled through her news feeds before opening Pinterest.

A text message pinged in her notifications, interrupting her search for newborn photo session inspiration on Pinterest. She looked at the messages and her stomach flipped.

"Happy Thanksgiving" read a text from Graham.

It pinged again,

"Happy Thanksgiving!! Xo"

Bea's brow furrowed until she saw that it was a group text, not just one to her specifically. The last message came from Olivia. Another few dings, and it was apparent that it was a locals only group, and Bea was thrilled to be included. She sent a quick greeting back, and then a message to just Graham.

"How's the orchard?"

She held her breath as she waited.

A message came through almost immediately,

"Everything is fine, holding down the fort. Potatoes on the stove to take to O's parents. How R U?"

Texting with Graham was something new, and Bea laughed to herself at his abbreviations. She thought he would be a stickler for whole words and accurate spelling, but he surprised her with his texting lingo.

They went back and forth with a few innocent texts, and she beamed as she ran into the shower, so much so that she chose to ignore the strained voices and the clatter of dishes from the kitchen below.

Dinner was an elegant affair, starting off with Champagne while Christmas music played quietly in the background, hand bell choirs and Bing Crosby. The dark-wood inlay table was covered down the center with a deep crimson woven table runner flaked with gold fibers, on top of which sat a basket full of decorative colored corn on the cob with stiff dried husks.

The Hampton's stood on ceremony, whatever ill words were spoken in the kitchen - and there were many - passed when they came together in the dining room. Eric stood at the head of the table and carved the turkey, Donna and Bea sat on either side of him. They passed the turkey and cranberry sauce, potatoes and gravy.

"Calories don't count today," chirped Donna, piling her plate high with a mountain of mashed potatoes. Bea didn't tell her mother that she never counted them. Bea didn't tell her mother a lot of things and her tongue paid the price, it was swollen in the places she chomped on to stop herself from speaking.

They fell into the same silence Bea remembered from every meal ever shared at this house. Her stomach ached and twisted with unspoken words. While the food tasted delicious, it left behind a bitter feeling of guilt and discomfort. Bea longed for home, for the orchard, for Cliff. Tears formed at the corner of her eyes and she swallowed through the lump in her throat. She looked up at the ceiling to collect herself. She knew neither one of her parents would notice her emotions, neither one were focused on anything but their plates and getting through the meal.

"So what are we thankful for this year?" Eric's voice boomed over Nat King Cole's Christmas Song.

Donna cleared her throat, "I'm thankful that we're all together. It's been so long," her voice dipped with a guilt inducing pout, and she looked right at Bea, "and of course, I'm thankful for my family. For my wonderful husband, and my daughter. I'm thankful for this day and the food I slaved away for hours on, and I'm thankful for the stability you've always given me, Eric." She patted his hand and they shared a gaze. He smiled at her briefly and then lowered his eyes.

"I'm thankful," he started, "for the opportunity that Bea has been handed, and the security of her new role."

Bea scoffed and moved her potatoes around on her plate. He continued, "I'm thankful for Cliff," Bea looked across the table and saw her mother's eyes wide with surprise, "and what he was able to do for our daughter," he patted Donna's hand again, "and I'm thankful for this incredible meal you masterfully whipped up." He smiled at her and then looked to Bea, "Bea?"

Bea was gobsmacked, and suddenly fifteen again, twelve again, ten again, and was looking for the right answer. One that wouldn't disappoint or cause a fight or end up with a shameful reproach from her parents.

Donna and Eric both put down their forks and waited for her answer. Donna's gaze was amused, Eric's expectant.

It felt like a test.

And so, like a dutiful daughter, she said, "I'm thankful for my parents," she looked from one to the other, and then back

253

down to her plate, "and for this incredible meal. I'm thankful for the hidden blessings in this year, the past few months especially. And I'm thankful for new friends and old ones." She was thinking of Graham and Olivia, Henry and Cliff, and the countless others who were waiting for her in Cumberland.

She grabbed her wine glass and smiled, raising a toast to gratitude. There were clinks all around and Bea took a long pull of red wine, and let the contents go straight to her head. Earlier she had looked at the bottle, it was a Turley Mead Ranch Zinfandel, out of her price range, but a staple at her parents' home.

"You know, Cliff was storing a few boxes of Grandma's things for me," Bea was testing the waters. The wine made her brave.

Donna raised an eyebrow, "I thought we emptied her place, I should have known he would go over there, though I gave explicit orders for him not to."

"It sounded like they were left behind."

Eric put down his fork and asked, "What was in them?"

"Her chickadee figurines and some old books. I took the books over to Graham for him to appraise. They're probably nothing, but they looked old."

"Your grandmother and those damned chickadees. You know, she made a point of telling me, right before we got married, how I reminded her of those birds," she took a big gulp of her wine, leaving Bea and Eric waiting for the rest of the story.

Bea took the bait, "How so?"

"Because they're social climbers," said Donna dryly.

Bea looked down at her plate. The clink of silverware against china and jingle bells playing softly in the background filled the space left by Donna's words.

"One time," Bea said, "Grandma was telling me about how chickadees don't really migrate, except for the young ones.

Every now and then the young birds will fly south to explore, but the older birds, the more mature ones, stay close to home. They know that home is better than anything out there, but they had to have the experience to know that, " Bea smiled at the memory. It was right before Bea went off to college. She was devastated at the idea of less time in Cumberland, the unknown of how often she'd actually get home to see her grandmother and Cliff and the orchard. She'd miss the best parts of picking season. It turned out she would make it home for more weekends than not, but she didn't know it then. Bea and Sylvia sat on the front porch, Bea looked across the street longingly at the orchard, and her grandmother told her the story about chickadees. Somehow, it comforted Bea.

"Well," Eric cleared his throat, "You'll have to let us know what this Graham says about the books."

Donna's shrill laughter echoed through the room, "I can't imagine she had anything worth much. But yes, let us know," she took another long drink of wine and when she put her glass down a wave of crimson liquid sloshed onto the table cloth. Donna didn't notice, but Bea did. Bea always noticed when things were starting to get messy.

After dinner Bea and Donna settled into the kitchen. The turkey carcass was on the counter, meat stripped and ready for someone - probably not Donna - to make it into soup stock. There were containers full of turkey, potatoes, and even cranberry sauce. A jar of gravy sat congealing on the counter top.

Eric was hidden away in his study. Bea and Donna were both tipsy from the wine and drowsy from the turkey. Bea's defenses were down, and she assumed the same of her mother's. It was the perfect time for Bea to ask questions.

"Hand me the skillet from the stove, Bea," commanded Donna. Her lips were stained purple, and as she wiped her hair away from her face with the back of her hand a few wisps stuck to her forehead.

The skillet felt heavy in Bea's hands as she brought it from the stove to the sink. Donna sprinkled kosher salt over the bottom of the pan and scrubbed it with a dish cloth.

She caught the question in Bea's gaze.

"Don't tell me you've never seen me do this," Bea shook her head, so Donna continued, "You must have a bunch of these at the orchard, you'll have to know how to take care of them."

"There's a few skillets hanging on the wall, I haven't used them yet. I knew there was something special you had to do with them, but I wasn't sure. I haven't had a chance to look it up yet."

"Your grandmother taught me. This," she raised the pan a bit, "is one of hers. You have to season them well, take care of them and they'll see you through years and years. They'll outlive you," she paused and arched her back before continuing. "First of all, you never use soap in a cast iron pan. Ever. You'll damage it, and then have to start all over again. These pans have been seasoned properly, every so many years. You heat it to a very high temperature in the oven, and then coat it with oil. Heat it again, and coat it again. And so on. From then on you should be able to wipe it out after each use, but if there's bits left you can use salt as an abrasive, or scrape it out with a metal spatula. Then you heat it on the stove top to get rid of any moisture, and rub a bit of oil in it. Simple." she said with a weak smile and used the back of her hand to wipe the hair out of her face once more.

"Thanks, Mom. I'll have to remember that," Bea paused as she watched Donna scrub and scrape, her mother's face softened with each scratch of the pan.

"I found something at Cliff's," said Bea. Her heart was in her throat, it beat fast and her face turned red.

"Oh?"

"It's a photograph," said Bea, Donna kept scrubbing, "of you." The scraping stopped for a brief moment and then started again, Donna moved faster, her movements were more erratic the quicker she went. "Why would he have a photo of you?"

Donna shrugged, "Maybe it was from mom's house? It sounds like he helped himself to some of her belongings when we weren't looking," her voice had a wine fueled edge to it, at least that's what Bea told herself, but it could have been Donna's regular edge.

"But why would he do that?"

"I don't know, Beatrix. Maybe Cliff had his secrets."

"Are you one of them?"

"I'm just saying, you don't know everything about everything."

"Obviously," said Bea, "that's why I'm asking you. I thought you could help. The only other person who could answer my questions is dead."

"Cliff? If he hadn't told you anything by now, he never would have."

"Grandma."

Donna stopped scrubbing the pan. She wiped out the contents, the salt soaked with cooking grease and leftover bits of gravy. She slammed it down against the gas burner so hard the stove was lucky it didn't break under the force.

"And I think you're wrong," Bea said to Donna's back. Bea's irritation masked itself as bravery, "I think Cliff would have told me whatever secret he was keeping, eventually. But we were cut short. He died before he could share parts of his life that I had just started asking questions about. Why he left his family for the orchard, why he never married, if there was someone special for him - he said there was, once, long ago. But it was a story for another time. A time that never came."

The kitchen went quiet, and Donna's back straightened with resolve as she turned to Bea. She put one hand on the counter, the other on her hip.

"Are you finished?" she asked.

Bea gawked at her. Donna left the room, ending the conversation, leaving Bea with an open mouth and tears in her eyes.

Night fell and there was no Wizard of Oz. The house echoed with loneliness. Bea took a hot bath and tried to figure out how long she could stay at her parent's and keep her sanity. How long before anger took over and ate away at her.

The scalding bath turned her skin pink. Steam filled the air. Her head pounded, especially when she started thinking about how many baths she had taken over the years, for escape purposes only. For years there was nowhere else to go, nothing to do, and she locked the door and escaped the tension for a while. She could imagine that she was in a sauna, someplace exotic and far away, a steam room, or a Grecian bath. It was during those baths that Bea started to plan her escape, to anywhere but here. When she was young she spent time dreaming about Sylvia's house, but then she eventually needed someplace even farther away.

Her travels yielded incredible photos and experiences. She saw the faces of life and death and all stages between. She met strangers who turned into spiritual guides and friends who turned into strangers. But through all of her travels, there was never a place that felt like home. No place that she yearned for the way that some spoke of a childhood home or a current space. Even a favorite town. She didn't realize it at the time, but from the very start, she was searching for her very own place in the world.

And the orchard was it. All that time, it was across the street from her Grandmother's house.

Out of the bath she wrapped herself in a fluffy terry cloth towel. It was thicker than three of the ones she used at the farmhouse.

Even if she couldn't get the answers she was looking for while she was here, maybe she could get started on planning for the winter months. Back in the bedroom she pulled on her pajamas, they felt soft and cool against her overheated skin, and she felt an energy swell within her as she reached for her phone and scrolled through pictures she took before leaving on Wednesday. Bea didn't know what she was thinking, maybe that her parents would want updates, visuals, of her work. Maybe they'd be interested in more than the business aspect of it. But why would they? Cumberland was never a place of happy memories for them, at least not together.

She started jotting down bits and pieces of thoughts in her notebook, things she wanted to try and other things she needed to look into, reminders for herself about the last few weeks that she didn't want to forget. She spent a page per person she knew who was related to the orchard, and listed questions for each. For Henry. For Graham. For Olivia. For Bert, Ron, William, and Anna. She filled more pages than she could count before her stomach rumbled with hunger.

After poking her head out of the doorway, she found the house quiet and still. Downstairs the lights were dimmed for the night, and she knew not to open a door for fear of setting off the alarm. Bea didn't know the passwords to disarm it any more. She was told the last time she visited that they had been changed, but the new codes were never shared. She never got the memo.

In the kitchen the remains of Thanksgiving were swept away, hidden in the refrigerator and within cabinets. The counters were clean and the sink was empty. No one would have guessed there was an expansive meal served just hours earlier.

In the fridge Bea found an entire pumpkin pie and a can of whipped cream. She hesitated over its perfection only briefly before cutting herself a double slice and topping it with a hefty swirl of whipped cream, though she winced at the noise from the aerosol. The pie tasted silky and smooth. Without anyone watching her, she shoved in bite after bite, her hunger grew deeper with each forkful.

Bea's mouth was full of pie when she heard footsteps. She quickly brushed away crumbs from her mouth to try and make herself look a little more presentable.

"Midnight snack?" Donna said as her head came into view. She was wrapped in a soft pink bathrobe, her face scrubbed free of makeup and she had swapped her contacts for wire rimmed glasses.

"Want some?" Bea asked, gesturing to her plate.

Donna shook her head, "No, I just wanted some tea." She filled the kettle with tap water and set it on the stove. Standing across the island from Bea, she was quiet. She fidgeted with the tag of the tea bag that hung over her cup as she waited for the water to boil.

Bea chewed a bite of pie so much that it began to lose its flavor.

Moments dragged slowly before the kettle whistled. Donna was dunking her tea bag in and out of the mug when Bea opened her notebook. Wordlessly, Bea slid the photograph across the counter and took another bite of pie.

Donna inhaled sharply. "I was so young, you understand,"

she whispered.

"No," said Bea, "I don't." She put her fork down, and pushed away the plate. Her arms crossed in front of her and she leaned on them heavily. "Tell me."

Donna sighed, and then she told her daughter about the photograph.

TWENTY-FIVE

"We had a summer together," Donna started. "You and Cliff?" Bea's stomach flipped and she couldn't help the curiosity that stemmed from that one statement, it was even more than from seeing the picture.

Donna nodded and continued, "Eric and I met at college, you know that, but the summer before we were married I had an opportunity to visit a friend of mine on the Cape for the season. Her family summered out there, they had an extra bedroom and Trish was always looking for company. Eric was already working in the city, and we thought it would be good for me to relieve some stress while the wedding coordinators did their thing. He could answer most of the questions leading up to the day, and I could visit with friends and get a good tan," she stopped to sip her tea, she laughed a bit to herself, "back then it was all baby oil and laying out for hours on end. We had no idea of the consequences and the money we'd spend later to repair the damage," she sighed.

Bea sat quietly, waiting for her to get back to Cliff.

"One evening Trish and I went out to a hole in the wall for dinner, real salt of the earth type of place. Dingy, but they had the best fried clams, and back then the fried food didn't go straight to my waist," she sighed. "The line snaked out the door and around the building, and we were waiting forever. I was getting pretty fed up, and we almost left, except I bumped into this guy behind me."

"Cliff?"

"Cliff. He was so tall, and his smile was so," she paused while she looked for the right word, "honest. He apologized for being in my way, imagine that, when I was the one who bumped into him. I was done for. His eyes, well, you know what they looked like, but back then I swear they were even clearer, brighter, they drew me in."

Bea pictured a young Cliff. Between his kindness and his looks, she could never understand why he was perpetually single.

"Didn't he see the ring on your finger?"

Donna shook her head, "I took it off, left it at the beach house in a safe so I wouldn't lose it on the beach or in the ocean. I was so sure of myself, and of Eric, that I didn't think there would ever be a time that I looked elsewhere." Her voice was hushed, quiet, but there was still very little emotion. She was telling Bea a story over a cup of tea, with a hint of gossip but otherwise it was a story of people who were so far removed from the ones at the table.

"It was an instant attraction, even Trish noticed. She took her food to go, I stayed and sat with Cliff that evening, our first date. Trish had never liked Eric, and so she thought she was actually doing me a favor." Bea realized she'd never heard of Trish before. "We sat at the restaurant for so long that the people behind the counter started to stare at us, it was one of those places with a quick turn over of tables, and they were losing business

263

every time someone walked by and saw the place was full. But we didn't care. We talked for hours, and then he walked me home, the long way past the harbor and the boardwalk, I can still remember the smell of the Cape," she paused, as if taken by the memory.

"Not like Cumberland?"

She shook her head, "No, that was the thing. It was similar enough to make it feel like home, but the smell of the ocean was so much more intense everywhere on the Cape. You become immersed in the sea, the fish and tide. In Cumberland the main smell was still land, at the Cape, it's the sea. And at that time, I didn't realize it but I guess I was looking to get swept away by something. Cliff was both familiar and exotic in his own way. He wasn't like Eric or the like the boys I knew from home, but he somehow felt like the best of both of them." She sipped her tea, the edges of her eyes crinkled. Donna shrugged, "It was a wild few weeks, really. Trish encouraged every encounter with Cliff, and Cliff and I were head over heels for each other. He showed me the Cape during his free time, and told me about his hopes of getting off island. He wanted to follow his own dreams and pursuits, to connect with land, not the sea, and he desperately wanted to forge his own way.

"I told him about Cumberland. How the landscape rolled from marshes to farmland. How the community was tight, almost oppressive. How, at the time, land was coming up for sale because the older generation was tired, worn out, and so many of my peers left for college and never came back."

"You led him to Cumberland?" Bea asked, incredulously.

"No," she said firmly and then her face softened, "well, I never meant to." She straightened and walked to the kitchen sink, filled the kettle again and set it back on the stove top. She walked back to the island slowly, not making eye contact. She fiddled with her tea cup, the paper tag of the already used tea bag. Bea's cheeks burned and her heart raced. This story was not what she had imagined, though right now she was not sure exactly what it was she had hoped for.

"I was of course smitten with Cliff, but always knew it would only be a summer fling. We had an intense attraction, but Cliff's plans were far from stable. Eric offered a secure future and the life I wanted. I wanted to get away from Cumberland and all the memories it held, I didn't hold any romantic notion of it."

"But Cliff didn't know that?" said Bea, wondering to herself what memories of her mother's were so bad.

"No, I didn't tell Cliff any of that. By the end of the summer he had fallen completely in love with me, but I think more so with the idea of where I came from. He talked about coming out to visit me after the summer ended, but I always left things vague. Said I might be moving, that I wasn't sure I wanted to live in the same place I grew up, just like he had said about the Cape. At the end of the summer I didn't give him any contact information. I left a day earlier than I had planned, and gave him a letter via Trish. It explained everything. I told him I was getting married and not going back to Cumberland, that the summer was something I would hold onto forever, but he'd never hear from me again."

Bea sat back in her chair, stunned.

"I just left. I went to Cumberland for a quick visit with Mom before going back to live with Eric. She knew something was going on, but I didn't say anything. I just went on with the plan. We got married that September, and started our lives together. In the days leading up to the wedding, Trish tried to talk me out of going through with it. She told me about her last few days on the island, how Cliff reacted to the letter. He was calm, quiet, but it devastated him."

"You devastated him," Bea corrected her. She wanted to be kind, but there was something in the way Donna was distancing herself from the story, her actions, that made Bea want to prod.

Donna cocked her head to the side and gave Bea a warning look with a raised eyebrow. "By Thanksgiving I was settling into life as a married woman, the summer was behind me and I rarely thought of Cliff. Eric had an overseas business trip over the long holiday weekend, and so I thought it would be a perfect time to go back to my mother's to get the recipes of hers that I never knew I wanted. To see how she prepared a big feast. Well, I came back and found that the orchard across the street had sold, and my mother had taken on the new owner as a charity case of sorts."

Bea's eyes went wide, "And it was him."

"It was him," she said solemnly. "At first he had no idea his neighbor was my mother. But once he got to know her, once he was invited over for dinner and saw the family photos on the wall, he knew. My mother got hints of our acquaintance, she put two and two together without him even saying a word. When I saw him that first time at Mom's it was like no time had passed, and the letter was never written. My Thanksgiving visit became a whirlwind affair with Cliff."

"How long did it go on after that?"

"It didn't. That was the end of it. When I left after that visit, I made it clear. There was very little room for Cliff in our lives."

"How could you compartmentalize?" Bea asked, once again indignant.

"You have always been just like your father - driven by emotion."

"Dad's not like that."

Donna's stare was hard, and yet there was a little bit of laughter behind it. A cruel bit of laughter revealing that the wool had been pulled over Bea's head for so long.

"But Cliff was," said Bea, and her mother looked at her and the cruelty disappeared for only a moment, and in that brief stretch of time relief spread over Donna's face.

"I can't believe you never figured it out," she said, the brittleness of cruelty returned, "Eric knew. He knew the moment he laid eyes you."

"But we don't look that different, me and," and for the first time, Bea was not sure what to call him, Dad or Eric.

"Just enough though. Mother sent me a copy of the Cumberland Times the first winter of our marriage, there was a write up about Cliff and the orchard, picture included. Eric of course wondered why she sent it to me, but I played it off as just her wanting to keep me in the loop. He was suspicious, and must have committed that photo of Cliff to memory. Eric always assessed his competition. He knew his enemies better than his friends."

"I don't understand, why would anyone want to live like that?"

"We have certain agreements. This was an unspoken one. Our relationship might not look like any other, but it works for us."

"Does it really?"

"Resignation is a part of every marriage, it just comes at different times for everyone. It came earlier for us than most."

Silence and a stark new reality spread within the space between them.

"Cliff knew all along," said Bea, dumbfounded. Her stomach was in knots, and at the same time there were butterflies giving wings to truth.

Donna nodded her head, "I never had to spell it out for him. He just knew," she cleared her throat and stood tall, "and he knew not to say anything. We had a few moments here and there, but mostly he got word about you through your grandmother."

"Grandma knew," it was hitting Bea just how many people were involved in the deception of her life.

"She did. She told me she didn't agree with what I was doing, but she understood why. She also never failed to mention how I was hurting Cliff. She had to convince me to start bringing you to her house. I didn't until you were three. I kept you to myself those first few years, your Grandmother would come visit, and eventually it seemed like a good idea to send you up to Cumberland with her, to give me a break and I suppose part of me thought I was doing a good deed by sharing you. But then it all changed when you fell in love with Cliff. Mom told me how it tore him up not to be known as your father. I never caught wind of anger. Sadness, maybe, but I looked at it like we shared custody. He got to see you more than he would have if we were to arrange an actual custody agreement. And Eric, well, Eric never really wanted children. He wanted them on paper. You know how that worked out."

"I still don't understand, it seems like such a shit deal for Cliff."

"Cliff was realistic. Once he realized I wasn't going to leave Eric, he knew not to try to fight. Eric is a powerful man, with money to fight any battle."

"Except a paternity test."

"Even still. Cliff would never have won custody. This way, he was able to save face, and still see you. Really, I gave him a huge gift, without strings. I could have made it difficult, I had every right to. But it worked out for everyone. And in the end, he knew what he was doing, leaving you the orchard like that. He left you with the truth in his own way."

Donna was cold. She showed little remorse. Her voice didn't strain or waver.

"He must have loved you very much to go through all of that," whispered Bea.

"He may have, or he just knew what he was up against. He was no match for the life I wanted to live. What I wanted to have."

"Would you have ever told me?" asked Bea, not sure if she really wanted to know the answer.

Donna didn't hesitate, she looked Bea straight in the eye, gave her a cold, chilling stare. "No."

"What kind of mother…" Bea's voice trailed off, but Donna stood straight up with fire in her eyes.

"Beatrix Hampton. You listen to me. I was a good mother. I did the work. I picked up used tissues when you were sick, I bathed you, I dried tears and picked up dishes and fed you. Clothed you. I signed off on report cards and went to parent teacher nights. I was here. All the while you were ungrateful. You still are. You came home from Cumberland all those times thinking Cliff was amazing. Thinking your Grandmother was so much better than me. Do you know how that hurt me? Do you know what that did to me? But I still let you go. You're welcome. That was my gift to you and to him, I let you go knowing you liked it better than being with me. That's the kind of mother I am."

Bea had heard enough, she took her dishes to the sink, and then turned without looking at Donna and headed towards the stairs. There was nowhere to go outside of the house, it was cold and dark and without a car, her options were limited. The only thing Bea knew was that she couldn't stay in the same room as her mother.

She started up the stairs and glanced through the doorway. Donna stood at the kitchen island, staring resolutely at the wall in front of her. Closed off to the end.

Bea woke with a start, she must have just fallen asleep, when her bedroom door opened. Sitting up on her forearm she looked through the darkness to see a familiar shape walk in. It had been years, but Bea remembered.

Donna slipped in next to Bea, gently moving covers. Bea's head hit the pillow, she was flooded by grogginess and her mother's breath on her neck.

Donna stroked Bea's hair just as she did when Bea was a child, before she stopped visiting in the middle of the night. Only now, she smelled of cold cream and the lavender oil she sprayed her pillow with every night.

"Bea," she whispered, her edge left behind in the kitchen, moonlight stripped her of coarseness.

Bea was still on her side, turned away from Donna. She didn't want to move for fear of breaking the spell.

"I didn't want to end up like her," said Donna quietly, her mouth so close to Bea's ear.

"Like who?" Bea whispered back.

"Your grandmother," she said.

Bea's mind raced, Grandma was one of the strongest women she knew. Not only in the sturdy sense, but in every other way as well. She was kind, fair, honest, and true. Diligent, loving, and thoughtful, she was exactly who Bea wanted to be when she grew up.

Donna's words were breathy, "My father, your granddad, got bored with small town life. He wanted more. And so he played around, and he was rough with her when she called him out on it."

Bea rolled over and their faces were next to one another, Donna's eyes were closed but her face was open. Bea put an arm around her and drew her in tightly.

She pulled away slightly and shook her head, "You have to understand this. Because it's the reason I couldn't stay with Cliff. I was terrified that he'd get bored with the life he wanted. And then," she shuddered, "and then I'd end up trapped like my mother."

"Why didn't grandma leave?"

She shrugged, "All the reasons battered women don't leave their husbands."

"But she seemed so strong. Like nothing could touch her."

"That was after he died. She became a new person. You never met your granddad. He was charming, suave. The whole town knew about his running around before she did. And they said nothing. I could never forgive them. So I left. That house was never a happy house, even after he died. Even after you were born. I couldn't stay overnight without having nightmares. Memories resurfaced. It wasn't Cliff that I left. It was what I feared he would become."

So she found someone completely different, but ended up trapped in a different way. In an equally difficult marriage. Bea shook her head and mulled over the word irony for a moment.

The tables had turned and now Bea played with her mother's hair, stroked her back. Donna's eyes were open and wide with memories, her cheeks damp from tears.

Bea closed her eyes and let the information sink in. Pictures of her grandparents flashed in front of her, memories she wasn't a part of. Their wedding picture, a photo of Donna as a baby sitting between her parents on a picnic blanket, her grandmother's hand on her hip, a tight smile plastered on, details Bea never looked too closely at, or could be read a million ways depending on the context.

271

Now she had context.

Donna kissed the top of Bea's head and gave her a squeeze before she slipped out of bed as quietly as she came in. Bea remembered this part, that the moments shared in the middle of the night went without explanation, clouded in a haze somewhere between a memory and a dream.

TWENTY-SIX

B ea thought her body would fight sleep, but instead it
welcomed slumber like an old friend. She slept more
soundly than she had in forever. It was as if the newfound
knowledge made sense of her world, and with that, she could
finally rest.

She woke up the day after Thanksgiving in a place that,
while it still did not feel like home, it felt settled. There was
understanding in the walls and the floors echoed with familiarity
that Bea, for once, welcomed.

Downstairs she found a pot of coffee, still warm, and an
array of bagels and muffins on the counter. Bea knew from years
past that Donna was out searching for Black Friday deals, and her
father - Eric, she corrected herself - was probably working. She
helped herself to a pumpkin muffin and filled a mug to the brim
with coffee. With a paper towel serving as a plate she ate
unceremoniously at the kitchen table, overlooking the suburban
backyard and neighbors on either side and behind. Fences all

around, of course.

After eating she wandered the first floor, gazing at everything with new eyes. The sitting room, the family photos, the perfect display. Her feet led the way to Eric's study, the door was wide open, and she peeked in. The lights were on but Eric was nowhere to be seen. The room was a cave full of ornate dark wood furniture, shelves of heavy books - Bea wonder if there were any treasures that Graham would be able to point out - burgundy drapes and a small wet bar in a corner. A businessman's room.

Amid the books were picture frames, and as Bea walked closer to inspect the contents her heart leapt into her throat and goosebumps pricked her skin.

They were hers. Her photographs. They not only sat on the bookshelf, but they hung on the wall with a sense of purpose, grandeur even. Landscapes blown up to poster size proportions in heavy, expensive frames, familiar scenes of Bea's life from the past ten years.

Eric cleared his throat from behind her.

Bea turned and gaped at him, from the doorway he looked around the room a bit nervously which made her smile. For the first time, he truly endeared himself to Beatrix.

He walked into his study, crossed the room and leaned against his leather desk chair. She turned back to the frames.

"Your latest work," he said, "isn't nearly as inspired as the photographs from the beginning. Funny, given how the intensity of the locations grew with your career."

"You followed my career?" she asked, unable to meet his dark brown eyes, his thoughtful stare.

"Of course I did, and I'll continue to. Business is my specialty, and I always liked to know what was going on in your professional life. I've tried to understand it, but I do think board rooms are more my speed than creative entrepreneurship. I'm looking forward to being able to keep up with the business end of Finley Orchards."

Bea stood there, rubbing the palm of one hand with the other's thumb, staring at her work. She didn't know if this was something she wanted to hear, or something she wanted to shove away and not feel. She didn't even know what to call the man in front of her anymore. Father? Even on a good day, she had a hard time thinking of him as such. Someone who cared for her, looked out for her, showed his love in his own way, supported his daughter emotionally - not just financially, that's not who he was. Or at least, that's not who she let him be.

"I had no idea you were interested in my life," she said quietly. They were treading on thin ice, she wasn't sure if he heard the conversation in the kitchen last night, if he knew she knew. "You never asked, never came to see me when I was in college, or talked on the phone at all when I called. Even when I was a kid, you didn't seem to care."

He crossed his arms and raised an eyebrow, "I think you now understand why."

So he had heard, or Donna told him.

"So why keep up the charade now?" asked Bea.

"Why not? Cliff is dead. I don't see how this changes much."

Bea scoffed, speechless.

"Listen, he gave you something I never could have. Hell, he gave your mother what we later found out I couldn't," he paused, Bea looked at the floor, thinking about all those times she wished for a sibling but one never came along. "But I gave your mother everything he couldn't."

"You knew everything, and never said a word."

He nodded.

"And that's why…" her voice trailed off, sadness crept in,

275

thinking about all those years that she wondered if she had done something wrong. All those times when Bea was young enough to not understand it wasn't her fault, that she wanted to be different so that maybe, just maybe he'd like her.

"I tried, Bea, I really did. But at one point I gave up. You were hers, and more so, his. I had, and still have, a very specific purpose to serve. I'm Donna's husband and provider. And I have fulfilled that duty well."

Bea stifled a sarcastic laugh, old habits die hard.

"Was I unkind to you?" he asked earnestly, uncrossing his arms and sitting in the desk chair. His head hung down in what could be construed as shame, but Bea was skeptical, she knew his negotiating skills, his business persona that took hold of him when he was trying to get what he wanted. What did he want?

Bea had to think for a moment. She had to think about the cold words, the detached emotions. Was that kindness? No. But could kindness also come by way of a roof over your head and a college degree, in security instead of affection?

Bea shook her head in confusion, in the absurdity of the situation. And yet, it felt right. Knowing that the man in front of her was not her father. He never was, and never would be. Even after all the years he played the part the only way he knew how.

She now knew who her real father was. And that was enough.

As she turned to walk out of the study when he stopped her, "Bea, about Graham Winters," he said. Turning, she nodded for him to continue, "I knew the name sounded familiar. There's a woman at the office, Charlotte Brown, who says he was her ex fiance."

The name didn't ring any bells, but then, Graham kept a tight lip about his past, especially his ex.

"I knew he was engaged, I haven't heard much of the

story though, just that he ended up buying Grandma's house."

Eric shook his head, "Yes, and at a bargain. I looked into it, and the people we sold it to took quite a hit when they sold it to him. He must be a shrewd businessman."

She started to turn around again when he said, "Let me just say this, be careful who you trust." Bea bristled, and Eric extended a hand to wave off the offense he knew she was taking, "Listen, I'm not trying to cause trouble, I want you to succeed," his voice softened as he spoke, "Charlotte never said exactly what happened to end their relationship, but she led us to believe Graham left a trail of devastation in his wake. I know you're a grown woman now, and can handle more than we've ever given you credit for, but please take my word for it. It might be hearsay, but still, be careful."

"I find that hard to believe," said Bea, surprising herself with the loyalty she felt growing towards Graham. It had taken so long to build trust between them, she wasn't ready to give it all away.

Bea's pajama pocket vibrated, startling her. She turned to walk out the door and to find a text message from Graham. "Speaking of the devil," she muttered to herself as she opened the text.

"Come home, emergency" was all it said. Bea stared at the phone, willing a second message to come through the air waves or however text messages magically appear.

"Everything okay?" said Eric from the back of the room. He stood over his desk, one hand in his chino pocket, the other mindlessly sorting through the items in front of him. A paper weight, a stray letter, a dozen pens in an upright holder.

"I don't think so. Something happened at the orchard, I need to go."

There were a million scenarios that flipped through her

mind in a matter of seconds, from an accident with farm equipment, to Henry's safety, a water leak in the house, to a protest or a riot of townspeople who didn't want Bea to take ownership of the orchard, Olivia's pregnancy - Bea tried to remember her exact due date. She ran down a list of every single person she knew associated with the orchard and various things that could have happened to them.

"I need to make a call."

Eric stood and crossed his study in only a few steps, suddenly he was larger than himself, but his presence didn't frighten her. It was quite the opposite.

"Go grab your things, then tell me what you need. I can drive you home faster than you could get there any other way."

Bea looked at him, and saw the years of both their lives they missed. In that moment, forgiveness began working it's way into Bea's heart.

"Thank you," she said to him, looking into his chestnut eyes. She ran upstairs to make a phone call and collect her things. Good thing she'd packed lightly.

TWENTY-SEVEN

On the phone Graham was elusive and simply said she was needed, quickly. No one was hurt, but something happened to the barn, though he wouldn't say what. He then asked if the orchard's insurance was up to date - yes - if there were any documents left in the barn - no - and if she could get there by end of day - yes. And then he hung up, with the sound of fire engines in the background.

While she was packing her things, Donna walked into Bea's bedroom, fresh from shopping. Dressed in slacks and a cashmere sweater in an autumnal shade of burgundy, she didn't look ruffled in the least. She held a mug of coffee in her hands and stood in the doorway, leaning against the door frame.

"Leaving? I knew you'd be in a rush to leave after last night, but seriously Beatrix," she tutted, the soft vulnerability of the night before long gone. "Is that really what you brought? Just a flimsy bag? What happened to that nice suitcase we gave you for your college graduation?" Not a hint of kindness for a woman, her own daughter, who had just found out the truth that had been coursing through her blood since before her birth.

Bea rolled her eyes, ignoring her mother's question.

"Something happened at the orchard," said Bea, without looking at her mother, stuffing her things back into the canvas bag. "Dad," she stumbled, "Eric is taking me home."

"It's business, then," said Donna with a smile, "you two have more in common now than you ever did before." Like she planned it, like she was happy about the turn of events.

"You're unbelievable," said Bea as she pushed past her and continued down the stairs, where Eric was waiting with a travel mug of coffee and his car keys. He wore a canvas barn coat, the fabric looked stiff and hardly used.

"So you're not coming back tonight?" Donna called down from the second floor.

"Darling, Bea's livelihood is at stake, so no, I don't think she'll be coming back here tonight," he paused for a moment and looked at Bea solemnly before saying softly, "or ever."

"I thought with everything you now know, you would stick around. I thought you would have cared about our relationship now, since you never did before," said Donna.

Bea turned to her mother and said, "I've cared far too much. If I didn't show it, it was to protect myself."

Donna's eyes sharpened, her voice raised, "To protect you from what?"

Bea took one last look at her mother, at the pearls she clung to, at her perfect hair and her perfect make up. Her fake smile and her glaring eyes. One last look before Bea gave a pointed nod and turned and walked out of the house without a word.

The car ride was quiet except for the drone of NPR news and Eric's questions. He tried to ask about the incident at the orchard, but Bea had no answers to give. Her tone became more impatient with every mile, and with every passing moment Bea's hands grew sweatier. She went from wanting Eric to drive faster to wanting the journey to never end, not sure of what was waiting for her at the orchard.

She sent Olivia a text, but the response didn't calm her nerves or answer any questions. "Steve's with Graham, everything will be okay. We're all here for you."

What the hell did that mean? Thought Bea.

They were about twenty minutes away from the orchard and her patience and resolve escaped her. Eric lowered the volume on the radio. Bea prepared for another question.

"Do you remember when you were five or six, and you went to your grandmother's for the summer?"

"I remember bits and pieces from all of the visits." Outside the world blurred as they sped past familiar roads.

"You forgot Tiny at home, and when your grandmother called she said you were inconsolable. Donna had a migraine, she claimed it was from the strain of dropping you off, she couldn't make the trip twice in one day. It was a Sunday, and I knew how sad you would be if you had to sleep without Tiny, so I went up to your room, found it, and headed up north myself."

Bea pulled her feet up onto the passenger seat and rested her chin on her knees. She was trying to steal glances at him without staring, this stranger she had known her whole life.

"When I arrived in Cumberland your grandmother was waiting for me on her porch, but you were nowhere to be seen. I got out of the car with Tiny in my hand, and she just sat in that rocking chair. I could never figure her out, you know. I don't know why she detested me from the start, my only guess is she thought I was stealing Donna. But she had to have known, Donna had a plan from the moment she met me, a timetable. I was more or less a vehicle to get what she wanted," he paused and wiped his brow, Bea tried to remember Eric ever being at Sylvia's house during her childhood, but she couldn't think of a single instance. "Sylvia pointed across the street, and through the trees I could see you, with him. He was laying on the ground with his legs up in the air, and you were on his feet pretending to be an airplane. Beatrix, I had never seen you so happy," he paused, his voice was thick and his eyes were sad, "Sylvia dared me, she said, 'go ahead, she'd love to see Tiny.'"

Bea pictured the scene and her grandmother. How she must have protected Cliff's time with Bea, how she helped to give him what Donna stole.

"Cliff set you down on the ground and you ran off, but when he stood up he saw me. He waved," Eric shook his head, "I couldn't even wave back at him. I was so angry. Up until that point I could ignore the facts. But after that, there was no way. You were with your father, and you were happy."

"All these years," she said, "were you jealous?"

"More than I'll ever admit to anyone else," he said, "but it didn't hit me until I saw you with him. It took so long for you to warm up to being with us after your visits to Cumberland, it got harder and harder, and I started resenting the visits, and you. I'm sorry, Bea. It was easier for me to focus on other things."

"Work."

"Work," he conceded, "but I never stopped caring. Please know that. It's why I have your photographs up in my office, I'm so proud of the work you've done. And now, I'm so proud of what you're doing. I know your mother doesn't think you'll stick it out, and I may have had my doubts, but I've seen how dedicated you are when you find something that ignites a fire in you, and I can see the orchard has done just that. It always has, and it makes sense that he left it to you."

They drove in silence for a moment, then he turned down the road that would take them to the orchard. "I don't think I ever gave you my condolences," he said softly, and Bea looked at him in wonder, "Bea, I'm sorry for your loss."

Before she could react, they arrived at the orchard. They couldn't pull into the driveway, it was full of fire engines, an ambulance, and police cars. Bea saw Olivia and Steve's jeep and a handful of cars she didn't recognize parked on the side of the street. She smelled smoke before she saw it. It seeped into the car ventilation system and Bea gasped and fought to suppress a gag.

She couldn't find her breath, and she didn't even know what had happened.

Eric pulled the car to the side of the road and she was out the door before he turned off the ignition.

She ran fast, her breathing was hard, her heart pounded in her chest. She didn't look back to see if Eric was following, she ran as if she had blinders on the sides of her face, she was focused only on the path forward. All of her senses were in overdrive.

Her eyes were drawn to the barn, or what was left of it. A charred expanse of wood greeted her and she dropped to her knees. The sounds around her began to whoosh and echo in her head. She thought she heard her name being shouted, but she couldn't tear her eyes away from the remains of the building.

The sky was bright blue, and the only sound that made its way to her ears was the bright chirp of the chickadees. They surrounded her in the trees and bushes that lined the driveway and the front porch.

"Bea," Graham's voice pulled her out of the fog that had enveloped her mind. "Bea," his arms were around her and he crouched next to her. Her body sank into his. He smelled like smoke and sweat, of desperation and strength.

"Is Henry?" she asked, unable to finish the thought.

"Henry is fine, he wasn't in the barn at the time."

"What happened?"

"They think it was the space heater, or some electrical work. They're investigating."

"I want to see," she said as she stood, the earth swayed under her feet and Graham stood quickly and put an arm around her. She had the feeling she should be comforting him, wiping his brow, making him a cup of tea or a stiff drink, filling a tub of hot water for a long soak.

"I don't know that it's safe," he said, he squeezed her arm and pulled her into his side as they walked, "but I'm sure the fire department will want to talk with you, they can fill you in on the details."

He guided her over to where the firemen stood, and the chief, Chris Taggert, gave her the break down. Ron was being modest earlier in the season, his son wasn't just a firefighter, but the man in charge. He smiled kindly at Bea and told her that they were waiting for the last of the hot spots to die down, for the fire to be completely out before investigating further. No one was hurt, the barn wasn't salvageable, and it was not safe to poke around. What was left of it needed to be removed, but the insurance people would have to come out first to assess the situation. It was an accident, they thought. No foul play, he said.

"The apples? The trees?" she asked.

"The storage shed looks untouched, and the trees look fine. I had someone poke around, though I'm sure you'll want to have a botanist or whatever come out and take a look, but I think they'll be alright," he paused, glanced from Graham back to Bea and said softly, "I'm sorry it took so long to get over here, and extreme circumstances at that. Dad mentioned you were back, I meant to stop by to say welcome home." Chris was tall, Bea had to crane her neck to see his eyes even as he leaned towards her. Graham cleared his throat and Bea said diplomatically, "Thanks, Chris. We'll have to catch up soon."

As Bea digested the information, a circle formed around her. Eric had joined them and introduced himself around simply as Eric Hampton. Bert showed up in the diner's catering van and walked towards them with an arm full of bagged lunches, for those at the scene, the spectators and firemen.

"I don't think I could eat now," said Bea, suddenly very cold.

"But you will," said Bert, "I'll leave some food in the kitchen."

From the driveway came a sob that echoed throughout the property and everyone turned to look.

There was Vicky, wearing a bright red puffy coat and jeans, along with a pair of rubber boots. It looked like she had a total transformation to country living, aside from her perfectly coiffed hair and full face of makeup.

"Vicky," said Graham, he walked over to greet her, "I'm surprised to see you."

She waved him off, "I wasn't far when I got your message, so I thought I'd see if I could help."

Bea's attention went from the barn, to Graham, to Vicky, and back to the barn. The scent of wet fire kept her attention, the damp charred smell that would linger in her clothes and hair and seep into everything on the orchard.

"Oh Beatrix," Vicky walked over and wrapped an arm around Bea, who stood stiff with her arms crossed in front of her, "I'm as devastated as you must be, my brother's orchard."

"It looks like it's just the barn, and insurance should cover everything," Bea told her, going into fact mode.

285

"All his hard work, his legacy," Vicky looked at the barn, or what was left of it, and mustered up tears, "gone."

Graham piped up, "It's not, though. The trees are what's important, and they said they weren't touched."

"The pristine property is no longer, Cliff must be rolling in his grave, I'm so glad he didn't have to see this."

Everyone looked at Vicky, some with sympathy, but Bea didn't have any patience for her. Eric was giving Vicky a puzzled look, and he came to stand closer to Bea.

"If only he'd left me the property, I'd never have let something like this happen."

"Excuse me?" said Bea, shrugging off Vicky's arm, voice rising with the heat in her face.

"You can't blame yourself, dear."

"She wasn't," said Eric, the gruffness in his voice surprised Bea.

"It's just that you're so young, I can't imagine all the pressure on you, of course there were things that were overlooked. And the fact that you had someone living in the barn."

Graham said, "That has nothing to do with anything. And it wasn't Bea's fault, or Henry's. It was a complete accident."

"Graham, I'm so glad that you called," she gushed, "thank you for keeping me informed."

Bea looked from her to Graham, catching his eye. When he saw, he offered, "She had asked about a book," he said, his voice quiet and even, "we had a conference call arranged for this afternoon, but obviously I didn't think I'd make it so I called to tell her."

"Once I heard, I just had to come and see for myself."

"Why exactly are you here?" Bea asked, and as she waited for an answer she stared at Vicky and tried to find Cliff inside of her somewhere, some hint of family resemblance, because now

286

Bea looked at her with new eyes, eyes of a niece, eyes of a daughter who was protecting her father from a woman who didn't seem to have his best interests at heart.

Even the chickadees stopped singing, and the only sound was from the beeping of a fire truck as it reversed onto the street.

"I came to help," said Vicky indignantly.

"You came to try to get your hands on the orchard. You came because you are opportunistic and want the orchard, the property, and you think you can insert yourself into this situation if you make me less credible."

Vicky's eyes narrowed and she stood taller, her cheeks colored, "There's no reason for you to have this orchard, you're not family. Cliff owed his family, he owed me."

"Cliff owed you nothing."

"He left me there, with our parents. He left me because of your mother, and she didn't even stick around."

There were audible gasps and the air become very still.

"If he had any decency, he would have made amends for what he did, and left me the orchard. I've had a lifetime of cleaning up his mistakes, making up for the son who deserted my parents, you have no idea the toll that took on me."

There was a bubble rising in Bea and she couldn't push it down. She knew it wasn't the time or the place, but she felt simultaneously threatened and empowered, and wanted to be left alone. Coming home to the orchard with the knowledge of Cliff being her father had changed everything.

Before she could say the words that were swelling inside of her, Eric stepped forward and said, "He was Bea's father."

"It's true," Bea said, standing taller, thankful for Eric and the pride he must have swallowed to help her.

She closed her eyes as another round of gasps made their way around the orchard. When she opened her eyes, she saw each person who was still standing there, watching her. There was sadness in Eric's eyes, though also a bit of pride as he looked at Bea. Graham was looking at Bea with bewilderment, while Anna smiled with recognition and the rest of those that had gathered showed reverence in their gazes. Vicky put her hands on her hips and was shaking her head. It looked as though she was riling herself up to say something, and Bea was sure it would be neither kind nor sympathetic.

"This place is rightfully mine," said Bea, "and there's no need for anyone else to be here right now. "

Vicky shuffled her Hunter boot clad feet past Bea who couldn't help watching her. Vicky's eyes were filled with fire, her face was bright red, if she was a cartoon character she would have had steam coming out of her ears.

Vicky mumbled as she walked by, a low grumble. All Bea could make out were the words "paternity test".

"I had no idea," said Graham. He stood, seemingly paralyzed with the news, "Do you want me to stay?"

She thought for a moment, stared at the debris and the orchard. "No, I think," she reached out and put a hand on the inside of his elbow and rested it there for a moment while her words found her, "I think I'd like to be alone for a little bit."

He tried to hold her gaze but she had closed her eyes, out of fatigue and overwhelming emotion, so he put his hand over hers. His lingering touch was comforting, and Bea wanted nothing more than to rest her head on his shoulder, to have his arms around her to protect her from all that was unfolding. But she had spoken the truth, she wanted to be alone, and so she straightened and squeezed his arm before retracting her hand and putting it into her back pocket. Then she watched him and the others walk away, down the driveway.

Once the only people left were the authorities and Eric,

Bea looked down the road to make sure everyone was really gone. Vicky had waited at the end of the driveway and was now talking with Graham. Bea bristled at the sight, remembering Eric's warning earlier, and then watched as they walked across the street towards his house.

Eric placed the tote bag he'd been holding on the ground next to Bea. "Your mother and I are only a phone call away," he said.

Bea looked up at him, she parted her lips to say something, but nothing came out.

"Give us a second chance. Maybe not as parents, but as allies. Your mother, she'll come around. It'll take time to let go of all the anger she has, and to adjust to no longer carrying such a secret."

"Thank you, for everything," said Bea, and she hugged him.

"It'll be okay," he said, pointing to the barn, "you'll figure it out. I believe in you."

Bea watched as he walked down the path towards his car. She brushed away a tear that had slid down her cheek, and took a deep breath of sooty air.

The sun was still shining brightly, but the air was thick. Wet leaves lay beneath her feet, stomped and trampled on by the weight of fire trucks and hoses, sopping wood and debris. Even though the sun was warming her back, she was chilled to the bone. The chickadees sang in the distance, and after she decided there was nothing she could do outside, she headed to the house.

The porch seemed smaller than it did before, there was something more intimate about the house, something more personal. She stared at the door, unable to bring herself to open it, and noticed a shape moving from the far side of the porch.

"Henry," she said, not at all surprised to see him. She

dropped her bag and walked over to him. He had a blanket wrapped around him, it was coarse and smelled of moth balls and dust. "I'm so happy to see you," she embraced him, at first he stiffened, but then she felt his body sigh as she kept her arms around him for a moment.

"I always hoped," he said, eyes twinkling. Bea tilted her head in question, "I suspected, and never asked, because with Cliff, you didn't ask, you couldn't push him. He was so open about so much, but the things he wanted to keep private, well, he kept them private."

"Will you come in?" she asked with a hint of hope. She had wanted to be alone, but Henry's presence was unobtrusive, and with the fire Henry was the only other person who lost something as dearly as she had.

He followed her inside, and on the kitchen table, they found a large brown bag filled with Styrofoam containers of food from Bert.

"I'm going to take my things upstairs, can I fill the tub for you?"

"I'd rather just take a hot shower, if you don't mind," said Henry, his gaze hovered over the food.

"Not at all, let me pull some towels out for you."

Upstairs in Cliff's bedroom she rustled through the drawers of his bureau to find something for Henry to wear. The clothes were a bit big, but they'd do. The photographs on the bureau gave her pause. She saw everything in a new light. These were my father's things, she thought to herself. These were my father's clothes, she thought as she lined the bed with tee shirts and flannels and corduroy pants for Henry to choose. This was my father's bed, she thought as she laid her hand flat on the comforter, smoothing the edges on the now dusty fabric.

Next she found clean towels and put them into the

bathroom, flipped on the light switch and turned on the shower to take the chill off the room. She watched as the bathroom filled with steam, she felt her body grow weary with the heat. She paused and gave herself a moment to feel everything. But the emotions were too heavy, and she left the bathroom, shutting the door, steeling herself as she walked downstairs to the kitchen.

On the kitchen counter her phone was vibrating. By the time she reached it the call had gone to voicemail. Expecting it to be a local caller about the fire, she was surprised to instead recognize the number as the editor of an online travel magazine she had worked for in the past. She pushed the phone aside and vowed to listen to the message later, when and if things ever calmed down.

TWENTY-EIGHT

While she waited for Henry, Bea set out the food Bert had brought earlier. The aroma of apple pie overpowered the smell of deli meat sandwiches and fries lining the table, and stamped out the undertones of soot and water logged debris. She tried to sit down at the table but she couldn't sit still. She started a fire in the wood stove, more mindfully than ever. Mesmerized by the flame, it was like watching a story as the logs caught fire and light filled the dark chamber, flames danced in shapes of trees and faces.

Later, when Henry came down, he found Bea standing at the sink, staring at the remains of the barn. She watched as the firefighters walked away from the site, as the police wrapped yellow tape around and around, blocking entry and inquiry, as the last fire truck backed down the driveway and out onto the road. They were alone, Henry and Bea. She turned around and smiled at him. His green eyes twinkled as he looked at the table filled with food, and he stroked his fluffy beard in thought. The flannel shirt and brown corduroy pants Bea laid out for him were indeed too big, mostly in the length, though the belt looked to be tightened as far as it would go.

She pulled herself away from the sink and they sat down together, passing noisy Styrofoam trays.

Henry sat back and stared at Bea, "Cliff's daughter," he said with a grin spreading from ear to ear and through his beard.

"I think you're the first person to say that and be happy about it," she managed a weak smile.

He shook his head, "That can't be so, all those people who were out there, they might not have found the words, but this makes sense. And it'll make them happy. No one wanted that money-hungry lady to run the place."

"Do you think she would have?"

"I think she'd have put up a good fight."

Bea popped a fry into her mouth and chewed slowly, then licked the lingering salt off her finger.

"I just don't get why Cliff didn't say anything."

"He did" said Henry, "in his own way. Leaving you the orchard. But Cliff also protected those he loved, and he loved your mother something fierce. Not as much as you, but enough to protect her secret. I can see that now. He spoke of her only a few times, mostly after too many bottles of Gabe's cider," at this he chuckled to himself, "but he never spoke ill of her."

Bea shook her head. It all sent her head spinning.

"Did you find everything you needed upstairs?" she asked around a mouthful of a turkey club and fatigue.

"I did," he said, staring down at his plate. He moved slowly through his food, methodically, appreciatively.

"Will you stay here tonight?" She had her hopes set on not being alone tonight, and she thought Henry might feel similarly.

"I don't know, Bea," he said, his voice trailing off.

293

"It wouldn't be any bother, Cliff's room is empty," she regretted the words as soon as they were out. The fact was she hadn't even changed the sheets since he was gone, and she sunk under the weight of the very thought of changing anything in his room, let alone the bedding. "It's just, I'd love for you to stay," she said with as much sincerity as she could.

Henry's face turned downcast and he said, "I don't think I could stay in his room."

Bea looked around and thought about the various options, realizing she was unwilling to sleep in Cliff's room as well. "How about you take my room and I'll sleep on the couch?"

"No, I couldn't do that," he said, and her face fell, "but I'll take the couch," he offered.

"That's perfect," she grinned.

Henry looked around the kitchen and then turned to view the living room.

"I haven't been in here in ages," he said, peaking Bea's interest. She raised an eyebrow and hoped he would continue. He didn't disappoint, "I still am not terribly comfortable indoors," he said, and she could detect a faint blush in his cheeks. "I'm sure Cliff mentioned, but when I had my breakdown I just couldn't stand to be inside of houses. It makes no sense," he shook his head, "unless you've been through something like that."

She cupped her hands around her mug of tea, stealing leftover bits of warmth, "Cliff said you left everything behind and didn't want anything to do with material things," she played with the tag of the tea bag.

"I've always thought maybe you'd understand a bit of that, with your traveling."

Bea agreed, "I do pack lightly, and I've never stayed in one place for very long."

"Cliff collected all of our stories, there's lots of them. And he held space for them, right here," he tapped his chest with an overgrown fingernail. "Me, I couldn't come to terms with things after my wife died. We had everything. A house, a fancy car, friends and jobs. Lives. Everything except for children. It was cancer that took her, far too young," his head shook almost imperceptibly, like a tic that he tried to hide over the years. "I figured, there was no reason for all that we worked so hard for, because in the end she died and I was alone. The stuff, it took too much out of us. If I had just worked a little less," his eyes gazed off towards the window, he shook it off again.

"You couldn't have known," she reached across the table and patted his hand gently.

"No, I couldn't. After Maureen died I didn't want all of the stuff, especially if I was going to be alone. It just didn't matter, and took up space, in my mind and my heart. I wanted time to grieve properly, and I couldn't do that with all of our things, the physical reminders of her."

She gave him a quizzical look.

"I know it sounds strange, but it's the truth. I couldn't move forward in my grief without moving away from all of it. Cliff helped. He'd just bought the orchard the year before and we knew each other a little from town. He stepped up like no one else did during that time. Like he knew what real loss was," he looked at Bea, stared into her eyes, "In a way, I guess he really did. That man, the whole town is grieving for him. And now this happened," he pointed out towards the barn, "I'm so, so sorry, Bea." She waved him off, stood and started clearing the table.

"It was an accident, by all accounts," said Bea with a resigned sigh.

"Thank goodness we saw the smoke as soon as we did, and it didn't spread through to the orchard, or the house."

"You were with Graham?"

He nodded, "He's another one, like Cliff. A good man who knows about loss and heartache." Bea stifled her inner groan, thinking of what Eric had told her, what she didn't want to think about. "He's opened his home up to me just as Cliff used to do, on my own terms. A shower and a meal for bits of labor. Swapping resources, I guess you could say."

Bea had her back turned towards him as she tossed the takeaway containers in the trash and stared out at the barn. A fog had rolled in, the gray mist hovered over the orchard.

"Am I missing something?" asked Henry, "Did Graham upset you?"

She turned, grabbed a dish towel and dried her hands. She held onto the cloth, ringing it over and over, "Ever since I came back, everyone and their mother has been asking me to give Graham a chance. I want to, I really do. I want to believe in him. But Eric, my mother's husband," her cheeks flushed and her voice lifted higher with every word, "mentioned something he heard about Graham's ex-"

At that Henry raised his hand up like a child wanting to be called on, "Just a minute. His ex? The ex that left him and ran off with all of his money?"

Bea was at a loss for words, she stood with her mouth gaping.

"If that's the one you're speaking of, you've got nothing to worry about. Graham showed up here penniless except for the loan his parents gave him to buy your grandmother's house. His ex took all of his money and ran for the hills, or the city I guess, with a colleague. Graham was, he may still be, heartbroken. Cliff helped him to pick up the pieces. He was in rough shape when he got here. He looked the way I felt when my wife passed. Being treated like that, it does a number on a person."

Bea sat down, feeling like a chastised child.

"Why didn't he say?"

Henry shrugged, "Why would he? He probably felt shame over the whole situation. It wasn't pretty, and people here have a way of picking each other up and dusting each other off, and not mentioning it again. That, and no one really besides Cliff and me knew the whole truth of it. I'm sure folks wondered, but everyone's too polite to ask. Or if they did ask, he kept it close to him as everyone knows Cliff was the only one around here who could keep a secret."

He stood up to clear the rest of the food from the table, "Your grandmother did that for Cliff when he came, I think. Among other people. He felt that generosity and wanted to pass it along. I think he helped her out quite a bit as she got on in age. And then Anna, well, she and her sons stayed I don't know how many nights in that bedroom of yours until her husband left. Everyone knew he was a bad egg, but Cliff gave her refuge on nights that she and her boys needed it."

The hem of Bea's shirt suddenly needed her attention and she looked to it, rolling it between her thumb and forefinger, "And I wondered why people considered me an outsider, there are so many stories I haven't heard. I'm really not from here," she said and started to feel the loss of so many things, so many people, all at once.

Henry sat down across from her, leaning on his arms, his watery eyes were on display, "I wouldn't say that, Bea, especially now. This place is in your blood. It's funny," he smiled warmly, "technically your mother was more from here than Cliff was. But the fact of the matter was she never wanted to live this life. And this was the only life Cliff ever wanted." He paused and then added, "And I think it's the only one for you," she lifted her eyes and gave an exasperated look and sighed. "Bea, think about it. I know it looks dim, with the barn and all, but you can make this

297

work. If anyone can, it's Cliff's daughter."

"It's a lot to think about. A message about a freelance gig landed in my voicemail while you were upstairs."

"And you're considering it?"

"I'm not dismissing it," she said softly, "but it's just one option. I've got a lot to think about."

Henry stood, "Yes, you do. I think I'll leave you to it, if you don't mind. Whatever choice you make, you'll be supported. We just can't let Vicky get her hands on this place," he shook his head, "I think she'd either commercialize the hell out of it or raze it to the ground. Either way, the town wouldn't be better for it." Bea stood and walked over to the kitchen door and turned the porch lights on, flooding the driveway. Beyond looked darker than usual.

"Let me grab some more blankets," she said, but he shook his head.

"Looks like there's plenty on the couch already," he walked by and gave her arm a squeeze. "You've done good, farm girl," he said. The words echoed Cliff and her eyes automatically teared up.

"I'm going to make another cup of tea and sit on the porch for a bit, I'll try to be quiet when I come back in."

"Don't worry, I have a feeling I'll sleep like a rock tonight, I haven't talked this much in ages and it tires me out," and then he said with a small, sheepish smile, "but if you don't mind, I think I'll go ahead and put the fire out first."

Outside the air was thick, filled with debris and the overpowering smell of a campfire that had just been put out with gallons of water. A soggy, thick soup of mess, even though the sky was clear and the fog from earlier dissipated into nothing. Her mug full of peppermint tea warmed her hands and thighs as she curled herself into a ball within the big, wooden chair. It supported her, and yet she felt it's frailty. With just one match, one faulty wire, one breath of flame in the wrong direction, all of this could have been gone.

She was lost in her own thoughts when a light flickered in the corner of her eye. Turning, the glow of a flashlight could be made out across the road. At first her heart lifted, her spirit soared for a split second before it came crashing down. She stood up and walked back inside, her flashlight partner in crime dangling in the night.

TWENTY-NINE

L ight spilled into the bedroom and Bea began to stir at the smell of coffee brewing. It was Saturday, and her alarm didn't go off because she didn't plan on being in the orchard. She was supposed to be at her parent's house, her mother's house. She awoke and the reality of what had occurred in the last forty-eight hours washed over her and she pulled the sheet and multiple quilts over her head and curled up on her side.

Eventually she crawled out of bed, washed her face and pulled back her hair into a loose bun. Still in a pair of Cliff's old flannel pants and a sweater, she headed downstairs where she found stillness and quiet. The couch looked like a couch rather than a bed, blankets were folded neatly and placed on the back. The only sign that someone had been there was the coffee waiting for her in the pot, still warm.

In the kitchen she poured herself a big mug of coffee, using Cliff's favorite cup, the lopsided one with chips on the handle. She made it and a matching one for her grandmother in pottery class during her sophomore year of high school. The morning light was crisp and yellow, outside frost danced in the corners of the fields.

The quiet was interrupted by gravel crunching under the wheels of a vehicle. Bea's guard flew up and her back straightened, she shuffled across the kitchen in her slippers. They were Cliffs, and they swallowed her feet. Yesterday when she went through his things to find clothes for Henry she found a few things to put aside for herself. Flannel pants, slippers, a couple of work shirts that must have been from earlier years when he was slim. They swam on her, but she could roll the sleeves up and layer multiple shirts underneath. She could wear them here or on a photo shoot, she thought to herself when she was going through his drawers.

Opening the door she found Olivia climbing out of her Jeep. She walked up the porch steps with a sympathetic smile on her face and a brown paper bag in her hand.

"Breakfast?" asked Olivia.

"You're up early," said Bea as she made her way over to the coffee maker and poured another cup for Olivia.

Olivia sat down and rubbed her belly gently, "The baby, it keeps me up all night and then wakes me super early," she shrugged, "they say this phase prepares you for all the sleepless nights ahead."

Bea handed her coffee in the mug decorated with the Bert's Diner logo, and then went to find two plates in the cabinet.

"I didn't know what to get, so there's an assortment of donuts and bagels. And some fruit salad," said Olivia as she unpacked the bag, laying out a spread. There were tiny containers of cream cheese and jam, square cardboard containers of orange juice and plastic forks. "There's also a couple slices of pie," she looked up with a guilty face, "I couldn't help it. It all looked good!"

They laughed and piled food onto their plates.

"So," said Olivia around a mouthful of jelly donut, "I heard about yesterday."

"The fire?" said Bea, avoiding her eyes.

Olivia's hands flew up in the air, "Hardly. The other bombshell."

"Yeah, it's been quite a few days."

"Steve said as much. The whole town's talking about it."

Bea rolled her eyes. "That's exactly what I wanted," she shook her head, "I know, small town, big news, it flies. But how long until it dies down?"

"I'm not sure. News flies but it also gets swept under the rug pretty quickly."

"That's sort of what Henry said last night."

"Is he staying here?" Knife and cream cheese container stilled in her hand as she looked up at Bea.

Bea nodded, "He was, I hope he'll stay again tonight. I'm not sure where else he'll go, or where he is now. He made coffee and his bed, but I haven't seen him this morning."

"Normally gossip doesn't last long, but this, this is huge. You're like the town's long lost daughter now, not just a granddaughter."

Bea's chair creaked as she sat back, "Huh, that makes sense. I guess it didn't feel like Mom was ever from here, she didn't want anything to do with it. But Grandma certainly was. So yeah, another step closer makes all the difference."

"It does, trust me," she paused and set her bagel down, licked the stray crumbs off her finger and said, "how was it with your mom?"

Bea took a deep breath and let out a sigh, "It wasn't pleasant, I'll tell you that," she dove in and told Olivia the details of how and when the truth came out.

"She must have really loved Eric to let all of this, and Cliff, go," said Olivia.

"No, I think it was quite the opposite. She didn't love all of this enough to let Eric go."

They ate quietly for a few minutes. Bea got up for a coffee refill and motioned to Olivia's cup, but she covered it with her hand. "I have to watch my caffeine, that was my one cup for the day," she sighed.

"Are you feeling ready?" asked Bea, realizing she should ask more questions about the baby, but didn't know what else to say. Babies were so far from her mind, just about as far as settling down and owning an orchard were two months ago.

Olivia smiled and said, "We've still got a few months, but yeah, I think so. We're both so excited. Nervous, but mostly excited."

"I can't even imagine what it must be like," Bea pulled her feet up on the chair and wrapped her arms around her knees, the flannel of her pants smelled like coffee and sleep, like soft pillows and moth balls, "watching your caffeine and avoiding lunch meat and having a tiny person growing inside of you."

"I still don't know what it really feels like. Having the business and all, we keep waiting for the baby to arrive to slow down, you know? But in the quiet moments, especially when I can feel the baby kick and roll around, I kind of freak out a bit," she spoke quietly, with trepidation seemingly from a place of wanting to be understood, but not wanting to voice your fears. Bea recognized her tone instantly.

Bea started to say something but Olivia changed the subject as she stood, arched her back in a stretch, and walked over to the window, "So, do you need names for contractors or are you thinking of a do it yourself build?" she smirked.

"Oh goodness, I haven't even thought that far. I'm still trying to figure out all of the insurance stuff."

"Graham didn't take care of that yesterday?" she raised an eyebrow and leaned against the sink. Bea had to turn to talk to her, so she swiveled around on the kitchen chair.

"I know the insurance people were called, I think June was over at some point as well. Today is for getting all of it in order. Thank God we moved all of the paperwork in here the other week!"

"I thought about that last night, imagine if all the paperwork was lost, or even just the journals," Olivia shook her head and rested her hands on the top of her stomach.

Bea's heart sunk thinking about Cliff's journals going up in flames. Instantly she had a longing to hold them, to look at his handwriting.

"I had a job offer come in," she said quietly, looking down at her hands around the mug.

Olivia walked back over to the chair and sat down.

"It's a freelance job covering hotels in southern California for a travel magazine I've worked for before. It'd be a couple weeks worth of easy work. I don't know that I'll take it, but, it makes me wonder even more about what makes sense for me career wise. Can I really do this whole orchard thing, or do I even want to? Rebuild something that wasn't mine a few months ago?"

Olivia tilted her head to the side and her eyebrows furrowed, "It was always yours, Bea. Once you realize that, you'll be better off."

Bea sat, stunned, chastised by the bluntness of Olivia's words, the truth.

Olivia stood, picked up the leftover donuts and said, "I'm taking these, for the baby," she winked. "I've got to run, I told Steve I'd be back to help open the store. Not that he needs the help," she sighed, "but we've reached the stage where he worries if I don't show up places when I say I will."

"That's sweet," offered Bea, and started clearing the remains of breakfast.

"It is, but it's also cramping my style. This is what cell phones are for, text updates won't even suffice these days."

"You can't blame him. Pretty soon the whole town will be on baby watch and you'll be required to update everyone you walk by," they both laughed and then embraced in a quick hug.

"Oh, I've got a bunch of tarps in the back of the jeep for you, you'll probably need them. Want to grab them?"

And this, Bea thought to herself, is what community was all about. Breakfast and tarps, lifting spirits and putting you in your place.

She followed Olivia out the door, piled a stack of tarps on the side of the lawn and waved when the Jeep turned out of the driveway.

After spending some time on the phone with both the fire department and the insurance company - there was something to be said for having property insurance through someone right in town who calls on a Saturday morning - Bea knew how her Saturday would be spent. She was to secure the damage until they could do a full assessment, which meant picking out the easily accessible things from the rubble, and covering the rest to make sure there was no further damage done by the weather.

Knowing that it was a dirty job, she didn't bother with a shower. She found her jeans and steel toed boots, and put on one of Cliff's flannels. In the coat closet she found a pair of work gloves and tucked them into the back pocket of her jeans.

The weekend's forecast included a warm front, probably the last of the year. It was a surprise, and the warmth felt unnatural instead of the colder temperatures from earlier in the week, even from the morning. Bea walked outside and the wind didn't bite her nose, it said hello with a balmy caress.

Grabbing the deceivingly heavy pile of tarps she headed over to the remains of the barn. The yellow caution tape was easily lifted to climb under. The tarps fell with a thump at her feet. The task at hand was to assess what was left. To remove anything that wouldn't stand the elements. There was the metal desk and what looked like a chair within the pile of burnt rubble. The ceiling had collapsed and there were heaps of burnt wood, so far gone that splinters weren't an issue.

And the smell. The smell was unforgettable. It clung to her clothes and her hair, and she knew even after several showers the smell from spending just a few minutes in the remains would linger.

She cautiously watched her step as she walked around, realizing there was nothing left to save. No equipment that could be fixed. No corner untouched by flame.

Bea walked back to the edge and pulled the first tarp off the pile and started to spread it open. It crinkled and swayed. She was struggling with it, but then Henry's figure appeared at the edge of the barn and he silently started to work with her. He grabbed the opposite end of the tarp and together they opened it wide. They carried it to the far end of the building and laid it down, anchoring it with rocks and bricks of charred wood.

When they got to the third tarp Graham walked up the driveway. His hair was flopped over his forehead, hands in his pockets. His tee shirt looked slept in, his pants wrinkled. He was wearing work boots, proper shoes for the job, which surprised Bea and her gaze lingered and then traveled to his upper arms where his shirt sleeves were filled out. He caught her stare and gave a nod and a wry smile.

Wordlessly he picked up the next tarp and set to work.

The three of them worked with determination and the job was quickly finished. After climbing out of the rubble Bea stood with her hands on her hips, assessing the bright blue covering. It would be an eyesore from the kitchen, and hopefully the snow wouldn't come soon. According to Cliff's journals, the proximity of the orchard to the ocean meant there was less snowfall than a few miles inland. For the orchard's sake she hoped he was right.

Flanked by her coworkers, she couldn't help but gaze appreciatively at the two men. Henry had put on his trench coat and hat once again. He wasn't wearing either of them yesterday, and she assumed they were left at Graham's when the fire started and they ran towards it.

They ran towards it.

These two, she thought as tears pricked her eyes, saved the orchard.

She reached both hands out, and grabbed Graham's right hand and Henry's left. She looked straight ahead for fear of crying, her chest heaved with a sob. She felt a squeeze on her left, and a squeeze on her right.

After a moment she gripped both of their hands tightly in acknowledgment and then let go, turned and walked back to the house. Her legs were tired from navigating the debris, her heart heavy from covering up what was left of the barn. She didn't turn around to see if Graham and Henry followed or stayed put, she knew they would find their way to wherever they needed to be. Instinctively, she knew Henry would come back to sleep on the couch that night. She knew Graham would be across the street with his books and his stability, and his story that maybe one day he'd tell her. She knew she could only do so much alone and that if she was going to stay she needed to accept that the orchard may be hers, but it wasn't hers alone. There was a community that depended on it, and not just for the fruits of the harvest.

She took her boots off at the door and left them on the porch. Upstairs she stripped down and left a pile of soot covered clothing in the hallway and headed into the bathroom. It was the middle of the day, and she felt pangs of hunger, but she needed to rinse away the grime. She turned the shower on hot as it would go. As scalding water ran over her, it took with it the first layer of soot. She bowed her head and watched the dirt fall to the shower floor, it swirled around the drain, eventually escaping down the pipes.

Dried and dressed she made her way back down to the kitchen, where the options were slim aside from leftover diner fare. So she put on her boots and headed into town. It was time to properly fill the refrigerator, at the very least to offer Henry a decent dinner.

THIRTY

"Brunch at Bert's?" texted Olivia on Sunday morning. "Can't, heading to the beach for new Sunday tradition" replied Bea. She was sitting in the study, finishing up sorting invoices and bills.

"Tradition? Does that mean you're staying?"
  "It means I'm here now."

The door creaked as she opened the driver's side of the truck. Bea tossed her bag into the passenger seat and put her travel mug in the cup-holder by the radio, the bottom scratched against dirt and pebbles.

She looked down the driveway and out past the road

where Sylvia's house caught her eye, and suddenly she wanted to look at it with fresh, knowing eyes. Her feet carried her slowly down the driveway, and she stood at the end looking across the empty two-lane road at the little yellow cape. It looked the same as it always had, except now it held a much more complicated history. Bea wondered where in the house her grandmother stood when she waited for her husband to come home. Where she was when she found out that there was another woman. Did she crumple to the kitchen floor and lean against the cabinets, heaving with sobs? Where were the corners that her own mother cowered in when the arguments happened? Did she have a stuffed animal she snuggled, or spoke to, or looked to for comfort? And did Cliff stand where Bea stood, hoping, praying that Donna would change her mind?

There must have been too many misunderstandings, and understandings, to count.

"Have you decided?" A voice drew her out of thought. Graham stood in the front doorway leaning against the frame, arms crossed.

"Decided what?" Bea asked, half shouting.

"Do you want to come over or not? You look like you're deliberating," he smiled at her and gestured at the space between them.

She walked across the street and up his driveway, over to the walkway. But she didn't step onto the porch.

"I'm on my way to the beach. Are you working today?"

He ran a hand through his hair and looked down at the ground, a slow smile grew. "No, I just finished up with a client. Hopefully for good."

Bea gave him a puzzled look.

"Vicky," he said, and Bea straightened her back. "She had me going on a wild goose chase for months. I was hoping to end it

310

once and for all during the conference call we had scheduled, but then the fire broke out and I let her know I couldn't talk. I didn't call her to tell her specifically about the fire, I don't know why she gave you that impression. Anyway, I tried to tell her after the fire, she came over and I showed her once again what I found. She claimed it wasn't what she asked for, and I didn't have anything left in me to fight her. But, just now, I finally told her to stop playing games with me, and that should be it."

"What was she looking for?"

He shook his head in irritation, his eyes darkened, "A book with an illustration of the property where she and her husband got married. The place was supposedly the inspiration for illustrations of the dwarfs house in a version of Snow White, and she wanted the original edition. She said it was going to be an anniversary gift for her husband."

Bea leaned against the banister that led up to the porch, "Did you find it?"

Graham let out a deep sigh, "I found the only book it could have been, but she claimed the illustrations weren't what she remembered, and there must have been another version by the same artist. Either she doesn't know what she's talking about, or she just wants to keep me close by, a reason to be in contact."

"That sounds more like it," said Bea with a little laugh, "she's not all that nice of a person."

He looked at her with apologetic eyes, his face sincere, "I'm sorry I didn't recognize it sooner." Graham stuck his hands in his pockets and rocked back on his heels, "I think I wanted her to be an extension of Cliff, all his good qualities."

For a split second Bea felt badly that she hadn't given Vicky a chance to show her that side of her, she wondered what would come next for her aunt, if they would ever have a relationship.

311

A gust of wind swirled the leaves at Bea's feet, and they both looked down.

"So, the beach?" he asked.

"Yes," she almost forgot where she was going, "I was heading down to the beach. I just, after everything that's happened I wanted to see Grandma's house, your house."

"Want company?"

She looked at him, puzzled.

"At the beach?" he added.

It took her by surprise, his request. But then, maybe it shouldn't have. They had been on their way to friendship on and off for months. Maybe this time, after all they'd been through, they could take a shot at friendship. Or at least, being friendly neighbors.

"Okay," she said, surprising herself.

"Great, give me five minutes. Want me to drive? I have a parking pass, I'm not sure Cliff's is up to date. Not that they check that often after Columbus Day, but just in case."

"I'll go grab my things," said Bea.

Bag in hand, she stood on the porch of what used to be her grandmother's house, and peered through the screen door. Bea heard Graham puttering around, but she thought he was far enough away that she could sneak a peek of the house. Her nose was pressed up close enough to feel the fine metal that made up the screen.

"Bea?" called Graham from inside, "I'm just waiting for my computer to shut down, it shouldn't be long. Come on in," he said.

She let herself in, noticing the squeak of the screen door,

wondering if he'd put the storm door on soon. She had to do the same soon enough. There was so much that needed to be done, but she could only tackle one thing at a time. Today it was sorting paperwork, tomorrow she could think about the screen door.

Graham closed the office door and was walking up the hall as Bea made it into the kitchen.

"I have to keep the door closed even more now. The smoke," he continued, sniffing his shirt sleeve, "hasn't come out no matter how many times I put my clothes through the wash."

"I haven't even tried," said Bea, "it must be in the air, too. I hadn't thought about your books, was there any damage?"

He shook his head, "No, I don't think so. The room was sealed up for the day, so it wasn't an issue. But the rest of the house, I'm not sure how to get it out. It must be almost uninhabitable at your place."

Bea liked that he called it hers. "I stopped noticing it after a while. I think I must reek of wet fire."

Graham pointed to thin air, as if recalling something. "I'll be just a minute," he said, apologetically. "Have a seat if you want," he gestured to the living room before he disappeared back into his office.

Bea was standing in front of his bookshelves in the living room when he returned with the stack of books Bea had given him prior to Thanksgiving. "I finally looked at the box of books you brought over. Turns out you could have quite the inheritance on your hands."

"Really?" she said.

"Really," he said, "There were a few that are worth pennies, but buried at the bottom was a collection of very valuable books, there's a set by the name of An Inquiry into the Nature and Causes of the Wealth of Nations, by Adam Smith. Have you heard of him?"

Bea shook her head.

"It's the bible for economic thought, and the books you have," he was getting excited, his eyes danced and he looked as though he was about to start bouncing off the wall. It made Bea nervous, "are first editions of the first publication in the US, dating back to the 18th century."

It was obvious to Bea that he was telling her some very important information, but it wasn't registering. To her, they were simply old books.

"So what are they worth?" she asked.

"They could be worth over fifteen thousand dollars."

It was as if the wind got knocked out of her, like the time she fell off a swing as a child and landed flat on her back, her chest felt devoid of all air.

"I'd be happy to help you find a buyer for them, it shouldn't be hard. What's more," said Graham, "is that I found a note. You'll want to see it." He handed her a piece of paper and motioned for her to sit down. "I'll give you a minute," he said, and touched her shoulder gently.

Bea had every intention of reading the note she held in her hand, but instead her eyes wandered around the room, landing on the staircase. Her curiosity got the better of her and one step led to the next, and before she knew it, she was in the hallway upstairs. At the top of the staircase was an empty wall, and she shook her head when a flash of a painting flit in front of her. The lady in the orchard painting in her bedroom at Cliff's smiled a coy smile in Bea's imagination. The woman in the painting belonged there, watching over Graham as well as across to Finley Orchards. She shook off the thought and walked without thinking into what used to be her bedroom. Now, it looked as if it was a guest room. There was a single bed, and boxes lined the floor. Graham obviously

314

hadn't spent a lot of time in here, and Bea noted that while the bed was made, it looked as though a layer of dust would jump up if she sat on the comforter.

She made her way to the window and touched the pane of glass that looked out toward the orchard. This was her safe place. Her home away from home, but more so just her home. A rush of emotions flooded her, and she sniffled a bit. She told herself it was the dust.

Bea moved towards the stairs and walked halfway down, sat and looked at the note in her hand. The paper was thin and yellowed. As she unfolded it she saw that the top had been torn hastily from a notepad.

Dear Sylvia,

I won these in a poker game. I know you won't think much of them, but Charlie says they're worth something. Put them in a safe place. Maybe they'll make up for some of my mistakes.

Love,
Jerry

"Bea?" she heard Graham call from the living room.

She wiped her eyes and stood before she walked the rest of the way downstairs. Even with the stinging history, this space, she realized, was still sacred and safe. She felt it in every step, in the smooth handle of the banister, the pockets of memories she walked through in the hallway, in the hope of friendship in the entryway. The note only solidified that while there were mistakes made in this house, there was also hope.

"I'm sorry," she said when she found him looking for her on the porch, "I needed to see the upstairs. I didn't go into your

315

bedroom, just the guest room."

Graham paused, and looked at her with a soft, gentle look, his brows creased and his mouth drawn in a thoughtful pause, "Does it feel strange, being here?"

"Not anymore," she smiled.

"You're willing to get your new car sandy?"

Graham's car still smelled of leather and glass cleaner and hints of lemon, the distinct scent of a new car.

"It's a Subaru, that's what it's made for," he smiled at her and shrugged, then turned into the beach parking lot. "Plus," he said, "I have towels and a thing of baby powder in the back."

Bea turned her head towards him and waited for an explanation. "To get rid of the sand," there was a twinkle in his eyes, "don't tell me you don't know the trick, with having spent so much of your childhood here."

"I've never heard of it. For as close as she lived to it, Grandma wasn't a fan of the beach, and Cliff never worried about sand in his truck."

They hopped out of the car and he walked around to meet her. "Well, you put the baby powder on your feet, or wherever you have sand," he tried to give a wink but instead it just looked like an eye spasm, Bea couldn't help but laugh, "and then you give it a second and wipe with a towel. It's like magic. The baby powder dries any moisture in the sand, and then it brushes right off. Good as new."

"Well, you learn something new every day," said Bea. Graham put his hand on the small of her back and ushered her down the path and onto the beach.

They found a place to lay out a blanket, and Bea

316

immediately took her shoes off and sunk her feet into the cold sand. The surface was warmed from the sun, but just underneath was a reminder that yes, indeed, it was late autumn. The sand on this beach was unlike any other on the northern coast of Massachusetts. Where there were normally rocky beaches covered in coarse sand and seaweed, all that was found here was soft, pale, fine sand. This spot was a hidden treasure, and the locals did their best to keep it to themselves for fear of tight parking and less peace.

"I'm going to stretch my legs, I've been at my desk all morning. Do you want to come?" Graham asked.

Bea shook her head and looked down at her bag, "No, I've brought some reading I'd like to get to."

He took off down the beach, and even though Bea held a journal in her hand to read, she stared past the words and watched him. He stood tall, even as he walked with hands in his pockets. His back was broad, and he rolled up his pant legs. There was something boyish about him, carefree, a skip in his step, and as the wind lifted his hair, he didn't fix it. It got messier and messier, and Bea's heart exploded and her chest constricted as she watched as a ray of sunshine followed him down the beach. The sky was filled with clouds, big puffy ones that looked more threatening than they were in reality. The worst they could do was block the sun for a few minutes, otherwise they were harmless.

Bea pulled her sweater around her tighter when the sun went behind a cloud, and she immersed herself in Cliff's handwriting. The journal she was reading was from that past summer and into fall, and although it was filled with figures and diagrams, there were notes scribbled throughout on daily happenings. It felt like more of a diary than the others did, a running tally of the happenings of not only the orchard, but of Cliff's life. There was a note he must have taken after talking with

317

Bea relaying flight times and an airline name. She flipped to the most recent update and she gasped, it was the week before his death.

There were lists in the notebook: grocery and to do lists with check marks next to most items, but also lists of questions. It was a notebook of a man who was feeling age's pull on memory.

On one to do list an item caught her eye: "See June" and another "Tell B"

In his notebook she was simply B. This made her smile, as did the rest of the shorthand she had gotten to know through his writings.

But tell B what? She wondered if he was going to tell her everything, or just about the orchard. There was a calendar tucked into the back fold and as she pulled it out it flapped gently in the wind. Opening it, Bea found there were a few marks on each day. It looked like a symptom tracker, and on the back was a list of questions one might ask a doctor. Blood pressure med check? Dizzy spells normal?

He knew.

Maybe he didn't know what exactly, but he knew something was wrong with his body.

And he never got the chance to tell Beatrix.

Bea was laying down when he walked up. She felt him before she heard him, his footprints vibrated through the sand and into her back. The journals were back in her bag, she'd read enough for today. There was no point in pleading with the past to give her more time, to give Cliff a chance to say the things he needed to, to visit the doctor before it was too late, to change the course of events.

As Graham laid down next to her, she felt the warmth of his side and smelled his aftershave mixed with sea breeze.

"So," he said, his voice deep but soft. Bea turned onto her right ear and squinted through sunshine to see his face. His eyes were closed, his hands rested on his chest.

She turned back and rested on the back of her head. Her hands played with the edge of her sweater.

"So," she replied.

He propped himself up on an elbow and looked directly at her with piercing eyes. "Are you taking the photography gig?" There wasn't a hint of anger in his voice, just curiosity and fact.

"How-"

He cut her off with a smile. "Olivia. Small town. Remember?"

She sighed with exasperation and closed her eyes again to collect her thoughts. "I haven't decided."

"No one would blame you if you didn't want to stay," he said. He rolled over onto his stomach and played with the sand in front of him.

"Are you trying to get rid of me?" she sat up, she wasn't angry. She was tired, and she didn't want to play the game they'd been engaged in since they met.

"No, not at all. I was going to offer to keep an eye on things until you can sell. I'm not sure I'd be able to manage it, or if I'd want to do it alone for very long." He looked at her and she felt any lingering anger and suspicion melt away. Graham's voice was calm, almost sad, his shoulders hunched forward over his elbows.

"It's just," he continued, sat upright with his legs crossed in front of him in a pretzel shape, "with the fire, it's a chance to start over, one way or the other. To either rebuild, or to sell to someone who wants to create something new. And if you have

319

people wanting you to return to photography..." she looked away but he touched her arm, "You're an amazing photographer, Bea. I've seen your work."

"Thank you," said Bea. The wind turned and the gusts came off the water, and a chill ran through her. She wrapped her arms around her legs and pulled them in tightly. "I keep thinking that there has to be a way to do both, that maybe I don't have to choose one or the other."

"For as much as Cliff wanted you to stay and have the orchard, he appreciated your photography, and of all people he understood needing to do what your heart calls for."

She nodded, "What if it pulls you in two different directions? Or worse, what if something you thought you wanted all along, turns out to be unimportant after all?"

Graham held her gaze until a noise came from behind them and they both turned. A family walked down the beach, a mother and father with two children, a boy and a girl. They looked familiar, but Bea couldn't place them. The parents held hands, the children chased each other in circles around them. There was laughter, so much laughter. Graham lifted his arm to wave and the parents both waved back.

"Friends of yours?" she asked.

"Neighbors, really."

She gave him a puzzled look.

"They live down the road from us, they're relatively new in town too, maybe in the last five years? They keep to themselves, Gabe and Charlotte, they're the ones who make cider."

"You know just about everyone around here."

"And they'll all know that we were down here together in no time," he smiled an apologetic smile. "Small town. Anyway, it's thanks to Cliff that I know everyone. He thought the cure for a broken heart was to jump into work, and his work was the community. I guess now we know that he knew a bit more about that than we thought."

"What happened, Graham? Before you moved here?"

He sighed, "My ex-fiance decided that a higher up in her company was better suited to give her the life she wanted."

Sounded familiar, she thought to herself as a picture of her parents, or rather, her mother and Eric, floated through her mind.

"And when she told me, two weeks before our wedding, I lost it. I just couldn't see life without her in it, and I went to a really dark place. Meanwhile she took everything, aside from my business. She took the house and all of our belongings, and then sold everything. Said that she bought them all and had been carrying my business on her shoulders for the last few years. She hadn't, but I didn't have the energy to fight her, or the rumors that she started when they both transferred to the Boston office, and I haven't seen her since. I had to borrow money from my parents to get set up here, it was awful. I'm still ashamed at having to ask for help like that. But after a few months I was able to get back on my feet.

"There's really no such thing as a fresh start, I know that now. Your past stays with you, no matter how many fresh starts you have. I think all you can do is learn from it, and let your past make you a better person. I think that was possibly Cliff's legacy. Or at least the one I'll remember."

Graham's eyes were intense and focused solely on Bea. All she could do was think of Cliff, and the life he led that she knew little of. He was always there, when she visited, and he always made room for her. He probably thought he had years ahead to share the stories of his life. And now she would only know them through others. Maybe that was best, she thought, maybe it was the way Cliff would have wanted. He hated talking about himself, anyway.

"I think I'll remember it, too," she said to Graham, and a thought popped into her head, "What do you mean when you said you didn't want to man the orchard alone? As you've reminded me many times, there's plenty of people who will always help. And you were right, if the last month or so has taught me anything, it's that the orchard isn't a one person endeavor. It takes a village. You wouldn't be alone." He gave her an unreadable look. She added, "I mean, not that I want you to take over."

Graham looked down and her eyes followed to where his strong and capable hands were shaking.

"Graham, if anyone could run the place, it's you. You've got the whole town on your side," she said with earnest while at the same time picking up sand and letting it fall between her fingers.

She heard him laugh nervously, caught his eye and saw him blush. She thought for a moment that she'd been blind not to see it, but then, it must have happened gradually.

He put his hands over his eyes and groaned, "It's not that," he said stumbling over his words. "It's just that there's not much I want to do without you these days," he looked at her shyly with pleading eyes, and Bea couldn't help but smile at him, at his nervousness. For the first time, she felt she held the upper hand in their friendship, their relationship. But it didn't last long, because the butterflies that filled her stomach gave way to a blush of her own.

The feeling was mutual, she knew. They were at the beginning of something, and it was much more than just friendship.

"Well look at the two of you, getting awfully neighborly, aren't you?" Anna's voice carried on the wind, and her golden retriever, Rusty, rushed up to greet Bea and Graham, smelling their necks and faces, looking for food and play. Anna was barefoot and carried a bright pink plastic ball thrower that had a tennis ball on the end. Her dog's leash was in her other hand, a neon blue plastic waste bag cascaded out of her jeans pocket.

Graham got up to his feet, looked at Bea and rolled his eyes a bit, "Just finding some quiet before the beginning of the week," he said and gave Anna a hug.

Bea stayed seated, smiling up at Anna and Graham, mostly at Graham. She couldn't take her eyes off him, it was as though she could see him fully for who he was, and she liked everything she saw.

Anna chattered on about the fire, and Graham tried to deflect the questions to Bea. "Really, you should ask Bea, she's the one who…" but Bea stopped listening, instead she buried her face in Rusty's neck. Sometimes Rusty found his way to the orchard alongside Anna, and he had become overly friendly with Bea these past few weeks. Her smile hid in his sandy fur, her mind full of the future.

"Well, I'll leave you two alone. Do you need me at the orchard tomorrow?" Anna asked Bea.

"I'm not sure what I need help with yet, but I bet we can find something to work on if you're up for it," said Bea. Rusty lapped at Bea's face one last time and then followed Anna's command to start walking again. They headed towards the pathway, Anna waved at Bea and Graham as she made her way through the sand.

The clouds grew thicker and Bea pulled an edge of the blanket up around her shoulder. Graham sat back down and ran a hand through his hair and looked at Bea with a hopeful gaze.

"Small town," she said and shrugged her shoulders.

"Small town," he said.

Bea closed her eyes and leaned back on her hands. Her

face lifted to the sun and she surrendered to the breeze. It carried salt and seaweed, hints of a change in the tide. She opened her eyes and saw Graham watching his hands, his brow furrowed. Her heart swelled as she leaned forward, and then into him. He looked at her with surprise, but without a word he put an arm around her back.

"So," he whispered into her hair.

"So," she replied.

"Give her five minutes, and the whole town will know," he nodded in the direction of the beach bath. Bea looked to see Anna standing there watching them, and when Anna realized she'd been seen, she turned and hustled off the beach with Rusty following close behind.

"Is that a bad thing?" Bea asked, smiling into his shoulder. She felt his arm tightening around her, and it felt like coming home. The sea air, the man beside her, the orchard waiting only a few miles away.

"No," he said, "I think it's so perfectly imperfect, just like us."

And Bea couldn't agree more.

EPILOGUE

A pair of cameras thudded lightly against Bea's side as she walked toward the orchard. The sun was beginning to lower through the trees, and the light was golden and low, perfect for a photo shoot.

"She's here!" said Olivia, as she bounced her baby on her hip. Steve looked proudly at his daughter and then back at his wife, even from a distance Bea felt the love they shared between the three of them. Olivia's parents looked on, arms around each other. Bea swung one of the cameras in front of her and took a few unplanned and unframed shots quickly.

Olivia had spread a quilt under an apple tree, the ground was covered in spring grass and apple blossoms. The drop was in progress and blossoms covered the trees and the ground, blooms landing in the hair of anyone walking by, fairy crowns formed and drifted down from above and landed atop heads.

"Are we ready?" Bea asked as she approached with confident steps.

"Bea!" called Graham from behind. He was running to catch up, Bea left him at home unpacking a sea of boxes from the farm house. At their home. She still wasn't used to calling it theirs, the novelty had yet to wear off.

"You forgot this," he handed her a small children's book, "it was on the kitchen counter, thought you might want it for the shoot."

"I do, thank you," she said and leaned in to kiss him.

"Do you want a hand?" he asked, and though she knew he couldn't take a good photograph if his life depended on it, Bea nodded a yes.

She handed Olivia the book.

"What's this?" asked Olivia as she looked with surprise at the gift.

Bea swung the camera to her side and said, "Graham started looking for it around the time of your baby shower, but he couldn't find it until just last week. It's our gift to Millie."

"Comical Customers, by Beatrix Potter," Olivia read out loud and then laughed, "sounds perfect for our family of shopkeepers!"

Graham came up next to Bea and said, "That was the thought, it's not a first edition, so a little drool will be okay," he put a finger out and Millie grabbed it and looked at him with bright blue eyes and a toothless grin.

"Alright everyone, let's get started," said Bea, and continued to orchestrate the photo shoot. For the next twenty minutes she took photo after photo; Graham helped by fixing the edge of the blanket when it got caught up in the wind, and to rearrange people for various combinations of family photos. Millie was a sweet, good-natured baby, but she was still a baby and they worked quickly to ensure they got the best light and the best moods without pushing the limit.

At the end Bea scrolled through the photos and when she knew that there were at least a dozen that would make Olivia happy, she called it a day.

Back at the yellow cape there was tea and lemonade on her grandmother's old porch, as well as an assortment of baked goods that Bernie and Nathan brought with them.

Millie was passed from grandmother to grandfather, dad and then over to Graham. Olivia and Bea stood on the far end of the porch and watched.

"He's a natural with her," said Olivia, giving Bea a bit of a look.

"More than I am," replied Bea.

Olivia grinned, "I'm so glad it worked out that we could get the photos with the drop, with the weather and schedules and all. You never know exactly when it'll happen."

"It worked out well."

"It all has. I think Cliff would be so proud of how you've managed so much in such a little amount of time."

"I think so, too. Who would have thought the fire would bring it all together like it did."

"And you think Henry will come around to the changes?"

Bea nodded, "Henry is taking quite a liking to the idea of being assistant manager of Finley Orchard. He hasn't wrapped his head around it all yet, but he'll get there. Not only will he help me with the orchard itself, but he's most looking forward to keeping up the rooms and working with the homeless shelter. They're open to the idea of having a few extra beds to utilize, especially in the winter."

"Cliff would be so pleased, Bea," she looked at Bea, and

Bea had to look away before the tears that threatened finally spilled.

"Speaking of Henry," said Bea.

Henry walked up to the porch and went straight over to Millie.

Bea watched as Olivia stole a glance of Graham handing Millie to Henry.

"Maybe he just needed a little push," said Olivia. "For all Cliff's good qualities, he wasn't one to push people out of their comfort zone."

"Except for the whole giving his daughter an orchard thing."

"But don't you see?" she said to Bea, "that was the safe thing for you. This, what you've made here, this is you creating your own life, pushing boundaries. You're making the orchard into even more of a gift for the community, that's incredible. It's so far beyond what Cliff could have even imagined."

"I see your point," said Bea, and smiled into her tea cup. She yelled across the porch, "How's the to do list coming, Henry?"

He threw Bea a thumbs up and gave his attention back to the baby.

"How is it all coming?" Olivia asked Bea, "Honestly?"

"The focus right now is on the offices in the house, and they're perfect, thanks to the contractor you suggested. Simple, clean lines, new paint. With how quickly the building was able to go back up, since it's just a simple barn, the rest is coming along really well. The upstairs shouldn't take too long. Henry spent a few of the colder nights in one of the bedrooms, even though they're a mess. I think he's getting more comfortable with the idea of it all."

Between the insurance money, the sale of her

grandmother's books, and the travel magazine spread, there were plenty of funds to get the orchard ready for the upcoming year and then some. Bea came home from a two-week stint in California, and knew she'd never leave again for that kind of work. Her heart wasn't in it any longer, but she had to try in order to be sure. Soon after her return they broke ground, and with a mild winter were able to make the kind of progress contractors only dream of. Construction went without a hitch and then it was time to start remodeling the farm house into a few offices on the first floor and bedrooms upstairs to serve as an extension of the local homeless shelter. At the same time, Bea and Graham were falling head over heels for each other and when Graham asked Bea if she wanted to stay with him during the renovations, and then maybe longer, she didn't hesitate to say yes.

The first thing she did to make herself at home was to hang the painting of the woman in the orchard in the upstairs hall. Right where it belonged. After that, she didn't look back, she knew she was home.

The baby cried and reached her arms out towards Olivia from across the porch. "That's my cue," said Olivia as she rushed over to Millie.

Bea leaned back against the rail of the porch and watched the people she had grown to think of as family laugh and smile together. Graham walked over and put an arm around her, his hand rested on her hip.

"What are you thinking about, farm girl?" he asked, the term of endearment made her smile.

"I'm thinking about what Cliff would think of all this," she said, wiping away tears from the corners of her eyes.

"Cliff," Graham said quietly into her ear, "would be so proud of you."

Bea looked at him and said, "Of us. I don't think he'd

want it any other way," Bea leaned into him, closed her eyes and breathed a sigh of content. "It must have been lonely for him. I think it was his plan all along for the two of us to have each other. That's why he wrote the will as he did."

"I didn't peg him for a matchmaker, but he was always full of surprises," said Graham, and then he kissed the top of Bea's head.

The wind blew across the porch and Bea smelled the fragrance of the apple blossoms wafting from across the street, surrounding her and the ones she loved. A chickadee flew by and perched on the railing and began to serenade it's audience with a familiar chick-a-dee-dee-dee. Bea and Graham looked across the street to the little orchard that patched their broken hearts together at last.

The end

ABOUT THE AUTHOR

Corinne Cunningham is a writer, mother, avid reader and knitter, and tea enthusiast. She lives with her family on the northern coast of Massachusetts. FARM GIRL is her debut novel.

You can find her on Instagram and Twitter at @crnnoel, and more information and writing on her website:
www.corinnenoelcunningham.com

Made in the USA
Middletown, DE
11 January 2020